Face Blind

Deborah Rine

Face Blind is a work of fiction. The characters, incidents, and dialogue are drawn from the author's imagination and are not to be construed as real. Any resemblance to actual events or persons, living or dead, is entirely coincidental.

ISBN-13: 978-1497430143
ISBN-10: 1497430143

For

Kenneth Williamson

My father

Other books by Deborah Rine

Banner Bluff Mysteries:

THE LAKE

Acknowledgements

Thank you to Diane Piron-Gelman, my editor, who continues to instruct me in the art of writing.

Thank you to Susan Garrett, former Illinois State Senator for taking time to talk with me.

Thank you to David Naftzger, Executive Director of the Council of Great Lakes Governors who provided creative ideas.

Thank you to Priscilla Chabot of the Lake Bluff Post Office.

Thank you to the fine officers of the Lake Forest Police Department.

Thank you to my husband Larry for his encouragement and help in producing this book

Cast of Characters

Francesca Antonelli – Editor of the *Banner Bee*. Chief sleuth.

Tom Barnett – Chief of Police – Francesca's significant other. Detectives **Ron Puchalski, Cindy Murray, Brendan O'Connor**

Colman Canfield – Hardworking young man, Francesca's friend.
Royce Canfield – Colman's father, inmate of Federal Prison.

The Captain – Petroff – Manager of Service Department of Zimmerman Motors.

Ramses Crenshaw III, Governor of Illinois
Harrison Rand – lawyer who works for the Governor.

Luis Gonzales – Buildings and Grounds worker
Yahaira (Yari) Gonzales – Luis's wife

Anya Kozerski – Phlebotomist, Cancer Ward - Banner Bluff Hospital
Alexei Kozerski – Anya's husband, inmate of Federal Prison.

Lorinda Landers – elderly busybody.
Sadie – Lorinda's maid.

Carrie Landwehr – young woman who overcame drug dependency.
Julie Robinson – Carrie's friend.

Martin Marshall –College Professor who is face-blind.
Kate Marshall – Martin's wife, teacher.

Daphne Meriwether – Owner of Hollyhock Farm.
Carina Meriwether – Daphne's daughter.

Robert Newhouse – Candidate for governor.
Connie Munster – Robert's campaign manager

Hero Papadopoulos - Owner of Hero's Market and Cafe

Frank Penfield – Francesca's friend and assistant at the *Banner Bee*

Marcus Reynolds – physician, Francesca's friend

Isabelle Simmons – *teenage girl*
Brett Atkins – *Isabelle's boyfriend*

FACE BLIND

Face Blind

Do I know you? Do I not?
A fluid face, a smooth façade,
A brilliant smile, a wavering grin,
Ginger hair or ebony locks,
Sapphire eyes or dusky pools,
A sketchy nose, a pointed chin,
My love, a stranger, hiding there,
Behind a veil, a swirling mist.
Do I know you? Do I not?

Prologue

Martin got out of the car and pulled up his hood. He was glad the parking lot was empty. He didn't want to have to face anybody. The tension he felt in public was exhausting. Here he could let down his guard and breathe free.

It was almost dark and the air felt cold and damp. They'd had a surprisingly mild fall but now in November, winter was looming. Overhead, trees creaked as they swayed in the wind. Leaves spiraled away like miniature helicopters. He took a deep breath and felt the cleansing power of cold air fill his lungs.

He opened the back door of the car and Jack, his golden retriever, bounded across the parking lot and into the undergrowth. Undoubtedly he was onto the scent of a rabbit or squirrel. Martin pulled on his gloves and headed down the dirt path whistling for Jack to follow.

He'd had to get out of the house for a little while. This had been one of those bad days. That morning, after Kate left, he hustled Rosie upstairs to get dressed for school. Meanwhile eight month-old Stevie had spilled water from the dog's bowl all over the kitchen floor. After Martin had mopped up, Rosie still hadn't come down. So he'd picked up Stevie and gone back up to check on her. She was sitting on the floor in her underpants and socks playing with Legos. He glared at her and she glared back.

"Come on, Rosie, we have to get going. You're going to be late. Here, put on these striped leggings and your pink daisy dress.

She scowled at him. "Those leggings are too tight and that dress scratches."

He reached into the drawer for another outfit. "How about these polka dot tights?"

"Daddy, I don't have a dress that matches them."

After extensive negotiations, he'd finally gotten her dressed. They had barely arrived at Banner Bluff Elementary on time.

Then he'd gone over to Appleby's to pick up a few groceries. They were going to have tacos for dinner, and he located the box of taco shells and the taco seasoning packet. Stevie was sitting placidly in the grocery cart mouthing an animal cracker. Martin left the cart in the aisle for just a second to run back and grab some grated cheddar and a gallon of milk. When he came back, he smiled at Stevie and started to push the cart towards the checkout counter. Just then a woman came up behind him screaming, "Hey! What are you doing? That's my cart. That's my little boy."

He turned as the woman pushed him away and grabbed the shopping cart. Her cheeks bore bright red spots and her mouth

4

formed an angry slice across her face. "What are you anyway; some kind of pervert?"

As she pushed the cart away down the aisle, he felt a hand on his arm. He turned to see a friendly face: Yahaira Gonzales. "Mr. Marshall, your cart is in the next aisle over." She'd led him like a child over to where Stevie was smearing cracker into his blond hair. Blond and wearing a blue parka, just like the other kid.

Later, at home, the morning had crawled by with Stevie crying off and on. Kate thought he was teething, and that was why his nose was running and he was so grumpy. Stevie didn't want to play with blocks or watch Baby Einstein videos; he just wanted to be held. After he refused applesauce and rice cereal for lunch, Martin grabbed a bottle out of the fridge and warmed it. He'd taken Stevie upstairs and they had settled into the rocking chair. Martin crooned some lullabies in his atonal voice. Finally, Stevie had fallen asleep in his arms and he'd put the little boy down in his crib.

This was Martin's time to do some reading and a little research. Although he had the semester off from the University, he wanted to begin formatting the curriculum for a course he would teach in the spring. But every day it was the same story. He just couldn't get started. Exhaustion descended upon him like an iron weight.

After easing Stevie's door shut he'd gone into the master bedroom, pausing at Kate's dresser to look at himself in the mirror. Who was this rumpled guy with wild dark hair and frightened eyes behind steel-rimmed glasses? He didn't even recognize himself. Then he'd walked over to the unmade bed and lain down fully dressed. He'd fallen asleep in minutes.

At 2:30 Kate came home. Martin awoke to banging cupboards and slamming kitchen drawers. He'd gone downstairs and found a whirling dervish cleaning up the kitchen and picking up toys and books in the living room. She was ticked.

5

"Martin, you're here all day with nothing to do but take care of Stevie. This place is a mess. You didn't even do the breakfast dishes."

"I'm sorry, honey," he said. He couldn't think of an excuse. There was no excuse. The days went by in a fog and he was useless.

"I know you're having a hard time, Martin, but you've got to chip in here. I can't do everything." She was tossing toys into the box under the stairs. "Could you please go pick up Rosie."

"Sure." he paused. "Kate, I'm sorry."

She hadn't looked up. "Remember, Rosie is wearing a red parka with fur around the hood and she has two handlebar ponytails with blue ribbons. I tied them before I left this morning."

At the school he got out of the car and waited by the side door with the other second-grade parents. He heard the bell ring and pretty soon kids were pouring out into the yard. He kept looking until he saw a little girl with handlebar pony tails and a red coat. He bent down, held out his arms and called, "Rosie, over here." But the little girl wasn't Rosie. She frowned at him and ran right past. A moment later he'd felt a tug on his sleeve. "Here I am, Daddy," Rosie said quietly.

He tried to cover up his mistake, leaning down for a hug; but she pulled away.

"Can we go home now?" she whined.

"Sure, honey." He reached for her hand, but she pulled it away. In the car he tried to elicit some conversation. "How was school? Did you play outside for recess?" But he got no response.

At home, she dropped her coat and book bag by the back door. That did it, and he lost his temper. "Rose Marie, please come back here and hang up your coat," he shouted. But she ignored him and ran upstairs where he could hear Stevie wailing and Kate's comforting voice. A minute later, Rosie slammed her bedroom door.

6

He'd stood there in the back hallway looking out at the barren trees and the crumpled perennials. He hadn't done the usual fall clean-up in the garden. The hose still snaked its way through the grass. Buckets, shovels and Tonka trucks were strewn across the yard. The broken swing hung by one rope from the oak tree, where it squeaked and spun in the wind. Tomorrow he would get out there and clean things up, he promised himself.

Martin had felt a cold nose in the palm of his hand. It was Jack, currently his only friend in the world. Gosh, he probably needed to go outside. Martin had forgotten to let the dog out at noon. He'd let everyone down. "Come on, old boy. You and I are going for a walk."

He'd yelled up the stairs to Kate that he was taking Jack for a walk and would be back soon, but she hadn't answered. Apparently, he was being punished for his transgressions.

Martin turned right at the entrance to the forest preserve and walked along the creek. Jack zipped by him, running ahead down the path. In the summer months, Jack liked to take a dip in the creek; but at this time of year there was very little water. When they came to the stone bridge, they turned right over the creek and went up along the meadow. The path was on a slight incline. Local lore said that this trail had existed for over two hundred years. A sign indicated it had been used by Indians before the white man even arrived. To the right were woods. To the left was a natural prairie that was a field of flowers in the summer. Now, in the November gloom, it looked like a rutted minefield with clumps of dirt and haphazard tufts of straw.

As he walked, Martin realized he was angry, angry with himself. Damn, why couldn't he just shape up? He had to pull himself together and get on with life. Today was a washout, but tomorrow would be different. Maybe if he made a list and set some goals, he could reestablish a sense of purpose.

In the distance he heard a high-pitched wail, the keening of some bird or woodland creature. He stood motionless and listened. Maybe it was an owl? Or maybe a coyote had made a kill. Jack stopped on the path, his ears back, listening. Then he dashed into the bushes. He came running back with a stick, and Martin yanked it out of his mouth and threw it with force into the field. He should be concentrating on the positives in his life. He had a wonderful wife, wonderful children and a job he loved. "Come on, Martin, get with it," he said to himself.

As he trudged along, tossing the stick for Jack every now and again, he thought he smelled smoke. Where could it be coming from? In the spring, the caretakers of the open lands burned off the prairie grass but that wouldn't account for the acrid odor he smelled now. Dark had fallen; Martin pulled out his flashlight and turned it on. He continued up the path among the trees. Jack came and went, running and sniffing.

At the top of the incline the trail meandered to the left across the prairie and along an old wooden fence. To the right, back among the trees, there were a couple of decrepit houses that dated back to the last century. There was some talk of their being refurbished by a local artists' colony to provide sanctuary for writers and painters who needed quiet and solitude. For the moment they were inhabited by field mice.

As he neared the top of the path, Martin heard voices and the smell of smoke grew more pronounced. Curious, he turned right into the undergrowth. The voices grew louder and there seemed to be a disagreement. One voice, with a thick accent, was hard to understand. As Martin came closer he heard the crackling of a wood fire and someone yelling, "It's too late."

Jack crept up beside him and was staying close to his master's legs. Moving cautiously, Martin used the flashlight to find his way.

"Let's cut her down," one of the voices said.

8

"It is imposs-i-ble. We cannot reach her. We will be burned."

"If we had a bucket of water we could put out the fire."

Martin stepped carefully over fallen trees and brush. He wondered who had started this fire; probably a couple of teenage kids. He should help them put it out. He could see a dilapidated building now among the trees. Flickering light danced above the walls. He smelled something cooking, maybe a steak or hamburgers.

The building had no roof, just wooden rafters spanning the gap between two stone walls. The third wall had crumbled away and the fourth wall retained only half its height. Martin approached the fourth wall, stepping over fallen rocks and heavy brush. As he peered over the ragged stone rim, he went rigid with shock. Hanging from the rafters was the nude body of a young woman. She was dangling by a rope over a crackling fire. At her blackened, burning feet stood a wooden chair, partially consumed by the flames. Two men were nearby, bent over picking up some rope and a backpack from the ground.

Jack growled. The men looked up. One was dark and stocky, the other taller and wearing a hoodie. They stared at Martin, who was illuminated by the fire. Then they looked at each other. An unspoken message seemed to pass between them. The shorter one pulled out a gun while the hooded man moved rapidly toward the half-crumbled wall.

Martin ducked back and ran. Careening through the underbrush, darting between trees, driven by horror and fear. The smell of smoke and the image of the naked, dangling girl whirled in his mind as he ran. Somewhere he found the strength to keep going. At first, he heard footsteps behind him—crashing through the undergrowth, snapping twigs, then someone tripping over fallen branches. Gradually he realized he was no longer being followed, but he kept going. He knew these woods and he knew

9

all the trails. Jack was racing beside him. They crossed a leaf-strewn path bordered by bushes. Martin slipped between the bushes and slid down a slope on his back. He pulled Jack to him and held his muzzle closed. They lay there for some time, listening and breathing hard. Martin didn't hear any movement from above except the wind in the trees. After a time he took out his cellphone and called 911.

Prosopagnosia (Greek: "prosopon" = "face", "agnosia" = "not knowing") is a disorder of face perception where the ability to recognize faces is impaired, while the ability to recognize other objects may be relatively intact. The term originally referred to a condition following acute brain damage, but a congenital form of the disorder has been proposed, which may be inherited by about 2.5% of the population. The specific brain area usually associated with prosopagnosia is the fusiform gyrus.

—Wikipedia, 2012

Chapter 1
July—Four Months Earlier

He was deep under water. It was murky, grey-blue, opaque. He was swimming up; swimming toward the daylight. Above him he could see the sun filtering through the water. As he swam up through the multi-layers of heavy liquid, it became easier and his strokes were long and fluid. The water changed color from cobalt blue, to sapphire, to cerulean, to deep turquoise and then he was almost there; to a light, clear turquoise and then all color was gone and it was white, bright white.

He opened his eyes to an unfamiliar room. He heard a beep and a whoosh and background murmurs. His arm hurt and his head was pounding. He closed his eyes again and melted back down into the viscous liquid.

Later, there was a voice, a voice he recognized.

"Martin, Martin, hello darling."

He opened his eyes. He was in the same room, a pale beige room, and he wasn't alone. His whole body felt sore and tender. Ah! His head ached, his arm and his torso. He wanted to look at his right arm but he couldn't lift his head. It felt like a ten-ton bowling ball wrapped in cellophane.

The voice again: "Are you awake, Martin? I'm here."

Slowly he moved his head towards the sound. Just a bit, sliding his eyes in that direction. Then another slight movement of his head and he could see his guest. It was a lovely blond lady, encircled in an aura of pale light. She smiled at him and bent over to kiss his cheek. Then he saw tears in her eyes. She was upset about something. Did he say something to upset her? He couldn't remember. He tried to smile but even that small gesture hurt.

The door to the room opened. He heard footsteps but he couldn't see who had walked in. A doctor in a white coat came into view, standing beside the pretty lady.

"Hello, Martin. We're happy to see you awake. You gave us all a scare."

Who was this man? He didn't remember meeting him before. He tried to smile. "Hello, Doctor." It hurt to talk, and the words came out in a rasping whisper, but he tried again. "What happened?"

The doctor frowned and then smiled, first at him and then at the woman. "You had a terrific fall."

"A fall?" Pain shot up the back of his head, and he winced.

"Does it hurt to talk, Martin? I think you should just lie quietly." The doctor looked down at a chart in his hands. "Don't try to talk for now. We're going to continue to sedate you until the swelling in your head has abated."

Martin tried to process what he'd learned. Fallen? How had he fallen? He closed his eyes to rest. He didn't feel like talking to these strangers now.

The next time he awoke it was night. A nurse moved into view and bent to take his temperature and check the monitors beside his bed. When she saw he was awake she said, "Hello, Mr. Marshall. I'm Marie, your night nurse. I'll be taking good care of you. Is there anything you need?" She was wearing light green scrubs and bent over to fuss with his sheets and then the bandage on his head.

"Water," he whispered.

She bent closer and he repeated his request.

"Water? Certainly. Let me get you a fresh pitcher with some ice. This one has been sitting here for quite a while."

She left and he heard the door close. A few minutes later another nurse came back and filled a cup. She placed a straw in it and held it to his lips. He took a sip. The cool water tasted wonderful: cold, tingling, a gift from the gods. He took another long sip.

"Thank you," he said carefully as he looked at her. "Who are you?"

"I'm Marie, your night nurse. Remember?"

He looked at her again. He didn't remember having seen her before.

A while after that, it was daylight. He could see the sun streaming through the blinds. His eyes roamed from the window to the pink plastic chair beside his bed. Another lady was sitting in it.

"Hello, darling, how are you feeling?" she said.

He recognized the voice. It was Kate's voice, but who was this woman? She leaned over and kissed him ever so gently. He recognized her perfume. Fragonard's *Belle de Nuit*, the scent Kate always wore. She had bought it in Paris a year ago. He could envision the little bottle on her dresser. But who was this stranger? His mind was playing tricks on him. He felt oddly disconnected.

"Martin, Rosie is dying to come and see you. Maybe when you feel a little better…"

He looked at the woman. She sounded and smelled like Kate; but who was she? Was this some nightmare? He closed his eyes and wished her away.

Sometime later he woke up again. An older woman was sitting by his side. Her curly grey hair framed a lively face. She was holding a Starbucks cup and reading the paper.

As if feeling his gaze, she looked up and smiled. Who was she? A hospital volunteer? An aged candy-striper?

He recognized her voice when she spoke. "Hello, Martin. It's so good to see you open your eyes. Kate went home to take care of the children. I took care of them this morning. I think she's exhausted. She's been worried sick about you." The woman cocked her head and continued. "How are you feeling?"

When she tilted her head just so, he knew it was Emma. Their neighbor, dear friend and surrogate grandmother for his children. He tried to smile. Emma mustn't know that he hadn't recognized her until a second ago. He had to put on a good act.

"Emma?" he said tentatively.

She nodded eyes bright and questioning. "Yes."

"Well, I'm sore all over and my head is killing me." He took a breath, then hesitantly said, "What happened, exactly?"

"You took a horrendous fall. You were on a ladder in the front hallway, painting the stairwell. Somehow or other you slipped or the ladder moved, and you crashed down on the hardwood floor. You don't remember anything?" She cocked her head again, her eyebrows raised.

"No. No, I don't."

"Well, you and Kate picked a nice orangey-pinky color; it will look lovely with the white molding." She took a sip of her coffee. "But you won't be able to finish the job in the near future. No more climbing ladders for you! I say get a professional and he'll get it done in a jiffy."

Martin heard the door open and a white-coated doctor came into view. He said hello to Emma. He seemed to know her. Then he smiled and turned to Martin. Martin felt he should recognize this man, but he didn't. Was it the same doctor who had been here

14

the other day? He was frightened. Had he stepped into the twilight zone? Had he lost his mind? Right now he wanted to lose consciousness and plunge back down into oblivion.

He turned his head carefully. "Do you suppose you could get me a Coke from downstairs? It sounds good to me. Would that be all right, Doctor, if I had a Coke?"

"Sure. If it sounds good to you, it's probably fine."

Emma got up and bustled out of the room, looking happy to be useful. There was a moment of silence. Martin looked at the ceiling and then said in a trembling voice, "Do I know you, Doctor?"

"Yes, you do, Martin. I'm Marcus Reynolds."

"Marcus, I don't recognize you. I don't recognize anyone, not even Kate. I think I'm going nuts." Martin's voice wavered. "I'm frightened. What's going on?"

"You haven't lost your mind, rest assured." Marcus gave a faint grin. "If you had, you would not be communicating with me and dreaming up reasons to get Emma out of the room. But you might have some neurological issues that we need to address. I'll get Dr. Hanson in here to talk to you. He'll probably want to do some tests."

Martin clung to every word. He needed some reassurances. "I've been feeling as though I'm alienated from the world. Maybe it will just take a few days for this to pass?" he asked hopefully.

Dr. Reynolds' response was noncommittal. "Let's see what Hanson has to say."

Anya sat in the parking lot in front of the Jordanville Federal Prison. The car window was open and the warm summer breeze wafted in. The prison was surrounded by green fields of corn and above them she could see a hawk swooping through the air. White puffy clouds hung motionless in the blue sky. Along the soggy ditch beside the road, redwing blackbirds warbled as they dashed about. A golden butterfly alighted briefly on the side mirror, its wings beating rhythmically. How was it, she thought, that the world was so glorious and her life so miserable? Nature was mocking her in all its beauty.

She'd left home at the crack of dawn so she could be here on time. Even with a stop for coffee and a bagel, she'd still arrived too early. Sunday was her usual visiting day. Her schedule at work fluctuated, but she usually had Sunday off. Anya worked as a phlebotomist in the oncology unit at Banner Bluff Hospital. Her duties required drawing blood but she also helped out readying patients for chemotherapy. Working with these cancer patients was sometimes difficult, but Anya offered solace in a quiet, gentle manner. Patients often asked for her.

"Where's that beautiful Russian girl, Anya? She's the only reason I come back here, you know," Mr. Morris often said. He was an elderly gentleman suffering from colon cancer.

"I want Anya to hold my hand," Rusty said, who was fighting a losing battle with leukemia.

Anya had been lucky to get this job and she liked the people she worked with. They invited her along for lunch and included her in family get-togethers. No one knew she was married to a criminal and spent every Sunday at Jordanville Prison with her husband Alexei.

After Alexei was incarcerated here in Illinois, Anya had left New York. She hadn't wanted to be seen in Brooklyn ever again after the Feds had swooped down and arrested everyone in the Bayford clinic. The story of the Medicare fraud perpetrated by her husband and his cousins had been front-page news for days. Alexei was a doctor, a fine doctor, and yet he had been drawn into an easy money scheme. He'd let those "cousins," those rapacious rats Burlachenko and Sikorski; use his clinic as a front for their organization.

16

They had lured poor, elderly Russian immigrants into their scheme, as "patients" who were paid from $50 to $100 a visit in exchange for their Medicare numbers, plus bonuses for recruiting new patients. The Medicare numbers were used again and again to bilk the government for bogus lab tests and phony medical procedures. Alexei said the old people didn't really know what they were doing was wrong, but Anya didn't believe that. Nothing in life is free; even her eighty-year-old grandmother knew the difference between right and wrong.

After a lengthy trial, Alexei, Burlachenko and Sikorski all went to jail, in three different federal prisons. When Anya learned that Alexei would be jailed in Illinois, she had packed up her few belongings and moved to Banner Bluff. Now her life was the hospital, her tiny apartment and prison on Sundays.

Other visitors were camped in their cars listening to the radio or taking a nap. Coming down the road between the fields, she could see the bus from Chicago. It would be bringing the wives and children who were here to visit their husbands or daddies. She quickly closed the window, got out of the car and locked it. She didn't want to have to wait behind all those people to get through security.

As the doors to the prison entrance hall opened, Anya was standing behind an old man. He was there every time she was, always wearing a grey tweed cap and a beige jacket. He turned and winked at her. "You here to see your man, honey?"

She nodded. "Yes."

He smiled. "I missed you last week. But your man had another visitor."

Anya frowned. Alexei had not told her about any visitor.

"Don't worry your pretty head. Wasn't some lady. It was some other Russian guy."

Probably one of Alexei's cousins, she thought, one of that family of cockroaches. They could crawl out of the woodwork and

17

visit him if they wanted; but she wanted nothing to do with any of them. The old man chuckled as he turned back around and moved forward in the line.

At last it was her turn at the front desk. She had to show her driver's license, sign in and explain which prisoner she was there to visit. The police officer made a call. A few minutes later, they shouted her name and she went through the first security door. She stowed her purse in a locker provided, keeping only what little she was allowed to have on her: $25 in cash and her handkerchief. Once she'd locked up her belongings and put the usual plastic bracelet around her wrist, a no-nonsense female guard beckoned her forward. Anya opened her legs and spread out her arms so the woman could pat her down. This was the moment she hated the most. She felt violated by this silent woman who took unwanted liberties with her body. Today Anya had worn black capris and a fitted royal blue blouse, but standing before this woman, she felt naked and defenseless.

After the body search, a male guard took over and led her through another heavy door, followed by a narrow hall and yet another security door. Each time, the guard used a key and let her pass through, and then the door slammed shut behind them. With the closing of each steel door, she felt increasingly claustrophobic. She wanted to turn around and run back out to the cornfields and the freedom of that swooping hawk.

Carrie was clean. She was clean thanks to her friend Julie. It had been a long three months, but she had not swallowed, puffed, inhaled, smoked or injected any illicit foreign substances into her body. Julie had basically been her bodyguard for the entire time. She'd spent every daylight hour with Carrie. At night Julie had locked Carrie in the bathroom of her apartment, knowing Carrie would be tempted to go out and find a supplier if she could get free. In the large old-fashioned bathroom she had a mattress, a bunch of pillows, her little reading lamp, a stack of books and a couple of cans of Diet Coke. The first weeks were pure hell. She had banged on the door and screamed; but only Julie knew she was in there and Julie had gone home until morning.

The days weren't so bad. Carrie taught fitness classes at The Modern Method five days a week. The Modern Method was an exercise regimen that combined ballet, yoga and muscle strengthening. Carrie would teach her classes and then stick around and help in the office or participate in other classes taught by her colleagues. Anything to stay busy and around people; anything so she wasn't tempted to pop a pill or take a drink. Sandra Sorenson, who ran the place, said she had become the ideal employee. If she only knew, Carrie thought.

In the evenings, Julie came by and they would make dinner and watch a movie and then Julie would lock her up. It was really Julie who had turned Carrie's life around. They'd met at Modern Method where they were both instructors. Julie was into this "healthy mind in a healthy body" thing. She'd convinced Carrie to adopt a vegetarian lifestyle and then she'd kept after Carrie to clean up her act and stop abusing.

The previous January, Carrie had flunked out of her freshman year at the University of Illinois. She'd spent the first month in her room during the day and out partying at night. Finally, her parents drew the line: either she got a job and settled down or they were going to kick her out. She'd been lucky to land the position at Modern Method. Sandra Sorenson was just opening the center and had hired Carrie with the provision that she participate in a two-week training session in Chicago. She and Julie had done their training together and been inseparable ever since.

After she landed her job, she'd asked her parents if she could move into the apartment over the garage. It had been the chauffeur's apartment back when her grandfather lived in the mansion. The old-fashioned garage was at the back of a long driveway, some distance from the main house. After arguing with her mother and wheedling her father, her parents had agreed to let her move in. Carrie had some independence and her parents got her out of their hair.

Now she was ready to take the next step. She picked up her phone and dialed Julie's number. "Hey, Jules, it's me!"

"Hi, Carrie! Whaz' up?"

"It's been two months! I feel like… really great!"

Julie's reaction didn't disappoint. "You go, girl!"

"It's all thanks to you, you know. You're the best friend ever!" Carrie's voice caught. "Today I'm going to get my hair cut, kinda to celebrate, you know."

"That's cool."

"Then I'm going for an interview at Zimmerman's Mercedes, you know, down on the highway. They're looking for a cashier in the service department from five to eight PM. I could really use some more cash."

She could practically hear her friend smiling through the phone. "Well, good luck! With a new haircut and you doing so well, you're sure to land the job. See you later?"

"Yeah, right. And thanks again, Julie, you're the best!"

Mikhail Kozlov made his way down the streets of Baltimore towards the harbor. It was drizzling but still about eighty degrees even at this early hour. The night breezes off the Patapsco River had done nothing to clear the air. It felt like a citywide sauna. Sweat dripped down his back and his face felt oily and sticky. The air conditioning didn't work in his car and he had the windows wide open.

Mikhail was a man of medium height, lean and muscular, with black hair that curled like an apostrophe across his forehead. He had an aquiline nose in a thin pock-marked face. He sat erect behind the steering wheel. His deep-set piercing eyes scanned the street as he drove down Dundalk Avenue towards the docks. His gaze went from the rearview mirror, to the side mirrors and then to the occupants of passing cars; always searching, always on the alert. He had been working for two years at the Port of Baltimore Auto Terminal, at the Mercedes-Benz lots.

Even after all this time, he was amazed as he approached the lots. The surrounding area was a wasteland of derelict buildings and abandoned factories. Rusted metal pipes, old tires and industrial debris were scattered across the emptiness. Yet amid the detritus rose a massive fence topped with barbed wire, protecting millions of dollars' worth of luxury vehicles. It was mind-boggling.

Every day, starting just after sunrise, a caravan of nearly a thousand new Mercedes cars would come streaming down the ramps of massive cargo ships. The procession continued until evening. The shiny new cars arriving from Germany were driven off the ship where they'd been lashed down just inches apart and taken to an auto-processing plant, where they were washed and then inspected for the least little scratch. Then the cars would move along to an inspector, who made sure the wipers wiped, the horns honked and the seats warmed up quickly. This was Mikhail's job. He was continually astounded at the organization and efficiency of the process.

Each car officially became part of the inventory once it was logged in on a hand-held scanner. The parking lot held 12,000 vehicles, so this system was crucial. After each car was fully examined, Mikhail placed the Monroney label in the window and then the cars were ready for shipment. From Baltimore cars were sent by truck to dealerships from Maine to Virginia and as far away as Colorado.

As Mikhail drove down Dundalk Avenue, a dark grey car swooped in front of him and slowed down. *Asshole*, he thought,

21

just as a car to his left caught his eye. Another vehicle, herding him over to the right. Forcing him to slow down and pull over onto the shoulder. He was boxed in, the lead car in front and the other behind him. He swallowed, dry-mouthed with dread. He knew this would happen sooner or later. He'd let his mind wander and now he was screwed.

The dark grey car backed into his bumper while the rear car drove up close. Two men, one of them heavy-set and very familiar, got out and came up behind him. The heavy-set man pulled opened the passenger door and maneuvered his bulk into the car. It was Smirnov, better known as Крюк—the Hook. In the early morning dimness his face was obscured; but the metal hook that served as his left hand glimmered in the light of the street lamp. His companion slid into the back seat and Mikhail felt the cold barrel of a gun against his neck.

"Доброе утро, Mikhail. Как поживаешь?" (Hello, Mikhail, How are you?)

"Плохо (Bad), said Mikhail, "now that you're here."

The gun dug deeper into his neck. "Respect, Mikhail. Do not disrespect Mr. Smirnov. Understand?"

"Yes, I understand." Mikhail fought to keep his voice from shaking. "What is it that you want from me, Mr. Smirnov, sir?"

"Dear Mishka, it's time to help out your cousins. Family is family, is it not?" Smirnov stroked his metal hook with his right hand, smoothly caressing its curves.

Mikhail swallowed nervously. Sweat dripped down his forehead, and he wiped his face with his shirtsleeve. It had become unbearably hot in the car. He felt the smash of the gun against his right ear and he heard a ringing deep within his brain.

"You have no choice, Mishka, no choice at all. You work at the processing plant, right?"

Isabelle met Brett last summer at the BBYC, The Banner Bluff Youth Club. Her mom had actually pushed her into the club. She hadn't wanted to join. It seemed so lame. She'd noticed Brett at one of the jives. She'd seen him from across the room. He had that kind of blond hair that didn't lie flat. His bangs made a jagged line across his forehead. He was skinny and tallish but he had a baby face. She figured he might be sixteen already but she wasn't sure.

When she pointed him out to her friend Rachel, they giggled at his crazy hair. "Hey, Rach, do you know that dude?" Isabelle only used the word dude when she was joking around with Rachel.

"Yeah, he just moved here from New York. He wasn't in school last year so he probably doesn't know anybody."

They watched him standing alone, slouched against the wall on the other side of the dance floor watching the band. It was Upstairs, *a bunch of local kids who were always looking for a place to play. They did pretty good covers of hit songs, but Isabelle thought they always blasted the sound too much.*

When the band took a break, Rachel went over to talk to this guy she was hot for. Isabelle got a Sprite and looked around for somebody to talk to. She actually recognized just about everybody there, but that didn't mean they were her friends. Up on the stage the guys were putting down their guitars and hopping down to get something to drink. Isabelle saw the new kid pull himself up onto the stage and start talking to one of the guys. They were laughing and then he picked up a guitar. He strummed it slowly, moving his fingers, his head cocked over the strings. Then he started to play. Whatever he was playing, it was simple and beautiful; nothing like the usual stuff she heard at these jives. Silence fell in the room as everyone listened to the blond kid's fingers making magic from the guitar.

Chapter 2
Saturday, November 4th   Four Months Later

It was a foggy morning with a cool, heavy mist rolling off of Lake Michigan. Tom Barnett and Francesca Antonelli were going in to Chicago. They decided to take the train so they didn't need to worry about parking. During the hour-long trip they discussed their plans for the day. They were going to take in the sights like tourists from Omaha.

Upon arrival at Ogilvie Station, they headed downstairs to the French market. After perusing the aisles resplendent with fresh produce, artisan cheeses and bakery delights, they settled down with lattes and flaky croissants fresh from the oven.

"Let's walk to the Art Institute," Francesca suggested.

"You're sure you won't be too cold?"

"No, we'll walk fast. I love to feel the city vibes. Do you know what I mean?"

He nodded, smiling at her and raising his cup for a toast.

Outside, the streets were practically empty on this Saturday morning. It was as though they were walking through a futuristic abandoned city. The office buildings were vacant and many of the restaurants and shops were closed for the weekend. A lone taxi trolled the street.

"How about you give me an art lesson today," Francesca said as they walked down Monroe Street. She knew that although Tom was Chief of Police of Banner Bluff, he had studied art history as an undergraduate and often visited the museum.

Tom laughed. "Hey, you've got a great eye for art. Look at the prints you've got up in your condo. What am I going to teach you? Ultimately it's about what you yourself like."

24

"Yes, but I want more than a gut reaction, I want to understand what I'm feeling and why I respond the way I do."

When they arrived at the museum, they posed in front of one of the stone lions and asked a friendly tourist to take their picture. Then they went in and strolled through the different galleries, stopping to study the tiny dots that made up Seurat's famous painting *Sunday Afternoon on the Island of the Grande Jatte*, and to enjoy the familiar paintings *American Gothic* and *Night Hawks*. Tom explained styles and techniques without being pedantic. Francesca asked questions and absorbed his explanations. After two hours, they agreed that cerebral overload was setting in.

"Let's blow this place," Tom said as he reached down and took Francesca's hand. "Have you seen enough for today?"

Francesca gave his hand a squeeze. "It's been great, but I'm ready to call it quits."

Outside the November sun had broken through the clouds. The lake was glittering and the windows of the tall buildings reflected the blue sky and sparkling water. They started north along Michigan Avenue and stopped in a café for a cappuccino and some people-watching. The sidewalks were packed with families from the suburbs; visitors from as close as Iowa and as far away as China.

"I forget Chicago is a destination for people from all over the world," Francesca said. "Did you hear all the different languages in the museum?"

"Yeah, lots of French I think, and some German."

"Speaking of which, have you noticed the influx of Russians west of Banner Bluff?

Tom nodded.

"They're a hard working group of people," Francesca went on. "I was thinking of doing a feature on that for the *Banner Bee*.

25

They've landed jobs in everything from the Banner Bluff Hospital to my beauty spa."

"Beauty spa?" Tom reached over, cradled her chin in his hand and looked into her dark brown eyes. "You don't need the spa treatment. You're perfect just as you are."

She blushed. "Tom. I just get my hair cut there, but they provide just about every service you can think of... Anyway there are several really nice Russian girls."

His easy grin turned sober. "You're right about them being a hard-working group, but I've heard some troublesome stories lately about an increase in crime—prostitution and drugs—that may be connected with the Russian mob."

Francesca was taken aback. "Right in town? In Banner Bluff?"

"Not yet. Some towns nearby have reported an increase in heroin usage, though." He stood up. "Let's not talk shop talk today. Come on, let's head up Michigan Avenue."

They spent the afternoon window-shopping and people-watching. Tom insisted on buying Francesca a raspberry-pink cloche hat and matching scarf. She never would have bought them on her own, but they would look great with her black Patagonia down jacket. In the late afternoon they decided on an early dinner at Spiaggia Blu, an upscale Italian restaurant off Michigan Avenue. Once seated, they each ordered a glass of Chianti Classico and enjoyed crusty bread dipped in rosemary and garlic flavored olive oil.

"Look at us;" Tom said, "we're gobbling this up as though we were starving!"

Francesca smiled. "Well, I *am* starving. We practically didn't eat anything all day. Let's have the fried calamari and the sausage and spinach lasagna. That way we won't have to eat for a week."

With all the fresh air, long walk and delicious food, Francesca fell asleep snuggled against Tom's shoulder on the train home. He felt a deep sense of contentment. For one whole day he hadn't thought of Candace, his deceased wife. Francesca was easy to be with, bright and sensitive. He looked down at her, smoothing a strand of hair from her forehead. Then he peered out the window at the buildings and trees flashing by. In the glass he could see their reflection: a sleeping beauty and her stalwart guardian.

Daphne Meriwether and her daughter Carina sat at the kitchen table enjoying bowls of steaming hot vegetable soup. Daphne was an attractive woman in her early sixties. Despite the difference in their ages, the two women could almost have been sisters with their tall, elegant bearing. Carina's blond hair was pulled into a casual pony tail; her mother's in a loose bun burnished gold with streaks of grey. With high cheekbones and classic features, they formed a graceful pair despite their working attire: jeans, plaid flannel shirts and heavy sweaters.

By the kitchen door, on a muddy red mat, stood two well-worn pairs of dark green Hunter boots. That morning Carina and Daphne had been mucking out stalls in the barn and cleaning the indoor and outdoor arenas. This was the heavy work of running a horse farm. They had their own horses, which were used for riding lessons and rented to local equestrians. They also boarded eight horses, which provided additional income.

Beside Carina's bowl of soup was a printout of the current financial statement of Hollyhock Farm. Things were not looking good. The Meriwethers had cut back on a multitude of extras in running their business. An increase in fees for their boarding horses had not been well received. Last summer, they had skipped painting the sprawling white farmhouse with its well-worn red trim as well as the red barn. Inside, they kept the house at sixty degrees and closed off unused rooms. They wore warm sweaters and wooly socks as the temperature dipped and winter approached.

"We're not doing too well, Mom," Carina said as her finger traveled down the list of figures.

"Let's not talk about that now while we're eating lunch," Daphne said, her voice scratchy. She took a sip of soup. "I think I'm coming down with something. My throat hurts and I feel achy."

"After lunch you should take a nap. You're probably just exhausted." Carina reached for a piece of thick toasted bread and spread some creamy butter on it. "You're also worried sick about the farm. Admit it." She looked directly at her mother. "Maybe it's too much for the two of us."

Daphne put down her spoon. "What are you saying… that we should just give up? What would your father say if he were alive?" She put both hands on the edge of the table as though ready to stand.

"I don't really know what I'm saying..." Carina looked her mother in the eye and the words tumbled out. "When I look at the current figures and the budget we made… This continued recession has really hurt our business. People can't buy, let alone board, a horse. Horseback riding lessons are a luxury few can afford." She swallowed and clasped her hands together so hard her knuckles whitened. "Mom, you know as well as I do that our riding camps were half the size of previous years. And did you know the wood shavings we use in the stalls have nearly doubled in price since new house construction is down?" She took a breath and shook her head. "This morning I got a call from Marybeth Schroeder. She's discontinuing her private lesson. That's one more nail in our financial coffin."

Carina saw her mother's shoulders droop. Too late, she realized she'd chosen the wrong moment to assail her with these depressing figures. "Sit back down, Mom. I'm sorry. Let's talk about something else." She rubbed her eyes with her palms.

Daphne spoke softly. "Carina, I am well aware of our financial situation, but I refuse to give up on the farm. I promised your father that I would take care of Hollyhock, that I would maintain its buildings and its reputation. I intend to keep my promise."

Carina nodded. "I know, Mom, but I don't know how we're going to do that."

Daphne sat back down and wrapped her fingers around the warm soup bowl. There was a long moment of silence while they sipped their soup. Then Carina began to talk about the antics of the cute Wegner children in that morning's classes. Before long peace was restored and they were both laughing. In the midst of it they heard the front door bell ring, followed by insistent knocking. "What on earth?" Daphne said.

Carina shrugged. "Somebody's impatient." Both women got to their feet and went down the hall to the front foyer.

Carina opened the door. On the front step stood two middle-aged men in summer khakis, cotton shirts and lightweight jackets. The chilly wind blew at their backs and they looked cold and miserable. Without introducing themselves, they held out letters of introduction and what looked like government badges.

Carina barely glanced at the papers. "May I ask what you want?"

One of the men, taller than the other and rumpled-looking, said, "We're geologists working for the government. We need to do a geological survey of your property that borders Lake Michigan. We'd like your permission to go down to the beach and take some measurements, do an initial study of the land."

Carina looked at her mother as she accepted the proffered papers.

"Why is anyone interested in our Michigan shoreline?" Daphne asked. She eyed the papers skeptically. "Where did this order come from?"

"Listen, lady, said the shorter man. "It's in the paperwork. We don't know the whys and wherefores, we just do our jobs."

The taller man jabbed with his finger at a paragraph on the document. "Read that, you can see we're legit."

After perusing the documents, Daphne invited the two men into the hallway and shut the door, cutting off the cold air and the wind. "Let me call down to our handyman, José. He can accompany you to the beach." She went down the hall to the kitchen.

Carina remained in the foyer. She eyed the two men. Their ruddy complexions bore the burnished color of a recent tan. "May I offer you some coffee? You look like you're about frozen."

"No thanks, lady." They seemed eager to be gone.

Carina looked down at the documents in her hand. "I'm going to make copies of these." The two men looked at each other and shrugged. Carina stepped into the office that was off the entryway. While she made her copies, she kept her eye on the hallway. The men were whispering to each other and looking into the living room across the hall.

Daphne came back a few minutes later and opened the front door. "There's José in our farm truck." She gave him a wave. Then, turning to the two guests, "You can follow him down to the beach. He will remain there with you if you have any questions."

Carina handed them back their documents and they left without another word. The two women stood by the window looking out.

"I don't know, Mom. This all seems a little fishy to me. Maybe we shouldn't have let them in?"

"Maybe you're right. What's done is done. José will keep an eye out and report to me later."

The next time Isabelle saw Brett was on the trip to the Indiana Dunes, another set-up by her mother. "You'll have fun instead of moping around telling me you have nothing to do." The problem was, Rachel wasn't going and Isabelle was worried about who she would sit next to on the bus.

That morning she purposely dragged her feet. Her mom kept after her: "Are you ready? Don't forget the sunblock. Put your bathing suit in this bag, honey. I packed you a lunch and some snacks but you might want to buy a drink or some ice cream. Here's a ten-dollar bill." Blah, blah, blah!

Her mom drove her down to the recreation center on the Green. The bus was there, surrounded by a lot of sleepy-looking kids. Isabelle was one of the younger ones. You had to be fourteen to join the BBYC. She was just fourteen and she could see that the older kids thought she was a baby. She held back as they formed a line. When she boarded the bus there seemed to be no seats available. She went down the aisle looking to the right and left. Everybody was busy talking to their friends. There was only one seat available at the very back on the right. When she got there, she found herself looking at the new kid who was busy texting. "Can I sit here?" she asked.

"Might as well, but you might catch cooties." He barely looked at her and went back to his phone.

"Right," she murmured. "Whatever." She sat down with her backpack on her lap. Then she opened it up to get out a book. When she zippered it back up she bumped the kid's arm. He started to laugh.

"Hey, look what you made me write." He showed her the screen. It said: Talk to you soon, Good Fuck. *He looked at her from under his jagged blond bangs, laughing. He had one brown eye and one green eye. She didn't know whether to laugh or not.*

31

"So," she said.

"So, I obviously wanted to write 'good luck.' Right? I'm texting my techy grandma."

"Oh my gosh, I'm so sorry." And then she started to laugh too, thinking of her own grandmother who didn't even know how to use a cellphone let alone text.

After that exchange they talked the whole way to Indiana about all sorts of stuff. He had moved to Banner Bluff from New York with his mom and his sister. His parents were divorced and his dad was back east. His mom had a job in the city and worked long hours. She was a project manager for some big company. His seventeen-year-old sister already had a job at Appleby's, the grocery store in town. So Brett spent a lot of time alone. He'd been jamming with the guys from Upstairs. *But they hadn't asked him to play at any gigs.*

"Why did you come today?" Isabelle asked. "I didn't want to come but my mom made me."

"I actually want to see the dunes. They're like the eighth wonder of the world. I was reading about them online." He looked out at the Chicago skyline that was spread before them. "Now that is totally cool. I love cities." He turned to her. "Do you go to Chicago often?"

"Not really. My dad takes the train every day but we just go down to the aquarium or a museum once in a while. When I was little we used to go to the zoo a lot." She reached into her bag and pulled out two granola bars. "Want one?"

"Sure. Thanks. I'm starving and I forgot to bring a lunch."

They spent the whole day together. They went swimming, sliding down the sand dunes and hiking along the paths among the tall grasses. It was the most fun Isabelle had ever had in her life. On the way home they told jokes and riddles. Later some kids started singing and they joined in doing a parody of the latest contestants on American Idol. *Back in Banner Bluff, in the rush to*

32

get off the bus, they never really said goodbye. Isabelle's dad was there and she would have died to have him see her talking to a boy. He would tease her non-stop.

Chapter 3
Monday Morning, November 6th

Francesca was almost glad to be back at work. She'd had a super busy weekend but there was something nice about the familiar daily grind. She looked out on the Village Green from her second-floor office. The mature trees were barren, their black branches forming twisted arms reaching to the sky. Below, orange, yellow and red leaves covered the grass like a multicolored crazy quilt. In the summer, Francesca had a limited view of the busy village below her; but in winter she could see across the Green and up and down the streets below.

Today was a bit nippy with a bright blue sky. Fall leaves danced in the wind. There was a feeling of energy and purpose in the air. Francesca was editor-in-chief of the *Banner Bee*, an online newspaper that covered news and local events and provided a forum for the citizens of Banner Bluff to discuss, comment or just plain bitch about issues and happenings. She had begun the *Bee* on a small scale and it had grown considerably since its inception. She now had a large raft of advertisers and an ever-growing number of readers. This was exciting.

However, every day brought its challenges because every day there had to be fresh stories as well as content about local clubs, service organizations and church activities. Readers also loved pictures of themselves and their children, so almost every story included an eye-catching photograph. These were supplied by David, the staff photographer, as well as helpful amateur shutterbugs.

The *Banner Bee* office occupied a large sunny room over Hero's Market, a small grocery and café. Francesca's Greek friend Hero rented her the space for a very reasonable amount. When she was hungry she could pop down for a piece of crispy baklava dripping with honey or a cup of fragrant lemon rice soup. Hero also had crunchy salads adorned with olives and feta as well as gourmet sandwiches. As a foodie, Francesca often thought she couldn't have asked for a better locale.

With fall in the air, Francesca had dressed in chocolate-brown corduroy jeans and a bulky beige and brown turtleneck sweater. Her wavy dark brown hair was pulled into a smooth ponytail. Small gold hoops graced her earlobes.

From downstairs, she heard murmurings and a man's booming laughter. She decided to grab another cup of coffee before sitting down at her computer; and besides, she wanted to know what was going on. As she descended the stairs that led into the shop, she found herself looking at the back of a tall, imposing man who was shaking hands with two ladies seated by the window, enjoying coffee and blueberry scones. Just past him, through the glass front door, Francesca could see a shiny black town car complete with chauffeur. Two hefty body-builders were sprawled against the oak counter inside the market, their beefy arms covering its length. Colman Canfield, the morning barista, caught sight of Francesca and rolled his eyes in her direction with a can-you-believe-it look.

Could it be? Yes, it was! Hero's Market was being blessed by a visit from the current Governor of Illinois. Ramses Crenshaw III, known as RC by his cronies and as the Pharaoh by his enemies, was making an appearance right here in Banner Bluff. Although the election was one year away, everyone knew RC was making random drop-ins all over the state. Francesca thought he ought to spend more time down in Springfield doing his job. But like all politicians, once he'd won the election and secured the post, he spent half his time running for the next election.

Crenshaw must have had eyes at the back of his head, because he turned swiftly toward Francesca. "Hello, what have we here? Another Banner Bluff beauty?" He stretched out his hand. It engulfed hers.

Francesca gave an offhand smile. "Hello, Governor. It's nice to meet you." She took full advantage of the opportunity to size him up. The governor was wearing a dark-grey silk Gucci suit, a pink shirt and a silk patterned necktie with matching pocket square. Strongly built, he had thick grey hair and deep-set steel grey eyes. His welcoming grin displayed perfect white teeth between thin lips. He was handsome and he knew it. In Francesca's mind he resembled a shark with all those teeth and those cold eyes.

His smile widened and he drew her closer. "To whom do I have the pleasure of speaking?"

"I'm Francesca Antonelli, upstairs tenant and Editor-in-Chief of the *Banner Bee*."

"Ah! I've heard of the *Banner Bee*. Didn't you win a prize recently from the Chicago Media Society?" Governor Crenshaw was known for his fabulous memory and Francesca figured she was being entered into his mental Rolodex. She would probably get a letter soon asking for a donation.

"Yes, I did. I was honored that they recognized the work we've done." She turned towards Colman, who was barely visible behind the bodyguards. "Let me introduce you to Colman Canfield, who's a stringer with the *Bee* when he has time between two jobs and college." She pulled her hand from the governor's grasp and moved towards the counter.

The two attendants leaped out of the way as Crenshaw came over to shake Colman's hand. "Aren't you the young man who brought down the Lake Monster last year? It's a pleasure to meet you, young fellow."

Colman turned bright red with embarrassment and pleasure. "Thank you, Governor," he stammered.

36

What the governor probably also knew and didn't say, was that Colman's father was currently in federal prison, convicted for wire fraud in connection with a real estate investment Ponzi scheme. The story had been in the national news a year ago.

Hovering in the background was Hero himself speaking in precise English with a heavy Greek accent, "Governor, what can we offer you today. Would you like a coffee and perhaps a freshly baked pastry?" His smile was warm and genuine; his brown eyes alight with pleasure at the presence of a famous person.

"I don't need anything, but thank you for your hospitality. It's great to see a small business such as yours flourishing in this economy." He shook Hero's hand and then turned back to Francesca. "Ms. Antonelli, perhaps you would be my dinner guest some evening in the city. I am frequently in Chicago and I would be interested in hearing more about your e-newspaper. Online media is the future of journalism these days."

Francesca felt momentarily flummoxed by the invitation. She was thinking, *not in this lifetime.* But she gave him her best professional smile and said, "That would be a pleasure, Governor." She could always refuse when the invitation arrived.

Crenshaw headed out the door followed by his henchmen, or bodyguards, or whatever they were. The chauffeur jumped out of the car and stood in attendance as the great man got in.

"Wow," Colman piped up. "Like, is he impressive or what?"

"Impressive, yes; honest and sincere, no!" Francesca responded.

"Come on, Francesca, you don't really know all that much about him do you?"

"What I've read online and in the paper...he has a lot of questionable friends and he's been implicated in multiple nefarious schemes. Granted, they've never been able to indict him on anything." She smiled at Colman. "But you're right; he can charm your socks off."

Hero stood shaking his head. "I believe I think like Francesca." He wiped his hands on his fresh white apron and turned to Colman. "Now that the royal visit is over, we had better get to work."

"Yes sir!" Colman said.

Rameses Crenshaw III leaned back in his seat and looked out at the town of Banner Bluff as the car went slowly down Elm Street. He observed the village green and the people walking briskly in the chilly air. This town was Americana par excellence. He needed to come back here for a photo shoot in the near future.

He tapped Roscoe, his chauffeur, on the shoulder and asked him to stop at the next corner. He wanted to step into the post office and shake some hands. Then he would amble down the sidewalk for a block to the café on the corner. Inside the post office he complimented the postal workers on their fine efforts and discussed the weather with two old guys who were picking up their mail from the P.O. boxes. At the cozy restaurant called Churchill's he accepted a cup of coffee and sat down with two young mothers and their children. He cooed at the babies and flattered the two young women. He complimented the proprietor on the coffee and signed an autograph for the grandson of an adoring crone.

Back in the car, he asked Roscoe to drive down to the bluff overlooking Lake Michigan. Today the lake was ten shades of blue, sparkling in the sunlight. The water rippled as far as the eye could see. This was truly an inland sea, so precious and so beautiful, like a jewel.

He stepped out of the car and told his attendants to follow him at a distance. After a few steps, he pulled out a prepaid cell phone and punched in a number. "You called earlier?"

He listened to the brief response. Then he said, "I'm thinking over your little proposition."

He gestured with his other hand and listened some more. Then: "No, you listen. I don't want to be hurried in my decision. There are details that my experts need to evaluate."

Another pause while he inspected his buffed fingernails. "I understand that this will be mutually beneficial; but I don't like your tone of voice and I don't want to be pressured." He scowled. "Don't call me. I'll call you." He jabbed at the little red phone icon, ending the call, and walked back the way he had come. He had the feeling someone was watching him, but in the houses facing the street he saw only the reflection of the sky and the lake in the windows. No one was there, so far as he could tell. To his right were the bluff and a sheer drop to the lake. Feeling paranoid, he headed back to the car, stopping at the plastic-lined garbage bin at the corner long enough to toss in the phone. He signaled to his bodyguards, and they got into the car and drove away.

Luis Gonzales had been manning the leaf-blower for a couple of hours. He always wore earplugs because he was sure all that noise would lead to hearing loss. This was his fifth year with the Banner Bluff Department of Buildings and Grounds. He liked his job and he liked the guys he worked with. At times his manager could be a jerk but on the whole he was fair and just.

The leaves were now in a neat row beside the curb. A truck would soon be along to vacuum them up from the street. He headed into the Village Hall to grab his thermos of coffee, and then he went down the corridor for the keys to the city utility truck.

Luis was a short, powerfully built man with a ready smile and intelligent, warm eyes. People liked and trusted him. He said hello to several other employees and waved to Gloria Jimenez at the front desk, then went out to the parking lot.

He got into the truck and drove down Banner Bluff Boulevard, enjoying the sunny day and blue sky. He was going to empty garbage cans down at the beach. Usually he did this in the early morning, but now that winter was setting in he preferred to wait until later when it was light. He didn't empty them as often this time of year since the kids were in school and the beach was empty except for dog walkers.

Lake Michigan was bright and sparkling. He opened the gate and drove down to the beach along the access road. He checked the three dark green receptacles and found them empty. Then he drove back up to Lake Avenue and pulled over to the side of the road. There was one garbage can at the top of the bluff. He pried off the heavy metal cover and pulled up the black plastic bag. It was almost empty except for an object at the bottom. After pulling the plastic liner all the way out, he rolled back the edges and peered into the bag. Nothing in it except for a cellphone. Why would anyone throw away a cellphone? Maybe it was one of those prepaid phones and was out of juice. A little thrill of excitement shot through him. Maybe some drug dealer? That was always the deal on TV shows. Then he smiled at his own foolishness. Of course it wouldn't be anything so dramatic. He pocketed the phone and then looked at his watch. It was almost noon, time to go home for lunch.

In August Isabelle went out to California with her parents to visit her Aunt Suzie and her cousins. After two weeks her dad went home, and she and her mom stayed on for another week. When she got back it was time to get ready for high school. This would be her first year and she was really nervous. Her mom took her shopping. They bought new clothes and a new blue backpack. She attached two cute little teddy bears to the handle. She'd gotten them at Disneyland.

She didn't see Brett that whole time. But she thought about him every day. She relived their conversations and the way he had looked at her when they were hiking the dunes and how he had taken her hand when they went splashing into the water.

She never told her parents anything. Her mom said she couldn't have a boyfriend until she was sixteen. She knew Rachel thought Brett was kind of weird and different, so she didn't talk to her either. Brett was locked away in her heart.

Once, Isabelle saw Brett at school. He was crossing the courtyard and she was sitting on a bench with a friend. He didn't see her and she didn't call out. She didn't want to look like a dork. The next day, she sat outside again but he didn't walk by.

Banner Bluff High School had 2,700 students and the facility was enormous. She never saw Rachel all day long and she didn't run into Brett again. But in her daydreams she relived their summer day together with added embellishments. They were walking in the tall grass on the dune and he reached down and pushed her hair off her cheek. Then he kissed her, gazing into her eyes. It made her feel all squishy inside.

Chapter 4
Monday Afternoon, November 6th

Lorinda Landers sat by the window looking out at Lake Michigan. Her legs were wrapped in a pale blue blanket. She wore a pink woolly cardigan over a pink blouse. Her glasses hung around her neck by a crocheted cord. On her lap was a crossword puzzle. But she hadn't been very successful this morning. Some days the words just escaped her. They were on the periphery of her psyche, but she couldn't pull them up.

Outside she watched the remnants of fall. The trees had just about lost all their leaves and the squirrels were ever so busy gathering and storing nuts for the winter. In the sky she watched a flock of geese heading south in perfect flying formation. Through the stark trees the lake looked cold and brittle to her tired eyes. Lorinda's stone and shaker house stood in all its magnificence on the bluff above Lake Michigan. In winter it bore the full strength of storms and ferocious winds coming from the north. But in summer cool breezes wafted through the open windows.

In the kitchen, she could hear Sadie making lunch and keeping up a running dialogue with Herbert the cat. Today they were having tuna sandwiches. Herbert had jumped down from his perch on the window seat and raced into the kitchen when Sadie opened the can of tuna. He was making quite a racket in there, deep in discussion with Sadie about his rights to the empty can.

Sadie was a gem. She'd been with Lorinda for years. Their relationship had evolved to one of deep friendship. After Lorinda's husband died, Sadie had left her rented apartment and moved in. She was ten years younger than Lorinda and was spry enough to help her get around the house and up the stairs at night. Now, when they went to the market, Sadie did the driving. She dealt with gardeners in the summer and instructed the Polish cleaning ladies when they came each week. Lorinda didn't know what she would do without her.

Outside, Lorinda watched a large black car pull up and stop. A tall man got out with two big burly fellows. The tall man pulled out a phone, jabbed at it with his finger and put it to his ear. He waved off his two companions and walked along the bluff, listening to his phone and gesticulating with his free hand. Lorinda reached for the telescope that she kept at hand for bird-watching and general curiosity. With her gnarled fingers she adjusted the sight. When the man turned back towards the car, she could see his face. He looked familiar somehow. Maybe she'd seen him in town or at church? Now that his phone call was finished, he walked with determination towards the garbage can and threw the phone into it. Then he gestured angrily at the two burly men and they all got back into the car and drove away.

Lorinda was shocked that he'd thrown the phone in the garbage. How wasteful and irresponsible! If she had a cellphone, she wouldn't throw it away. My goodness! People were so wasteful these days.

Yahaira Gonzales had the day off. She hadn't worked at Appleby's Grocery Store that morning and she wasn't working at Hero's Market this afternoon. Of course, this meant no money coming in, but having a day off with no children was pretty special. She had taken the boys to school and then walked slowly back home, enjoying the fall weather.

She hadn't gone far when she saw Martin Marshall, who'd dropped his daughter off as well. When she approached him to chat for a moment, he frowned and looked a little worried, but once she introduced herself he broke into a smile. She always said her name so he would know who she was. "Hello, Mr. Marshall, it's Yari Gonzales."

"Yari, yes, so good to see you. How are Luis and the boys?"

"Everybody is doing fine. And how about little Steven?" She bent down to smile at the toddler in the stroller.

"Things are going downhill," he joked. "Stevie started crawling yesterday. He'll be into everything before you know it."

They both laughed

Yari said goodbye and headed across the village green. She was deep in thought about the Marshalls' difficulties—the poor man, he hadn't been able to recognize anyone by sight since his fall a few months ago—when she looked up to see Gloria Jimenez crossing the green on her way to the Village Hall. Gloria was the receptionist and knew just about everyone in town. She was a pretty, plump woman with a million-dollar smile.

"Hola, Yari, how are you?" Gloria said. "I never get to see you these days. You're so busy!"

"I'm taking the whole day off to run errands and get things done at home. I feel almost guilty having a free day, kind of like an escaped convict."

"Do you have time for a cup of coffee? Let's celebrate your freedom!"

Gloria only had thirty minutes before she had to get to work, but they had a good time catching up. They agreed to get their families together soon.

At home Yari spent the morning doing laundry and cleaning their apartment. They had a large kitchen, a nice-sized living room with high ceilings, two bedrooms and a bath. Their flat was on the second floor of a Victorian house. The landlords, Mr. Smith and his wife, lived downstairs. They were a wonderful warm couple who helped out babysitting whenever Yari was in a pinch.

At noon, Luis came home for lunch. This also was a special treat. Usually, he ate in the lunch room at City Hall. "Hola, *mi amor.*" He kissed her on the back of the neck as he walked in and she turned to give him a hug.

"I've made chicken tortilla soup and fresh tortillas. Everything will be ready in a minute." She set the bowls of soup on the table.

"Look what I found this morning." He took a cellphone from his pocket. "Found it in a garbage can on the bluff. I'm going to post it in the Lost and Found section of the *Banner Bee*. Maybe someone threw it away by accident."

"How could anyone do that?" She lifted a tortilla from the hot griddle and put it on a plate with three other ones. "Let's eat!"

Luis laid the cellphone on the kitchen table and sat down. "What have you been up to today?" he asked as he added some hot sauce to his soup.

"I ran into Gloria on the way home from dropping off the boys. She and I went for coffee. It was so nice to just relax and talk. Oh, and I also saw Mr. Marshall. I feel so sorry for him. He always looks panicked when I say hello."

"Yeah. But think how frightening it would be if you never recognized anyone. I can't imagine what that would be like."

"I'll bet it's hard on his wife too."

"I wonder how he recognizes her...maybe her voice..."

"Or how she does her hair, or the clothes she wears, things like that.

"Right."

They smiled at each other. Having a quiet lunch together without children created a certain intimacy. After lunch Luis took Yari's hand in his, bending to kiss her small palm and then her wrist. Then he stood up and led her back to their bedroom.

That afternoon, she was making chocolate cupcakes with chocolate buttercream frosting for Raul and Roberto as an after-school treat. Then she would take them over to the park. As she pulled the cupcakes from the oven, she heard a phone ring. It wasn't her phone. Where was the sound coming from? She looked over at the kitchen table and saw the mystery cellphone light up. Maybe if she talked to the person calling, she could find out who it belonged to.

The phone screen read PRIVATE. As she pushed the green button to answer, she cleared her throat. The person on the other end seemed to think she *had* answered and just started talking. It was a spiteful, vicious voice that sent shivers down her spine.

"I don't like being hung up on. The Agua Corriente project *will* go through. You have no choice. You need our money." There was a pause. "Remember that your life is in my hands." Then the phone went dead.

She stood there staring at it. The menacing voice still rang in her ears. She dropped the phone as though it were a snake and ran her hands through her hair. She was frightened; of what, she didn't know.

Francesca was researching tar spot, a fungus that afflicted the leaves of maple trees. This fall many of the yellow and red leaves blowing to the ground were covered with ugly black spots. The *Banner Bee* had received many emails about it from concerned citizens. Francesca was looking it up on the internet and had called Calabrese's, the local gardening emporium. She was preparing an article with pictures to be posted tomorrow. David, her photographer, was out taking some shots of afflicted maple trees in Banner Bluff.

She heard footsteps on the stairs. Either Vicki, Hero's granddaughter, was home from school or she had a visitor. Francesca looked around her sunny office with its spring-green walls and white woodwork. The room was in a state of disarray but still presentable for guests.

"Hi." It was Colman, who had finished his shift. "Thought I'd come up for a visit."

Francesca swiveled her chair to face him. Colman was a lanky young man with longish dark brown hair that curled around his ears and large sensitive blue eyes. Although only twenty years old, he had been on his own for the last year and a half. Two summers ago, after his father was indicted for participating in a real estate Ponzi scheme, his mother had left for Grand Haven, Michigan, taking his sister with her. Now his father was in the Jordanville Federal prison and Colman lived on his own in a studio apartment above Churchill's restaurant and café.

"How about this morning…a visit from the Pharaoh!" she said. "I can't believe he picked Hero's for one of his famous drop-ins."

Colman shrugged. "I thought it was cool. Whether you like him or not, he is pretty impressive."

"Come on, Colman, you've got to see what a pompous, egotistical jerk he is. I can't stand him."

He started laughing. "Wow, like don't mince words or anything…you're positively toxic!"

She couldn't help grinning back. "So do you want some tea or something?"

"No thanks, but I'd love a cookie if you've got any in the jar." He sat down at the round oak table in the center of the room, looking expectant.

"You're in luck." Francesca went behind the Chinese screen and brought out her grandmother's antique cookie jar. She took off the top and pushed it over to Colman as she sat down across from him. "I've got some chocolate chocolate-chip cookies, kind of overkill for your average chocolate fiend."

He helped himself to two of the dense, chewy cookies and leaned back in his chair. "Thanks."

"Tell me how everything is going: school, jobs, social life?" Francesca leaned forward and helped herself to a cookie too. "Are you managing everything?"

"Yeah, I'm doing all right financially, just making it though. Hey, but you know what, Francesca? I really like my classes. In high school I basically didn't do anything and I just felt like it was all about making my parents happy. But now that I'm studying for myself it's totally different."

"What are you taking, currently?"

"Modern Literature, biology and calculus."

"Wow, that sounds like a heavy load with your work schedule."

"I've become pretty good at juggling work, classes and studying." He swallowed a bite of cookie. "But I don't really have any time, let alone money for a social life. Vicki and I watch movies on Netflix and make popcorn. That's about all I can afford, and half the time I fall asleep during the film."

"I admire your determination, Colman. Where do you think you're heading with your courses at the college?"

"I want to become a doctor, but I know it will take forever and I'm going to need to get straight A's to make it into medical school."

"Hey, I firmly believe that if you set your goals, you'll succeed." She reached over and patted his arm. "What about your parents?"

"Well, I don't see much of my mom. I went up there once this fall. They're living with my grandmother. Samantha is enrolled in high school and my mom has a job in a gift shop."

"And what about your dad?"

Colman stared out the window for a moment and then looked into Francesca's eyes. "I visit him about once a month. That's all I can manage time-wise. It takes all day to drive down to Jordanville, visit him and drive back." He sighed.

"Listen, how would you like me to go down there with you some time?" Francesca asked.

"Would you? Really?" His eyes lit up. "I would…like, really appreciate it."

"When are you going next?" Francesca pushed the cookie jar over to him.

"I'm going this Sunday. But I'm telling you, the trip down there sucks. It's flat and boring."

"If you'd like the company, I'll go with you this Sunday. Have you got some funky music to listen to?"

"We'll listen to anything you like….R and R, hip-hop, blues, classical, you name it."

Five minutes later, Colman left, whistling as he went down the stairs two at a time. Francesca went back to her desk but she couldn't concentrate. Colman had a difficult road ahead but she knew there were people in town looking out for him. She gazed out at the grey clouds scuttling across the sky, wondering what it would be like to enter a prison.

On a Monday night in September Isabelle ran into Brett at the library. He sat down at the same round table. It was illuminated by a green shaded reading lamp. She looked up and smiled nervously. "Hi!" Her voice came out in a squeak. She wanted to seem cool and nonchalant. She'd been thinking about him every single day for weeks and now he was actually there beside her.

"Hey, how are you?" He leaned in close. She could see the sprinkling of freckles across his nose and those mismatched eyes.

"Fine, except I've got a math test tomorrow." She was thinking she must look terrible. She had on some old sweats and her hair was in a messy ponytail.

They started talking about high school. Brett was new to BBHS just like she was. Then Mrs. Faraday, the librarian, shushed

49

them. "Isabelle, you know the rules. No talking in the periodical room." The librarian was a friend of her mom's. Her mom had spies everywhere.

Brett leaned closer and whispered, "Why don't we get out of here? Come on over to my house. It's only a block away."

"I don't know." She frowned. "I've just about finished studying, I guess." She looked at her phone. It was eight o'clock. "I could come over for a few minutes. I have to be home by nine."

They grabbed their backpacks, got up and went out. Mrs. Faraday was not at her desk. They went out the back door, across the parking lot and around the corner. Brett's house was a few doors down the block. Isabelle had never been to a boy's house before. She was pretty sure her mom wouldn't approve.

Brett lived in a boxy sort of house. There were no lights on as they went up the front walk. "Is your mother here?" she asked.

"No, she's working late."

"I don't know if I should go in, then." She hesitated on the walkway.

"Listen, you know me. Do I scare you?"

She shook her head.

"I thought we could just talk...maybe I'd play something for you on my guitar."

"Well, okay." She was feeling pretty freaky as he opened the door and turned on the light. She didn't know where to put her hands. They were in and out of her pockets. The living room looked real modern; hard straight surfaces and a linear sofa, nothing like her living room at home.

Brett headed through a doorway into the kitchen. "Do you want a Coke or something?"

"A Coke, I guess." She followed him into a stainless steel and granite kitchen. It was small but impressive. "Wow, this is like a kitchen on the food channel. My mom would probably love all the cool appliances."

50

"Well, she should come on over because my mom never cooks anything. My sister grabs something at work and I eat frozen pizza."

"Where's your sister?" Isabelle was still having second thoughts about being in this house with a boy she barely knew.

"She works until nine at Appleby's on Mondays and Wednesdays. My mom is never home until around nine-thirty. So I'm on my own."

Isabelle was thinking about her own life. Her parents were always home and her mother insisted on a family dinner every single night. It would be nice to be alone once in a while without her mom checking up on her every five minutes. But she thought Brett's life must be way lonely. Brett handed her a Coke.

"Let's go upstairs to my room. I've got some weed and we can smoke a joint."

"Oh, I don't do drugs." She tripped over the words.

"This isn't drugs. This is marijuana. Hey, you don't have to if you don't want to, but I'm going to smoke a joint."

In the end she tried a few puffs and it didn't seem to do anything. She didn't feel any different. They sat on the floor leaning up against his bed and talked. Brett put on some Jimi Hendrix. She didn't know anything about guitar music but Brett said Hendrix was the best. Sitting there breathing in the smoke that curled around them, she felt as though she was in another world. The music pulsed through her and she began to relax.

51

Chapter 5
Thursday Morning, November 9th

Winter is upon us, thought Francesca as she looked out the kitchen window. Angry clouds scuttled across the sky. The world had become shades of black and grey. She switched on the light over the kitchen table and the rosy glow of the red lamp shade cheered up the room. After brewing a cup of coffee she added a good two inches of warm milk. Currently she was on a health kick, so she'd better make herself a nutritious breakfast. She scrambled an egg and plopped it on a piece of multigrain toast. After adding a spoonful of spicy salsa, a spoonful of black beans and a very, very small dollop of sour cream, she was ready to eat. A glass of pink grapefruit juice completed her virtuous meal.

There was no time for a run this morning. Francesca had promised Frank Penfield that she would pick him up at 8:30. Frank was her right-hand man at the *Banner Bee.* He had retired from the *Chicago Tribune* several years earlier and had shown up at Francesca's door when she was just getting the *Bee* off the ground. He had given her much useful advice about the world of journalism and had become a close friend and a major contributor. Frank refused payment of any kind except for fresh baked scones in the morning and homemade cookies in the afternoon. They both enjoyed their afternoon tea time when they discussed politics, goings-on about town and innovative reporting techniques.

Last summer Frank had been diagnosed with cancer. He'd gone through an operation, radiation, and was currently completing his chemo sessions. His prognosis was excellent and after today he could hopefully put this episode behind him. Francesca had been driving him back and forth to the Oncology Department at Banner

Bluff Hospital. Today was to be his last treatment and they were both overjoyed.

Frank had a wonderful perspective on life, taking each day as it came and rarely complaining. His consistent cheerfulness made Francesca feel guilty at her inability to accept the vagaries of life. He told her it was all about age and wisdom, and quoted St. Francis: "Lord, give me the strength to accept the things I cannot change, the courage to change the things I can, and the wisdom to know the difference." Great advice; but Francesca so often found herself drawn into wanting to change things that couldn't necessarily be changed.

After a shower, she donned a pair of jeans and a black wool turtleneck. Downstairs she tucked her jeans into a pair of black riding boots and pulled on her down jacket. She was ready for the cold. Then she remembered her new hat and scarf. Looking in the mirror, she could see that the warm raspberry color would do its share to combat winter. The soft wool against her cheek reminded her of last Saturday and Tom.

Frank came right out when she pulled up outside his house in her bright blue Mini. She leaned over and pushed open the passenger door.

"Hey there, gorgeous! I love the hat and scarf." Frank sat down, balancing a box with a big bow on it in his lap. He slammed the door shut. "It's a perfect color for you!"

"Thanks, Frank. Hey! How are you feeling today?"

"Pretty good. I will be pleased when this last session is over."

She pulled away from the curb. "Can you believe it? This is the last one. In a week or two when you're feeling better, I want to have a little dinner party in your honor."

"You needn't do that, my dear."

"I know, but I want to." She turned to smile at Frank but he was looking out the window. "What's in that box?"

53

"I've brought some Belgian chocolates to leave with the staff today. They've been unbelievably kind and caring. I'll miss them."

"Yeah, they've been an intimate part of your life these last few months."

Several minutes later they pulled up to the side entrance of the hospital and Frank got out.

"I'll go park the car and be back in a jiffy," Francesca watched until he was safely inside.

A few minutes later, her Mini parked and the ticket in her pocket, Francesca came into the waiting room, spotted Frank and sat down beside him. She had brought a book and her iPad. She could get some work done and maybe read a chapter or two.

They were chatting, awaiting Frank's turn, when a lovely, tall blond woman dressed in blue scrubs came into the room. She was striking in her simplicity, straight blond hair pulled smoothly back from a sculpted face, no makeup, just a warm smile that lit up her face and her clear blue eyes. "Hello, Mr. Penfield. How are you?"

Frank nodded happily. "This is my last treatment, Anya."

"I am sure you are pleased about that, but we will miss you."

Frank turned to Francesca. "Have you two girls met? Francesca, this is Anya, my lovely Russian angel. Anya, this is Francesca my dearest friend and colleague."

Francesca put out her hand and clasped Anya's. "I have heard lots about you, Anya. I understand you're a very special person. It's so nice to finally meet you."

Anya blushed and nodded. "Thank you both," she mumbled. "Mr. Penfield, you are to come with me now."

Francesca watched as Frank got up and walked slowly to the door. Her heart went out to him. Hopefully, in a few weeks he would be back to his old self; charging around, laughing uproariously and giving her orders.

For Royce Canfield this day started like every single day in the last year. His life in Jordanville Federal Prison was as regimented as a military boot camp. He awoke at 5:30 AM for the first official count and was in the dining hall by 6. Breakfast might be powdered scrambled eggs, canned peaches, a roll, juice and coffee. Then he was off to work, which began at 6:30. Currently he had been assigned to the laundry. On Mondays and Wednesdays, inmates handed in their laundry bags and his life had become a mountain of sheets. At 10:30 the lunch service started: baked chicken, beans, rice, everything carefully measured so that each inmate got his due. Riots had been known to start if one inmate got an extra piece of bread.

Then back to sheets and underwear until 3 PM when the official workday was over. He usually went outside and walked around and around the yard, and tried to focus on his current case load. Dinner service began at 4:15 after the count: meatballs, corn, potatoes au gratin, and applesauce. It sounded all right but it all tasted the same. He had lost a lot of weight since he'd arrived. He knew he had to eat, but it was a chore to force it down.

After dinner he went to the law library and worked. He had agreed to examine the records of several fellow inmates' cases to see if there were grounds on which their convictions could be reversed. These were the lawsuits of acquaintances he had made in Jordanville; "acquaintances," because he had made few friends. Several inmates had asked him for help, once they knew he'd been a successful lawyer on the outside. They were using him, but he was using them as well—to fill up his mind and to fill up his time. The only way he would survive was to keep his brain active and agile.

He shared his cell with a Russian doctor, Alexei Kozerski. He liked the guy. Here was another intelligent person who had done something stupid. They belonged together. Alexei was in for Medicare fraud. He claimed he had been dragged into it by his cousins, that he had no choice. Nice cousins!

Their cell was 60 square feet with a bunk bed, closet and small desk and chair. They wore prison khaki pants and shirts. In their pockets they each carried a photo ID that needed to be on their person at all times. Life was humdrum. He tried to follow the advice from the counselor when he'd been admitted: "Accept your fate, set some goals and try to meet them."

Every week Alexei's wife came to visit. Royce rarely had any visitors. His wife, Amanda, had divorced him shortly after the indictment and she had never come to visit or to bring his sixteen year-old daughter, Samantha. Apart from his lawyer, his son Colman was his only visitor. Although Colman's visits were awkward and their conversation superficial; he looked forward to them for weeks ahead. They usually played chess or cards to fill the time. Neither of them seemed able to break the barrier that separated them. And yet, Colman came because he was a decent kid and more honorable than his father. He would be coming for a visit in three days. Thinking about Colman brought tears to Royce's eyes.

As Francesca sat in the waiting room, her cellphone rang. She looked at the screen and saw it was Tom. She got up and stepped out into the hallway so she wouldn't disturb the other people.

"Hi, Tom," she said, a smile in her voice.

"Hey there," he said quietly, intimately. "What are you up to?"

"I'm at the hospital, waiting for Frank. He's having his last chemo session. He's feeling pretty happy right now.

"I bet. Now he'll start putting on some weight and growing back his hair."

"Right, we actually laugh about that, considering Frank didn't have all that much hair to begin with."

"So I'm calling to see if you want to have dinner tonight over at Sorrel's. The deal is I have a meeting at three and another one at seven-thirty. I was thinking we could meet at five-thirty for an early dinner." He paused. "I miss you."

"I miss you too. I would love to have dinner. I can tell you all the exciting things that have happened in the last three days!"

He chuckled. "Deal! See you at five-thirty."

"Can't wait, bye." As she rang off, Francesca looked over at the revolving door. There was Martin Marshall coming through. She walked over. "Hi, Martin. It's Francesca. How are you?"

As she said her name, his wary expression changed into a big smile. "Francesca, good to see you. I'm actually here for an appointment with Dr. Hanson, my neurologist."

"Is there anything new? Has anything changed?"

The smile vanished, replaced by pain and resignation. "You know what, Francesca? Nothing has changed. We'll see what the tests show today; but I think I won't be able to recognize anyone for the rest of my life."

"Gosh, how are you dealing with all this?"

"One day at a time, but I can't seem to get on with my life."

People were walking around them, heading over to the front desk, into the Oncology Department and down the hospital halls. This was a busy thoroughfare. "Listen, this isn't the right time or place to talk about all this." He looked frazzled. "I think I'm going to be late for my appointment. I've got to go." And he walked off without saying goodbye.

Brett met her again on Wednesday night. After about fifteen minutes they left and went over to his house. He got her a can of Coke and they went upstairs. His room looked neater than the last time. He must have cleaned up for her. That made her smile.

Brett lit up a joint and passed it to her. She took a tiny puff; they passed it back and forth. Brett talked about moving to Banner Bluff. He hated it. He hadn't wanted to move away from his father and all of his friends. Now he was alone and couldn't seem to pick up with anyone; anyone, that is, except Isabelle. He turned and smiled at her. "I'm glad I saw you Monday at the library."

"Yeah, me too," she mumbled. She was feeling way strange. She looked into his eyes. "Hey, can I ask you about your eyes? Why are they different colors?" she blurted out.

Brett started to laugh. "Do you think I look weird?"

"No, no, I just wondered is all." She looked down at her lap and then glanced up. "Sorry."

"Listen, it's called heterochromia of the eye. It's hereditary and depends on the concentration of melanin or pigment in the eye." He held her gaze.

"It doesn't bother me at all. I think it's kind of cool."

A smile spread from Brett's eyes to his mouth. When it reached his lips, he bent over and kissed her softly. She closed her eyes, feeling warm all over. When she opened them Brett was still smiling at her. She sat there feeling as though the earth had shifted under her. Then she jumped up, knocking over the can of Coke and spilling it on the floor.

"I b-b-better go home. I mean, I don't know what I'm doing here. Oh, I'm sorry about the Coke. I've got to go." She flew down the stairs and grabbed her backpack by the door.

Brett watched her from the top of the stairs. "I didn't mean to scare you off. I just felt like kissing you." She could hear him calling after her as she left the house. "Come back, Isabelle. I'm sorry."

58

Her first kiss; her life had radically changed in one night. She practically ran home the whole way, as if Brett were chasing her. When she barged into the living room, out of breath; her parents were placidly watching TV and didn't look up. It was as though time had stood still. Nothing had changed. But for her the world had been turned upside down.

"You better get ready for bed, honey," her mother said. "You've got that test tomorrow." She didn't look up from her knitting and the TV show.

Isabelle didn't sleep much that night. She couldn't stop thinking about Brett's lips when they touched hers. In her mind she went over and over their conversation, how Brett looked, how she felt. Why had she bolted out of there? What was she afraid of, anyway? In the morning she was exhausted. At breakfast, she sat staring blindly at the box of Cheerios.

"Hello, Dad to Izzy. Dad to Izzy. Are you there? Over and out."

She looked up to see her father staring at her over the paper. "Sorry, Daddy, I'm just tired."

"Maybe you need to think about going to bed a little earlier?"

"Yeah, right." She picked up her spoon and began to shovel in the Cheerios and bananas without really tasting anything.

Chapter 6
Thursday Afternoon and Evening, November 9th

"There's been a marked increase in drug activity recently in Lindenville," said Detective Mark Sanders of the Lindenville police. He and several other detectives from towns up and down the North Shore were at the Banner Bluff police station for a meeting of the North Shore Drug Task Force. Sanders was of average build, with sparse blond hair. A large port-wine birthmark covered his right cheek. "We've arrested several kids on heroin charges. Heroin! These are fifteen-year-olds that have procured the drug somewhere around here."

"Yeah, it's the same in Lake Woods," said Pete Smith, the Lake Woods police chief. "We had a kid nearly die of an overdose. He was at a party and claims not to know where the drugs came from." Smith shook his head.

"I'm telling you, the source is somewhere nearby," Sanders said. "These kids are not driving down to Chicago. They've found an easy buy right around here."

"We're seeing OxyContin among factory workers in Somerset." This came from Brendan O'Connor, a burly red-haired detective with bright blue eyes. "We found a treasure trove in the basement of an abandoned building. An anonymous tipster told us they saw people going in and out. I don't know if this could be the same source."

"Things around Lake Woods used to be pretty calm," Smith said. "What about Banner Bluff?"

"Not much sign of heroin here yet," Tom Barnett said. He turned to his detective sergeant, who sat next to him. "What do you have for us, Puchalski?"

60

"We raided a party a few days ago…the kids were smoking pot and we found some ecstasy. But last week a woman called 911, frantic about her husband…another overdose. *That* was heroin. Nice middle-aged couple. Not who you'd expect."

"We should increase our undercover operations," O'Connor said. "Anyone have staff available to go undercover for a few months?" He looked around the table.

A brief silence fell. Tom gave O'Connor's question some thought. He knew each town was stretched to the limit and that losing an officer was asking a lot. Still, they clearly needed to do more. "I think we could offer somebody," he said, turning towards Puchalski again. "Lewis might make a good choice. He's young-looking and would blend in well. He's been asking for increased assignments."

Puchalski grinned. "This one should be right up his alley."

The task force agreed to meet again the following week to iron-out any problems.

Robert Newhouse had the greatest smile. When he turned his eyes on you and broke out that smile, you couldn't help smiling back. When he made eye contact, you felt as though he was riveted to your very being. You became clever, fascinating and wise through his encouraging gaze. You might think this was an act. But the truth was Newhouse was really a nice guy.

Bob Newhouse was born and raised in Banner Bluff. He had delivered newspapers as a kid. In high school he achieved Eagle Scout, was captain of the football team and graduated valedictorian of his class. In the yearbook he was voted "Most Likely to Succeed" and "Most Friendly." He'd gone on to study history and economics at the University of Illinois. In the fraternity and on campus he had made a lot of friends. People naturally gravitated towards him.

After college he joined the army. There was no draft but Newhouse felt that he owed his country his allegiance and wanted to give back. He spent a couple of years in the army and served in Desert Storm with distinction. Upon exiting the military he returned to Banner Bluff, became a social studies teacher and married his high-school sweetheart, Alicia Morgan.

But Bob was a mover and a shaker. He needed a larger stage than the classroom, teaching American history and high school economics. He served on various committees in town and was bitten by the political bug. Friends in Banner Bluff encouraged him to run for the state senate seat, which he won after a hard-fought campaign. The press talked about his forward-thinking ideas and his willingness to listen to others. In Springfield his intelligence and ability to get fellow senators to talk to each other resulted in some landmark compromises that moved the unwieldy Illinois government forward. Now there was talk about his running for governor against his Majesty, the Pharaoh. Bob Newhouse was being catapulted into a political battle field as Mr. Nice Guy up against Mr. Power and Evil.

Bob's headquarters were on the village green, on the second floor of a building just two doors down from Hero's Market. He and his wife sat at the conference table with Connie Munster, Bob's campaign manager. Outside, darkness had fallen and the room had taken on a sudden chill. Alicia grabbed a heavy cardigan from the back of her chair and slipped it on. She looked at Connie, smiling. "So how do things look?"

Connie sat with perfect posture, her elbows tucked into her sides, her hands resting on the edge of the table. Before her was spread her most recent report, carefully organized with multicolor Post-it tabs. Her dark grey eyes surveyed her work through rimless spectacles. In her twin set, pearls and wool skirt, she looked a bit like an indomitable great-aunt or a no-nonsense schoolmarm.

"I have all the numbers here: both committed donors and a list of companies and organizations that seem ready to take the plunge. Conrad is working on the website. It should be up and running next week. You need to make your intentions public the week of Thanksgiving. In December, I've set up several speaking engagements for you both in Chicago and downstate. We need to get you out there addressing Rotary Clubs and kissing babies. Spreading holiday cheer is a great image." She centered the papers and aligned them with the edge of the table, then looked up. "I've been working with the team on a new slogan: something that resonates, that excites, that brings hope. Any ideas?"

Bob had been listening intently. It always amazed him that this seemingly unpretentious lady was actually a capable and astute strategist. She understood every aspect of the election process and left nothing to chance. She would be running a very tight campaign, and when necessary, a ruthless one. He smiled at her and shook his head. "Connie, what would I do without you?"

"Mr. Newhouse, do you know why you need me?"

"Why?" he asked, leaning back in his chair and folding his arms across his chest.

"Because I believe in you and in your ability to clean up the state of Illinois." Her gaze bore into his. "Conviction is a strong motivator. Together we will win."

There was a moment of silence. Then Alicia clapped her hands: "Hear, hear, hail to the chief and all that."

Bob actually blushed. That was part of his charm. He still had not wrapped himself in a veneer of self-importance. "I am honored to be held in such high esteem. And also honored that we're working together to bring about the changes we both believe in." He paused as his own words sank in. "Hey! What about just the word 'believe'?"

"Believe in change?" Alicia said.

"What about 'hope'?" Connie said. "Hope for change?"

63

"I like 'believe'…something about… 'if you believe, you will bring about change.'" Bob stood up and began to pace. "How could we best get that idea across in as few words as possible?"

"How about 'Believe in the future'?" Alicia said.

Bob and Connie both nodded.

"It has a nice ring," Connie said as she wrote down their ideas in her neat handwriting.

Francesca shut down her computer and grabbed her coat from the rack. It was 4:45. She would have just enough time to go home and get ready for her dinner with Tom. Downstairs, she found Yari Gonzales busy stocking the candy shelves of Hero's small grocery store. They exchanged smiles and greetings, and then Yari drew in a breath and spoke in a rush. "Hey, could I show you something?"

"Sure." Francesca waited while Yari went into the back room of the shop and came back with her purse in hand. She pulled out a cellphone in a plastic sandwich bag.

"Luis found this in a garbage can down on Lake Avenue above the beach. I was thinking I should maybe take it over to the police station."

"Did you want me to put a notice in the *Banner Bee* to see if someone lost it? Maybe we could find the owner."

"Maybe, but I think I should give it to Chief Barnett."

Francesca's instinct for news was roused. "Why?"

"Well, it's about what I heard on the phone, I mean, I answered it. It started to ring and I answered it. The person on the other end must've thought I was whoever owns the phone." Yari looked upset now, even a little frightened.

"What did you hear?" Francesca asked.

"I can't remember the exact words but it was something like, 'Don't hang up on me. Don't forget the *agua corriente* project.' It was the Spanish words that I noticed. 'Agua corriente' means running water." She shivered. "But then he made this threat. Something about money and 'your life is in my hands.'"

"When did Luis find the phone?"

"Monday morning. The phone call came Monday afternoon."

Francesca laid a sympathetic hand on her shoulder. "I agree with you, Yari. Take it over to the station and let them handle it. Maybe they can figure out who called."

Yari nodded. "I'm closing up here at seven. I'll take it over there on my way home."

At home, Francesca took a quick shower and then went rummaging through her closet for her favorite black pencil skirt and creamy Ralph Lauren silk wrap blouse. She'd debated about buying the blouse for a couple of weeks before she actually bought it. Now, eying herself in the mirror, she was pleased to see it fit perfectly. She completed the ensemble with rosy-pink pearl earrings and a matching necklace that nestled between her breasts.

She was searching around for her cashmere drape cardigan when the phone rang. She really didn't have time to talk. She glanced at the caller ID and saw it was her mother. Best to let the call go to voice mail and she would deal with it tomorrow. She loved her mother, but these conversations were always trying. Last summer, when her parents came for a visit, her mother had mostly grumped about the rainy weather when she wasn't chiding Francesca for her 'bachelorette lifestyle'. Not like Francesca's sister Sandra, who'd done the expected thing by getting married and producing two adorable grandchildren.

She eyed the ringing phone as she headed toward the door. Her mother would expect to hear wedding bells the moment she knew there was a man in Francesca's life. All the more reason not to tell her.

When Francesca arrived at Sorrel's, Tom was already there. As usual he was seated facing the door, a precaution taken by police officers.

As he rose to greet her his face broke into a smile and she felt herself beaming in return. He came forward, giving her a light kiss on the cheek.

"Hi, am I late?" she said.

"No, you're right on time. I was here early." He led her back to the corner table. They basically had the restaurant to themselves. "Good day?"

"Yes, how about you?"

She was interrupted as a nervous-looking waiter handed them their menus. "Good evening. My name is Kevin. I will be your server. May I get you a glass of wine or a cocktail?" the young man blurted. Behind him, Francesca spotted a concerned waitress hovering.

"Kevin, are you in training?" Francesca asked with a smile.

"Yes, ma'am, this is my first night." He looked back at his trainer and she nodded her approval.

"Well, relax; you're going to do just great. I would love a glass of the house cabernet."

"Make that two," Tom said.

After Kevin had scurried off, they picked up the menus. "Let's order right away when he comes back and then we won't be rushed," Tom said.

"Well, I know what I'm going to have," Francesca said. "Steak frites and the house salad." She plopped the menu back on the table.

Tom nodded in agreement. "Sounds good to me." He put down his menu and reached over to cover her hand with his. "I like meeting like this in the middle of the week."

"Me too, it makes a hum-drum day seem special!" Francesca smiled into his eyes but then pulled her hand away as

66

the waiter returned with two glasses of wine. He placed them very cautiously on the table. Then they gave their order, which he wrote down with care.

Tom raised his glass. "Happy Thursday." They clinked glasses. "What have you been up to today?"

"This morning, I was at the hospital when you called. Right after we hung up, Martin Marshall came through the door. We talked briefly."

"How's he doing?"

"Not well. He was going to see his neurologist. It sounds as though his face blindness has not improved. He looked frazzled and seemed disoriented. I feel so bad for him... and for Kate."

"With all they've been through, it doesn't seem fair." His expression was sober, and she knew he was remembering when the Marshalls' daughter, Rosie, had been kidnapped by the maniac dubbed "the Lake Monster" a year ago. Francesca and Colman Canfield had followed him down to the beach and rescued the little girl just before the kidnapper was about to drown her.

"Oh, and I learned about something a little bizarre this afternoon." Francesca proceeded to tell him about the cellphone Yari had found and about the strange phone call. "Yari was pretty freaked out. She's taking the phone to the police station."

"We're too busy right now to do a follow-up on this. Somebody will take down her story, but if no crime has been committed, there isn't much we can do."

"How about if I put a blurb in the *Bee* just saying the phone was found?"

"Go for it. Maybe someone will show up." He smiled at Francesca and took a sip of wine.

"What about you? You said you had a meeting earlier?" Francesca asked.

"Right, the North Shore Drug Task Force. Lindenville, Somerset and Lake Woods have all been seeing an increase in heroin usage. There have been some overdoses among teenagers."

"Heroin, wow, that's scary. Where are they getting the drugs?"

"That's the big mystery. It used to be that kids went down to Chicago, but our informants tell us the current supply is available locally. This is making it too easy for kids who smoke a little marijuana to try something stronger."

"Yes, and then get hooked." Francesca took a sip of wine. "Somebody must be infiltrating the schools."

"That's the problem. There's no trail to follow. We're going to send in an undercover cop." Tom looked up as the waiter placed their salads in front of them. A panicked expression crossed the young man's face; he ran over to the counter and then hurried back, asking if they wanted some freshly ground black pepper. Considering his effort, both Francesca and Tom said yes.

"This looks wonderful," Francesca said as she took a bite and chewed slowly. Julienned carrots, beets and Fuji apple atop a bed of baby lettuce dressed with lemony vinaigrette and a sprinkling of fresh herbs—the salad tasted delicious. "You know, whenever I hear about the war on drugs and the enormous amount of money spent incarcerating drug-related felons, I wonder why we just don't legalize drugs. Maybe there wouldn't be all the crime and the lure to try drugs."

Tom shook his head. "I know that's a familiar argument, but the DEA has done a great deal of research. When they legalized marijuana in Alaska in the seventies, even though the law only permitted marijuana use for over-nineteen year-olds, usage shot up among younger teens." Tom stabbed at a piece of apple.

"But if drugs were legal everywhere, maybe things would be different. Look at alcohol and cigarettes; not everyone is a lush or a chain-smoker."

"Well, I would tell you that in Banner Bluff, there are a lot more alcoholics than you might think." Tom cocked his head and raised his wine glass. They both started laughing. "Hey, let's talk about something else. Okay?"

At that moment Kevin arrived with their main course. The steaks were perfectly cooked, topped by a pat of herb butter. Beside them was a mound of golden matchstick fries seasoned with sea salt. There was a moment of quiet appreciation as they each took a bite.

"What about this weekend," Tom said.

"Remember, you're coming to the wedding shower for Susan and Marcus. It's at five o'clock."

He nodded. "So who's coming?"

"I think you'll know most of the people. Marcus invited a few other doctors from the hospital and their wives. Susan's invited a few fellow employees from Oak Hills Country Club. And I've invited some mutual friends, such as you."

"Didn't you and Marcus date for a while?" Tom asked as he stabbed at the fries.

"Yes, we did," Francesca said, "but we never really connected. Then I introduced him to Susan and that was that. I was actually a little chagrined at first."

Tom smiled. "Marcus obviously doesn't have discriminating taste."

"Maybe he just likes blondes. Don't gentlemen prefer blondes?"

"Not this gentleman," Tom said, over a loud clatter and the sound of glass breaking. Francesca winced. Poor Kevin had just upturned a tray of glasses filled with water and ice.

Tom took a bite of his steak. "I bet they won't keep him. Sorrel's prides itself on a quiet dining experience."

"Poor kid," Francesca said. "It's not easy to find a job these days. Speaking of kids, I'm going to Jordanville Prison on Sunday with Colman."

"What?" Tom put down his fork, frowning. "Why are you doing that?"

"Colman has been driving there by himself and I thought it would be nice to keep him company."

Tom looked irritated. "Francesca, you don't want to do that. Prisons are ugly places."

"I know that. But I actually think it might be an interesting experience."

"I don't want you to go. I know about prisons. I know all too well the dregs of society."

Now it was her turn to feel irritated. "*You* don't want *me* to go?" She put down her fork with exaggerated precision. "I have never been in a prison and I am a journalist. I want to have this experience; but more importantly, I want to accompany Colman. And..." she searched for words.

Tom's eyes blazed. "And I should mind my own business? Is that it?"

"Well, yes, as a matter of fact. I'm a big girl." The heat in her cheeks told her how pink they must be.

A momentary silence fell. "Are we having an argument?" Tom asked in a pained voice. "I'm sorry. I guess I just want to protect you from…I don't know from what…from the sleazy side of life."

Francesca took a breath. "I'm sorry too. I guess the thing with me is that I fought hard to be independent and to stand on my own two feet…to make my own decisions. I don't want to be told what to do." She looked at him, her gaze unwavering.

Kevin arrived to clear their plates and hand them the dessert menus. He appeared unaware of the uncomfortable aura surrounding their table.

70

"I'll skip dessert." Tom said. "How about you, Francesca?"

"I would just like an espresso."

"Make that two," Tom said, his expression impenetrable. When the coffee arrived they continued to make small talk, but their sense of intimacy was gone.

At 7:15 Tom looked at his watch and said he'd better get going. He signaled to Kevin to bring the check and got up to put on his coat. "Finish your coffee, I'll be in touch." He leaned over and kissed Francesca's cheek.

After he left, Francesca sat fingering the handle of her demitasse cup. Suddenly, she felt very alone.

Colman was tired. He'd worked that morning from 6 AM to 12 at Hero's Market. Then he'd gone to classes at the college. In the late afternoon, he pounded down the stairs to Churchill's Restaurant beneath his studio apartment. Mr. Churchill was waiting anxiously for him at the door.

"I've got to get going, Colman. Mrs. Churchill is waiting for me at home. Fix yourself some dinner. There is some pastrami left and some Italian bread."

"Thanks, sir. I much appreciate it," he said.

His employer rushed to his car.

Colman worked in the café four hours each evening. He did some food prep for the next morning but primarily he cleaned the restaurant and kitchen so everything was spotless. The restaurant was decorated with an English motif: London street signs, a picture of Winston Churchill and a bright red telephone booth in the far corner.

Tonight Colman's job took longer than usual. Someone had spilled something red and sticky in the large refrigerator. He had to pull out lettuce, tomatoes, jars of pickles mayonnaise and mustard, meat and cheese; all of the essentials for making a good

71

sandwich. Then he had completely washed and dried the walls and floor of the refrigerator and loaded it again.

While he was taking the last bag of garbage out to the dumpster behind the building, his cellphone rang. It was a number he hadn't seen for well over a year.

"Yeah," he said with little warmth in his voice.

"I need to talk to you." There was no preamble, no *how are you*, no *sorry I dumped you*; just this "I need."

"What about?" he asked as he heaved the bag into the dumpster.

"I can't talk on the phone. Can we get together?" He could hear her breathing heavily, as if she'd been running.

"I don't know. Why call me?"

"Colman, please, I can't think of anyone else." She paused. She sounded nervous, maybe even scared. Then she hung up, just like that, without a goodbye.

He stood there in the dark, watching the glowing screen of his phone slowly fade. Well, if she really needed him, she could call back.

The following week, she was back at the library, half hoping that Brett would show up. She never saw him at school. About 7:30 he came in and looked around. He sat next to her and pulled out his chemistry book. Inside was a note that he slipped to her.

It said: Isabelle, I'm sorry I kissed you like that. I just couldn't resist. I would still like to be friends. I didn't mean to scare you off. Would you like to be friends if I promise not to kiss you? Brett

She read it twice and then looked up and smiled, nodding yes. "I'm sorry, I was such a dork."

They got in the habit of meeting every Monday and Wednesday. Isabelle would arrive at the library at seven. She told

her mom she could study better there. Her mother said she was glad Isabelle was serious about her schoolwork. Isabelle actually did want to do well so she would study hard in study hall at school and finish up when she got home after school. Then she was free to just be with Brett on Mondays and Wednesdays.

When she got to the library she would say hello to Mrs. Faraday and then head for the periodical room. She would slip out the back entrance, where Brett met her. Then they would head over to his house. Usually they shared a joint. At first they mainly talked with just a few kisses. Then they began to kiss more. They moved onto Brett's bed and couldn't stop touching and rubbing each other. Brett would tell her to close her eyes and his hands would outline the planes of her face and he'd follow his hands with kisses. Then she would touch and kiss him. They giggled a lot.

Chapter 7
Saturday Afternoon and Evening, November 11th

It had been a brilliant sunny day, cold and crisp, but Francesca hadn't been outside to enjoy it. Instead, she had spent the day getting ready for that evening's wedding shower. The tablecloth was yellow, the napkins and plates patterned with decorative geometric designs in yellow, white and lime green. In the center of the table was a glass bowl filled with white and yellow roses atop a twelve-inch round mirror. She'd found some clear crystal votive candle holders, and the mirror reflected the flowers and the gentle light.

A variety of tasty bite-size hors d'oeuvres graced the table, along with a tray of strawberry, balsamic vinegar and goat cheese bruschetta. As a sweet finish, mini cupcakes from Bonnie's Bakery sat between a bowl of crystalized fruit and a basket of perfect, golden clementines. Beer, wine and sangria were ready to go along with coffee and tea.

Early in the day, Emma Boucher had come over to help make the hors d'oeuvres. Although she was thirty years Francesca's senior, they had become close friends. They chatted comfortably as Emma filled cucumber cups with crab Louis and Francesca made the filling for the mini chipotle chicken tostadas.

"How is Martin doing, Emma? I met him coming into the hospital Thursday morning and he seemed frazzled."

"Not well, not well at all. He seems depressed to me."

"How about Kate?"

"Well, she runs out of patience periodically. She wants him to accept his limitations and move on."

"It must be hard if he doesn't recognize her sometimes."

"Yes, well there's that. And then Rosie gets upset with her daddy if he doesn't recognize her. I think she really can't understand what has happened; she's only seven."

"Well, tonight I hope everyone remembers to introduce themselves to make it easier for Martin."

"What's in the oven?" Emma asked as she covered the cucumber cups with plastic wrap.

"I'm roasting a small filet. I'm going to slice it paper-thin and serve it with a choice of blue cheese or spicy Asian dipping sauce."

"Francesca, you are a fabulous cook. What shall I make next?"

"How about the brie and smoked salmon pizza?" Francesca pulled the ingredients out of the fridge, then turned back to the roasted chicken she'd been chopping. Emma was an avid fan of the Weather Channel, and they talked about that morning's story on the "water wars" going on all over the United States. "We're experiencing the worst drought in seventy years," Emma said, smearing the softened Brie over the prepared pizza crust. "They compared the western part of the Midwest to the Dust Bowl back in the thirties. Nothing will grow. The Colorado River is drying up, and they're having to dredge the Mississippi so the barges can go down it."

"We're lucky to be living here in Banner Bluff right next door to Lake Michigan with its abundance of fresh water." Francesca took the filet out of the oven and then reached for the kettle. "Let's stop and have a cup of tea and you can tell me all about what you're going to wear tonight."

Emma laughed. "As if that was a topic of interest."

Tonight, Francesca was wearing her "little black dress", a sheath that fit perfectly, with gold beads and gold earrings. She had swept her dark, wavy hair into a chignon. She looked like a modern-day Audrey Hepburn. As she applied some cool red lipstick, the doorbell rang. She went to the door, and there was Tom. She felt a little nervous, wondering what to say. They hadn't spoken since Thursday night.

"Hi," he said warmly as he stepped inside and hugged her. His cheeks were cold and his lips felt smooth as they brushed hers in a light kiss. "Francesca, I'm sorry about Thursday," he whispered in her ear.

Her anxiety vanished. She whispered back, "Don't worry; I'm super sensitive about being told what to do."

"I guess I want to protect you from unpleasantness. It's the cave man in me." He held her away from him enough to look at her. "Wow, you look great…I like the dress."

"You look pretty spiffy yourself." Tom was dressed casually in grey slacks and a French blue dress shirt. "Thanks for coming a little early. You can be my co-host."

The doorbell rang again. This time it was Frank.

Francesca gave him a hug. "I wasn't sure you would come." His tweed jacket and slacks hung on him and his coloring was not the best. His last chemo session had been only three days earlier.

"I wasn't so sure either. This morning I felt pretty lousy; but I think I need to get out and be around people. I'll probably just sit in that armchair by the fireplace and watch the action."

Francesca had lit the gas fire earlier and it looked cozy and welcoming. As soon as they had Frank ensconced in a chair with a glass of San Pellegrino, the doorbell rang again. Pretty soon the condo was filled with people. With little encouragement, they helped themselves to the food and to glasses of wine and sangria.

The guests of honor, Susan and Marcus, arrived at 5:15 and were warmly welcomed by the crowd. Susan wore a blue silk high-collared Chinese jacket embroidered with small flowers, black velvet pants and velvet embroidered slippers. Her blond hair was wrapped in a loose chignon. She looked exquisite. Everyone applauded their arrival and they said a few words of thanks.

Even though Susan had insisted on no gifts, some of the guests had brought surprise presents. Bottles of wine, theatre tickets, restaurant vouchers, even a skimpy negligee from Victoria's Secret that brought forth guffaws. Francesca had found an antique silver love cup and had it engraved with the date of their engagement across entwined hearts. They shared a sip of wine from the cup as they were toasted by their friends.

After making sure Frank was still comfortable, Francesca picked up a platter of mu shu wonton cups and made the rounds. The first small group she went to included Robert and Alicia Newhouse. One-armed, she hugged Alicia and complimented her on her dress, and then turned to Bob. "So, guess who was in town on Monday?"

He flashed his dazzling smile. "I give up."

"Your nemesis, Ramses Crenshaw the Third!"

"The Pharaoh? Where?"

"In Banner Bluff. He was in Hero's Market to glad-hand the common folk. Then he went down Elm Street and spent time in the post office and some shops."

"God, he pops up everywhere. I wish he'd go back downstate and sign some of the bills that are waiting on his desk."

Alicia looked nervously at her husband. "Maybe he knows your plans and is moving in on your base territory."

Francesca raised her eyebrows. "What are your plans, Bob?"

He cleared his throat and glanced at his wife, then back at Francesca. "It's not official yet, but I'm planning on running for governor next year."

"Wow, that's great. I'll do anything I can to help."

"For now, maybe you could just keep it under your hat? I haven't made a public announcement yet."

77

"Mum's the word." She patted his arm and moved on. As she approached Tom and Marcus, she caught some of their conversation.

"What do you think, Marcus? Is that kid going to make it?" Tom asked.

Marcus shrugged. "It was touch and go last night and into this morning. But I think he'll come out of it all right."

"What are you two talking about?" Francesca asked.

Marcus helped himself to an appetizer. "Last night Ron Puchalski brought in a kid who had overdosed. We were working on him much of the night."

Francesca turned to Tom. "This is what we were talking about Thursday night, right?"

He nodded. "There's definitely been an increase in drug usage in the last six months. We're working closely with the hospital's ER."

Martin Marshall came over and joined their little group. Tom and Marcus both introduced themselves. Instead of relief, Martin looked irritated. "Does everyone have to say who they are all the time? It's driving me nuts. I feel like an idiot."

"I'll bet a party like this is pretty stressful," Francesca said. "But you know you're among friends. Relax!" She put her arm through his, and saw Kate looking at them from across the room. Her face reflected her husband's anguish and something else: impatience and anger.

Sometimes Brett was moody. Usually, it was on Mondays after the weekend. It sounded like he had a lot of run-ins with his mom. He said she wasn't happy with anything he did. She was always harping about his grades and the kids he'd started hanging out with. His mom didn't know anything about Isabelle. That was their secret.

"Who are you hanging out with on the weekend?" Isabelle asked. She was jealous of the time he spent away from her.

"Kids I met at school. We go to this one guy's house. There's a back entrance and we jam, hang out, smoke, you know…"

"Do I know them?"

"Probably not. They're juniors. They're not your type."

"What's my type?"

"Isabelle, you're a good student and you're on the Math Team. Give me a break. These kids are not like you."

She tried again. "Whose basement do you hang out in?"

"His name is Mickey. His parents don't have a clue what goes on in their house."

She was quiet thinking about his other life. All they had together was a couple of hours, two days a week. At school, she didn't run into him. He was a junior and she was a freshman so their classes were in different parts of the building. She had told him that if her mother ever learned she had a boyfriend, she would be grounded for life. Now, she was thinking she would like to sneak out on the weekend. But where could they go?

Chapter 8
Sunday, November 12th

Francesca had set the alarm for 5:45 in order to be up in time for her trip to Jordanville Prison. Colman would be coming by at 6:30. She got right out of bed and took a shower. While she was brushing her teeth, she wondered what one wore to prison. Maybe jeans weren't a good idea, maybe you needed to look more respectable? In the closet she found a nice pair of dark grey wool pants and a royal blue turtleneck sweater.

Downstairs she had time to make a quick cup of coffee. Her kitchen was back to its normal state. Last night Susan and Marcus had insisted on sticking around after the other guests left. Together they'd cleaned up the kitchen, stashed the few leftovers in the fridge and restored order to the living room.

As they were cleaning up, Susan and Marcus discussed their wedding plans. Rather than getting married in the spring, they were opting for a January wedding. Susan's job as manager of the Oak Hills Golf and Tennis Club was slow in January. She could take off a couple of weeks with no problem. They both wanted to honeymoon in a warm spot, Bermuda or St. Bart's.

This morning, Francesca thought escaping to sunshine and warmth would be heavenly. January in Chicago could be pretty miserable. As she sipped her coffee, she looked out the window at total darkness. It wouldn't be light for another hour. She felt a sense of anxiety, and dread of the winter that was looming.

Colman was right on time. He got out of the car and came around to open the door for her. "Look, I cleaned up my car for you. There's actually a place for you to sit down. Normally the front seat is piled with junk," he said.

"Well, that's great. It would have been pretty chilly up on the roof." Francesca sat and belted herself in. "So how long did you say the trip was again?"

"About three hours. We can make good time at this hour on a Sunday."

As it turned out, the trip went by quickly. They stopped once at an oasis for coffee and a sausage McMuffin that tasted pretty good. Conversation was easy. They talked about writing and Colman's literature course. Colman had read *The Great Gatsby* and *The Grapes of Wrath* recently. They discussed the social perspective those books portrayed, and agreed that even today there were inside traders in New York City living a Gatsby life-style and transient workers picking strawberries in the fields of California living in miserable shacks.

Colman wanted to know about Francesca, and she ended up telling him about her childhood in California, her marriage to Dan, her divorce and the creation of the *Banner Bee*. Driving along without eye contact was somewhat like a visit to the shrink. You could just talk without registering the other person's reaction except by their verbal responses. There was a certain intimacy to driving along in the semidarkness.

Three hours later, they arrived at Jordanville prison. Although they had made good time, they weren't the first to arrive. There was a line of visitors and they had to wait their turn. Francesca felt apprehensive. She unbuttoned her jacket and unwound the scarf she was wearing. She needed air. There was something frightening about the large main building and the barbed-wire topped fences that stretched out on each side of it.

At the front desk they each showed their driver's licenses and filled out a form. Colman had told his father that Francesca was accompanying him and Royce Canfield had put Francesca on his visitor list. Then they went into the security area. Colman told her she would have to leave everything in a locker but she could keep some cash.

Francesca was shown to the women's security area, where she was told to put her coat and purse in a safe and then was frisked by a female guard. The woman was massive, probably six feet tall with arms like a wrestler. She smelled faintly of garlic and cigarettes. Her hands traveled up and down Francesca's body checking for weapons. Again Francesca had the frightening feeling of needing air. She swallowed hard.

She was relieved to rejoin Colman and to escape the clutches of her Amazon security guard. They went through a series of locked doors before being admitted into the visitor reception area, a large room filled with square tables each surrounded by four chairs. Along one wall was a bank of vending machines that dispensed candy, snacks, pop and various sandwiches. On a counter were several microwaves, napkins and packets of ketchup and mustard. A second wall displayed a full-size mural of a Hawaiian scene complete with rolling waves, palm trees and a profusion of large bright flowers, kind of a Gauguin look-alike. The third wall was divided by a series of floor-to-ceiling windows that looked out on a small courtyard, surrounded by a high cement wall topped by barbed wire. In the summer, Francesca guessed, this area must serve as an extended visiting area. The fourth wall was unadorned. There were cameras high in the corners, but no guards were in the room.

Lively groups filled the tables, mostly wives and children visiting their husbands or fathers. People laughed, talked and played cards. It was almost a party atmosphere. In the back by a window, Royce Canfield stood and raised his hand. He had secured a quiet corner. Francesca followed Colman as he wound his way between the tables. Royce was visibly thrilled to see his son, but they didn't hug. He held Colman at arm's length and then

82

patted his back. Francesca found this restrained show of affection disheartening.

Royce turned to her, smiled and shook her hand. He'd lost weight, and looked older and frailer. His shoulders were rounded and his former arrogance was replaced by a reserved humility. "Thanks so much for coming. I know the trip is a long one for Colman each month."

"I've got to admit I was curious to see what a prison visit was like," Francesca said with a smile. "But I also thought it might be nice for you to see another friendly face." The word "friendly" had a certain irony to it, she thought as soon as she said it, considering that Francesca had been instrumental in bringing Royce to justice. After he was indicted, though, he'd come to talk with her several times at the *Banner Bee*. At that point, he was totally alone. His wife and daughter had left and his son wasn't talking to him. He had wanted to talk, to explain how he came to commit fraud and cheat so many seniors out of their life's savings. He had accepted full blame and clearly felt anguish about what he'd done. Francesca could not excuse him, but she had listened.

"Dad, let's get you something to eat."

Royce demurred. "I don't want you to spend your hard-earned money on me."

"Well, I'm going to have a hamburger and so are you. What about you, Francesca?"

"Just get me a Diet Coke. Okay?"

They both watched Colman weave his way toward the vending machines. "You've got a wonderful son, Royce," Francesca said. "He's amazing. You must be so proud."

Royce turned to look at her, his grey eyes reflecting pain and sincerity. "I am proud of him, but I feel so guilty that I let him down. It's because of me that he has to fight life's battles alone."

Francesca was silent. Then she said, "You know what I think, Royce? We are all alone. What we ultimately make of ourselves is up to each of us individually. That said you can still play a major role in encouraging him, listening to him. Whatever you may have done, you are still an important person in his life. That's why he's here." She looked up as Colman returned to the table with his hands full and his pockets bulging. He'd brought warmed-up hamburgers, pop, bags of chips and candy bars.

"I've brought some healthy snacks full of vitamins and minerals. This is what we do here, Francesca. We eat." He placed the bags on the table.

"Right," Francesca said with a laugh. The microwaved hamburgers left something to be desired, but they ate them anyway. Colman and Francesca told Royce all the latest news from Banner Bluff. He was interested in Ramses Crenshaw's visit. It seemed one of RC's former associates was incarcerated in Jordanville. The guy had been involved in a payola scheme. Although RC had to have known what was going on, he had managed to evade criminal charges.

"The Pharaoh is as slippery as a greased pig," Royce mused. "They can't catch him on anything; but his cronies aren't so lucky. They're willing to take the fall." He shook his head in disgust.

Colman ate a chip. "Dad, is Alexei here? I bet Francesca would like meeting him. He's really a nice guy." He turned to Francesca. "Alexei is Dad's cellmate. He's a Russian doctor."

Royce stood and scanned the room. "Yes, he's here. Over there by the mural."

Colman got up and found his way over to a tall, dark man who sat with a slim blond woman. They chatted with Colman for a minute and then came over to Royce and Francesca, Colman carrying their chairs. Before they even sat down, Francesca stood up and smiled.

"Hello, Anya. Remember meeting me at the hospital last week? I was with Mr. Penfield."

84

Anya looked worried. She glanced from right to left as though she wanted to escape. Then she faced Francesca. "I remember. Yes. Uh, how is Mr. Penfield?"

Francesca felt confused. She had thought this woman would be happy to say hello; but Anya obviously didn't want to be recognized. The fact that her husband was in prison must be a deeply held secret. Alexei looked embarrassed at his wife's reaction, while Royce and Colman stood still looking uncomfortable.

Francesca plunged ahead, "Mr. Penfield speaks highly of you." She turned to Alexei. "I hear your wife is the favorite of all the patients that visit the oncology department. She has winning ways."

Alexei smiled. "She does, indeed. Please, sit down." He moved Anya's chair closer to his and sat, then reached over and took her slim hand in his. She clutched his large one and looked down at her lap.

Francesca battled on. "I came with Colman to keep him company today. It's a long trip from Banner Bluff." *What else should I say? Tell me why you're in prison? Right. That would go over well.*

The awkwardness slowly eased as Royce began to talk about some of the cases he was working on. Currently, he was looking into some discrepancies in Alexei's trial. "This legal work keeps my mind busy and I don't have time to dwell on the long years ahead."

Alexei told them he was working his way through the prison's meager library selection. In addition, Anya sent him books through Amazon and he had subscriptions to various medical journals. He was in better physical shape than Royce and said he worked out every day. They discussed the monotony of the food and the overly sweet juice served with every meal.

"What I wouldn't do for a nice glass of cabernet," Royce said.

"Or a bottle of Stolichnaya," Alexei quipped. They laughed together. The lack of alcohol was obviously something they'd joked about before. Eventually, the conversation came around to Banner Bluff and the renowned hospital where Anya worked. Francesca asked if she knew Dr. Marcus Reynolds, and told them about the wedding shower the night before. When Alexei asked, Francesca explained it was a party to celebrate the engaged couple and shower them with gifts.

"I know Dr. Reynolds," Anya said. "Last winter he helped me shovel out my car from under a foot of snow. He is a very nice man."

Alexei frowned. "I don't remember hearing about this snow storm."

"I didn't want to worry you." Anya said, squeezing his hand and smiling.

Colman and Royce got up to get more Cokes. Francesca looked across the room. A couple three tables away were kissing passionately. Colman had told her there were no conjugal visits in federal prison. They looked like they could use some private time together.

Anya and Alexei were talking quietly, their voices barely audible above the general chatter. They had edged their chairs a little away from her, as if in quest of privacy that was clearly in short supply at Jordanville. Francesca tried not to eavesdrop, but her interest was piqued when she heard Alexei mention Banner Bluff. He was gazing out the window at the cold, deserted courtyard. "I heard talk about Banner Bluff from my cousin Sergei," he whispered.

"Why do you still talk to him? That family, they are nothing to you. They have ruined your life and mine." Anya's tone was both angry and pleading.

"Anya, you don't understand. They keep tabs on me, they send me money. And," he paused, turning to look at her. "They will help you if you need them."

"I will never, ever need them." Anya's hands were clenched into fists.

Alexei continued. "Sergei said Petroff thinks there's a snitch in Banner Bluff that will destroy the business. The Hook is angry."

Anya shivered. "What does that mean?"

Alexei put his arm around her and pulled her close. "Shhh, I shouldn't have talked to you. Don't worry, Мой дорогой."

At that moment Colman and Royce returned. Alexei fell silent, and Francesca wondered what she had heard. It didn't make any sense to her. What business were they talking about? And what—or who—was 'the hook'?

On the way home, Colman put on some music and they didn't talk. Somehow, the visit had been exhausting. Francesca was glad to be on the outside of Jordanville Prison. She wanted to go home and take a shower.

Once, they met on a Saturday. Isabelle got permission to go to the mall to buy a birthday present for Rachel. Usually, she wasn't allowed to go. Her mom didn't approve of the kids who hung out at the mall. "Mall rats," she called them. Isabelle assured her mom that she would be with a nice group of girls from the school choir. The word "choir" was her secret weapon. Her mom thought they were a more trustworthy group of kids. Actually, Isabelle thought the choir girls were ding-a-lings.

Her dad dropped her off by Macy's and said he would be back to get her at four o'clock. Brett met her in front of the Apple store. He wanted to look at the new iPhone. Then they just wandered around. She picked out a little jewelry box for Rachel from a costume jewelry shop. Then they went out of the mall and across the street to Game City. It was a little sleazy and there were a lot of boys playing video games. In the back there were dark wooden booths and vending machines. They got Dr. Peppers and two bags of Doritos. They sat close together on one side of a booth so no one could see them.

They fed each other Doritos and talked. Then they started to kiss. Time flew by. At five of four, Isabelle tore out of Game City and ran across the road. She just missed being hit by a red pick-up truck. The driver honked at her and then rolled down the window and gave her the finger. When she met her dad, she was out of breath.

"Sorry, Dad, I was at the other end of the mall when I looked at the time."

"Don't worry kitten, I would have waited." He smiled at her and ruffled her hair.

Chapter 9
Monday Afternoon, November 13th

Francesca stood looking up at the house. From this perspective it seemed massive. The grey stone and heavy masonry denoted strength and permanence. She started up the wide front steps. She had received a call from Lorinda Landers the day before, in response to a small notice in the *Banner Bee* about the cell phone found in the garbage can on the bluff above the lake.

"I know something about that cell phone," Lorinda had said when Francesca called back. "It may be important information. I'd prefer to talk about it in person." Knowing Lorinda was practically homebound; Francesca figured she was hoping for a visit. So here she was.

This house was one of the treasures of Banner Bluff. Beveled glass sidelights flanked the heavy oak door, and the doorframe was intricately carved with small birds and garlands of flowers. Francesca rang the doorbell and heard a shower of chimes inside. A moment later, the door was opened by a statuesque African-American woman wearing a dark blue dress and a crisp white apron. Her face broke into a big smile and she reached out to give Francesca a hug.

"How are you doing darlin'? You look pretty as a picture with that pink hat and scarf."

"I'm fine, Sadie, how about you?"

"I'm doing as well as can be expected at the ripe old age of seventy." She winked and drew Francesca into the house. "Let me take your coat. Mrs. Landers is expecting you. She's sitting in the front room." She gestured to Francesca and whispered, "She's been waiting for you since this morning." Then in a louder voice, "Mrs. Landers, here's our favorite visitor."

Francesca stepped into the parlor. Several lamps glowed in the afternoon light. A fire crackled in the fireplace. A table pulled up between two period armchairs was set with an embroidered tablecloth, delicate teacups, silver spoons and flowered plates.

"Hello, dear Francesca. How wonderful to see you," Lorinda Landers made an effort to stand.

"Please don't get up. Stay right where you are." Francesca went over and bent down to hug Lorinda. "Don't you look pretty with that lovely blue sweater?"

"It's cashmere. Seems like a terrible expense. My nephew Harold sent it to me for my birthday. He never forgets my birthday. I figure he's worried I won't include him in the will when I die."

"Now, Mrs. Landers, he's very fond of you," Sadie said.

"Maybe he is, but I know he has expensive tastes." She raised her eyebrows and rubbed her thumb and forefinger together.

Sadie left to fetch the tea, turning down Francesca's offer to help. Francesca sat down in the armchair across from Lorinda. She had met both of these ladies shortly after moving to Banner Bluff as a young bride. At the summer outdoor market Francesca had been looking at a display of fresh produce and wondering how to cook it all. An offer to come and take cooking lessons from Sadie had swiftly grown into friendship.

Francesca looked out at the flat, cold lake. It was nice to be inside. Sadie returned bearing a tray with a silver pot of tea and three plates of cookies. "I made you some shortbread, Francesca. I know you like it." The shortbread was cut in small triangles and bars. There was also a plate of almond tuiles and one of blackberry jam cake.

"This looks like a feast." Francesca said. "Thank you, Sadie."

Sadie poured them each a cup of tea and then she retired to the kitchen.

They spent a few minutes eating and chatting, and then Francesca turned things to the reason for her visit. "So what do you have to tell me about this mysterious cell phone?"

Lorinda looked pleased to begin her tale with a captive audience. "I was looking out at the birds and squirrels the other day and I saw a gentleman walking along the sidewalk." She gestured toward the spyglass that lay on the table near her chair. "He was talking and gesturing. I think he was angry with the person on the other end of the line. He had a couple of friends following along behind him." Lorinda took a sip of tea. "He went to the end of the block and then he retraced his steps. He kept jabbering on his phone the whole time. When he got down near the garbage can at the top of the access road to the beach, he threw his phone in. Can you believe it?" She shook her head in disgust. "What a waste."

"Do you know who the man was?" Francesca inquired.

Lorinda's pale blue eyes met Francesca's. "Yes, I do." Then she sighed. "The problem is, for the life of me, I can't remember his name."

"Is he somebody from Banner Bluff?"

"No, no, he's someone you see in the paper and on TV."

"In the paper and on TV," Francesca repeated. "Is he famous, like an actor or sports figure?"

"No, no. Someone else."

"Don't upset yourself, Lorinda. It will come to you." Francesca reached over and patted her friend's hand. "Do you remember what day it was?"

Lorinda bit her lip. "I think it was last Monday because Sadie was making tuna sandwiches and Herbert was meowing up a storm. We always have tuna sandwiches on Monday."

What had happened last Monday? Then it hit her. "Lorinda, did you see Governor Crenshaw?"

Lorinda's eyes lit up with relief and pleasure. "My stars, that's who it was, The Pharaoh. He threw that phone away, and it was probably purchased with taxpayers' money."

Francesca's mind was racing. Yari Gonzalez had heard a call on that phone. A threatening call, something about *agua corriente*. She needed to get back to Yari and have her repeat that phone message word for word.

It was a Wednesday night.

"What's the matter, Brett?" They were lying side by side on the floor, their heads on a pillow, sharing a joint; but he was barely communicating.

She tried again, "Are you mad at me?"

"No, I just feel shitty."

"Why?"

"Isabelle, you're the only good thing that's happened to me since I moved here." He fell silent gazing at the ceiling. "My dad isn't even calling anymore. He doesn't call and he doesn't text. It's like I'm dead as far as he's concerned." His voice sounded low and plaintive.

"Well, he's probably busy."

"Right...too busy to call his only son."

She could see tears running down his cheeks. She turned toward him and licked them away. Then she kissed him tenderly. He reached for her and they rolled together on the carpet.

Chapter 10
Monday Evening, November 13th

At 8 PM, Tom Barnett was at his desk doing paperwork. He wondered if anyone realized that police work involved a myriad of forms, documentation, fact-checking and research. Probably not! He thought of the popular image of the hefty cop sitting in the coffee shop enjoying a couple of doughnuts and a mug of java. Wouldn't that be nice?

This evening he meant to stay at his desk until he had filed every last report. Most of the "paperwork" involved electronic files, so he was punching away on his computer. Down the hall he could hear Arlyne, the dispatcher, talking to someone. Her voice was raised and she spoke with intensity. A few moments later she appeared at his door.

"Chief, we've got a nine-one-one call from a Martin Marshall. He claims to have seen a woman, hanging by the rafters in some shack in the woods." Arlyne's normally ruddy complexion was pasty white. "Chief, he said her feet were on fire. He could smell it."

"What woods?" Tom got up and came around his desk, reaching for his coat.

"In the forest preserve, sir, off of Eastern."

"Where is Marshall?" Tom asked as he zipped up his jacket.

"On a slope behind some bushes near the creek. I told him to stay put."

"Where did he say this woman was located?" Tom was heading down the hall to the parking lot. Arlyne trailed behind him.

"At the top of the prairie path, back off the track. You know those old buildings that are falling apart? That's where. We have officers converging on the area."

Tom turned toward her before heading out the door. "Notify the Homicide Task Force coordinator and get Hollister over to the crime scene."

"Yes, sir."

The wind swirled dry leaves across the parking lot. There was a heavy chill in the air. Maybe they would get some early snow tonight, Tom thought as he drove down Banner Boulevard towards the forest preserve.

He turned off Eastern Road onto a rutted dirt track. Someone had removed the heavy chain that normally hung between two posts barring this entrance to the woods. This was the back way into the preserve and was not intended for vehicles. Tom drove down the narrow track, tree branches brushing his car. His headlights illuminated dark tree trunks and heavy underbrush. As he came around a bend he saw a floodlit clearing. Several patrol cars were parked along the periphery.

Deputy Chief Conroy greeted him as Tom got out of the car. Two other officers were stringing yellow crime scene tape to form a boundary in the open clearing. "Chief, this is horrific," Conroy said. "Holy moly, I've never seen anything like it. These are some perverted bastards."

Tom viewed the open area and the lights coming from the woods. "Where do we stand here?"

"We've cordoned off part of this area. There are some tire marks that could be from the killer's car. We've also cordoned off the pathway back to the crime scene. We're using an alternative route through the trees. Evidence technicians from the Homicide Task Force should be along any time now."

Tom nodded. "What about Martin Marshall?"

94

"Some guys came in from the other way, from the entrance to the forest preserve. They say he's pretty shook up. They're taking him in to the station now."

"I want Puchalski to talk to him, to get his story while it's fresh."

"Puchalski is back at the crime scene."

"Okay. Let's go back there."

Following Conroy, Tom wove through the trees past one dilapidated structure and then around a tumbledown fence towards another ramshackle building. It was missing a wall, and Tom could see right into it. Floodlights lit up the other three walls. The scene had the eerie feeling of a stage set.

Directly in the middle of the open area, hanging from the rafters, was the nude body of a young woman. A girl really. She had a slim, muscular body with small breasts and jutting hip bones. As Tom got closer he saw the nylon rope around her neck and smelled the lingering odor of burning flesh. Her hands were tied behind her back. Her head hung slightly to the side, her mouth open. A swollen, darkened tongue protruded through her teeth. One eye was open, the pupil dilated. Her features were contorted into a ghastly grimace.

On the ground was a smoldering fire. The remnants of a wooden chair lay among the ashes, the spindles and top rail fallen away out of the fire's reach. Above the fire, the young woman's feet were blackened and charred. That explained where the stench came from.

Tom turned away, breathing in the cold night air. Footsteps and voices behind him announced the arrival of the evidence technicians. He looked up at the trees, steeling his mind and his racing heart. Then he turned back to the crime scene. The technicians were ready to go, dressed in their white PPE's, their hoods up, their hands gloved and their feet shod in protective booties. They looked like purposeful ghosts. To the right, talking to one of the newly arrived ET's, was Detective Sergeant Ron Puchalski. Tom went over to him.

"Ron, glad you've had a chance to view the crime scene. I want you to go back to the station and interview Martin Marshall while everything is fresh in his mind. We need his statement and any evidence he can give us."

"I'm on my way." Puchalski glanced over at the body. "This looks like some kind of torture; like they had her stand on a chair until it burned away and then she suffocated to death. I just hope she was dead before her feet caught on fire."

Tom grimaced. "Here comes the man who can answer all those questions."

Approaching through the woods came Edmond Hollister, the Medical Examiner. Tom walked over to greet him. Hollister was a small, energetic man with quick hands and a wry sense of humor. He accomplished his job with vigor, no matter how gruesome the task. He had a round, bald head with a ring of grey hair. In his PPE's he looked like a jolly gnome.

Acknowledging Tom, he whistled and then said, "Talk about putting her feet to the fire."

Martin was freezing. The new recruit, Officer Romano, had gone down to the jail in the basement to get a couple of blankets. He brought them up and helped Martin wrap himself in their warmth. "Can I get you some coffee?" Romano asked with concern.

"Not coffee. Have you got a tea bag? I think I'd rather have tea."

"Sure, I can make tea. No problem."

"Actually, I'd rather have a double scotch."

"I know what you mean. Unfortunately, we never applied for a liquor license." Romano chuckled as he started out the door of the interview room.

Martin wished he could laugh about something. After tonight, he had the feeling he'd never laugh again.

A little while later, Detective Puchalski entered the room. Martin started to stand, still clutching the blankets around him, but Puchalski waved him down. "No, no, don't get up. How are you doing, Mr. Marshall?"

"I think I'm in aftershock mode. I can't seem to warm up."

"Romano will be back with that tea in a jiff. In the meantime, I need to go through your story. We'll be going through it a couple of times. You might actually feel better after you've talked about it."

Martin nodded, his eyes questioning.

"Do we need to call your wife?"

"Someone drove my car home with the dog. I told them to just tell Kate I was helping you out with an investigation, and to go ahead and have dinner." He paused, tears filling his eyes. "I don't want her to know anything about what I saw. I don't want to frighten her."

Puchalski nodded his face full of sympathy. Martin had always liked the tall, methodical cop with the kind and friendly manner. He also knew first-hand that Puchalski was a brilliant detective. Two years ago, he'd helped rescue Martin's daughter from a deranged kidnapper. Now, Puchalski looked into Martin's eyes with understanding. "Let's get started. The sooner we start, the sooner it will be over." He reached up and turned on the video-recorder. "Tell me what happened in your own words."

Martin cleared his throat and began to talk. "You know I had a fall and I've been having some problems since." His long, thin hands clenched the edge of the blankets. "The university gave me the semester off. Anyway, I needed to get out of the house and get some air."

Ron nodded, his eyes reflecting sympathy and interest.

"Going up the path, you know, by the open prairie, I heard this weird keening sound. Jack heard it too. Jack's my dog. Anyway, I thought it was an animal or a bird. But now I'm thinking it was the girl. I think she was screaming in pain. Oh God!" He began to shake. When Puchalski reached out as if to steady him, Martin took a deep breath and mastered his emotions. *He could do this. He had to.* "And then I smelled something cooking." He hid his face in his hands and mumbled through his fingers. "It was her, it was her feet."

Puchalski laid a hand on Martin's shoulder. "Take your time. I know this is hard."

Martin began again. "When we got to the top of the path, I heard a couple of guys talking about putting out a fire." He looked up at Ron, "I thought it was teenagers. I thought they needed help."

"What did they say?"

"Something about not being able to cut her down…I wasn't thinking." He stared into space. "I went through the trees and then I looked over the wall…and I saw it…her."

Martin described everything he saw in fits and starts. Then he talked about the two men, the tall one in a hoodie and the short darker one. "One of them had an accent. I don't know which one. They saw me. They looked straight at me and I looked at them."

"That's good," Puchalski said. "So you'll be able to recognize them in a photo series or a line-up."

Slowly, Martin shook his head. "I'll never be able to recognize them." He paused. "I'm face-blind."

Last Tuesday, Isabelle got the flu and was out of school for a week. Her mom brought her homemade chicken soup and tea with lemon. Brett texted her between classes. She texted him back when she knew her mom was downstairs. Then, over the weekend, he stopped contacting her. She couldn't leave; her mom was holding her under house arrest, making sure she'd be well enough for school Monday. She left message after message but he never responded. Was he angry with her? Was he sick too? Monday morning at school she waited by his locker but he never showed up.

    Tonight she'd gone to the library like usual. Brett never came in. He wasn't at the back entrance so she headed over to his house. If his mom or sister were there, she'd make up some excuse. She went up the front steps and rang the bell. The lights were on in the living room. She climbed up on the wrought iron banister and leaned over so she could see in. Brett was on the sofa.

    She hopped down and tried the front door. The knob turned. She went inside and walked over to the sofa. Brett looked a mess. His eyes were unfocused and his crazy hair was sticking straight up. He didn't seem to see her. On the coffee table were a straw and traces of white powder.

    "Brett, what's wrong?"

    He moved his head. He looked like he was trying to focus. His pupils were like pinpoints, and he was trembling. "Everything is wrong." His speech was slurred.

    "Brett, are you sick? What can I do?" His skin had a bluish cast; his lips were a deeper blue. He was having trouble breathing. "Brett, what's the matter? Do you think you've got the flu?"

    He seemed out of it now. He was murmuring. "Mickey...bad stuff."

    What should she do? In the kitchen there was a landline. She went in, picked up the phone and called 911. When the dispatcher answered, she blurted out, "A boy is very sick at 233 Elm."

    "Miss, can I get your name?"

"He's very sick. Hurry! Did you get it? 233 Elm! Please send an ambulance." Before the woman could ask her any more questions, she hung up.

In the living room, Brett's cellphone rang. It was on the coffee table beside him. He didn't react. She stared at it, frozen in place. She had to get out of there but the phone was calling to her. She ran over and picked it up. The screen said PRIVATE. She put the phone in her pocket and bolted out the door.

She ran most of the way home. It was raining. Wet leaves covered the sidewalk. They were slippery under her feet. She fell down twice and scraped her hands. By the time she got home, her wet jeans clung to her legs and her coat was smudged with dirt. She opened the front door and then slammed it shut.

Her mom came out of the kitchen. "Isabelle, what's wrong, honey? You're as white as a sheet!"

Isabelle stood there shaking. She couldn't talk, couldn't focus.

Her mom walked over to her and gently gripped her shoulders. "Tell me what happened, honey. Did you fall down? Your coat looks filthy."

"I'm sick, Mom. I ran home from the library and I fell down. I'm going up to bed." She dropped her backpack on the floor.

"Let me see if you have a fever. Does your head ache?"

She couldn't stand all the questions. She needed to get away. She eased out of her mother's grasp.

"Do you think you haven't fully recovered from the flu? Maybe you should stay home from school tomorrow."

Isabelle was on her way up the stairs. "Yeah, Mom, I want to stay home tomorrow. Right now I need to sleep." Before her mom could say anything else, she charged into her room and slammed the door behind her.

Brett, Brett. What was wrong with him? He could barely breathe and he looked so weird.

She took off her coat and pulled Brett's phone out of her pocket. She put it under her pillow. Then she took off her wet clothes and threw them in the hamper in the bathroom. By the time her mother knocked at the door, she was in bed with her eyes closed, one hand clutching the cellphone to her chest.

Chapter 11
Tuesday Morning, November 14th

Julie decided to go over to Carrie's apartment. She had a key so she could just let herself in. Carrie wasn't answering her cell phone. Julie had tried a zillion times since she got home last night and heard Carrie's message. She'd left messages of her own, and she'd texted several times. Julie knew her friend was supposed to work on Monday and Tuesday, so she should be around. She pulled on her down jacket and grabbed her purse.

Outside it was cold, grey and windy, a real November day. At Carrie's apartment, Julie pulled up in front of the ancient garage next to Carrie's red Prius. She got out and went around to peer inside. Carrie's workout bag was on the back seat. She must have forgotten to bring it in. In the cup holder there was a Starbuck's cup and several bunched-up Kleenexes. The rest of the car was empty.

Julie felt a little nervous as she walked up the worn wooden steps that flanked the building. What would she find in Carrie's apartment? Something terrible might have happened. Carrie hadn't sounded normal when she'd left that message. She'd sounded upset, maybe even scared. Maybe Carrie had fallen; or she'd started using again and had overdosed. Julie held on to the railing as a gust of wind whipped around the corner of the building. *Please, let me be wrong.*

She knocked on the door several times. Nothing. Then she tried looking through the side window into the main room. The curtains had been pulled across and she could only see through a slit.

She slipped her key into the lock, but to her surprise the door swung open. "Hey," she called out. "It's Julie. Are you here? Carrie, are you here?" There was no answer.

She moved into the front room that served as living room and kitchen. Everything looked normal. Carrie had turned into a neat freak once she had her own place, and the apartment was clean and tidy. In the back, a little hallway led to a bedroom and a bathroom. With trepidation, Julie went down the hallway and checked out the bedroom. The bed was neatly made. Julie looked in the closet and under the bed. She felt like a CIA agent, spying on her friend. In the bathroom the towels were carefully hung on the rack. She pulled back the shower curtain. No one was there.

She went back to the main room and took a closer look. On the counter was a box of quinoa and a knife next to a cutting board that held shriveled-up, diced sweet potatoes and onions. On the other side of the board lay a tired-looking zucchini. Little black flies buzzed around the vegetables. Julie felt slightly nauseated. Something wasn't right.

As she walked back toward the door, she caught sight of Carrie's purse on the floor. She'd missed seeing it when she walked in. Everything had been dumped out. Julie looked down at the lipstick, wallet, pencil and small notebook scattered across the floor. Carrie's phone wasn't there. Her car keys were hanging in their usual spot, on the tail of the carved wooden monkey Carrie and Julie had found at a garage sale.

Julie stood still, trying to think. The silence inside the apartment was oppressive. She needed to get out. She jerked open the door. Her key was still in the lock. Fighting with a gust of wind, she pulled the door shut and locked it. Then she ran down the stairs, feeling as though she was being chased.

She backed down the driveway and pulled over next to the front porch of Carrie's parents' house. She yanked open the car door, got out and ran up the steps to the front door. She rang the bell several times, and then knocked frantically. No one answered. Then, she remembered that Carrie's parents were in New York attending some shows. They were theatre buffs and went to New York and London several times a year.

Back in the car she folded her arms across her chest and rested her forehead on the steering wheel. What should she do? Go to the police? Would they think she was nuts? She tried calling Sandra Sorenson. Maybe Sandra had seen Carrie around.

"Where are you?" Sandra said when she heard Julie's voice. "You've got a class at ten. I thought you'd pulled a runner like Carrie."

"What do you mean?"

"Carrie never showed up yesterday and she was supposed to do the eight AM class today. Never called, never answered her phone. Do you know where she is?"

"No. But I'm worried. Listen, Sandra, something's wrong. I'm going to report this to the police."

Someone had been murdered in the forest preserve last night. Francesca had heard the sirens in the early evening. When she drove over to the preserve, she found the entrance cordoned off. Curiosity seekers as well as TV and newspaper reporters were milling around trying to glean information. But the police stayed tight-lipped and refused to divulge anything. She had joined the throng for a couple of hours, and then gave up and went home.

This morning she'd been plagued by reporters from the big-name papers who wanted to know if she knew anything. They figured her small local online news source might get inside information. She had checked Facebook and Twitter, but it was all innuendo and hearsay. She was as much in the dark as anyone, and Tom didn't return her calls. Finally she got Arlyne over at the station, who told her there would be a press conference at eleven. She would just have to wait until then like everybody else.

A teenaged boy had also died last night, from a drug overdose. Francesca had gone to the hospital earlier this morning and managed to talk to Mary Frances, a nurse she knew. Apparently the boy, Brett Atkins, had died on the way to the hospital. No one else had been able to fill her in. She would have to talk to Tom about all this, and hope he didn't shut her out of the investigation.

The police station was humming. Along with the small Banner Bluff force, the Homicide Task Force had taken up residence in the basement meeting room. Detectives and evidence technicians had been sent in from surrounding communities to assist in the murder investigation.

Chief Barnett was talking to Detective Mark Sanders from Lindenville about the teenager who'd died of an overdose. "A girl called in to say this kid was in a bad way. All of us were out at the forest preserve. It took an extra ten minutes to get someone over there. When Sergeant Lister arrived at the house, the front door was wide open. He found the boy passed out on the sofa, barely breathing. The paramedics arrived, but it was too late."

"What do they think? Heroin?"

"Yeah, there was a straw and traces of heroin on a coffee table. This is another drug case, Mark. We've got to get on top of this river of poison that's pouring into our towns." Tom balled up his right fist and punched the palm of his left hand in frustration.

"What about the girl who called in?" Sanders asked.

"She was gone."

"Do they know who she could be?"

"Not a clue. The boy's mother and sister arrived home at about nine-fifteen. Lister had to give them the terrible news. The mom works in the city and often stays late. The sister works over at Appleby's until nine."

"What about his friends?"

"The mother claims he had some questionable friends. His sister said he'd started smoking pot after they moved here."

105

"How long have they lived in Banner Bluff?"

"Only since last summer." Tom paused. The horrors of last night flashed through his mind. He swallowed, trying to regain control. "You know what makes me mad? This mother really didn't know what her son was doing. She left him alone night after night." He punched his hand again. "And the boy, Brett Atkins, was only sixteen."

Sanders avoided Tom's eyes. "I hear you." He paused. "Getting back to our murder, so far we have no idea who the victim is, right? No one has come forward?"

Before Tom could respond, Officer Romano came charging down the hall. "Chief Barnett, there's a girl who's here to report a missing person. It's her friend who's missing."

"Bring her through. I'll speak to her in my office." Tom turned to Sanders and raised his eyebrows. "Maybe this is what we've been waiting for."

Romano went back through the security door to the lobby. A moment later he reappeared, leading an attractive young woman down the hall. She wore a red jacket over a yoga outfit in turquoise and dark blue. Tom noted details with a cop's long practice: she was of average height with shoulder-length black curls framing a pretty, round face. Her skin glowed ebony and her dark eyes reflected worry and apprehension.

He greeted her at the door of his office. "Please come in. Why don't we sit at this table and you can tell me why you're here." He nodded thanks to Romano and led her over to the round conference table.

She started talking even before she sat down. "I'm Julie Robinson. I'm here about my friend Carrie, Carrie Landwehr. She's missing. She called me this past weekend but I was gone and I didn't have my phone with me. And then I went over there and she's not there and she hasn't been to work and…" She looked up at Tom. "I'm really scared something happened to her."

"Let's start at the beginning." Tom reached over and grabbed a pencil and a pad of paper off his desk. Although his laptop was right there, he still felt more comfortable with paper and pencil when he took down information. He thought and listened better when he had pencil in hand. "You said your friend's name is Carrie. Carrie what?"

"Carrie Landwehr. L-A-N-D-W-E-H-R."

"Where does she live?"

"Over on Sycamore. I don't know the number but I can show you where it is. She lives in the garage apartment behind her parents' house. I went over there. She's not there, but her car and her purse are." The young woman unzipped her coat. She was perspiring and her gaze darted around the room.

"How long has she been missing."

"I don't know exactly. I just know she called me and sounded weird." She pulled her cell phone out of her pocket and punched a couple of buttons. "Here, listen." She held out the phone.

"Julie? Julie? I'm way scared. I think they're coming to get me. It's because of what I saw. I don't know what to do. Where are you, Julie? I—" Then the phone call cut off.

Tom handed the phone back to her. "We'll need to make a copy of that."

She nodded. "I was gone all weekend for my granny's birthday and I didn't have my phone." She pushed her hair out of her face, her eyes filling with tears.

Tom's face reflected concern. "Would you like some coffee or tea?"

"No thanks, but I would like some water. I don't do caffeine."

Tom reached over and made a call to the front desk. Then he turned back to her. "Do you know what she's talking about in this voice mail...about what she saw?"

107

"I don't have a clue." Julie sniffled. "Who would be coming to get her? Her parents are out of town. It couldn't be them."

A chill crept through him. "Julie, can you tell me what Carrie looks like?"

"She's about 5'5" like me. She's pretty thin. White. She's got short brown hair and blue eyes."

Tom felt his breathing accelerate. He continued to write on the pad, but his mind was racing. "Do you have a picture of your friend?"

"Yeah." Julie opened her purse and took out a zebra-striped wallet, pulled out a picture and handed it to him. "They took this at work." It was of herself and a young white woman, both of them dressed in turquoise and blue workout clothes. They were laughing at the camera, their arms around each other.

Tom gazed down at it and swallowed. Then he looked back up at Julie.

"I think we've found your friend," he said slowly.

Chapter 12
Wednesday Morning, November 15th

Carina Meriwether rode up from the eastern pasture on Cinnamon, her silky brown quarter horse. She had been checking the fencing along the bluff over Lake Michigan and up along the southern pasture. In the weeks ahead, she and José would need to do some repairs. A strong breeze was blowing off the lake, bringing occasional sprinkles with it. She was glad she had put on a sweater under her worn leather jacket. A brown cowboy hat kept her head warm, and a china-blue scarf was wound around her neck.

She was about to dismount at the entrance to the barn when she saw a sleek Lexus snaking its way up the driveway towards the house. With her knee she nudged Cinnamon forward. As she approached the house, a tall, lean man unfolded himself from the driver's seat and stood leaning against the car door.

"Mornin', ma'am, sure's nice ta meet ya."

"Well, good morning to you." Carina looked down at him, sizing him up. He had sharp brown eyes under dark brows in a tanned face. His teeth were shiny white and his dark brown hair was neatly cut. He wore a dark blue suit, white shirt and a striped blue and red tie. This guy must be a lawyer, Carina thought. What was he doing here?

He grinned at her. "I can't believe there's a real, live cowgirl in these parts!"

"Sorry to disappoint you, but there are no cows in the vicinity." She dismounted smoothly and tied Cinnamon to the newel post, then stuck out her hand. "I'm Carina Meriwether. I live here." She gestured toward the house.

"Well, Miss, or is it Mrs. Meriwether?" He took her hand in both of his. They were warm and enveloped hers.

"It's Miss." Carina extracted her hand. "My mother, Mrs. Meriwether, is in the house, but she's in bed today with the flu. Was she expecting you?"

"No, but perhaps I can present the situation to you, then," he said. "My name is Harrison Rand. I'm a lawyer for the state of Illinois. Let me get my briefcase out of the car.

Present the situation? State of Illinois? What could that possibly mean? She felt uneasy as she watched him retrieve a black leather briefcase from the back of his car.

When Mr. Rand returned, she led the way up the front steps to the house. She retrieved a key ring from the back pocket of her jeans and opened the door. It used to be that they never locked the doors, but ever since several scruffy men had come by looking for work, the Meriwethers had decided to keep the place locked up. After all, they were two women living alone and José went home at night. Carina had a gun and knew how to use it but she kept it locked away in the safe.

She stepped inside and ushered in their guest. Then she bent down and took off her dirty boots, leaving them on the mat. She felt foolish standing there in her stocking feet as she unwound the blue scarf from around her neck. "Why don't you follow me into the kitchen? That's the warmest place in the house."

He seemed to be taking her measure.

"Would you like a cup of coffee, Mr. Rand?" she asked as they walked down the hall to the bright kitchen.

"Please call me Harrison and yes, I would love a cup of coffee."

Carina was supremely aware of him following her past the library, the living and dining rooms. She chattered on nervously. "We've got a potbelly stove in the kitchen that my dad installed years ago. It's expensive to heat this big, old house so we stick to the kitchen much of the time."

110

"What's your first name?" he asked as they entered the sunny room.

"Carina. I was named after my maternal grandmother."

"May I call you Carina, then?"

"Yes, you may," she said, not looking at him.

Before measuring out the coffee beans, Carina picked up the house phone and called down to the barn. "José, I've got a guest here. I've left Cinnamon in front of the house. Could you please come up and take him down to the barn? Thanks so much." She figured it didn't hurt for Mr. Rand to know that a man on the premises was aware of his presence.

She whirred the coffee beans in the grinder and made a fresh pot of coffee, while Mr. Rand walked across the room and looked out the double French doors that gave onto a painted wooden deck. Beyond the deck were the barn, the rolling fields and a glimpse of Lake Michigan glistening in the sun that was peeking through the clouds.

"This is a beautiful spot you've got here. It must be great to be able to look at these fields and the lake every day."

"It is, but to us right now, it all represents a lot of work. The truth is we're suffering like everyone else in this economy. We've had to let go a couple of farm hands." *Why was she telling him all this? It wasn't as though he cared one way or the other about their financial situation.*

"In that case, you may welcome the court action that I'm here to present."

Carina felt apprehensive. She didn't know this man, and here he was standing in their kitchen. What court action was he talking about? She reached into the cupboard for the white cups with the red Hollyhock motif. "Mr. Rand, do you take cream or sugar?"

"No, I like it black and strong." He sat down on one side of the long oak table.

111

"So do I." Carina poured them each a cup of coffee and placed them on the table. She didn't feel like addressing him as Harrison. He was here on some official government business and he most definitely was not her friend.

He looked at her quizzically. "Harrison! Remember?"

"Listen, I don't know who you are or why you're here. Let's just get down to business. Okay? I've got a million things to do today."

A small smile played on his lips. Again he seemed to be taking her measure. Then he reached down, opened his briefcase and brought out a file folder. He opened it and handed her a multi-page document. "Miss Meriwether, I am here representing the state of Illinois, which is going to acquire one thousand feet of your beachfront property by eminent domain. You will be appropriately compensated in accordance with the current value of beachfront property. Do you understand the legal ramifications of eminent domain?"

Carina wasn't sure. She shook her head slowly. "Is that when they take over your land to build a road or a train track?"

"Right, it means literally the power to take private property for public use. It's a legal action for the public good. The state is taking some of your property, but you will receive monetary compensation from the state."

"How much?" Carina asked, trying not to sound too eager.

"Three million dollars."

"Three million dollars! You have got to be kidding!" Carina was stunned. "What land are we talking about? You aren't going to build a road through our land, are you?"

Mr. Rand shuffled some papers and pulled out a detailed map of Hollyhock Farm, complete with land elevations. He pointed to an area at the north end of their property just before the land jutted out into Lake Michigan to form a peninsula. At that point the bluff fell abruptly to the shoreline below.

"What does the state of Illinois want to do with that land that would benefit the general public?" Carina was skeptical.

"Do you see this rectangle and this heavy line up through the northern border of your property?" He pointed. She noticed he had strong fingers with nicely curved fingernails. He looked over at her.

"Yes." She felt slightly irritated and didn't know why.

"The rectangle will be the home of a new water pumping station and the line leading up to Eastern Road represents a pipe that will be laid underground connecting the pumping station to the main water lines on the other side of Eastern Road. This new pumping station will provide water to the suburbs west of here. It's a basic necessity for a large number of people. Those communities have grown terrifically in the last fifteen years and water is in short supply. With the drought we've experienced these last few years, the deep aquifers are not being replenished."

He spoke with little inflection, and Carina had the impression he was reciting a script. "Who determined that *our* land should be appropriated?"

"You had a recent visit from some geologists that have been studying the shoreline up and down the north shore, looking for the best location for the water plant. Simply put, you own the best spot." He picked up his cup and sipped the hot coffee. "This is good." He tapped the cup.

"How big is this pumping station going to be?" She was imagining a monstrosity.

"I don't know all the ins and outs of the construction; but with the new methods and solar pumps it shouldn't be that large. These are photovoltaic systems; they're quiet and don't require fuel. I was told it probably wouldn't be visible from your house." He gestured towards the window. "That's what I was trying to figure out when I was looking out the window a few minutes ago.

113

With those trees above the northern bluff, I don't think you'll even be able to see the structure."

"Do we have any recourse? Can the state just come in and grab the land?"

"In this instance the action being taken will benefit a large number of citizens. You have no choice. But considering the economy, you will be fairly compensated."

They were so deep in conversation; neither of them had noticed the arrival of Daphne Meriwether.

"What are you talking about? What's going on, Carina?" she croaked from the kitchen doorway.

Carina pushed back her chair. "Mom, what are you doing up?"

Harrison Rand stood up and walked over to introduce himself. He held out his hand, but she refused it. She stood trembling in the doorway, clutching the doorjamb. "No one is taking any of our land. This cannot happen. It *will not* happen. I promised." Her voice rose to a crescendo, and then she fell to the floor.

Chapter 13
Wednesday Morning, Nov. 15th

Francesca was in her office above Hero's Market. Downstairs she could hear the rumbling voice of Hero and the sing-song voice of a customer. She'd been down earlier to get a mocha latte.

Yesterday, she had eventually gotten the grisly details of Carrie Landwehr's murder and had reported on the story in the *Banner Bee*. Since then the *Bee*'s forum page had become a hotbed of questions and opinions about what had occurred and why. Plenty of people thought they had the answers. Francesca refereed the comments, only posting those that abided by the stated comment policy. She'd recently changed it to exclude anonymous posts.

The major theme from local residents was horror that this murder could have taken place in their quiet little town. Citizens of Banner Bluff had always felt safe in their insulated village, far from the crime of Chicago. Two years ago all this had temporarily changed when two children were abducted and drowned in Lake Michigan. After the murderer was apprehended, the town returned to its sleepy complacency. Now, they again felt their safety threatened.

Thursday morning, Francesca planned to go over and talk with Mrs. Atkins about the death of her son, Brett. She'd made the call that morning and the woman seemed open to a visit. She said she wanted to tell the story of her son in the local paper. She had refused to speak with reporters from the *Tribune* and the *Sun-Times*.

This morning, Francesca was researching the phrase "agua corriente." She googled the Spanish words and found a series of sites giving their definitions. Basically the term meant running water, but it was also translated as tap water, water pipe system or water supply. In her mind she went back over what Yari Gonzales had told her. Seemingly, the governor had been threatened by someone who wanted him to do something about an *agua corriente project*. What could all this mean? Who had called Governor Crenshaw? With Carrie Landwehr's murder and the Atkins boy's overdose, Francesca knew the small police department would not have time to check the caller ID on the mystery phone. So she would have to wait for that information.

She got up and walked over to the window that looked out on the village green. Today, a brisk wind was blowing the last leaves through the air. The sidewalks were empty. She recognized Martin Marshall pushing a stroller on the path across the green. He moved rapidly and turned around twice to look behind him. When he arrived at the post office on the corner, he picked his son up out of the stroller. He looked furtively up and down the street before entering the building.

Poor Martin. The guy was freaked. She knew he had discovered Carrie Landwehr's body. But she also knew the police had not revealed his identity to the media, for his protection. That didn't seem to matter to Martin, though. He looked scared to death. This was not the man she'd known six months earlier.

She went back to her computer and googled Governor Ramses Crenshaw. She got thousands of results. Every imaginable topic was addressed: Crenshaw's budget, pension reform, the Pharaoh's latest girlfriend, the governor's approval rating. Francesca clicked on the last topic. In spite of all the scandals that swirled around him, RC had managed to maintain a favorable approval rating. Maybe he should be nicknamed the chameleon governor, she thought; bad karma just rolled off his back.

What was she looking for? She really didn't know. She clicked through hundreds of articles and pictures. When she looked at the time, two hours had flown by and she hadn't learned a thing. It struck her then that she did know someone who might help her out: Connie Munster, Bob Newhouse's campaign manager. Francesca sent Connie a quick email.

Chapter 14
Wednesday Morning, November 15th

The Homicide Task Force was meeting downstairs in the conference room. Down the hall were a small workout room, showers, evidence lockers and the department's two jail cells. The walls of the conference room were covered with white boards. Tom Barnett liked organizing information and evidence on the boards as it came in. The information was color-coded, a visual representation that clarified facts for the viewer. They could also tack up pictures and paper documents using magnets.

The Homicide Task Force, like the North Shore Drug Task Force, was made up of detectives from nearby towns. Each community volunteered detectives, technicians and funds to maintain the force. This gave all the towns a core group of policemen providing a variety of skill-sets to the team. Whenever a homicide occurred, the force came together.

Tom looked around the room. The Banner Bluff team looked exhausted. They hadn't had much sleep in the last twenty-four hours. The atmosphere was tense. On one wall was a blown-up picture of Carrie Landwehr that her parents had provided. She was smiling out at them. Next to this portrait was a series of pictures taken at the scene of the crime. The dissimilarity was mind-chilling.

Tom welcomed the members of the task force. They all knew each other except a new addition from Lake Woods: Cindy Murray, a detective in the Lake Woods Police Department. Tom had been told she was an ace investigator. She came from a larger metropolitan area and brought big-city experience to the town. Her being a woman also made her an asset, though even as the thought crossed his mind, he wondered briefly if it was sexist. But in his experience, women and men reacted to situations differently. Having another perspective was a rich addition to the team.

He introduced her to the others. Cindy was a short, slight redhead with a perky face and a ready smile. Initially, he wondered if she could hold her own with this group, but it soon became apparent that she was equal to the challenge.

Detective Puchalski took the floor. "Carrie Landwehr's parents arrived earlier this morning and identified the body of their daughter. ME Hollister's preliminary findings indicate she died of asphyxiation by hanging. She was still alive when her feet were set on fire. It seems they initially put a chair under her feet. When it went up in flames, she lost her footing and subsequently was hanged. We're assuming this was a form of torture in order to obtain information."

All the faces in the group reflected horror, although they were experienced homicide investigators and had seen other gruesome crimes.

Puchalski continued, "There were ligature marks on her wrists and considerable bruising." He paused, looking down at his printout. "She had also been raped. The lab will be doing a forensic DNA analysis and search, which we should get back in a week."

He went over a few more details, including an analysis of the rope used to hang her. "It could have been purchased anywhere. But they did find traces of motor oil on the knot."

"Any fingerprints?" Cindy asked.

"No. Nothing could be lifted, they were too smudged."

"Who discovered the body?" Brendan O'Conner asked.

"Martin Marshall discovered the crime scene while walking his dog. We are not revealing his name to the media at this time, because the killers saw him."

"Can't he ID them for us?" Mark Sanders asked.

Puchalski sighed. "This is where things get complicated. Martin is face-blind and can't identify the faces of the two men."

"Face-blind? What's that?" O'Connor spoke for them all, judging from the bewildered looks on everyone's faces.

Tom took over briefly and explained what face-blindness was. "We tried showing Martin a photo line-up, but it was useless."

Cindy Murray was frowning. "That means they can ID him but he can't recognize them."

"Exactly," Barnett said.

A moment of heavy silence fell as everyone absorbed this information.

Puchalski said, "He did tell us one guy was dark and on the short side, the other one taller and wearing a dark hooded sweatshirt. He thought he heard one of them speak with an accent, something Eastern European, but he wasn't sure which man."

Puchalski continued going through the details of the case. Then Tom assigned tasks. Cindy Murray and Brendan O'Connor would interview Sandra Sorenson and the crew at Modern Method. Puchalski and Tom would go to Zimmerman's Mercedes. José Ramirez would conduct an assessment of Carrie's apartment with several evidence technicians. Her car would be towed to the Lindenville crime lab for analysis. Later, Puchalski and Sanders would interview Carrie's parents. Yesterday evening they had refused to be interviewed, claiming exhaustion. Officer Johnson of Banner Bluff would continue to field calls and follow up on any leads.

As they were getting ready to leave, gathering up coffee cups and dumping the doughnut boxes, Mark Sanders asked, "What about the overdose on Monday night? Anything new there?"

"That seems to be a separate issue altogether," Tom said. "Conroy's team is handling the forensics. Fingerprints from the phone are being analyzed. Puchalski has been talking to the mother. We're still on the hunt for the 911 caller."

The meeting was adjourned. It was ten AM.

Chapter 15
Wednesday Morning, November 15th

Barnett and Puchalski drove over to Zimmerman Mercedes down on the North-South Highway. Gleaming new vehicles lined the driveway into the dealership.

"Man, I would love to drive one of those." Puchalski slowed the squad car and pointed at a dark grey S550. "That car is a shark."

"Yeah, it would only set you back a hundred thousand dollars."

"Hmm, maybe not quite in my price range."

Puchalski drove to the front of the dealership to park, but Tom said, "Let's drive around the building and get a feel for the location."

They drove slowly around the entire building. The showroom was in front, the service department in the rear. The entrance to the service department was on the south side. Parked along the north side of the massive building was a car hauler that seemed to have just arrived, judging from the ten new cars balanced on it.

"Where do they ship these vehicles from?" Puchalski asked.

"I read somewhere they're still primarily made in Germany and are shipped over here."

They continued driving up and down the aisles of new cars and over to the back entrance. The lot backed on to a small service road. Beyond that were the train tracks and a solid wall of trees and brush.

"This is the back side of the forest preserve," Tom said thoughtfully. "It must be a mile and a half over to the scene of the crime."

Puchalski continued driving through several rows of used cars and back toward the front of the building. He pulled into a parking space, and they got out and went into the showroom. It was just after ten o'clock and there was no one around. They walked towards an office where a young woman with purple spiked hair, dressed in black leather was at work on a computer. Tom tapped gently on the glass. She jumped up, startled. She opened the office door and came around to greet them. Up close, Tom saw her slightly protruding eyes were heavily outlined with black cyeliner.

"Hi, there. Did you want to see a salesman? They're all in a meeting."

Tom flashed his badge. "No, we're not here to buy a car, but we would like to talk to the manager. Mr. Jenkins, I believe."

Her eyes widened. "Oh, is this about that Landwehr girl?"

Tom nodded.

"None of us really knew her, you know. She worked back in the service department late in the day, so, you know, she didn't come up here." The girl twirled a bright blue key ring around her forefinger.

"Right," Tom said, nodding, "but we would like to talk to Mr. Jenkins."

"Well, he's not going to like it if I get him out of the meeting, I mean, if you're not going to buy a car."

"Please get him now." A command, not a request.

She shrugged. "Okay, I guess it will be all right since you're the law." She turned away and clumped down the hall in her black boots.

"Where did they find her?" Puchalski said. "Definitely not the brightest bulb in the pack."

"Maybe she's a genius on the computer."

A short, slim man came towards them from down the hall, walking briskly with an air of authority. He wore a tweed jacket and beige slacks. His dark blond hair was artfully arranged in boyish disorder.

"Good morning, gentlemen, I'm Paul Jenkins." He smiled briefly and shook their hands. "How can I be of service?"

Tom introduced himself and his detective. "We'd like to talk about Carrie Landwehr. You've likely heard she was killed Monday night."

Jenkins looked suitably grave. "Yes, we are all terribly saddened by her death."

"What can you tell us about her employment here?"

"I'm afraid I know very little about her. She was hired five months ago and only worked in the evenings back in the service department. I think it would be best if you go back there."

"Okay," Tom said.

"Is there a file on her we could take a look at?" Puchalski asked.

"Certainly, we must have her application on file. I'll ask Sheba to get it for you." Jenkins went into the glass-walled office and spoke to the leather-clad girl.

"Sheba," Puchalski said rolling his eyes. "Give me a break."

Jenkins came back with a manila folder that contained a single sheet of paper. He handed it to Tom.

"What about time sheets?" Tom asked. "We'd like to verify Ms. Landwehr's whereabouts for the last month."

Jenkins looked irritated. "For the last month? I suppose I can get a print-out for you." He poked his head back inside the office. They could see him gesturing to Sheba and then he wrote something on a piece of paper for her.

124

"Let me take you down to the service department and Sheba can bring the print-out when she gets it." He walked briskly down the corridor and gestured for them to follow. It seemed obvious he wanted them out of his hair.

Tom paused as they reached a glass-paneled door. "Depending on our investigation in the service department, we might want to interview the sales staff in the showroom."

"Whatever I can do to help, Officer Barnett."

"Chief Barnett," Puchalski corrected. From the look on his face, he really didn't like the guy. Tom felt about the same.

"Sorry, I'm not familiar with the various echelons of police rank. Now, let me introduce you to the Captain. Right this way."

They followed Jenkins through the glass door into a large, high-ceilinged garage with four large garage doors at each end of the building. Along one side was a raised walkway flanked by waist-high work stations containing computers, printers and stacked identification tags. Several service assistants worked at these stations, checking in the cars that arrived to be serviced.

Glass-enclosed offices were visible behind the stations. Inside one, a heavyset man on the phone seemed to be in the middle of an argument. He was gesturing with his free hand and shouting, to judge from the expression on his face. Jenkins tapped on the window and then opened the door into the office. Abruptly, the man ended the call and came around his desk. He wore a dark blue shirt with the Zimmerman's logo on the pocket, khaki pants and boat shoes. On his head was a dark-blue captain's hat complete with gold braid. Under its short brim, the man's dark eyes assessed them from beneath heavy brows.

"Captain, this is Chief Barnett and Detective Puchalski. They've come to talk about Carrie Landwehr. I told them we really didn't know anything about her up front. So perhaps you could fill them in."

125

"Yes, of course." The Captain shook hands with Tom and Puchalski.

"If there's anything else you need, please don't hesitate to contact me," Jenkins said, and he went back through the door into the service garage.

"Please sit down." The Captain gestured to two chairs opposite his desk. "Can I get you a cup of coffee?"

"No thanks," Tom said.

Puchalski declined as well.

The Captain sat down and clasped his hands together on the desk. "I'm terribly sorry to hear of Carrie's death. She was a fine employee." He shook his head in disbelief. "How could something like this happen in Banner Bluff?"

"That's what we're going to find out." Tom looked over at Puchalski, who got out a small notebook and flipped some pages.

They started by asking the Captain's name, which was Petroff.

"Could you please tell us about Carrie's employment here? What were her responsibilities?" Tom said.

The Captain sighed. "She worked Monday through Friday from five o'clock until eight, just three hours. Our service department shuts down at five but our clients can't always get here by then, so we're open for pick-up until eight o'clock. Carrie worked as cashier for these late pick-ups. Our regular cashier goes home at five."

"Where is the cashier's window?"

"It's just inside the hallway between the garage and the showroom. You must have passed it when you came through."

"Is it always busy at that late hour?" Tom asked.

"Until about six-thirty or seven, yeah. After that, it depends."

"Did she work until eight every night?"

"Sometimes, I suggested she go home early if I knew we were finished for the day."

"Do you work until eight every night?" Puchalski asked.

"Yes, I like to be here first thing in the morning and last thing at night. I run a tight ship." He said it with self-satisfaction.

"Ah, yes." Tom smiled. "You're the Captain. How did you get that name, anyway?"

"I started wearing the hat and the name stuck." He smiled at them, leaning back in his chair.

"Did you talk to Carrie on a regular basis?" Tom asked.

"No, not really."

Puchalski raised his eyebrows. "Even when the two of you were here alone?"

Petroff's smile vanished. He leaned forward against his desk. "Listen, I don't like what you're insinuating. She came in and worked and then she went home, period."

"Calm down," Tom said. "We're trying to learn who she *did* talk to and what was going on in her life that last week. We know she called some friends and that she was upset but we don't know why."

"Listen, I don't know anything about her life. And I never talked to her except in passing or if I brought a customer over to her. That's it."

"Did she hang out with anyone else in the dealership?" Puchalski asked.

"Sometimes the service assistants would talk with her but mainly she stayed at the cashier's desk. She did some filing and telephoning to remind people about their appointments, stuff like that."

"So the mechanics leave at five?" Tom asked.

"Oh, it's probably five-fifteen, five-thirty by the time they roll out of here."

"What about the service assistants? Do they stick around?"

127

"We have a schedule. They either come in early at seven AM and leave early, or they come in late and stay until seven PM."

"So everyone is gone by seven except you and your cashier, right?" Puchalski said.

"Yes, that's right."

Tom and Puchalski spent another hour at the dealership. They were taken to the cashier's station and met the daytime cashier, Mrs. Muffie. She was a plump, middle-aged woman who started to cry when they began talking to her.

"Carrie was such a nice young woman, so polite and friendly. She always asked after my cat at home. See, here's a picture of Bernie, my cat. I named him after my dead husband. That way I feel like my husband is right nearby."

Puchalski bent down to take a look. The photo showed an enormous tabby cat that probably weighed close to twenty pounds. "Wow that is one big cat."

Tom smiled at the picture of the massive feline and then said, "Did you notice anything special last week? Did Carrie act different? Did she tell you something was bothering her?"

"Well, she was really quiet when she came in on Friday. Usually she tells me about her plans for the weekend. She has a nice girlfriend that she likes to go to the movies with, but she doesn't seem to have any boyfriend."

"Did she tell you what was bothering her?"

"No, she just seemed like she was worried about something. I had to run so we didn't get a chance to chat." Her eyes filled with tears again. "That was the last time I saw her."

Chapter 16
Wednesday Afternoon, November 15th

Connie Munster was coming over for tea at four o'clock. Francesca put on the electric kettle and measured fragrant Tung Ting Oolong into a flowered teapot. She brought out the mismatched porcelain cups. On a hand-painted Austrian plate she placed triangles of hazelnut sugar cookies and several raspberry crumble bars she had made the night before. Everything was ready when Connie arrived.

"You-hoo," Connie called as she came up the stairs.

Francesca welcomed her and took her coat. "Come sit down at the table. I've just got to pour water into the pot."

As Connie sat down she asked, "So what is all this about?"

Francesca brought the teapot over from behind the Chinese screen and sat down. She poured fragrant tea into their cups and began to explain about the cell phone Luis Gonzales had found in the garbage can, and about the threatening message Yari had heard.

Connie interrupted her. "Where is all this going?"

"I'm getting to that. After I put an announcement about the phone in the lost and found section of the *Banner Bee*, this past Monday I got a call from Lorinda Landers."

"Lorinda Landers?" Connie raised her eyebrows in surprise. "It was her phone?"

"No, no, no. She happened to be looking out on the street, supposedly at birds and squirrels, when she saw Ramses Crenshaw dump that phone into the garbage can."

"The Pharaoh? My, oh my!" Connie picked up a raspberry crumble bar and set it on her saucer. "Go on."

Francesca continued, "Last Monday, the Pharaoh was here in Banner Bluff to schmooze with the locals. He visited Hero's grocery, the post office, and Churchill's Café. He made quite a stir. People reacted like they were being visited by the Pope or a king."

"My stars, Francesca, do I sense some antagonism here?" Connie smiled primly and sipped her tea.

Francesca took a bite of cookie and chewed it slowly. "I'm wondering why he came to Banner Bluff. This town is off the beaten track. What brought him here?"

"He must have had a reason. He calculates his every move."

"Anyway, I went online this morning and googled Crenshaw. I got thousands of search results and I read a slew of articles; but I don't feel like I learned anything. That's why I emailed you. I wondered if you might have some ideas. Who could have called him? And what is this *agua corriente project?*"

Connie patted her mouth with a napkin, folded it and placed it on the table beside her cup. Francesca could see the wheels turning as Connie chose her next words carefully.

"The Pharaoh has several questionable friends. He provides for them and they provide for him. His cronies are currently putting together a Super Pac that will be one of the largest campaign treasure chests ever seen in the state of Illinois." She paused and straightened her spoon. "What's interesting is that several of these powerful and rich individuals don't live in Illinois and yet they are particularly interested in getting him elected."

"Do you know why?"

"Some of the money will be coming from people within the Party, people that want another governor to advance the Party's platform. Others have business interests in Illinois. For example, I've recently become aware of a certain individual in Oklahoma who has considerable holdings in Las Vegas."

"So which of these people could be threatening Crenshaw? Can you get a list of names?"

130

"Actually, I've made up a little list for myself. We're currently doing a bit of research." She looked at Francesca over her spectacles. "Would you like to see the list when it's completed?"

Francesca smiled. "Yes, I would, very much." She could feel the adrenaline flowing. "Maybe I could come up with something that would be useful to Bob's campaign and to me?"

"Undoubtedly, my dear." Connie ate a corner of the raspberry bar. "This is delicious. Now let's have another cup of tea, and then we ought to get to work."

Chapter 17
Thursday Morning, November 16th

Francesca checked herself in the mirror. She was wearing black jeans and had layered a teal scoop-necked sweater over a turquoise t-shirt. She rummaged in a drawer for a teal and black scarf that she looped around her neck. Downstairs she let the dogs out the back door for a quickie run and took a last sip of coffee, then placed the cup in the dishwasher. The dogs came bounding back in at her call; she gave them both a dog biscuit and then headed out to her car.

Five minutes later, Francesca was pulling up outside the Atkins' home. The house reflected the Prairie school design with horizontal lines, flat roofs and windows grouped in horizontal bands. It wasn't large but it made a statement. She went up on the porch and rang the doorbell. Almost instantly the door was opened by a thin, blond woman in jeans and a heavy fisherman's sweater. Her light blue eyes were almost colorless, ringed by dark circles.

"Ms. Antonelli?" the woman said in a hushed voice. At Francesca's nod, she held out a hand. "Please come in. I'm Emily Atkins." Her smile was tremulous.

Francesca stepped inside the small vestibule. Straight ahead were stairs leading to the second floor and a hallway that led back to a kitchen. To her right was a living room decorated in a minimalist style. "Please call me Francesca. Thank you for inviting me to your home."

"Please, call me Emily." She led the way into the living room and gestured toward a grey-green sectional sofa. "Won't you sit down? Can I get you some coffee?"

"I just finished a cup at home, thanks. But please go ahead and have one yourself."

"No, no, I've had way too much caffeine these last few days. I've got to stop drinking it. Then maybe I'll be able to sleep. Or maybe I should switch to martinis." Her smile was brittle.

Francesca shrugged off her coat and sat down on the sofa. Emily took a seat across from her on a straight-backed chair upholstered in grey and green stripes. Her posture was rigid as though she was holding herself in check.

Francesca leaned toward her. "I'm so sorry about the loss of your son. This must be a terrible time for you. Is there anything I can do? Anything you need?"

Emily Atkins looked out the window, as if searching for words. "What you can do for me, is write our story. I want to warn other parents about the dangers that exist in Banner Bluff. I want to tell them to be present in their children's lives, to communicate with their teenagers. But most of all I want them to know about Brett." Her eyes filled with tears. "About what a special boy he was."

Francesca took a notebook and a freshly sharpened pencil out of her purse. "Tell me about Brett. I would love to learn about him."

Emily talked for a long time about Brett's childhood. She spoke of his love of music and how he had taught himself to play the guitar. A curious child, he'd developed into an excellent student. Her voice was low and brimmed with love for her son.

"Brett was a happy-go-lucky kid until his father, my ex-husband, left us to marry a young model he met on a business trip. Brett took it pretty hard. Both kids did."

Francesca looked up from taking notes. "How long ago was this?"

"Three years ago. After that, the kids saw him less and less. For Brett, his father was the moon and the stars. He was devastated." She'd pulled a tissue from her pocket and was shredding it. "Michael, my ex, wasn't paying child support on a regular basis. I was looking around for a job, and a headhunter put me in touch with the company where I work now. Groundswell Industries. "They offered me a great job as project manager. So we moved here." She picked at the skin around her thumb. Francesca saw it was red and raw.

"My job required me to work long hours. We have a deadline to meet and I've been working until seven-thirty every night because I have to coordinate with California and they're on Pacific Time. In the morning it's New York. In the evening it's L.A."

She got up and walked over to the window, looking out at the grey sky and the dirty, brown leaves that covered the grass. "I haven't been home much since we moved here. I left the kids alone. They had to face a new school and make new friends and I was downtown. I moved them here and I abandoned them. That was my mistake."

"That's right, Mom. That was your mistake." Francesca looked up as a skinny dark-haired girl came flying into the room. Her brown eyes were flashing and her anger was palpable. "I've been listening to you talk about how perfect Brett always was. But he's dead!" Her voice was strident. "And tomorrow we're going to have this funeral and no one will be there, because no one knows us and nobody cares about us." She stood trembling, her arms held straight at her sides and her hands clenched in fists.

Emily moved towards her daughter but the girl pushed her away. "Tell her about our life these last few months. Tell her, Mom."

"Grace, you're being rude to our guest."

"Who cares? She's probably out to make money off of our tragedy... she'll sell the story to *People Magazine*."

"Grace! Please, honey."

Silence fell. Emily sat back down. Then the girl flopped down at the other end of the sofa. "This is where my brother died.

134

Right here on this sofa." She stared at Francesca, eyes burning with defiance. "Are you sure you want to sit here?"

"You must be Brett's sister." Francesca said evenly.

"Du-uh!" Grace said, shaking her head.

Emily raised her voice. "Grace!"

"Hello, Grace. My name is Francesca." She held out her hand. "I will not write anything that you and your mother haven't looked over first. I am here because your mother asked me to come." She paused. "Truce?"

Grudgingly Grace shook Francesca's hand. The girl's fingers were long and thin, her palm, cold and moist.

"So Grace, what can *you* tell me about Brett?" Francesca asked.

Grace ran her fingers through her long, dark hair, then pulled it over her right shoulder.

"Well, I knew he was smoking pot in his room because I could smell it." She turned to her mother. "I can't believe you couldn't smell it too!"

"Do you know where he got it?" Francesca asked.

"I don't have a clue. But he probably got the heroin from the same source. You know, there're guys around school selling stuff."

"Who was he hanging out with?"

"Some guys that were in a band. He went over to somebody's house to jam. They were all losers. Once some guy came here when you were home, Mom, remember?"

"Yes. He had all sorts of piercings and tattoos. I told him Brett wasn't home. Brett came down later and got angry with me and stormed out." Emily pushed back a strand of hair. "I should have invited that kid in here and found out who he was."

"What about you, Grace, have you made friends here in Banner Bluff?" Francesca asked.

135

"Not really. There's a girl in my English class that I sit with at lunch. She's nice. And there's a guy at Appleby's that I work with Mondays and Wednesdays. He's really cute." She blushed, a reaction that seemed touchingly young to Francesca.

"What about this girl who made the 911 call? Do you know who she is?"

"We talked about this with the police yesterday. We don't know who she could be," Emily sighed. "Another example of how little I knew of my son's life."

"She was here before," Grace said.

"She was?" Emily leaned forward. "Why didn't you say this before? Why didn't you tell me?"

"You didn't ask. Besides, it was Brett's business. I didn't want to snitch on him." Grace eased an elastic band off her wrist, pulled back her hair and fashioned a ponytail.

"Tell us about it," Francesca said.

"Once, I got home early from work. Brett's door was shut and I could hear a girl giggling in there."

"You didn't see her when she left?" Emily asked.

"No, Mom. I went in my room and shut the door. I'm not going to spy on my little brother." The girl realized what she had just said. Startled she looked from Francesca to her mother; then she hunched over, her hands covering her face. She began to sob. Emily came over, knelt down and wrapped her arms around her daughter.

Francesca sat still, feeling the terrible pain this mother and child were suffering.

After a few minutes, Emily got up and sat down beside Grace. "We'll get through this together, honey." She pulled her close.

Francesca felt it was time to leave. She picked up her coat and purse. "I'll email you a copy of the article when it's finished. Thank you for talking to me."

Grace glanced up at Francesca. "I saw her backpack."

"Whose? "The girl's?"

"Yeah. She left it down here by the door."

"What kind was it?"

"Jansport. But everyone has a Jansport backpack."

"What color was it?"

"Light blue. But she must be a freshman."

"Why?" Francesca asked.

"Because she had two little teddy bears hanging on the handle: one pink and one baby blue. Definitely a freshman."

Chapter 18
Thursday Evening, November 16th

Francesca threw open the door to find Tom on the doorstep. It was 7 o'clock and he was a little late but she had planned for that contingency. They were going to have an easy chicken and polenta meal that she could prepare at the last minute.

She knew he had been working day and night for the last three days. The details of Carrie Landwehr's murder had hit the airwaves and the entire country was shocked by the grisly crime. Francesca had participated in several press conferences where Tom had outlined the basics of the murder and asked for help from the general public.

"It's so good to be with you." Tom said, hugging her close. "I needed to get away for a few hours."

"I'm glad you're here." They held each other and kissed, a slow, deep kiss, then pulled apart and smiled at each other.

Francesca took his coat and hung it up before leading him down the hall to the kitchen. "We're going to eat in here. Nothing fancy. Why don't you open the wine?" She handed him a bottle of pinot Grigio.

Tom pulled out the cork and poured them each a glass of wine while Francesca whisked the polenta flour into the simmering broth. "Anything new with the investigation? Did anyone come forward?"

"Nothing so far. Carrie's parents got home yesterday morning and identified the body. They're in a terrible state." He paced the kitchen, glass in hand. "They really have no idea what her life has been like recently. I mean, she lived in this garage behind their big house, but they rarely saw her."

"What about the girl, her friend, does she have anything to tell you?"

"We interviewed Julie several times. She said Carrie was into drugs but she'd been clean for six months."

Francesca slipped the floured chicken cutlets into the fry pan. "Is this Julie Robinson?"

"Right." He took a sip of wine.

"I know Julie from Modern Method. I met her during an aborted attempt to attend regular fitness classes." She laughed. "I was wooed by Modern Method's claims that through rigorous workouts, I could sculpt my body into 'the perfect female silhouette.'" She made quotation marks with her fingers. "I gave up after a couple of months… I couldn't stick to the schedule, and ultimately I prefer being outside and running."

She handed Tom the vinaigrette and salad bowl and asked him to do the honors. "So Carrie worked there too?"

"Yeah, that's where they met. Julie seems like an awfully nice kid. She's really shook up."

"What else was Carrie involved in?" Francesca deglazed the fry pan with white wine and lemon juice and added a few capers, then poured the sauce over the chicken.

Tom looked blindly at their reflection in the darkened window. "She worked five nights a week at Zimmerman's Mercedes as a cashier in the service department. We were over there today, Ron Puchalski and me. We interviewed the sales manager and the service manager. I didn't like the vibes I got from that place."

Francesca stirred mascarpone and grated parmesan into the polenta, then scooped it onto the plates. "Why? What did they have to say?"

Tom didn't answer her at first. His mind was clearly elsewhere. "Most of the employees there didn't really know her since she came in at the end of the day. She served as cashier for

139

people who picked up their cars after five o'clock in the evening." He was still thinking. "Francesca, would you go with me over to Carrie Landwehr's apartment after dinner? I'd like to look around again. We still haven't found her phone."

"Sure," she said, "but come sit down. Everything is ready."

Tom seemed to wake from his reverie. He came over and sat down. "Wow, this looks wonderful. This will be my first real meal in days."

As they ate, Francesca told him about her visit to the Atkins house. "I spent the afternoon writing an article that will go in the *Banner Bee* Saturday. It's a tribute to Brett Atkins, but also a plea to Banner Bluff parents to be active and present in their children's lives. That's the message Emily Atkins wanted to promote."

Tom nodded. "We've got a couple of detectives working the Atkins case. They're connecting with some undercover cops that are trying to flush out a drug ring in the area. We want to know where the kid got his heroin."

Francesca put down her fork. "After this morning, I've been thinking…I'm wondering…if it was an overdose or suicide. Brett was an unhappy kid these last few months, but would he take his own life? He was so young, only sixteen."

Tom reached over and took her hand. "Maybe we'll never know." He looked into her troubled eyes. "Let it go, Francesca."

She nodded slowly and then resumed eating. "Oh, I did learn something useful. Grace Atkins said that the girl who made the 911 call had been to the house before. Grace doesn't know who she is, but she thinks the girl is a freshman at the high school. Grace also described the girl's backpack. It's blue and there are two little teddy bears hanging on it. I bet we could find her."

Tom was laughing. "Two teddy bears, you say? Okay, you're officially in charge of the teddy bear brigade. Go for it."

Colman was sitting at his desk going over a list of figures. He had to get his car repaired and he was trying to figure out how he would pay for it. Ken Hopkins over at Hopkins Auto Repair had told him it would be three hundred dollars. Colman couldn't squeeze three hundred bucks out of his budget this month. What to do? There was no time in the day to work any more hours, go to class and still study to keep his grades up. He'd have to beg Ken to let him pay in installments over the next six months. He sighed, balled up the paper and took a shot at the wastebasket in the corner. His financial state was depressing. It didn't help that he had missed work the last two days because of the flu.

On the desk before him was a copy of *Middlemarch*. He couldn't keep his mind on his reading. The woes of Dorothea and Ladislaw were anything but captivating tonight. He found that he had to sit at the desk to read. When he tried sitting in the armchair or in bed, he would fall asleep.

Maybe a Coke would give him a kick. He went over to the mini-fridge and took out a can. This represented a luxury he couldn't afford, but he had to finish this book tonight. He sat back down on the hard chair. The phone and keys in his back pocket dug into his thigh. He reached back, pulled them out and placed them on the desk.

Colman knew what was really bugging him. It was that phone call from Carrie. Should he call her back or just forget it? He hadn't seen her for over a year but her voice had been so familiar, so painfully familiar. She had sounded afraid. He looked at his phone sitting there on the desk. Maybe if he got it over with, he would calm down and be able to concentrate. He picked up the phone and dialed her number.

Tom led the way up the wooden staircase to Carrie Landwehr's apartment. He was carrying a flashlight. It was dark and Francesca could see the wind swishing the branches of the trees overhead. The steps creaked under their feet. At the top, Tom handed Francesca the flashlight, pulled off the yellow caution tape and took out a key. He unlocked the door and reached inside, feeling his way until he found the light switch. They took a couple of steps into a large room that served as living and dining area. The kitchen area was along the wall to the right of the front door. A worn sofa and matching armchair faced a scratched coffee table. Across the room was a small TV on a low bookshelf. The entire apartment was in disarray; sofa pillows tossed topsy-turvy, books jumbled on the floor and fingerprint powder covering all flat surfaces.

Tom handed her some paper booties and latex gloves. "Let's just wander around the apartment. Maybe you'll see something we missed earlier. Okay?"

"Sure, but I don't know what I'll see that your techies haven't already uncovered." She looked around the room. It was obvious Carrie had made an effort to make the apartment comfortable. The walls were painted a muted yellow with white trim. There were decals of pink and orange poppies above the bookshelf.

She knelt down and leafed through the magazines on the floor: *Cosmopolitan* and *Woman's Health*. She saw that Carrie had filled out one of those self-quizzes on her eating habits. It looked as though she was leading a healthy life.

Francesca got up and walked into a small corridor. On the left was the bathroom. She stopped to look at the door, which had a sliding bolt. "Hey Tom, did you see this bathroom door? What's the deal?"

"What do you mean?" He came over.

"Check out this bolt. See, it's on the *outside* of the door. What's that about?"

"I don't know." He took out a small notebook and made a note. "Maybe someone locked a dog in here."

142

"Kind of creepy," Francesca said, walking into the bathroom. Above the ancient clawfoot tub was a shelf containing Dove shampoo, conditioner and body wash. *Definitely a Dove girl,* Francesca thought.

The medicine cabinet contained the usual: aspirin, deodorant, toothpaste and a small bottle of prescription sleeping pills. Under the sink were tampons, toilet paper and scrubbing powder. A white lacquered table beside the sink was laden with make-up paraphernalia, nail polish and a little jewelry tree dangling with earrings and necklaces. She fingered the jewelry. There were glass beads, gold and silver bangles, a tiny, intricate ruby-studded key as well as a thick black pen hanging among the baubles.

The bedroom was relatively neat. Appliqués of delicate branches covered with pink and white blossoms decorated the light grey walls, giving the room a Japanese feeling. A laundry basket near the closet contained jeans along with turquoise and dark blue workout clothes. The closet door was open, and Francesca could tell some police technician had pawed through the sweaters and dresses hanging inside. The thought that this girl was dead and all sorts of strangers were going through her things filled Francesca with distaste.

On the bedside table was a picture of two girls with their arms around each other, laughing. Francesca recognized Julie. The other girl must be Carrie. There was also a picture of a middle-aged couple and a small stack of books. The one on top was titled *Staying Clean: Living without Drugs.*

On the long wall opposite the window were a series of photographs of women in various yoga poses, performing stretches and other exercises. Some of them were taken in the reflection of a mirror. The light was translucent, the pictures arresting. The women seemed totally unaware that they were being photographed.

Francesca wandered back into the living room and went over to the kitchen area. A box of quinoa was open on the counter next to a measuring cup. There were dried-up diced vegetables left on the cutting board, as though Carrie had been surprised in the midst of fixing dinner.

"Her keys are hanging on this monkey's tail and her coat is still here," Tom said from across the room. He was going meticulously through the pockets of her coat. From an inner pocket he pulled out a piece of pink paper. He studied it for a minute, inspecting both sides. "This is torn from a telephone message memo pad. There are a couple of words and three questions marks written on the back. I can't make the letters out, though."

Francesca came over for a look. "It looks like Cyrillic script. You know, like Russian."

"We'll have to get someone to look at this." He pulled out an evidence bag and dropped the piece of paper into it.

Just then they heard a phone ring. The muffled sound seemed to be coming from the kitchen area. They rushed over and began pulling out drawers and looking into cupboards. Francesca felt as though the ringtone was coming from right in front of her. She opened an antique porcelain sugar canister and dumped out the contents. Nothing. The ringtone came again. She dumped out the flour canister onto the counter, right on top of the dried-up vegetables. A cellphone fell out, covered in white dust, its screen still lit up.

Tom looked over her shoulder at the fading screen: "Colman."

Chapter 19
Thursday Night, November 16th

Francesca and Tom were back in the car. By the time Francesca answered Carrie's phone, Colman had hung up. It was obvious to both of them that Carrie had purposely hidden her phone from whoever was after her.

"What are you going to do, Tom?" Francesca asked as she pulled on her seat belt.

"I'm going to bring Colman in for questioning." Tom put the key in the ignition and turned on the engine.

"You don't really think he's involved with Carrie's murder, do you?"

"I've got to find out why he called her."

"Well, we know *he* doesn't know she's dead, or he wouldn't have called, right?"

"Right, but maybe she's been talking to him."

"Just don't be too hard on him." Francesca's tone was insistent.

"Are you telling me how to do my job?"

"No, Tom. I just feel he's been through so much that he doesn't need a cop giving him a hard time."

"Whoa there! I'm in the middle of a horrendous murder investigation." He pulled up at a stop sign and turned to her. "I can't be worrying about the feelings of every suspect I interview."

Francesca voice rose. "Suspect? That's making a major leap."

"Okay, let's call him a witness or a person of interest in the investigation." Tom sighed, suddenly feeling exhausted. "Come on, Francesca, get off my case."

Francesca looked over at him. "Sorry. I overreacted. I've got this protective streak where Colman is concerned."

"Yeah, I can tell." He accelerated and drove down the street a little too fast. The silence was heavy between them.

When they reached Francesca's house, Tom accompanied her to her door. He always waited until she went in. "You never know who could be lurking in the bushes," he'd say, only partly in jest.

Tonight, he kissed her briefly and turned to head down the front stairs. Francesca called after him, "We're good, right?" She was angry with herself that she needed reassurance and yet she didn't want to end the night with this sense of discomfort.

He sighed. "Yes, Francesca, we're good." He gave her a thumbs-up, got into the car and drove away.

Ron Puchalski brought Colman Canfield into the station. Tom was waiting for them in the interview room. He sometimes thought of it as the grey room: grey walls, grey carpet and a grey Formica-topped table. Colman had been there before, a year and a half earlier. He entered the room tentatively. Puchalski hadn't told him anything on the way over.

Carrie Landwehr's neon pink cell phone lay on the table. Tom stood up, put out his hand, and smiled. "Hello, Colman. How are you doing?"

"Fine," Colman mumbled. He looked from Tom to Puchalski, his eyes questioning. "I'm wondering why I'm here. Did I do something wrong?"

Tom motioned to a grey padded chair. "Please sit down."

Once they were all seated, Tom leaned forward, his elbows on the table. He gestured to the neon-pink phone. "Do you recognize this phone?"

Colman swallowed. "No sir, I don't."

"About an hour ago you made a call to it." Tom eyed the kid, measuring his reaction.

Colman looked uncertain. "I did?"

"Yes, you did," Puchalski said. "You can't remember who you called one hour ago?"

Then it seemed to dawn on him. "Is that Carrie's phone? Yeah, I did call her, but she didn't pick up."

"Why did you call her?" Tom said.

"She called me last week and I never got back to her." Colman looked uncomfortable.

"Why did she call you last week?" Puchalski asked.

"I don't know. She said she needed to talk to me."

"So did you talk to her or not?" Tom asked.

Colman looked at him. "No, I didn't." Then he looked down at his hands, which lay tightly clasped in his lap.

"So," Puchalski said aggressively.

"Listen, Carrie dumped me a year and a half ago when I got into trouble. She didn't call me or text me all this time. Then all of a sudden she calls up and says I have to meet her. She needs to talk to me." He looked from one man to the other. "I was ticked that she thought she could just call me up like that and I would cave."

"Do you know what she wanted to talk about?" Tom asked.

"No, but she did sound kind of upset. She said she didn't know who else to talk to, whatever that means."

"Why did you call her tonight?"

"Because…because I was feeling guilty. I was trying to study and I couldn't concentrate. So I decided to call and get it over with." Colman cheeks were flushed.

"Why didn't you answer when she called back?"

"After I made the call, I felt like ridiculous, like I was doing what she wanted. So I turned off my phone."

147

Tom and Puchalski looked at each other. Colman genuinely didn't seem to know about Carrie's murder. How could that be when the whole town had been talking about it?

Tom cleared his throat. "Colman, Carrie is dead. She was murdered Monday night."

Colman's eyes widened. "Oh, my God."

"You seem to be one of the last people she contacted," Tom said.

"Oh, my God. I just can't believe it." He looked from Tom to Ron in shock.

"You don't know anything about this? Everyone in town has been talking about nothing else since Wednesday afternoon, when we released Carrie's name to the public."

Colman shrugged. He looked sick. "I really haven't talked to anyone the past few days. I had the flu and skipped class. I was really out of it.

Tom took all this in. He twirled a pencil in his fingers. "Colman, are you clean?"

"Sir, I've been off drugs for a year and a half. I've even been counseling kids over at the West Haven Behavioral Clinic." He looked aggrieved. "You know that."

Tom nodded. "We think Carrie's death might be drug-related. I believe you when you say you're clean; but do you have any knowledge of the drug trade here in Banner Bluff? Dealers? Local haunts?"

"I don't," Colman said. "All that is over for me. The guy I bought from was sent to jail last year."

They sat there in silence.

"I guess that's it," Tom said after a moment. "Detective Puchalski will drive you home. Thank you for coming in."

"Chief Barnett?"

"Yes."

"How did Carrie die? What happened to her?"

148

Tom paused, weighing how much he wanted to say. Then he said, "She was hung and burned."

Chapter 20
Friday Morning, November 17th

The Homicide Task Force met at 8 AM in the conference room. The blown-up grinning face of Carrie Landwehr seemed to mock the policemen seated around the table. Over forty-eight hours had gone by and they were no closer to finding her murderers.

Cindy Murray and Brendan O'Connor were reporting on their visit to the Modern Method fitness studio. "We met with Sandra Sorenson, the owner. She said Carrie was a good employee, always on time, well-liked by the staff and the clientele," Cindy said.

"What did she do?" Puchalski asked.

"She was an exercise trainer and sometimes she manned the front desk and acted as a receptionist," Cindy said. "She had some private clients but mostly she taught classes."

Brendan drew breath as if to add something, but Cindy continued, "Last weekend the place was closed for three days because the owner's son got married. It wasn't until Monday morning that Carrie didn't show up for work."

Brendan raised his voice to be heard. "I talked to one other trainer." He was visibly irritated. Tom wondered if these two would be able to work together, thinking idly about redheads and Irish tempers.

"Michelle Pirelli," Brendan went on, glancing down at his notes. "She seemed to have a problem with Carrie."

"I didn't get that feeling," Cindy said, frowning. "When was that?"

Brendan gave her a look. "She said, and I quote, that she was 'freaking tired of Carrie taking secret pictures of everyone'."

"Secret pictures?" Puchalski asked.

"Apparently she used her phone to surreptitiously snap pictures of staff and clients. Pirelli thought it was an invasion of privacy.

"I saw some photographs in Carrie's bedroom," Tom said.

"Right, I noticed them too. Pictures of women working out." This came from Detective José Ramirez.

"Michelle said they told Carrie she couldn't take any more pictures." Brendan glanced over at Cindy, whose cheeks were flushed as she assiduously studied her notes.

Tom broke the mini-standoff. "Last night I went back to Carrie's garage apartment and found her phone. It was in the flour canister, hidden away. She must have shoved it in there in a panic."

Cindy looked hopeful. "Were there more pictures on it? Anything that could help us out?"

"Nothing I saw. I sent it to the lab. They'll get back to me with an analysis of photos and calls." Tom turned to Ramirez. "Any news on her car or the laptop?"

"We're still going through the car but it seems to be clean. Her friend Julie said she had a laptop but it wasn't in the apartment or her car."

"If she was abducted from her apartment, they might have taken her laptop," Puchalski said.

Tom nodded. "Right."

"I'm thinking she probably owed someone a lot of money," Detective Mark Sanders said. "Maybe this was a lesson or a warning to her druggie friends."

Tom reached for a file in front of him and pulled out an evidence bag with the pink message slip he and Francesca had found in Carrie's apartment. "This was in Miss Landwehr's coat." He carried it over to the white board and carefully copied the

151

words, first in Cyrillic and then phonetically in the English-alphabet: крюк- *kryuk*.

"Last night when I got home, I googled these words. On the left is the Cyrillic Russian alphabet, on the right an approximate English pronunciation. The words mean 'hook'." He wrote the word in capitals and underlined it twice. Then he turned and looked at the officers, his eyebrows raised. "Any ideas?"

Silence filled the room. "Let's keep this little bit of information to ourselves for now," Tom said. "I don't know what 'hook' means but apparently Carrie thought it was important. I want to keep this from the media." He turned to Puchalski. "Let's move on. What about Carrie's parents?"

"They were in New York all week. We got the feeling they didn't know much about her life. Even though she was living right behind their house, she didn't see much of them." He looked down at his note pad. "Carrie flunked out of the U of I a year ago and came home in disgrace. In spite of that, she continued to party and was into drugs the first few months she was home. Her dad finally laid down the law, and she got a job and seemed to have straightened herself out."

"Right, her friend Julie said she was a changed person." Cindy said.

Sanders added, "But does anyone really know? I mean, she could have been back onto something and her friend wouldn't necessarily know about it."

"You're feeling like I'm feeling," Tom said. "This is all about drugs. It's the tip of the iceberg."

152

Chapter 21
Friday Morning, November 17th

Francesca was at the hospital, heading up to the sixth floor. She leaned back against the elevator wall and closed her eyes. She hadn't slept last night. There'd been too much to think about. Her mind jumped from Carrie's apartment, to Emily and Grace Atkins, to her relationship with Tom. She had ruined a perfectly nice evening. "We're good," was all Tom had said, before hurrying back to his car and pulling away.

She had stood in the entryway watching the taillights disappear down the street while an all-too-familiar push-me pull-you roiled her heart. On the one hand she wanted total independence, but on the other hand she wanted to lean on someone. Now that things didn't feel right with Tom, she was in a state.

She'd come to the hospital this morning to visit Daphne Meriwether and drop off a plant. She had chosen a Christmas cactus with several bright fuchsia-colored blooms and lots of small pink buds. When she arrived at Daphne's room, the door was ajar. She knocked softly and poked her head inside. Daphne looked thin and frail under the covers. She had an IV attached to her hand and an oxygen tube in her nostrils. She turned towards the door and smiled gently.

"Francesca, do come in. How lovely to see you."

Francesca entered the room and approached the bed. She unwrapped the cactus plant. "This is for you, a little cheer-you-upper."

"Oh, I love those Christmas cacti." Daphne looked delighted.

Francesca placed the plant on the bedside table and sat down so she was at Daphne's eye level. "I read you can keep them for twenty years or more; but they like to remain in the same location when they're blooming. They don't like change in their lives.

"Like so many of us," Daphne murmured.

"I thought I might see Carina here," Francesca said.

"She went downstairs to get some tea. She should be back in a minute. Francesca, she won't go home," Daphne said in exasperation. "She's been here day and night."

A knock on the door heralded Emma Boucher, armed with a cup of Starbuck's, the newspaper and a knitting bag. "Well, look who's here." She beamed at Francesca, came over and gave her a hug. Then she smiled at Daphne. "How are you feeling?"

Daphne smiled back wanly. "I think I'm doing better but I'm exhausted."

Emma bustled over to an armchair near the window and plopped down her things. "I'm going to settle in over here but I want you to rest. I won't even talk to you. I told your daughter that I would stand guard so she can go home and check on things at the farm."

"Oh, heavens, I don't need a babysitter," Daphne cried. Then she began to cough from the exertion.

Emma helped her sit up until the fit was over, then helped her lay back down. She poured a fresh glass of ice water from the pitcher on the table and held the straw to Daphne's mouth. "Take a sip, my dear."

"I'm going to leave now. I see you're in good hands." Francesca smiled at Emma and patted Daphne on the arm. Then she headed for the door. As she started down the hall, she saw Carina exiting the elevator. Carina looked terrible. Her unwashed hair hung limp around her face. Dark circles ringed her eyes and she appeared even thinner than usual. She managed a smile when she saw Francesca approaching her.

"Have you been in to see Mom?" Nervously, she pushed a lank strand of hair behind her ear.

"Yes, I have and Emma is there now. So you can go home." Francesca searched Carina's eyes. "You need to take care of yourself. You don't want to get sick, too."

"I know, I know. But Mom is all I've got and I was frantic when she collapsed." There were tears in her eyes.

Francesca ushered Carina into the nearby waiting room, sat her in a green padded chair and handed her a Kleenex, then sat down next to her. "Tell me what happened."

"It was Wednesday morning. God, it feels like an eternity since then." Carina held her fist to her mouth. "I was in the kitchen having coffee with this government lawyer, talking about eminent domain, and Mom came down and heard what he was saying and then she collapsed..."

"Wait a minute. What are you talking about?" Francesca shook her head. "Eminent domain? Government lawyer? What's going on?"

Carina told her about the visit from the geologists and then the arrival of Harrison Rand. "Rand said the government was going to expropriate a part of our beachfront and build a pumping station."

Francesca frowned. "Did you get any prior notification? It seems so sudden."

"Just those geologists, a couple of weeks ago. They were weird."

"Weird how?"

"I don't know. They acted a little devious. Nothing I could put my finger on at the time, but..." Carina balled up the Kleenex in her hand.

"Have you studied the court order you received?"

155

"I barely even looked at the paperwork. When Mom collapsed we called 911 and since then I've barely been home."

"Who is this Harrison Rand?"

"He's a lawyer for the state government. He was really nice when all this happened. He came with me to the hospital and sat with me in the ER while Mom was admitted."

"Hmm," Francesca said. Suspicious by nature, she pondered what she'd just heard.

"Since I've been here he's called me on my cell a couple of times. He's really nice."

"And why is the state taking your land?"

"I'm told it's the perfect spot. Across Eastern Avenue there's a pipeline that was used previously. They're going to pump Lake Michigan water to the western suburbs using that water main. Apparently, the aquifers are low because of the drought."

"It's odd that we haven't heard anything about this in the news," Francesca said.

"Well, I can tell you that it's official. I saw the Illinois State seal and Governor Crenshaw's signature on the last page."

Chapter 22
Friday Afternoon, November 17th

Tom was in his office looking at the information gleaned from Carrie Landwehr's phone. It was precious little. The photos she had taken were primarily from the workout studio. No pictures of drug buys or clandestine meetings. Her phone calls were local, to friends, the Modern Method, a local vegan pizza joint. Her voicemail contained nothing bizarre. He sat back, laced his hands behind his head and closed his eyes. What had this girl been up to? Outwardly her life seemed so straightforward.

In his pocket he felt the vibration of his cell phone. He pulled it out and looked at the screen. It was Lewis. The last time Tom saw him, Officer Lewis had looked appropriately scruffy and dirty in filthy jeans and a baseball cap turned backward over his scraggly blond locks. He had also looked exhausted and on edge.

Tom answered the phone. "Barnett. What's the latest?"

"I've made a contact in the high school and in a dive down on the highway. It wasn't difficult to find a supplier of heroin. I've discovered a couple of coping zones."

"Have you made some buys?"

"Yeah, no problemo. Several, but all from low men on the totem pole."

"Right, so who's supplying them?" Tom asked.

"That's what I'm working on...guys don't want to share info. I'm working on a raspberry who is *very* talkative."

"Have you heard anything about Carrie Landwehr on the street?"

"No, I haven't. People tell me she hasn't been part of the scene for a while."

157

"We've hit a stone wall in our investigation but we think her death was drug-related." Tom drummed his fingers. "Anything else?"

"Chief, the heroin is pouring in through one source. It's not random. We're talking about organized crime. I get the feeling people are afraid. Of whom, I don't know yet." He paused. "Gotta go."

"Don't take any unnecessary chances," Tom said but Lewis had already hung up.

Isabelle spent the day in bed. All she wanted to do was sleep. She didn't have a fever. She wasn't coughing or sneezing. What could be wrong with her? Isabelle knew. She had sleeping sickness. All she wanted to do was sleep and forget. Brett was dead. Brett was gone. She felt the darkness descend upon her like a heavy blanket pressing her down.

On Tuesday, she'd heard her mother talking on the phone about Brett and some other girl that had been killed. Her mother was whispering into the phone so Isabelle wouldn't hear. Isabelle had gone back to her room and cried into the pillow. She had been crying off and on for days.

On Thursday her mom took her in to see Dr. Reynolds. They drew blood and they had her pee in a cup. When she got home her mom asked her if she wanted to make a batch of S'mores cookies, something they used to do together. But Isabelle said no and went back to bed. She put Brett's phone inside the pocket of her stuffed frog and hugged the frog to her chest.

Chapter 23
Friday Afternoon, November 17th

Julie Robinson had agreed to come for a visit. She'd looked tired as she trudged up the stairs to Francesca's office. Her usual bounce was gone. Under her coat she wore her turquoise and dark blue Modern Method uniform with a turquoise scarf wrapped around her curls. Her complexion had a grey tinge.

Francesca gave her a quick hug. "Here, give me your coat. Can I get you anything? Coffee? Tea?"

"No thanks, I'm good. " Julie wandered over to look out the window. "You've got a great view from up here. You can see everything that's going on in town."

Francesca chuckled. "Beware, the *Banner Bee* knows all."

They stood together looking out. "So, how are you doing, Julie?"

"I'm kind of in shock. Carrie and I spent a lot of time together. I feel like there's this big hole in my life." She turned to look at Francesca. "I'm actually thinking about moving. There's a Modern Method opening up in Elmhurst and I'm thinking about moving down there. Ms. Sorenson said I could probably get a job and I have an aunt who lives nearby."

"I'm sorry to hear we might lose you, but I can see how you feel. Come sit down and tell me about Carrie."

They talked for an hour. From the picture Julie painted, it sounded as though Carrie had turned a corner and was living a happy, productive life. She'd set goals for herself and planned on returning to college the following year. Along with working two jobs, she had started writing poetry and doing some photography.

"What kind of poetry did she write?"

"She was sort of rehashing her life through poetry. Some of it was really good." Julie fingered an earring "I told her she should try and get it published."

"Do you have any poems she wrote? I would love to see some of her work."

"Yeah. She used to send them to me. But you could check them out on her computer."

"The police say her laptop was stolen, probably when she was abducted," Francesca said.

"What were they looking for? It freaks me out."

"I don't know and I don't think the police do either." Francesca sighed.

"Well, I'll forward all the poems to you. Maybe you could publish one in the *Banner Bee*."

"That's exactly what I was thinking."

"I read your article about the boy that died the same night as Carrie. It seemed so sad. You did a good job telling his story."

"Thanks. I feel so sorry for that family. But you know what? I think the two events are connected. I've just got to figure out how. Last night I went over to Carrie's apartment with Chief Barnett. He wanted to go through it again. We found Carrie's phone."

Julie's eyes widened. "Where was it?"

"In the flour canister."

"The flour canister… she must have hidden it there. She knew they were coming to get her." Julie looked frightened now. "Maybe they'll come looking for me?"

"The police have the phone now. These criminals don't know you exist." Francesca reached out and touched her arm. "Don't worry, Julie, they'll find these guys."

"God, I hope so, I really hope so… for Carrie's sake."

160

Isabelle heard her mother's determined footsteps coming up the stairs followed by an unfamiliar heavier tread.

"Isabelle, honey, Dr. Reynolds is here to see you." Her mother's voice was sugary sweet.

The doctor peered into her room. "Hello, Isabelle." He smiled. "Can I come in?"

"Uh-huh, sure." She sat up in bed and pulled down her t-shirt that had ridden up. She pushed the frog to the floor under her bed. She could hear her mother walking back downstairs.

Dr. Reynolds looked at the posters of One Direction and Justin Bieber. "So is that your favorite group? Who are those guys?"

She cleared her throat. Her mouth suddenly felt dry. "That's One Direction and Justin Bieber. But I don't like them anymore. They're for little kids. I'm into Jimi Hendrix and Eric Clapton now. I just haven't taken those posters down."

Dr. Reynolds sat in her desk chair. "I like Clapton too." He smiled at her. "How do you feel today, Isabelle?"

"I'm all right, I guess. I'm just so tired." She looked down at her hands. She had started chewing her nails again.

"Your tests came back A-okay. There doesn't seem to be anything physically wrong with you." He sat still, looking around her room.

Isabelle didn't say anything. There was a long moment of silence.

Then he asked her some questions that didn't have anything to do with her health. Was she worried about school? Had something happened that upset her? Was she having problems with friends? Was she worried about her grades? Her mom had said she was a diligent student...

She kept saying no, no, no. "I'm just tired." There was more silence.

161

Dr. Reynolds pursed his lips and put the fingers of both hands together like a little tent. "Sometimes sleep seems like a way out of life's problems. But it isn't really a solution. Just like adults who drink alcohol or people who take drugs to forget their difficulties, the effects eventually wear off and the problems are still there." He turned and looked right into her eyes. She couldn't look away.

"I think something is bothering you, Isabelle. But you don't have to tell me what it is. Here's what I want you to do. When I leave, I want you to get up and take a long, hot shower. I want you to put on clean clothes. Then I want you to go downstairs and eat a sandwich and drink a glass of milk. Then I want you to put on your coat. It's a nice sunny day and I want you to walk down to the lake."

She was nodding as he gave his directives.

"Will you do what I'm telling you to do?"

It all seemed exhausting but she said, "Yes, I will."

"On Monday, you should go back to school. Right?"

"Right."

He got up to leave. "Things will get better, Isabelle. We'll talk again next week." He left the room and she could hear him walking down the stairs.

After he left, she felt somehow relieved. She got up and took a shower, then put on her jeans and a sweatshirt. Downstairs her mom had made her a turkey and cheese sandwich with lots of mayo. She ate the sandwich, drank some milk and grabbed an apple.

On the way down to the beach, the blackness seemed to lift a little. She looked at the puffy clouds sailing through the sky and a flock of geese flying south. How did they know where to go? Their life seemed so simple. She didn't know where she was going.

Chapter 24
Late Friday Afternoon, November 17th

It was late in the afternoon and already getting dark. Francesca drove west down Lakeland towards the North-South Highway. The road went through the forest preserve and then over the train track. Just before the highway there was an entrance into Zimmerman's Mercedes. The stadium lights lit up the parking lot with its rows of shiny cars. She pulled into a parking space in front of the dealership.

As she entered the showroom a good-looking guy with slicked-back dark hair and a gleaming smile came out of a cubicle towards her. He wore a blue V-necked sweater over an open-collared white shirt and gray slacks. He looked kind of preppy with his shiny black loafers. "Hello, I'm Don Johnson. How can I be of service?" His smile almost knocked her over.

"Hi, Don, it's nice to meet you, but I'm not here to buy a car."

His smile dropped about fifty watts.

"I'm here from the *Banner Bee*, the local online paper. My name is Francesca Antonelli. I would like to talk to anyone who might have known Carrie Landwehr. Were you a friend of hers?"

"Not really." He avoided her eyes. "The service department is somewhat separate from the sales department. And she worked cashier exclusively for the service department."

"You never went back to talk to her in the evenings? She was an attractive young woman."

He looked up, visibly ill at ease, "Well, yeah, I did talk to her some when she first started but, uh…" He didn't finish his sentence.

"What happened?"

"She was kind of distant so I stopped going back there." He was blushing. Francesca figured he'd come on to Carrie and she'd blown him off.

Just then a young woman dressed all in black with wild purple hair approached them. "Don, you've got a call, a Mrs. Springer."

"Sheba, can you please take, Ms. Antonelli down to talk to the Captain." He turned away without another word and strode towards his cubicle.

"Yeah, sure, Don." Sheba glanced over at Francesca. Her slightly bulging eyes were ringed with black mascara. "Are you another journalist? We've had a lot of people in here the last few days."

"Yes," Francesca said as they walked down the hall, "I'm from the *Banner Bee*."

"Oh yeah, sometimes I read it; like to know what's going on..."

"That's great to hear," Francesca said. "Tell me; were you a friend of Carrie Landwehr's?"

"Nah, not really. She used to talk to Mrs. Muffie, though. You really should talk to her." Sheba opened the door into the service department and stopped in front of a small room with a cashier's window and counter. "Dottie, here's another newspaper person." She turned to leave.

"Well, I don't know. I've already talked to a lot of people." Dorothy Muffie didn't look up from the pink baby sweater she was knitting.

Francesca cleared her throat and gave her name, also mentioning the *Banner Bee*. Dorothy looked up over her reading glasses. "You don't look anything like that picture you've got online. You're much prettier in person."

Francesca blushed. "Well, thank you." She paused. "I'm sorry to bother you, Mrs. Muffie. I'm trying to learn as much as I can about Carrie Landwehr. I'd like to write a story about her."

Dorothy reached over and opened the door into her office. "Oh, call me Dottie. Everyone does. Come sit down in here so we can talk."

Francesca went in and sat on a stool beside a filing cabinet.

Mrs. Muffie was seated in front of a counter with a computer and printer at one end. There were a series of cubby holes underneath and several file cabinets. She went back to her knitting. "Carrie was a darling girl, very thoughtful. When I needed to leave early for an appointment, she would make sure to get here and fill in for me."

"Do you think she was a happy person?" Francesca had gotten her notebook out and was fishing in her purse for a pencil.

"Happy person? Yes, until last week, that is…when she was all upset." Dottie put her knitting down. "The police asked me about that."

"They did?" Francesca prompted, notebook balanced on her knee.

"I've been thinking about what I told them."

"What's that?" Francesca was alert.

"I told them she was worried about something."

"About what?"

"I think she was afraid of something here at Zimmerman's." Dottie frowned and picked up her knitting.

"What do you mean?"

"Friday when she came in, she kept looking over there." She gestured with her knitting needle toward a metal door across the hall. It was painted grey and had a small window with wire mesh at eye level.

"What's through there?" Francesca asked.

"That's where the service bays are. We're not supposed to go in there. Maybe she went in to deliver a message and the Captain yelled at her."

"The captain? Who's that?"

"He runs the service department. He's not really a captain. His real name is Mr. Petroff, but he likes to wear a captain's cap. You know…dark blue with gold braid."

Petroff. Wasn't that the name Alexei Kozerski had mentioned, talking with his wife at Jordanville Prison? She wrote it down on her notepad.

The phone rang. Dottie set down her knitting and reached for a pink pad and a pen, then picked up. "Good afternoon, Zimmerman's Mercedes." She had an easy, friendly manner. She listened and then wrote down a name and number. When she'd finished the call, she put the message in a cubby hole.

Francesca remembered the pink slip from Carrie's apartment last night. It could have come from that very pad.

At that moment a woman in a full-length mink coat swept through the glass doors down the hall. "Hello, Dottie," her voice rang out. "I'm here to pick up my car."

Dottie smiled. "Hello, Mrs. Pomeroy. Did the Captain say your car was ready?"

"He certainly did. The car hiker is going to bring it around. I need to settle with you."

Dottie entered information on the computer and the printer began printing an invoice. Meanwhile, Mrs. Pomeroy glanced over at Francesca. She wore bright red lipstick, and the tight skin on her face was a shrine to multiple facelifts. Her blond hair was lacquered into a smooth bob. "Are you going to take over the job of that poor girl who got killed?"

Francesca smiled, "No. I'm Francesca Antonelli. I'm here from the *Banner Bee*."

"What's that? *Banner Bee?*" Mrs. Pomeroy could barely raise her eyebrows; her face was stretched so tight. She bent over and signed the invoice Dottie had printed and handed her a credit card.

"It's an online newspaper." Francesca said.

"Oh, I don't read things on the computer. My husband Harry does, but I like to read a real newspaper. You must be here to talk about that dead girl."

Francesca nodded.

"Well, it's too bad. She was probably a druggie. That's what happens to you when you break the law." Mrs. Pomeroy signed the credit card receipt with a flourish. Dottie handed her a copy of the receipt and invoice.

"Thank you, Dottie. I'll see you soon." She turned to Francesca. "Nice to meet you, miss." She wiggled her fingers in their direction as she left.

As Mrs. Pomeroy approached the glass doors, a stocky man wearing a navy blue captain's hat held the door open for her. Mr. Petroff, Francesca guessed. They exchanged a few words and then the man came down the hall. He barely glanced at Francesca. "Dorothy, you've got to stay late again tonight. I'm going to need you until seven."

Dottie looked unhappy. "I'm supposed to have dinner with my sister tonight. It's Friday."

"Sorry. You'll have to call your sister and make it later."

"But..." Dottie looked down at Mrs. Pomeroy's paperwork.

"No buts, Dorothy. We all have to pitch in this week."

"Are they hiring somebody for next week? I just get so tired..."

"You'll have to talk to Mr. Jenkins about that."

He was about to turn away when Francesca said, "Mr. Petroff, may I speak to you? I'm Francesca Antonelli from the *Banner* Bee. I'd like to talk to you about Carrie Landwehr."

167

He eyed her warily. "Around here they call me Captain. And no, I have no time to talk about that girl. I've talked to the police. I don't have to talk to you."

He walked over to the gray metal door and looked through the small window. Then he turned back around and addressed Francesca. "I think it's time you leave. Mrs. Muffie has work to do."

Chapter 25
Saturday, November 18th

Ramses Crenshaw III stepped out of the limo and walked across the tarmac to the waiting Astra/Gulfstream SPX. He knew this plane ran about three and a half million used. This one looked new and shiny.

A curvaceous blond in a red stewardess outfit with an ultra-mini skirt was waiting at the top of the stairway. Her matching red high heels extended her legs about a mile. Behind her stood an equally beautiful brunette in an identical outfit. Crenshaw smiled in spite of himself, wondering what this "little flight" might include.

Inside the plane he found his major campaign donor leaning back in a black club chair. In front of him were a bottle of bourbon and two cut-glass tumblers with the word CIMARRON etched in block letters on the side.

"Ramses, my friend, please sit down." The man's smile did not extend to his eyes. He was tall, thick-set with a protruding stomach. Thin blond hair was combed carefully over his balding pate. Hooded eyes, a wide nose and petulant lips were set in a splotchy red face.

Crenshaw heard the engines rev up as he sat down. The twin stewardesses came back and bent over to attach the seat belts. The blond reached over him. Her thick hair fell in front of his face and exuded the dense smell of vanilla and something else…gardenias. Soft breasts brushed his chest.

"We're going for a little ride to see where our pipeline takes us. You're going to look down and enjoy the view," his host commanded. The brunette poured two glasses of bourbon and added two ice cubes in the shape of miniature buffalos.

169

"Here's to our partnership." The man chuckled and took up his bourbon.

Crenshaw raised his glass. "Yes, here's to our mutual collaboration."

They flew down over Illinois and into Missouri. They talked about the money. They sipped the bourbon.

They talked about the campaign. They sipped the bourbon.

They talked about the message Crenshaw would deliver to his constituents. They sipped the bourbon.

They flew over Missouri, Kansas and down to the Oklahoma panhandle. The land below was flat and brown. Nothing seemed to be growing. Crenshaw could see oil rigs spotting the land in the distance. Twice, the plane circled a massive construction sight.

"There she is. We're on schedule." His host was beaming with pleasure.

"Right," Crenshaw nodded his head in agreement.

On the way back, the stewardesses served them sandwiches loaded with beef brisket and dripping with barbeque sauce, crispy fries and coleslaw. Afterwards, Crenshaw's host went to the back cabin with the brunette and shut the door.

Crenshaw smiled halfheartedly at the blonde. Then he fell asleep.

Sperryville Missouri News
"The Town with a Heart"
Saturday November 18th

This week Sperryville is pleased to welcome the crew of Anderson Pipeline Specialists. They're going to be here a couple of weeks working on the natural gas pipeline that runs through Barry Johnson's and Rhett Crandon's farms. This pipeline has been out of use for many years and served in the past as a conduit for gas piped from Illinois to Kansas and Oklahoma. Apparently, it will be used again.

The crew is being housed at the new Sperryville Super 8 Motel. They will be taking their meals at Grandma's Café on Main Street.

Grandma Larson says, "These are right nice fellows. They loved the breakfast special this morning, and I hope they enjoy the meatloaf and lemon meringue pie tonight."

Chapter 26
Sunday Night, November 19th

Tom had agreed to come over for chili on Sunday night. He'd been working around the clock. Nearly a week had gone by and they still had no leads or suspects. The Homicide Task Force was sifting through every piece of information that came in. At first Tom claimed to be too busy for dinner when Francesca called, but it didn't take long for her to persuade him. He desperately needed a little time to unwind.

They sat on the sofa in front of the TV. The Chicago Bears were having a good season and their new coach was the media's darling these days. They each had a beer and laughed at some of the crazy ads on TV. Francesca told him about her interview with Julie and the visit to Zimmerman's.

"I liked Dottie Muffie. She's an odd bird."

"Did you see the pictures of Bernie?"

Francesca frowned, "Bernie? Who's that?" She passed Tom the basket of tortilla chips. He took a handful.

"Bernie is her cat. He's named after her deceased husband."

Francesca laughed. "That's one way of remembering him!" Then her face clouded over. "I didn't like that guy, the Captain. What an overbearing creep! Did you know his real name is Petroff? He must be of Russian extraction. I heard—"

Tom interrupted her. "Hey, did I tell you about that pink message slip we found?"

"No, but I saw Dottie Muffie fill one out while I was there."

"The words we saw on there were Russian for *hook.*"

"That's weird. They were talking about *the hook* when I visited Royce Canfield in prison. What or who could that be?"

"I don't know. There's a lot I can't put together right now." He took a long drink of beer and munched some chips. "So what did you learn from your interview with Julie Robinson?"

"She assured me Carrie was no longer into drugs."

"Francesca, a user knows how to hide their habit when they want to. Julie wasn't with her friend twenty-four hours a day. Carrie must have been mixed up with some hardcore dealers at one time, even if not recently. We're getting close to finding out who they are."

"But wouldn't you have found something in her apartment if she was still using?"

He avoided her question. "Hey, I'm starving. Let's have some of your fabulous chili."

Francesca went into the kitchen and warmed up the chili. She served it in large, orange pasta bowls. Tom carried in a tray with small bowls of sour cream, chopped onions and shredded cheddar. Francesca had also made a simple green salad with orange sections and sliced radishes. They settled down on the sofa and by mutual agreement they didn't talk about Carrie Landwehr or Brett Atkins.

After the chili, Francesca gathered up the bowls and went into the kitchen to get the apple pie she'd made. She cut two pieces and scooped out some vanilla ice cream. But when she came back into the living room, Tom was dead to the world.

She turned off the TV and all but one lamp. Then she covered Tom with a blanket. He was sleeping peacefully, his face smooth and relaxed. For a while he could forget Carrie Landwehr's murder and the depravity of mankind. She bent down and kissed him gently on the top of the head. His shampoo smelled spicy and masculine.

173

After cleaning up the kitchen, Francesca crept upstairs to her study and got to work writing an article for Monday on the upcoming Thanksgiving Turkey Trot. This half-marathon was a fund raiser to provide Christmas presents for disadvantaged children. Francesca wanted to give the event plenty of publicity. The money raised went directly to the kids and not to some bloated organization.

While she was working, an email from Julie came through. It contained Carrie's poems, as promised. Francesca clicked on the attachment and opened it up. She read a few of the poems and found them disturbing. She scrolled down to the last one:

Slippery slimy smiley sleuth
Deep door double delve
Snowy silvery silky sack
Dark dragon dissimulate
Anonymous alien nautical knight
Tonight.

What did it mean? She read it through a couple of times and once out loud. The alliteration gave it a rhythm. Was Carrie playing with words or communicating something dark?

Tom woke up at 3 AM. At first he didn't know where he was. His cellphone was vibrating in his breast pocket. He pushed off the blanket and yanked the phone out, checked the caller ID and pushed the respond button. "Barnett here."

"It's Lewis, Chief." The undercover officer's voice sounded strained and was barely audible. "Could you meet me, like, soon?"

"Sure. Where?"

"At the train station on the south side. No one can see us there."

"Have you got news?"

174

"Yeah. Can't talk." He hung up.

Tom stood up and went to the hall closet where Francesca had put his coat. He slipped it on and quietly opened the front door. There was no time to leave a note. Briefly, he thought about how he would like to climb those stairs and get in bed with Francesca. He wanted to press himself against her warm body.

His phone vibrated again. It was a text message from Lewis: *PP 847.* What could that mean?

Outside, it was pitch black. There was no sign of the moon. He started the car, did a U-turn in the street and headed west. He decided it would be better not to put on the siren or flashing lights. Lewis had sounded like he was on surveillance. Was he being watched?

Tom turned left on Eastern Avenue that ran parallel to the train tracks. He could hear a train in the distance. It was hooting at the crossroads, going fast as it approached Banner Bluff. An Amtrak train, it wouldn't stop in town. Tom sped up, heading toward the driveway that led into the parking lot north of the train station. The headlights of a car coming towards him on his left, plus the glaring lights of the train approaching on his right, momentarily blinded him. He blinked several times, trying to rid his vision of after-images.

The train raced by and then all was darkness. He pulled into the horseshoe drive in front of the train station and got out of the car. He grabbed his flashlight and felt for his gun. Except for the breeze, there was no sound. He had an unsettling sense that something wasn't right.

The light inside the train station illuminated the street entrance. Tom went up the short flight of stairs and edged towards the south part of the structure, his back to the wall, his gun drawn. When he got to the corner, he slowly peered around the wall. No one there. He walked carefully along the cement walkway. "Lewis," he whispered. "Are you there?"

Nothing. He turned on his flashlight and surveyed the area. There was an eighteen-inch drop-off to his left. Bushes grew along the walkway. He looked down. Nothing. He went forward towards the platform, pointing his flashlight in both directions. The benches were empty, and no one lingered nearby. He went to the polished wooden door of the station and tried turning the handle. It was locked.

He stood for a moment, thinking. He pulled out his phone and texted Lewis: *Where R U?*

A moment later he saw a light flash down on the tracks. He moved closer to the cement edge painted with yellow warning stripes and pointed his flashlight onto the track bed.

Lewis's mangled body lay crumpled there, his soul long gone. The cell phone down on the tracks blinked and went out.

Chapter 27
Monday Morning, November 20th

Francesca had slept especially well knowing Tom was downstairs. His presence made her feel safe and protected. These days, she no longer had to sleep with the lights on as she had for so many years. She had finally conquered her childhood fears after they apprehended the Lake Monster. Thinking back to that summer when he was terrorizing the town of Banner Bluff still gave her the heebeegeebees.

Her bedside clock read 7 AM. Tom must still be sleeping. He'd been exhausted the night before. She slipped out of bed. In the bathroom she splashed water on her face and brushed her teeth. Then she pulled on her running gear and a clean pair of socks. Her running shoes were downstairs. She would make a pot of coffee and then steal out if Tom was still sleeping.

Downstairs Benji and Bailey greeted her with wagging tails. They recognized her clothing and started jumping around. They knew they were going for a run. She shushed them and peered into the living room. It was empty, the blanket thrown on the sofa. Tom must have slipped out much earlier. With a pang of disappointment, she folded up the blanket and put it in the closet. She would have liked to have coffee together and maybe a little breakfast. It would have been like…yes, like they were a married couple. Was that what she wanted? She didn't really know. At least she didn't want to think it through.

Francesca pulled on her shoes and snapped on the dogs' running leashes. Outside, it was cold and barely light. She turned west towards Eastern Avenue, a familiar route: along the running path that ran next to the train tracks, through the village green, down to the lake on Elm, along the bluff and then back up to town on Lakeview. She was shivering, but once she hit her rhythm she would warm up.

When she turned onto Eastern, she could see flashing lights and multiple vehicles parked by the train station. Had someone fallen onto the train tracks? As she got nearer, she made out police cars and emergency vehicles. The train station was lit up like a football field. The dogs pulled her forward towards the action. Her heart was beating from the exertion of her run but also from fear of what she might find ahead.

A few minutes later she arrived at the train station driveway. The entire area was cordoned off. A lot of traffic was bunched up nearby; the police were not permitting anyone to approach the station. The people who planned on taking the train would have to drive into Chicago today.

Francesca approached Officer Lister, who was guarding the driveway. A genteel Southerner, Lister had recently joined the force. He had soft, dark brown eyes set in a chocolate brown face. Today his expression was grim.

"Hey there, Francesca. The Chief's over at the tracks. Busy now." He spoke with a soft drawl.

"What's going on?"

"Something terrible." He paused, looking down. "The Chief found Lewis on the tracks. He was hit by a train."

"Was it suicide?" She felt bewildered. Lewis had been a young man, full of life.

"We don't think so." He looked at her briefly and then bent over to pat Benji and Bailey, who were sitting obediently.

"Oh, my God!" She was shocked. Then she remembered Tom had told her that Lewis was working undercover, trying to infiltrate the drug scene. "What do they know so far?"

"Not much." He looked up as a car drove up parallel to them.

178

The irate driver yelled, "What's going on here, Officer? I have to be on the seven-thirty train."

"Sorry, sir. No trains will be coming through here for a couple of hours."

"Couple of hours?" The man banged on his horn in anger and then gunned the engine driving off.

Lister rolled his eyes at Francesca. "What can you do?"

"Listen, I better get going. I'm in the way here. I'll talk to the Chief later." She turned and walked with the dogs along the road, looking for a place to cross through the traffic and get over to the village green. A car in front of the station was blocking her way. She looked in at the driver to see if he would let her pass in front and recognized the Captain, apparently scrutinizing the crime scene. He didn't see her.

She turned to see what he was looking at. Technicians dressed in white jumpsuits had gathered together to study an object in an evidence bag. She looked back at the Captain. He looked concerned, even worried. About what? Francesca wondered.

Chapter 28
Monday Morning, November 20th

It was drizzling as Harrison Rand brought the car around to the front of the hospital. A nurse pushed Daphne Meriwether's wheelchair close to the passenger door of Rand's black Lexus. Carina and the nurse helped Daphne into the front seat. Harrison came around and opened the back door for Carina, taking two vases of flowers from her arms. Once she was settled, he handed her the flowers. He went to the back and put two plants and a small suitcase in the trunk.

Daphne was not pleased. Although she knew Harrison Rand had been very helpful to her daughter, she didn't trust him a penny's worth. She didn't really remember what happened when she passed out nearly a week ago. The experience was a fog in her brain. Once she got home, she would be able to think more clearly.

Harrison slipped into the seat beside her and put the car in gear. "I bet you'll be glad to get home," he said, looking over at her with an ingratiating smile. He was a handsome devil; she had to give him that.

"Yes, Mr. Rand, I will be very happy to be in my own house and eat some home-cooked food. Everything was so bland in the hospital."

"Please call me Harrison. I want us to become friends."

Her mouth firmed in a straight line. "Mr. Rand, I am grateful to you for helping us out these last few days, but I don't feel we're on a first-name basis and we most certainly are not friends."

Harrison glanced at Carina in the rear view mirror. She raised her eyebrows and shook her head.

"I made some of that spicy sweet potato soup you love, Mom, and also a pot of split pea. Francesca brought over a pan of lasagna and a loaf of focaccia, so we're good to go. No more bland food." Carina clearly wanted this homecoming to be a happy one.

"How are the horses? Any problems?"

"Everything is fine. José asked Luis Gonzales to come over and help out this past week. I wish we could hire Luis full-time. He's a good worker and a fast learner."

"I wish we could hire ten more people," Daphne murmured.

"Oh, and when I got home on Sunday, Yari Gonzales had come over with the boys and cleaned the house. Everything is spic and span. And she made a pan of enchiladas. She didn't even want me to pay her, but I did. That couple is so nice." Carina was babbling, as if trying to smooth over the tension.

As they turned into their long driveway, the sun came out from behind a bank of dark grey clouds and rays plunged down, illuminating the graceful red-trimmed farmhouse and red barn. The buildings seemed to shine surrounded by the barren ground and leafless trees. From a distance they didn't look in need of a fresh coat of paint.

Daphne's eyes lit up with pleasure. "Oh, I'm so happy to be home. Doesn't our house look lovely in this light?" She turned her head, looking from left to right, wanting to soak in the rolling hills and white fences.

Harrison pulled the car around to the front of the house. He came around to help Daphne out of the car. She refused his hand and pulled herself up holding on to the door frame. "I don't need any help, thank you very much." But when she took a step towards the stairs that led to the porch, she felt herself wobbling. Despite her protests, Harrison reached out and took her arm.

Carina rushed past them up the stairs to open the front door. She smiled at her mother. "Voilà! Welcome home, Mom."

Daphne shook off Harrison's hand and moved towards the door. She was determined to be independent. In the distance, she heard rumbling. "What in the world is that?" she said, looking back toward the noise and frowning.

Carina and Harrison shared a guilty look. Just then a heavy truck pulling an industrial-sized flatbed came up the driveway and turned towards the access road that led down to the beach. On the flatbed was an enormous bulldozer. The engine throbbed and the ground shook as it rolled by.

At that moment, everything came back to Daphne. She looked at her daughter. "What is happening? Are you letting them steal our property?"

"Mom, there's nothing we can do. It's eminent domain. We can't fight it."

Daphne turned to Harrison. "You're the one, you're a conniving snake and you have conned my daughter into this scheme."

Harrison stared her down, his eyes hard and calculating.

"Get off my porch, get off my property and don't ever set foot here again." She was shaking as she grabbed the door frame and pulled herself into the house.

Chapter 29
Late Monday Afternoon, November 20th

The Homicide Task Force had convened in the downstairs meeting room. Tension was high, a mix of anger, frustration and horror at what had occurred. Jesse Lewis was one of their own, a bright light in the force.

Lewis's photo was tacked on the board next to pictures of Carrie Landwehr and Brett Atkins. To Tom they all looked heartbreakingly young. Each photo depicted a smiling, trusting face. The crime scene photos of the mangled body on the train tracks made a painful, grisly contrast. As Puchalski projected each crime-scene slide on a screen, Tom wanted to look away.

"According to Hollister, we can't be certain how Lewis landed on the tracks, but we do know he didn't commit suicide. Someone pushed him or threw him in front of the train. Lewis was strong and athletic, so we're thinking it had to be more than one person." He paused and looked down at his computer keyboard. "The force of the train hitting him was such that his body literally exploded. These remains do not represent his entire body." Puchalski paused again, swallowed, and looked down, then turned to Tom. His face was white and he was perspiring. "Do we have to look at these now? Do they tell us anything?"

Tom looked around at the ashen faces. "Maybe we can wait on these until we get the full report from forensics. Let's discuss what we've learned from the crime scene."

Puchalski clicked his mouse and the images disappeared. He sat down heavily. The room vibrated with unspoken emotion.

Tom broke the silence and told the group about the early-morning phone call from Lewis asking him to come to the train station. "He was nervous and said he couldn't talk. I was half asleep when I got the call. Then when I was going out the door I got a text message." He went to the white board, picked up a red marker and wrote *PP 847*. "This was it. Does this mean anything to anyone?"

"It's the local area code," Sanders said, his hand unconsciously covering the red birthmark on his cheek. "Maybe he was starting to send a phone number and got interrupted."

"But what about the PP, does that mean anything to anyone?"

They all looked at each other blankly.

"Could it be a place? An address? Maybe a street or a town?" Cindy Murray asked. "Poplar? Or maybe something like Poplar Place, you know, two words like that."

"How about a license plate…or part of a license plate. Maybe it was a clue he wanted to send you," Detective Ramirez said.

They fell silent again, thinking.

"I'll research 847 license plates with the DMV and possible addresses in town with that number," Puchalski said. "If it's part of a telephone number, we've got no lead."

Ramirez cleared his throat. "We're processing the evidence from the scene. On the tracks, we found all sorts of stuff: candy wrappers, cigarette butts, coffee cups. They're all being analyzed. On the platform we found very little. The most interesting item was a set of IEMs that we think were torn from someone's neck, maybe our killer's. They were on the edge of the tracks."

"IEMs?" Cindy asked.

"Inner-Ear-Monitors, you know, ear buds to listen to music on your iPod. The headset we found was attached to a cord that got ripped out of an iPod." Ramirez looked around the room. "What's interesting is that these are Russian-made, by a company called Fischer Audio. They're top notch and are sold primarily in

184

Russia and Asia. Here in the States there's only one distributer that I could find."

"Another Russian connection?" O'Connor asked.

"It's worth considering. Of course we don't know if these particular earphones belonged to our killer, or killers, but the lab is analyzing them for fingerprints or DNA, maybe from earwax or skin tissue cells."

Cindy Murray took the floor. "O'Connor and I went over to interview Jesse Lewis's girlfriend Ellie…" She referred to her notes. "Ellie Masters. She was in a terrible state. We didn't stay long. She really didn't know anything because Jesse didn't talk about his undercover work. Aside from that, she said they hadn't seen much of each other this last month. She works days over at the electric company. He came home in the early morning, went to bed and left in the late afternoon. She thought he was on to something yesterday afternoon, though. He was jazzed and told her he might be wrapping things up…that he'd be getting his life back."

Why didn't he call or text earlier, Tom thought as he punched a fist into his palm.

Chapter 30
Monday Evening, November 20th

Connie, Francesca and Frank were having a cocktail pow-wow in Francesca's office. Francesca had opened a bottle of French Chablis and made three varieties of bruschetta: goat cheese with sun-dried tomato relish, a garlicky tapenade and a crunchy cucumber-radish concoction. Each kind was decorated with a sprightly sprig of parsley. Francesca eyed them with pleasure.

The weekend before, Frank had called to talk. He said he was ready to come back to work, though just part-time. They'd had a good laugh about that. "What's part-time of part-time?" Francesca had asked.

"Let's just say I need to get out of this house and do something, see people."

So she'd invited him to the office on Monday, timing his visit to coincide with Connie Munster's in the early evening. "Why don't you get here at five? A little earlier, so we can kibitz."

Now the three of them were sitting around the table. They each had a glass of wine and had helped themselves to the bruschetta while they discussed the day's events.

"What have you learned about the accident at the train station?" Frank asked.

"The person who died was Officer Jesse Lewis. You know him, right?" Francesca said.

"Is he that baby-faced policeman? The blue-eyed blond?" Connie asked.

"Yes, he was the youngest guy on the force."

"What happened?" Frank asked.

"The police aren't saying much. Lewis was undercover these last few weeks, trying to infiltrate the drug trade on the North

186

Shore. It sounds as though someone was on to him and he was thrown in front of the train."

Connie leaned back in shock. "This happened here…just a block from your office? Who are these monsters?"

Francesca shivered. "They could very well be the same guys that killed Carrie Landwehr. They're ruthless…evil."

"Sometimes I think society hasn't advanced at all since prehistoric times." Frank said. "We're still animals being controlled by our narcissistic desires and emotions."

A brief silence fell.

"Speaking of evildoers, what about that list of the Pharaoh's campaign donors you were putting together, Connie. We never discussed it again," Francesca said.

"I made a copy for you." She pulled a spreadsheet out of her leather satchel and handed it to Francesca.

"Let me make a copy for Frank. We can check it out together," Francesca said.

When they each had a copy of the spreadsheet, Connie clarified some of the information. Beside each name she had typed addresses, occupation, political interests and so on.

"I see there's a Chinese investment group buying property in Chicago." Frank slid his finger down the page. "Another group built a two hundred thousand-dollar wind farm in Lee County, Illinois." His finger continued. "And another one is constructing a forty-thousand solar panel facility in Rockford." He looked up. "The Chinese certainly want to be in Ramses Crenshaw's good graces."

"Yes," Connie said. "Bob Newhouse has been approached by some Chinese advance men as well. It's par for the course." She took a sip of wine.

"Here's Groundswell Industries," Francesca said. "Brett Atkins' mother told me she worked for that company. After talking to her, I researched them. They're planning to open a

187

humongous plant in the near future, but haven't decided whether to build it in Illinois or Wisconsin. The two states are battling it out; sweetening the deal with tax incentives and relaxed building permits." Francesca took a small bite of bruschetta, wondering if the governor had been in touch with Emily Atkins.

"Now what about this fellow, Rollo Perry?" Frank asked. "What are his interests in Illinois? I see he's from Oklahoma and owns several casinos in Las Vegas. I haven't heard about new casino construction in Illinois."

Connie reacted swiftly. "He's a scum-bucket, filthy rich with highly questionable morals. We've got a picture of him and the Pharaoh entering a hotel in Las Vegas. She passed Francesca the photo. Taken from a distance, it looked like the product of a surveillance camera. Francesca recognized Crenshaw coming out of a hotel with another tall man. The photo was unclear and grainy but she could see Crenshaw's companion was somewhat overweight with unattractive thick features.

Connie continued with vehemence. "I'm not sure what the connection is, but it's worrisome. I've heard Rollo has delusions of grandeur. Who knows what he wants."

"It sounds as though he would get along with the Pharaoh," Francesca murmured.

Chapter 31
Tuesday Morning, November 21st

Francesca was on her way to Churchill's to meet Carina. The cozy café, just a block from her office, was a good place for a chat over delectable muffins and cinnamon rolls.

She walked across the street towards the post office, which was busy at this hour. Through the glass window she spotted a couple of people in line. She recognized Lenny behind the counter. He had something to say to everyone, and sometimes he would burst into song. He always turned the tedium of a post office visit into a pleasant experience.

She wanted to drop a birthday card in the box, so she pushed open the glass door and waved at Lenny, who sang out, "Here she comes, Miss Francesca. How're you doing, hon'?"

Before Francesca could respond, a tall man in a black hoodie pushed past her, knocking her against the center counter. He didn't apologize or even turn around to look at her. He strode towards the P.O. boxes as though it was a matter of life or death.

"Some people are in a mighty big hurry," Lenny sang out, shaking his head.

"You could say that again," Francesca said.

She dropped her letter in the mail slot and looked over at the P.O. boxes. The man removed an envelope from one. As he locked the little door, he looked around, as if worried someone might be watching him. Then he stuffed the envelope into his pocket. As he came back towards the entrance door, he looked directly at Francesca. "You got a problem?" he asked. She noted an accent, but couldn't place it.

What a jerk, Francesca thought. "Yes, I do. You nearly knocked me over coming in."

He shrugged and moved past her. Along with the hoodie, he wore jeans and work boots. She'd never seen him before, and she'd just as soon never see him again.

When she got to Churchill's, she saw Carina at a small table against the wall, talking on her cellphone. Francesca ordered coffee and a morning glory muffin and took them over to the table.

By the time she got there, Carina was off the phone. She looked as though she'd lost more weight. Her face was pale and dark circles rimmed her bloodshot eyes. Francesca saw no food in front of her, just a cup of black coffee.

"Hi Francesca, thanks for meeting me." She put her phone in her purse.

Francesca sat down and cut her muffin in two. "Let's share. You could do with some sustenance." She pushed the plate to the center of the table.

Carina shook her head. "I can't eat right now. I just need to talk to someone."

"What's going on?"

"We brought Mom home yesterday morning."

"Who's 'we'?" Francesca asked.

"Harrison Rand and me." Carina wore a guilty expression as she continued. "Francesca, he's been so nice but Mom is ready to kill him. Just when we arrived at the house, this big tractor trailer drove by on its way to the beach. The construction crew is using our access road, so there's lots of traffic and..."

"Wait a minute, you've lost me."

"Mom is against having this water-pumping station on our land. But we have no choice. The state has appropriated the land. She doesn't want to accept that." Tears filled Carina's eyes. "I know this situation is bad for her. The doctor said she needs to relax and rest...absolutely no stress." She rubbed her eyes with her fingers and yawned.

190

Francesca reached over and put her arm around Carina's thin shoulders. Back when she'd first met her two years ago, Carina had glowed with health and beauty. Now she was a wraith of her former self.

"How can I help?"

Carina lowered her hands from her face. "Maybe you could look into the eminent domain business. Find documentation that would prove to my mom that we have no choice. She trusts you. She knows you'll get to the bottom of a problem."

"What about Mr. Rand?"

"She won't have him in the house. She doesn't trust him."

"What about the money? If they're appropriating the land, they have to compensate you. Did you receive it already?"

"No, no. I was told it would take time." Carina sighed heavily, gazing out the window. "When we get it, Mom will probably relax."

Francesca thought, *when and if?*

The Cimarron Missive
A Blog Serving Cimarron, Texas and Beaver
Counties, Oklahoma
Today's story:

The US Drought Monitor has changed the intensity level of drought in Cimarron County from severe to extreme. We all know that we've seen no rain for months. What does this portend for Boise City and the people living in the surrounding area? Are we reliving the 1930s Dust Bowl?

Chapter 32
Tuesday Evening, November 21st

By 7:30 PM the kids were finally in bed and Martin went downstairs to clean up the kitchen. Kate would have a conniption if things weren't neat and tidy. It had been a long day. Lately Stevie was into everything and Martin knew he needed to be more attentive. This morning he had been doing some research online, with his computer set up on the kitchen table. Stevie was sitting on the floor playing with some plastic trucks and cars. In addition Martin had pulled out all the Tupperware, and Stevie seemed happy.

Martin was researching the construction of Viking ships. The ships were clinker built, constructed with overlapping planks riveted together. They were incredibly strong and flexible which enabled the Vikings to rule the North Sea...

A muffled bang interrupted him, and he looked over toward the pantry. Stevie had pulled down the sugar canister and was sitting in a lake of white crystals. At first Martin felt like laughing. Stevie looked so cute, and he actually grabbed his phone to take a picture of his wayward son. But then he'd groaned at the mess he was going to have to clean up. Meanwhile Stevie was licking his fingers, patting them in the sugar and then licking them off again, humming to himself. A minute later Jack came in from the living room where he'd been soaking up the morning sun and started to lick up the sugar as well.

It had taken awhile to clean up. Somehow Martin had never gotten back to the Viking ships that would be the subject of a lecture in his new course on the history of the Vikings. Martin had spent nine months in Uppsala in graduate school and although he had not written his doctoral thesis on Scandinavian history he was very knowledgeable on the subject. He had done research in Denmark and Sweden some years ago. Last spring he'd proposed this new course and the history department at the university had readily approved his suggestion. That was before the accident and his leave of absence. Now he only had six weeks to finish his curriculum and plan the readings before returning to the university in January. But again, today, he had wasted precious time.

Tonight after Stevie fell asleep, he went in to read with Rosie. She was supposed to read every night, so usually she read a chapter and then he read a chapter. Kate used to do the bedtime reading, but lately it had become Martin's role.

After they finished, Rosie said, "Daddy, will you snuggle with me?"

"Sure, I will." Martin reached up and turned off the lamp. They lay together in the dark. After a while, Rosie spoke again.

"Daddy?"

"Hmm?" Martin was feeling a little drowsy.

"What if I got lost?"

"That would be terrible. But I would come and find you."

"What if I got lost at Disney World?" Kate's parents had taken Rosie to Disney World last summer to help them out while Martin was still recovering.

"We would have everyone looking for you, honey, and we would find you."

"But Daddy, there are so many people there. When you found me you wouldn't know if it was me?"

Martin was silent. He felt helpless. He was supposed to be a source of security, the dependable father. She was right. He wouldn't recognize her at first.

"Rosie?"

"Yes, Daddy."

"I would move heaven and earth to find you and when I did, I would recognize your voice and the way you bounce on your toes when you're excited and the way you shake your head when you giggle. And there's something else. Somehow I would know you with my heart."

Rosie was silent.

"Do you believe me? Please trust me, Rosie, okay?"

It seemed to him that she took a while to answer. "I believe you, Daddy." Rosie buried herself in the covers. "Daddy?"

"Yes?"

"I love you."

"I love you, too, pumpkin."

He had lain there, feeling helpless and overwhelmed, until she fell asleep.

Now, Martin was downstairs in the quiet house. He went from window to window and door to door, making sure they were all locked. Since the discovery of Carrie Landwehr's body he had lived in fear that one of those men would come looking for him. They had seen him and would probably recognize him. He had nightmares where he relived the horrendous scene. At odd moments during the day that acrid smell would fill his nostrils. He knew it was all in his mind, but still...

Banner Bluff was not a large town and it wouldn't be that difficult to find someone. Whenever Martin walked down the street pushing the stroller, he turned at the sound of footsteps behind him. In the store, he was aware of people who stopped to look at him. This pervasive fear along with his face-blindness was making him paranoid.

He looked up at the kitchen clock. Where was Kate? The School Improvement Team meeting should be over by now. She hadn't come home for dinner, saying she would eat a sandwich at her desk and correct papers until the meeting started. The School Improvement Team included three faculty members, three students, three parents and the principal, Glen Seybold.

194

Supposedly the meeting took place at 6:30 to allow students to finish their sports practice and parents to return home from work.

He did another window and door check even though he knew he had already done it once. He needed to quell his rising panic. Maybe he would have a drink. The doctor had given him a prescription for an antidepressant but Martin avoided taking it. He reached up into the cabinet above the refrigerator and took down the bottle of scotch. He poured himself a half inch and went into the living room, turned on the TV and picked up the remote. After switching through the channels, he turned it off again. He couldn't concentrate on anything.

The picture over the mantel piece caught his eye. It was a photograph of the four of them taken last spring. Stevie was just a little baby and Rosie was beaming at the camera. They all looked so happy, the perfect American family. How he would like to turn back time. Since his accident things had fallen apart. He and Kate used to be each other's best friend. Now their conversations were stilted. They said just enough to each other to keep their household running. He took a large gulp of scotch.

Martin and Kate had met when he was in graduate school finishing up his Ph.D. and she was beginning her teaching career. She had a sparkling personality, like champagne. She bubbled with laughter, her spontaneous cheerfulness a counterbalance to his overly serious nature. He had fallen in love with her inner sweetness and warm, deep femininity. They were perfectly matched and she seemed to delight in him as he did in her. When they moved in together they could never get enough of each other. If either one of them awoke in the night, they would reach for the other. Then they would make slow, intense love, half awake, half asleep. They had agreed never to deny each other this pleasure.

Since September, though, Kate had refused his advances. When he reached for her, she would remove his hand from her hip and turn away, saying she was too tired. Couldn't she see that in bed, in the dark, he *did* know her? He could recognize the feel of her silken skin and her full breasts, her floral scent. In the dark he was whole again. In the dark nothing had changed.

The night he came home after finding the dead girl, he had told her as little as possible. He hadn't talked about the state of the girl's body or about the two men he had seen. He had wanted to protect her and she had accepted his pared-down version. She'd been sympathetic and made him a hot toddy. They had sat together at the kitchen table as if maintaining a truce. In bed that night she had held him like a child as he trembled in her arms. But the next morning, that tenderness was gone.

Martin heard the car turn into the driveway. He finished the last drops of the scotch and looked at his cellphone. It was 9 o'clock. A minute later he heard Kate fumbling with the lock on the back door. He got up and went quickly to the kitchen to open up for her.

"Why do you have to lock the door before I come home? I couldn't see a thing out there. It's impossible to find the keyhole in the dark." She glared at him. "Of course the light is still out, right? Nobody put in a new bulb." Her sarcasm was palpable.

"Hello Kate, nice to see you too," he retorted in spite of himself.

She looked tired and disheveled. Strands of blond hair had escaped her ponytail and framed her face. She turned to hang up her jacket on the coat tree and then went into the kitchen, throwing her bag on the table.

He trailed behind her. "Where have you been, anyway? That was a long meeting."

"Ah, the third degree!" She bristled. "Well, we started late and then Mr. Jeffries wanted to hash out the current tardy policy. He could talk all night. Glen doesn't want to offend him so he lets the man go on and on." Kate took down a wine glass from the cupboard. She opened the fridge, took out an opened bottle of chardonnay and poured herself a drink. "I really don't want to go over all that now, if you don't mind. I've had it." She undid her hair and ran her fingers through the golden strands. Then she sighed and reached down, opened her book bag and took out a sheaf of papers. "I've still got to read these essays before I go to bed."

"I thought you were going to do your papers before the meeting. You had at least three hours to work."

"Yes, I had planned to do that, but kids came in to talk to me and I had to deal with a parent on the phone. Time just got away from me." She carried her glass and the papers into the living room and curled up on the sofa under the pool of light from the table lamp.

Martin followed her and stopped in the doorway. He knew there was an intangible line across the threshold that he should not cross.

Kate looked up at him. "I really have to get these finished, Martin. I don't have time to talk." In the rosy glow of the lamp her face looked wind-burned and her lips swollen. She shook her head and turned back to her work.

"Well, I guess I'll go up to bed," he murmured quietly. She didn't look up, so he went back into the kitchen to make sure the back door was locked tight. Before turning off the light, Martin glanced at the calendar hanging by the phone. He wanted to check if Rosie had an after-school activity tomorrow. His gaze landed on Tuesday, November 22nd. Today's date. Across it, Kate had penciled in *SIT Meeting 4 PM*.

If the meeting was at four, where had she been all evening?

Chapter 33
Wednesday Morning, November 22nd

Francesca was on her way to O'Hare airport, heading to California for Thanksgiving. In some ways she would've rather stayed in Banner Bluff and had a quiet little dinner with Tom and a few friends, but she hadn't been back to California for the holiday for several years. Her sister Sandra had asked her to come out as a surprise for her parents. When she'd agreed, she thought they would cook together at her parents' house. But last night she'd learned that Sandra's in-laws were hosting the Thanksgiving dinner. Sandra's husband, Charles, was one of seven kids and all of his siblings were married with children. This would be one of those gigantic family affairs with oodles of people Francesca didn't know.

She parked in a far corner of the remote lot. She pulled her small carry-on bag out of the car and yanked up the handle, then hiked over to the ATS train that would take her to the terminal. The platform was hopping with families of hyper kids. At the terminal, there were lines everywhere. Luckily, she had printed her ticket at home and could get into the long security line right away.

On the way to her gate, she bought a cup of coffee and a doughnut. There were no seats left in the waiting area once she got there, so she leaned against a wall and surveyed the crowd. Thanksgiving weekend was probably the worst time to travel but here she was. A tall, solid, red-faced man was arguing with the airline personnel at the desk, shouting about his seat and waving his arms around. Beside him stood two stone-faced guys who had to be bodyguards, surveying the crowd of travelers. Their gaze traveled from passenger to passenger.

Who was this guy? Someone important? A politician? The face was familiar but she couldn't place him. And why did he need bodyguards? It made her think of the Pharaoh. She sipped her coffee and took a bite of her doughnut.

The irate man finally left the desk and plodded heavily towards her. He was still gesticulating. He looked at her coffee and doughnut and turned to one of his flunkies. "Go get me coffee and two doughnuts. You know what I want." He surveyed the waiting area and said to no one in particular, "This is why I always fly private. This place is a zoo."

Francesca smiled noncommittally and surveyed the crowd. Just about everyone was stuffing their faces, with everything from McMuffins to pepperoni pizza.

The obnoxious man addressed her directly. "Don't you hate these crowds and all the waiting? I'm wasting time right now."

"That's what happens when you travel at Thanksgiving," Francesca said. "Might as well grin and bear it."

He didn't return her smile. Francesca finished her coffee and dropped the cup in the garbage.

The airline attendant announced boarding for first class. The man turned and followed his remaining bodyguard, who pushed through the crowd making a path for his boss. They showed their tickets and went down the ramp to board the plane. Just then the other bodyguard arrived, balancing two coffees and two bags of doughnuts as well as a duffle bag over his shoulder. He looked around, clearly trying to figure out where he could put down his load so he could extricate his ticket when he got to the head of the line.

"Can I help you?" Francesca said. "Let me hold something while you find your ticket."

The man gave her a suspicious look. *He probably never trusts anyone*, she thought. He had the physique of a body-builder. Over his bulging muscles he wore a tight black t-shirt that

199

displayed the logo *Ape Man*. His hair was cut in a mullet and his uneven complexion was pock-marked from bygone teenage acne.

After inspecting her, he said gruffly, "Yeah. Okay." He handed Francesca the coffees. As he pulled out his ticket from the back pocket of his tight jeans, the line moved up. They reached the gate, where the attendant took their tickets and put them under the scanner. Ape Man shoved his ticket back in his pocket and then took the coffees from Francesca. "Like, thanks."

They started down the ramp. "Sure," Francesca said. "So who do you work for? Who is that guy?"

Ape Man looked at her in disbelief. "That's Rollo Perry. He's the Man!"

Rollo Perry. Francesca wondered if he'd been visiting the Pharaoh.

Chapter 34
Friday Afternoon and Evening, November 24th

They had spent Thanksgiving quietly, just the four of them. Kate's parents had gone to Texas to be with her brother and his family. Kate had cooked a turkey with all the trimmings. Now they had a ton of leftovers because the kids didn't eat much. But that was all right, Martin liked turkey sandwiches.

This afternoon they were going to the tree-lighting on the green. It was 4 o'clock and it would soon be dark. He pulled the stroller down the steps as Kate came out the front door. She loaded Stevie into the stroller and Martin took Rosie's hand. It was just a few blocks to the Banner Bluff village green. The weather had turned much colder in the last few days, so they were all bundled up. Martin memorized the color of the coats and hats the kids were wearing. He didn't want to lose them in the crowd. As they approached the busy downtown he held Rosie's hand tighter.

"Remember to stay with me, Rosie, okay?"

"Okay, Daddy." She was bouncing along in excitement.

The tree was enormous and stood on a slight rise in the middle of the green. Nearby was the gazebo, where the high school band was ensconced. They were playing "Jingle Bells." On the sidewalk shopkeepers had set up tables. There was hot chocolate and hot cider for the kids. In Nickleby's Wine Shop, a large cauldron of spiced Swedish Glogg perfumed the air. Bonnie's Bakery had set out quantities of crullers and gingerbread men. Banner Bluff Bank and Trust was providing small bags of popcorn. Light poles and shop windows sported garlands and fairy lights.

At 4:30 a motorized sleigh arrived with Santa Claus and four elves in attendance. The band was playing, "Here Comes Santa Claus." Martin picked up Stevie so he could see Santa. The sleigh crossed the green and approached the tree. Santa stepped out and an elf handed him a sparkling wand. He tapped on the massive fir tree and the multi-colored lights came to life. The band began playing "White Christmas" and the crowd joined in. The holiday season had officially begun.

Kate took Rosie to get some hot chocolate and cookies. Martin held Stevie on his shoulder and hummed along to the music. Stevie was spellbound although he didn't have a clue who Santa was. A light snow had begun to fall.

Petroff and Sergei stood in the back, searching the crowd. The Captain had left his trademark hat at home. He wore a knit cap pulled low on his forehead and the collar on his pea coat was turned up around his neck and face. Sergei wore a black leather jacket. Their gazes moved over the crowd of revelers.

Petroff couldn't see over the taller people in front of him. The crowd was rapt listening to the choir from St. Luke's sing carols. "Let's walk around," he said. "I'll move through the crowd to the front. I'll meet you behind the gazebo."

"O.K.", Sergei said in Russian. Deep and heavy, his voice carried even when he tried to keep it low.

"No Russian," Petroff hissed. "English."

"*Da*," Sergei said.

"Shut the fuck up!" Petroff growled at him, and turned away. Sergei was a genius when it came to cars but otherwise he was an idiot.

Petroff had barely gone three steps when he nearly bumped into a grey-haired man holding the hand of a ten year-old boy.

The man smiled. "Is that you, Captain? I barely recognized you!"

"Yes-sir-ee." Petroff put on a jovial smile. "Is this your grandson, Mr. Roberts?"

"It certainly is. Aiden, say hello to the Captain."

Aiden looked up. "Are you really a captain, with a ship and everything?"

"No, no." Petroff laughed. "That's just a nickname."

Mr. Roberts laughed as well. "I'll be coming in next week, I think. We've got a problem with the S550."

"Well, be sure to make an appointment. We're real busy right now." Petroff reached out to shake hands. "It was nice to meet you, Aiden."

Aiden shied away.

Petroff continued to move through the crowd, inspecting the faces of the taller men. He didn't see the face he was looking for. It was getting too dark to recognize anyone. When he rounded the back of the gazebo, Sergei rushed over to him.

"I see him. He has little kid on his shoulders. I know it's him. You come, I show you."

Petroff followed Sergei around the gazebo and towards the east side of the green. Sergei pointed. "That's him. Look!"

Sergei's target was a tall, dark-haired man with a little blond boy on his shoulders. The man wore wire-rimmed glasses like the guy that night. That was right. But Petroff wasn't sure. A few people walked in front of them. He moved closer after they passed, pulling the collar of his coat up around his face. Yes, he realized with mounting excitement, it was him. The man was staring at the Christmas tree with an uncertain expression. The glow lit up his face, just as it had that other night. They'd found him. Now they had to find out who he was.

Petroff breathed a sigh of relief. The Hook had been angry when he learned what'd happened to the girl. "You're getting sloppy," he'd said. "You learned nothing from the girl and now

203

we've got to eliminate this new person, and you don't know who he is. Clean up your mess."

As Petroff watched, the man turned to look directly at him and Sergei. He frowned, gazing more intently. Then a pretty blond woman took his arm and a little girl handed him a cookie. Petroff took the opportunity to move a little away amid the crowd, out of their quarry's line of sight.

"He saw us. Quick! Let's get around behind him and we can follow him."

Chapter 35
Saturday Night, November 25th

Francesca was back from California. It had been a busy weekend with family and friends. Busy, but not always pleasant. She'd had dinner Friday night with three girls from high school. Every one of them was married now, had children or was expecting a baby. She'd spent the evening looking at pictures and hearing about the best car seats and the latest baby breathing monitors.

The girls did ask Francesca about the *Banner Bee* and two of them said they followed it periodically. But they had no clue how much time and effort went into publishing a news source online; the research, the interviews, the fact-checking. All that escaped them.

"Don't you get lonely?" Lisa had asked, taking a bite of cucumber. "I don't know what I would do without Sam and the kids." Lisa had gained a lot of weight during her pregnancies and couldn't get it off. For dinner, she had opted for a green salad with the dressing on the side.

"Sometimes," Francesca said, "but I'm usually too busy to think about it." She took a big bite of her hamburger and patted her lips. She had chosen the cowboy burger complete with onion rings, bacon and barbeque sauce, with a side of French fries.

"What about Dan? Do you ever hear from him?" Debbie asked. "You two were together for so long."

"No." Francesca steeled herself. She'd known this would come up, but it still irritated her. "Since our divorce, we've had no contact. He's remarried with kids." She took a sip of wine.

"What a shame," Lisa said. "You two were so perfect together." She eyed Francesca's French fries.

"Right," Francesca said. She held out her plate. "Want one?"

Lisa helped herself to three fat fries and an onion ring as well. She bit into the onion ring's crunchy crust. "Yum, these are to die for."

Francesca didn't want to have this discussion again. She had already debated the divorce with her mother several times over the weekend. "Listen, you guys. I'm happy without Dan and I've met a really nice guy."

Debbie looked eager. "Who is he? Tell us all about him."

"He's a policeman. Actually, he's the Chief of Police."

Lisa spoke with her mouth full. "A policeman? You've got to be kidding. Dan was a hotshot lawyer. Couldn't you do better than a cop?"

"Tom has a Masters in Art History. He's a very smart guy and a very kind person." Suddenly she was angry. Why did she have to defend Tom to these silly women? "But you know what? I'm tired of hearing about Dan and what I *should* be doing. I am *so* glad he is out of my life." She stood up, reached into her purse for a twenty-dollar bill and tossed it on the table. "Here, that should cover my share. Lisa, you can finish my fries and onion rings." She turned and walked out of the restaurant.

She'd left the next morning. During the four hours she'd spent waiting at the airport, she'd texted each of her friends and apologized. What had gotten into her? She'd known those girls since kindergarten. It was stupid to burn bridges.

The entire weekend had worn her out. She'd had some great times taking walks with her Dad and playing Scrabble. She'd enjoyed getting reacquainted with her niece and nephew and had taken them to see the latest Disney movie. But her mother's constant criticism exhausted her. She couldn't seem to do anything right, even now in her thirties. And of course, there was the divorce, which in her mother's eyes made her an embarrassment to the family. When he drove her to the airport, her father had tried to smooth things over, but it hadn't really worked. She was happy to have seen him, but she was all the more determined to live her life the way she'd worked so hard to make it.

Because of the flight delay it was already 6 PM when she landed in Chicago. On the plane she read through a stack of newspapers and magazines. She felt it was important to keep on top of trends in other forms of journalism. Often, an article sparked an idea that she could use in the *Banner Bee*. On arrival, she dumped the papers in the trash can and took the shuttle out to the remote lot. There was a light dusting of snow on her car, and after California it seemed especially cold.

She'd called and texted Tom a couple of times during the weekend. They'd talked on Thanksgiving and he had texted her once. On the way home she tried calling, but he never picked up. Then she tried calling the station. Gerry, the night dispatcher, said the Chief was downstairs in the war room.

Francesca decided to stop on the way home just to say hi. If Tom was still in the middle of a meeting, she would head home. She hoped he would be free. After the weekend, she needed a friend. She wanted to feel his arms around her. Was that being weak?

She parked her car in front of the police station. The building was lit up and Gerry was sitting behind the glass partition when she walked inside. Francesca greeted her and asked if they'd finished the meeting yet.

"Most of the Homicide Team left a little bit ago. I think Chief Barnett is still down there, though. Let me buzz you in."

The buzzer sounded and the door clicked open. She stepped into the inner hallway. "I just wanted to say hello. I've been away for the weekend."

"Do you know your way downstairs?"

"No problem." Francesca smiled. "Did you have a nice Thanksgiving?"

"Yes and no. The food was great. My mother-in-law is a wonderful cook. And the kids like playing with their cousins. But we got into a political debate. My husband can't stand the Pharaoh and what his party is doing down in Springfield. His brother thinks Ramses Crenshaw the Third walks on water. They really got into it. I finally had to drag my husband away." She sighed and shook her head in disgust.

Francesca nodded in agreement. "My family isn't that bad; but these holidays do bring out a lot of emotion. You should probably stay home for Christmas!"

Gerry started to laugh. "You are so right."

Francesca went down the hall and opened the door that led down to the basement conference room. The heavy door shut with a bang behind her as she descended the carpeted stairs. It was very quiet. At the bottom, she turned right and went halfway down the hall. She could see the door into the jails at the end.

The conference room door was shut. Behind it, Francesca heard the murmuring of voices. She didn't want to interrupt, so she peered into the room through the small wire-reinforced window at eye level. Inside she saw two people looking at a computer screen. One of them was Tom, seated in a chair. Leaning over him with her arm against his back was a curly-haired redhead in tight jeans, cowboy boots and a form-fitting turtle neck. On her hip was a gun. She was pointing at something on the screen. Tom turned to look at her with a smile. Their faces were three inches apart.

Francesca bolted down the hall and up the stairs, banging the door behind her. Gerry looked up, surprise on her face. "Aren't they finished?"

208

Francesca couldn't meet her gaze. "No, they're busy," she said as she pushed open the street door. All she wanted was to get the hell out of there.

Chapter 36
Saturday Evening, November 25th

Carina was in the kitchen beside the potbelly stove, polishing her boots and sipping a mug of mint tea. Her mother was asleep upstairs. Carina felt exhausted. Her life was monotonous. She worked hard all day, from 6 AM until 10 at night. In the evening she maintained a state of cheerfulness that she didn't always feel. Tonight was no exception. She had kept up a cheerful prattle all during dinner but her mother hadn't been fooled.

"Carina, you should be out with friends tonight. Not home with me."

"I'm too tired…and besides, nobody invited me out."

"Well, call a friend and go to a movie. Go out for dinner. Go hang out in a bar." Daphne smiled "Carina, I don't need you here."

Carina hadn't looked up from scrubbing the cast iron skillet. It was a relief when Daphne retired for the night.

Carina had worn the same jeans for the last three days. Over her plaid shirt she wore a heavy red sweater, plus a full set of long underwear under her clothes. It was cold in the barn and a stiff wind had been blowing all day. Even now, she couldn't seem to get warm.

She took the mug of tea in her hands and breathed in the minty perfume. It smelled like summer and sunshine. Outside the French windows she saw a winter landscape. The moon was high over the barren fields and she could just make out the sparkle of the lake beyond. The construction scaffolding for the pumping station wasn't visible from the house. She was glad her mother couldn't see it.

Carina and Daphne had spent a quiet Thanksgiving together. Carina had roasted a chicken and made gravy, cornbread stuffing, Brussels sprouts with chestnuts, creamed onions and a pecan pie. It was a feast for the two of them.

She had lit a fire in the dining room fireplace and brought in an electric heater to warm the room before helping her mother downstairs for dinner. The table was set with their best china and Carina had polished the silver. There were creamy damask napkins at their places and she had placed a bouquet of flowers in an antique silver pitcher. The flowers had come from Harrison Rand, but she didn't tell her mother that.

They had dressed up in their winter finery and opened a bottle of white wine. They'd stayed away from discussing the farm and the construction. Instead they'd reminisced about past holidays when Gordon Meriwether was alive. Back then, Thanksgiving had been a bustling affair with friends and family. They had always gone for a ride in the morning. Ina, their beloved cook of twenty years, had provided a fabulous meal. In the late afternoon, neighbors, grooms and field hands arrived for dessert. There was always a large selection of pies and cakes with coffee, tea and sherry.

Reminiscing had been good for Daphne. With the warmth, good food and wine, they had laughed together. Daphne hadn't wanted any visitors that day and Carina had honored her wishes. After the meal she helped her mother upstairs to her room for an afternoon nap.

Tonight, Carina knew she needed to go up to bed. It was past 10:30 already, and tomorrow would be another long day. She didn't attend church at St. Luke's anymore. There just was no time. She figured God understood. She put down the tea, picked up her rag and dipped it into the small tub of polishing wax, then rubbed the wax into the worn leather of her boots.

211

There was a tap-tap at the window. Carina jumped. What was that? Who was there? She and Daphne were so alone in the house. José wasn't around at night.

Even though she felt like hiding, Carina stood up and peered outside. The roof formed an overhang and the porch was in deep shadow. After a moment she made out a tall, masculine figure. The man came closer and met her gaze through the glass. It was Harrison Rand. With relief, she reached down and unlocked the kitchen door.

"What in the world are you doing here at this hour? You scared me to death."

Harrison stepped into the room, bringing in the wind and the cold. Shivering, Carina quickly shut the doors and then stepped back, her arms wrapped around her body.

"I've come with the check. I knew you needed the money and I came up from Springfield after having dinner with the governor. Crenshaw signed the check this afternoon." Harrison was smiling like a Cheshire cat. She smelled liquor on his breath.

"But why now? It's so late."

He stepped towards her. She took a step back. "I'm going to Oklahoma tomorrow on business and then on to California. I won't be back here again for a couple of weeks." He put his briefcase down on the kitchen table and took off his brown leather jacket. Then he walked over to the potbelly stove, rubbing his hands. "This baby puts out a lot of heat."

"But it's almost eleven o'clock," Carina said.

Harrison looked irritated now. "Listen, I drove like mad all the way up here. I brought you your check. How about being a little grateful?"

Carina stumbled over her words. "I...I am grateful but I'm also a little in shock." She gripped the back of her wooden chair. He was acting very different from the kind and caring individual she thought she knew.

212

"How about you get me something to drink?" He gestured towards her mug. "What are you having?"

"It's mint tea, but it's probably cold now."

"Do you have anything stronger? I could use a real drink." He was smiling again.

"Yes, yes, I'll get you something. It's in the dining room." Carina walked quickly across the kitchen, and went down the hall. The dining room was chilly and dark. She fumbled with the light and walked over to the liquor cabinet. She rummaged around until she found a bottle of scotch. No one had touched it since her father died. It seemed somehow wrong to be serving this prized bottle. But Harrison Rand was making her nervous. She wanted him gone, the sooner the better. She found a heavy crystal tumbler and brought the bottle and the glass into the kitchen, shutting the door behind her.

Harrison was looking at her computer, one hand on the keyboard. He looked up, challenging her with his gaze. She chose not to say anything. What could he possibly learn perusing her email account?

"Glenlivet Eighteen," he said when she handed him the bottle and the glass. "Very nice indeed. Would you like to join me?"

"No, I'll just warm my tea in the microwave." She reached for the mug, but he reached out and grabbed her hand. His was warm and strong. He pursed his lips in a pout. "Come on, this is a celebration. Have a wee one with me."

"Okay, but just a little." Carina slipped her hand from his grasp. She went to a cupboard beside the sink and took out a blue juice glass. "Here, just a wee one as you said." She smiled uncertainly.

Harrison served himself an inch of the scotch and poured her a small amount. They clinked glasses. Harrison gulped down a large swallow. Carina took a small sip. She could feel the liquor course down her throat. It burned in a satisfying way.

"Now, isn't that a hell of a lot better than mint tea?" His Cheshire-cat smile was back. He moved over to the heavy oak kitchen table, sat down and opened his briefcase. Carina sat opposite him holding the juice glass between her hands. She felt anxious and edgy.

Harrison handed her an unsealed envelope and removed a sheaf of papers. "Open the envelope. Look at what's inside," he commanded, raising his eyebrows.

Carina opened the envelope and pulled out a light blue check. It was made out in her name and signed by Governor Crenshaw, for the sum of five million dollars. She stared and blinked. Then she looked up at Harrison. "This is for much more than you initially said. Are you sure there isn't a mistake?"

"No, Carina. Another appraisal was done of the land and this is what it's worth. This is fair to you and your mother. The governor is grateful that you didn't seek legal action and is glad to remunerate you appropriately." He reached over and patted her hand as though she were a small child. "Now, you need to sign a few forms and we'll be all set." He smiled encouragingly.

Again she felt as though she were being placated. "Why is this check in my name rather than my mother's? Is it legal?"

"I verified the documents on ownership of the property. Either you or your mother, individually or together, can make decisions on the use of Hollyhock Farms. That's how your father set up the trust. I'm surprised you haven't looked into this."

Carina swallowed another sip of scotch. Her head was spinning slightly. Dinner was a long time ago and she hadn't eaten much.

Harrison lined up the papers and passed the first document over to her. "Sign down here on the right. This says you have received the check for five million dollars and you agree to the amount." He handed her a pen and then tapped at the signature line.

Carina started to read from the top.

After a few moments Harrison drummed his fingers and sighed heavily. "You don't have to read the whole thing. My God, this is just a standard document."

Carina ignored him and continued to read; although she wasn't sure she understood all the legalese. When she had finished, she picked up the pen and signed her careful, slanted signature. She took a gulp of scotch.

They continued this process for several more pages. Harrison got up and paced the room. He took long swallows of his drink.

What was going on with him? He wasn't the man who had sent her flowers a few days earlier. She tried to concentrate on her reading. Basically, she was promising to accept the payment for the use of her land and agreeing not to pursue the state in court.

The last form gave her pause. "I promise not to reveal the details of this agreement to others," she read aloud. "Why not, if this is official government business?"

"Primarily, when all this becomes public other people along the shore will want in on the money and will begin proceedings to negate this document. You might lose the contract and the money." He motioned towards the check.

Carina nodded. The scotch had made her brain a little fuzzy, but it seemed to make sense.

When she finally signed the last page and placed the pen on the table, Harrison looked relieved and the tension went out of his body. He gathered up the papers and put them back in his briefcase.

"I'd like to have copies," Carina said.

"You'll receive copies by FedEx in the next few days." He smiled playfully. "Right now you have a check for five million dollars. That should make you happy. Let's not get greedy."

She continued to feel that something wasn't quite right. Was it the liquor, or Harrison's manner?

Abruptly, Carina stood up and handed him his jacket. "Where are you going to stay tonight?"

"I've got a reservation at the Deer Run Inn." He poured himself a little more scotch and drank it down. His face was flushed when he grinned at her. "But I'd rather stay here." He moved closer, running his forefinger down her cheek, and bent to kiss her.

She stepped back. "I think you'll sleep better at the inn. Where did you park?"

His grin was even wider now. "In front. But I saw the lights on back here so I came around so as not to disturb your mother." He moved towards her again but she spun on her heel and headed toward the hallway.

"How thoughtful of you." Or maybe he was worried how her mother would react if she saw him, especially at this hour. "Let me show you out."

They went down the dark hall to the foyer. She was aware of him behind her. At the door, she turned to face him. He eased his briefcase to the floor and grabbed her shoulders, pulling her to him. He kissed her long and hard and she found herself responding. With his Jekyll and Hyde personality, he both attracted and repulsed her. She pushed against his chest and stumbled backward.

"Please leave now," she whispered.

He smiled knowingly at her, opened the door and was gone.

Chapter 37
Tuesday Evening, November 28th

Francesca was on her way to Chicago. Yesterday morning she had received a call on her cell phone from the Pharaoh. She'd picked up the phone without looking at the screen; thinking it was Tom. She hadn't talked to him after finding him with the redhead Saturday night. He had texted her twice but she hadn't responded. When the phone rang Monday morning she was planning on being cool and detached.

But Ramses Crenshaw had caught her by surprise, inviting her for dinner in downtown Chicago the following night. He was going to be in town for a luncheon and a talk on Illinois-Chinese economic relations at the Union League Club followed by a meeting with Mayor Blodgett in the afternoon.

"I would very much enjoy a quiet dinner with you to discuss your views on several issues," Crenshaw said.

Francesca was momentarily tongue-tied. Then she responded, "Yes, yes, I would very much enjoy dinner. What time were you thinking?" She wondered whether to drive or take the train. Tom could hang out with that redhead while she hung out with the governor. She found it mildly puzzling that Crenshaw had called her, though. Had she made that much of an impression, that day in Hero's Market?

"How about seven at the Metropolitan Club? I'll send my car. Roscoe will pick you up at your house at six. It's 1350 Hennessey, right?"

"Yes, Governor, but how did you know my address?" She paused. "And my personal cell phone number, now that I think about it?"

"Ms. Antonelli, I know a great deal about you. That's my business. See you at seven tomorrow night." He hung up.

Francesca had spent an hour getting ready, which was not the norm for her. She'd taken time to choose her dress, a side-draped sheath with long sleeves and a deep-v neckline. The emerald green color was perfect for the season. She also took the time to do her hair, leaving it long and wavy. With some gold earrings and black open-toed pumps, she felt ready to go into battle.

Roscoe had been on time. He'd settled her in the car and asked if she would like a glass of champagne. She refused, thinking she needed all her wits about her. He put on some light jazz and raised his eyebrows. She smiled and nodded her approval to his reflection in the rearview mirror.

Now, sitting in the comfortable town car with its buttery smooth leather seats, she wondered about her decision. Was it wise to enter the lion's den? But she wanted to know more about the Pharaoh and his cronies. Thinking of Connie's list of campaign donors, Francesca hoped she could bring the conversation around to Crenshaw's supporters and the formation of the Super Pac. Then there was the agua corriente project. Could she bring that up subtly, without raising his suspicions? This evening would be a game of cat and mouse. She would have to play her cards very carefully.

The trip downtown took less than an hour. Traffic was light and they arrived in front of the Willis Tower a few minutes early. Roscoe helped her out of the car, indicated the entrance she should take up to the Metropolitan Club, and told her he would be back to pick her up when the dinner with the governor ended.

Inside the building, Francesca went through security before taking the elevator to the 67th floor. When she entered the Metropolitan Club she was directed to the Globe Room where Ramses Crenshaw sat at a choice table by the window. The restaurant's décor was rich oak with ochre and yellow tones. A woman took her coat and then Francesca made her way across the room. The maître d' seated her in a plush armchair, placed her napkin across her lap with a flourish and smoothly pushed in her chair.

The governor was on the phone. He smiled at her, but looked distracted. She eyed the cut-glass vase on the table that held a perfect orchid, and wondered if he was talking about the agua corriente project. He appeared to be listening intently. Then he stood up, smiling and shrugging his shoulders. "Tell them it will happen, Harrison." As he moved away all she could hear was, "We've got the property and all we need is …."

Property where, she wondered. The window to her right showcased a fabulous view of Chicago at night. While she waited for the governor to return, she gazed out at the sweeping expanse of the northerly shore line with the John Hancock building off to the right. The waiter arrived and Francesca ordered a glass of Bella Sera pinot grigio from the wine list. If she was going to dine alone, she meant to enjoy it. The waiter handed her a menu. She zeroed in on exactly what she wanted for dinner. She was starving.

When the wine arrived she took a small sip and looked around at the other diners. She thought she recognized John Valintis from the *Chicago Tribune* and Judge Rachel Melos, one of the toughest judges in town. Then, she saw Crenshaw returning, shaking hands and patting backs as he came towards her. He seemed to know everyone in the room. Eventually he arrived at their table.

"Ms. Antonelli, please do forgive me. I've been terribly rude. I just couldn't get out of that call." He bent down and kissed her lightly on the cheek. "You look lovely. When you walked in, every head turned." He signaled to the waiter. "That's a fabulous dress, by the way."

She smiled demurely and then decided to plunge in. "What were you talking about; something exciting for the State of Illinois?"

He frowned and quickly recovered as he sat down across from her. "Everything I do is for the benefit of the Land of Lincoln."

The waiter appeared instantly. "Let's have a bottle of Dom Pérignon; nothing but the best for Mademoiselle Antonelli." The waiter disappeared. Crenshaw leaned over and took Francesca's hand. "I can call you Francesca, right? Call me Ramses." With his thumb he caressed the tender skin on the inside of her wrist.

It was oddly erotic, and definitely creepy considering she barely knew him and didn't much like him. What was this dinner about? "Governor…" She pulled her hand away.

"Now Francesca, I said call me Ramses."

"Okay, Ramses. Why did you invite me for dinner? Let's face it, I really don't know you. And I doubt you do this for all your constituents."

He smiled. "I invited you because you seemed like a bright, young woman who can enlighten me as to the interests of our citizens on the North Shore."

"There are lots of bright young women and men who have their thumb on the public conscience…"

"Ah, but Francesca, they're not all beautiful. And I like to surround myself with beautiful women."

Francesca noted the plural. This guy was something else.

The waiter arrived with the champagne, an ice bucket and two flutes. He made a show of opening the bottle and carefully poured each of them a glass. Crenshaw raised his eyes and looked into hers. "Here's to the beginning of a wonderful relationship."

Francesca added, "And here's to honesty in all relationships." She smiled demurely over the rim of her glass.

When the waiter returned, Francesca ordered the foie gras toast with apricot balsamic syrup as a starter, followed by pan roasted halibut with confit of savoy cabbage, fingerling potatoes and blood orange emulsion. It all sounded wonderfully exotic. Ramses chose a simple green salad followed by grilled filet mignon, extra rare. "I have to be careful what I order with all the restaurant meals I eat in a week." He took a long sip of champagne. "So what's happening in your neck of the woods? Enlighten me."

Francesca thought for a minute, her fingers on the long stem of her champagne flute. "Do you want to know our major concerns?"

"Yes, exactly."

"Couldn't you get this from the newspapers?"

"You *are* the newspaper, so let's hear it."

"I think a major issue is traffic. Banner Bluff itself doesn't have a problem. Our village is insulated from the world. But when we get on the major east-west roads or the North-South highway it's horrendous. I think everyone in Lake County would like better roads and a shorter commute time."

Crenshaw nodded. "There's a bill going through the channels right now, introduced by Bob Newhouse. It advocates appropriating funds to widen Lakeview and Deerlane west. It's being considered this very week."

The waiter delivered their first course selections. After he left, Crenshaw leaned forward. "Tell me about Newhouse. How well do you know him?"

Francesca felt uncomfortable lying, but she wasn't going to reveal much to this man she didn't trust. "I know him enough to say 'hi' on the street. His office is two doors down from mine. But, you know, we're not tight. Why do you ask?"

He leaned in again. "I think he's going to run for governor. He's going to be my competition. And that's worrying me." His eyes had turned dark. "He will be a formidable opponent." He stabbed at a bright red tomato atop his salad. "I'll have to crush him."

Francesca shivered. "Crush him? That sounds ominous."

He chuckled. "It's all hyperbole in politics. Let's say, encourage him to drop out of the race."

She saw right through his false smile. "Don't you believe in the democratic process? You know: differing views, a lively debate?"

"Francesca, my dear, a lively debate is not how decisions are made. That's entertainment for the populace and the media. Real decisions are made behind closed doors. It's a dog-eat-dog world."

Francesca had lost her appetite but she soldiered on, taking another bite of the creamy foie gras. This dinner had been a big mistake.

"You seem upset by this talk. Let's change the subject. Tell me more about the concerns of my constituents."

Francesca sipped her champagne, stalling. "This is really good."

"So?" He sounded faintly belligerent, pushing her.

"Well…" She cast around for something that might give her an opening to steer the conversation. "People are concerned about Lake Michigan. Because of the drought we've experienced, the lake level is down ten feet. In Banner Bluff, our beaches are important. Last year we were voted fourth happiest coastline town by *Shoreline Magazine.* We want to keep our status."

"I read about that. So?" He was looking belligerent again.

"So, people up and down the shores of Lake Michigan are worried. We're worried about pollution, about the invasion of foreign species like the Asian carp and zebra mussels."

His eyes narrowed. Was she being too obvious?

She decided to continue. "And people are worried that water is being siphoned out of the lake, even with the Great Lakes Water Protection Act. We need better stewardship of the lake, our most precious resource."

The waiter arrived and cleared away their plates. He gestured to his assistant, who placed their main course before them. Francesca's fish looked delectable. She was determined to eat every bite.

Crenshaw sliced into his steak. Bright red blood leaked onto his plate. "This is what I love, good red meat." He put a piece in his mouth, chewed and swallowed. He wiped a drop of blood-red juice from his chin and looked at Francesca. "That water is for everyone."

She frowned. "What do you mean?"

"Illinois, Michigan, Wisconsin, Canada, they don't own the water in the Great Lakes. They happen to be located near it, but the water belongs to the entire United States."

"You don't think Illinois should protect its major water source?" She was astounded. "Isn't that what the Great Lakes Water Protection Act is all about?"

"Not if others need the water. Not if they're willing to pay a hefty price for it. And you know, Francesca, everything has a price."

Looking at him, Francesca was suddenly struck with a barrage of jumbled thoughts: the agua corriente project, Carina Meriwether's property taken by eminent domain, the Pharaoh's visit to Banner Bluff. Connected, or not? She didn't know.

Later that night the Pharaoh was in his usual suite at the Peninsula Hotel, looking out at the Chicago skyline and Lake Michigan beyond. Deep in thought, he paid no heed to any of it. He was troubled by his dinner with Ms. Antonelli. She attracted him. He liked her type: brainy and beautiful. But there was

223

something unsettling about their conversation tonight. He'd meant to charm her, win her over, but he wasn't sure he'd managed it. He needed to be careful. After all, she was a newspaper woman and nosy was her middle name.

He loosened his tie, took off his suit jacket and threw it on a chair. Then he leaned in toward the mirror over the chest of drawers and peered at himself. This past week had been a long one. There were slight bags under his eyes and his coloring wasn't good. He needed to cut back on alcohol and get a facial. In the morning he would have Roscoe schedule the appointment.

He pulled out his phone and made a call while eyeing himself in the mirror.

"It's me again," he said. "Any glitches with the Meriwethers?" He listened for several seconds. "Good, so the check cleared and there will be no repercussions?" Another pause while he listened to the person on the other end. "Good, good. What about out there?"

The answer he got pleased him less this time, and he grunted his disapproval. "Humph. I won't negotiate on that point. Never!" One more time, he listened. "Okay, call me from L.A." He ended the call and turned off the phone, frowning. So much was riding on these next few weeks.

Chapter 38
Wednesday Afternoon, November 29th

Francesca lurked outside Banner Bluff High School, looking for a blue backpack with teddy bears dangling from the handle. A monumental task, but she didn't let that discourage her. Yesterday she'd wasted her time standing by the junior-senior exit. When the three o'clock bell rang, she was almost run over by a tidal wave of kids streaming out of the school. Not only could she not identify their backpacks, but the kids definitely weren't freshmen. Some of the boys sported goatees. Today, better informed, she waited by the exit for the freshmen and sophomore classes. Brett Atkins' sister, Grace, had been sure her brother's girlfriend was a freshman.

Last night she'd called Julie Robinson and asked if she would be free at 2:45 today. Julie didn't have a class until five, so she agreed to help out. Francesca figured Julie was young enough to blend in with the crowd. They stood on each side of the double exit doors.

"Remember, it's a blue Jansport backpack with pink and baby-blue stuffed teddy bears attached to the handle," Francesca said.

"Okay. I'm ready, Sherlock." Julie giggled.

The bell rang inside the school. A couple of minutes later, the doors burst open. A few students trickled out. Then the trickle turned into a rush as more kids charged out, talking and laughing. They headed towards the buses lined up at the curb or towards the side streets. Overwhelmed, Francesca did her best to scan every backpack that went by. So many black ones. How did they ever tell them apart?

Then Julie came barging through the crowd. "I found her. There she is." She was pointing at a girl with long brown hair, wearing a turquoise jacket and a matching knit cap. Francesca couldn't see the girl's face. She was walking towards the busses. Over her shoulder was a heavy-looking backpack with two little teddy bears dancing against its surface.

Francesca had decided not to approach the girl here at school. Accosting her in front of her peers might backfire, considering she hadn't wanted to be found in the house where her boyfriend lay dying. Instead, Francesca planned to follow her a bit and then try to talk to her.

Julie pointed at the driveway. "It looks like she's taking the fourth bus down. She's standing in line over there."

"Great! I'm going to get my car. The bus won't be pulling out for a few minutes." She gave Julie a quick hug. "Thanks, Julie, you're a gem."

"I guess you don't need me anymore? I'm going home. Call me if you need any more undercover work." Julie gave her a thumbs-up and headed off in the opposite direction towards her car.

Francesca hurried to her own car and got in, then waited to see which direction the mystery girl's bus was headed. When it pulled out, she followed at a distance. That turquoise coat would be easy to spot when the girl got off.

The bus made several stops and traffic crept along behind it. They turned a corner onto Maple. One block further down, the bus stopped in front of the Banner Bluff Library. To her surprise, Francesca saw the girl in the turquoise coat alight and go up the library steps.

Luck was with Francesca; she found a parking space in the same block. She walked quickly back to the library and hurried in. The interior was dark after the bright sunshine outside, and

Francesca's eyes took a moment to adjust. The librarian at the front desk smiled. "Can I help you find something?"

"No thanks." A flash of turquoise toward the rear of the building, near the periodical room, caught her eye. She gave the librarian a bright smile and headed down the hallway.

A door opened at the end of the hall. Sunlight pouring in lit up the turquoise coat. Then the door slammed shut.

Francesca hurried down the hall, feeling like Agent 007 on an undercover mission. She pulled open the heavy door and saw her quarry walking through the back parking lot towards Elm Street. At the corner the girl turned right. She was heading for Brett Atkins' house. Francesca ran through the parking lot, keeping the girl in sight.

At Elm, she saw the girl walking slowly down the block. The girl paused ever so briefly in front of number 233, taking a quick look, and then increased her pace. Certain of her quarry now, Francesca walked briskly after her.

At the next intersection, the girl turned left and slowed her pace. From behind she looked small and thin in spite of the bulky coat over her jeans and bright blue Ugg boots.

Francesca came up behind her and cleared her throat. The girl turned around and frowned. Her blue eyes looked dull and her face was pale.

"Hi," Francesca said.

The girl frowned. "Do I know you?"

"No, but I think I know who you are." Francesca held out her hand. "Francesca Antonelli, from the *Banner Bee*.

The girl squinted at her. "Are you a friend of my mother's?"

"No." Francesca paused. "I'm a friend of Brett Atkins."

The girl's eyes widened. Then she turned and began walking quickly towards the lake.

Francesca jogged behind her. "Talk to me. You must be suffering a great deal."

The girl started to run, her heavy backpack banging against the small of her back. "I don't want to talk to anyone. Leave me alone."

Francesca kept close behind her. "Sooner or later, you're going to have to tell what happened. Stop and talk to me."

The girl slowed enough to turn and yelled, "I don't know what you're talking about." As she whipped back around, she tripped on a crack in the sidewalk. Francesca reached out and grabbed her arm before she fell down.

The girl began to cry. She dropped her backpack and covered her face with her mittened hands.

Francesca reached over and picked up the backpack. "Wow, this is heavy. Let me carry it for a while."

The girl was still crying in choking little sobs. "My mother will kill me when she finds out."

Francesca considered this. "I'll bet your mother will be happy to know what's been troubling you. I'll bet she's been worrying about you." She pulled a tissue from her purse and handed it to the girl. "Here, blow your nose."

The girl took the tissue and blew hard, then stuffed the Kleenex into her pocket. She stared at the ground, not wanting to meet Francesca's eyes. They turned and began to retrace their steps, walking slowly.

"What's your name?"

"Isabelle, Isabelle Simmons."

"Well, Isabelle, why don't you come over to my office and we can talk," Francesca said. "I've got some great cookies you might like."

"Are you going to write a story about me, like you did about Brett?"

228

"Not unless you want me to…but I would like to hear what you know about Brett, since you were his special friend." She turned to look at the girl trailing behind her. "Okay?"

The girl nodded slowly.

Chapter 39
Wednesday Afternoon, November 29th

Ron Puchalski and Tom Barnett went down the hall for a late lunch. The break room was shared by all village employees. It was Gloria Jimenez's birthday and she had supplied pizza, soda and cake for everyone. Tom dropped his five bucks into the glass jar set aside for contributions to the celebration and took a paper plate. There were a couple pieces of pepperoni and onion left, and an entire veggie pizza. Tom took a slice of each, a can of Coke and a piece of double-chocolate cake. Puchalski did likewise. They sat down at one end of the table. A couple of the secretaries were at the other end.

"I'm going to warm mine up," Puchalski said. "Want to give me yours?"

"No, I'm fine. I've eaten a lot of cold pizza in my time."

"We should have gotten here earlier."

"How's that?"

Puchalski snorted. "Veggie pizza! Give me a break." He got up and went over to the microwave, then came back a minute later with warmed pizza and a knife and fork in hand. He tucked a napkin in at his neck and spread another one on his lap.

Tom grinned. "Swear to god, you're the only person I know around here who eats pizza like that. Most of us use our hands."

Puchalski grinned back. His fastidious habits bought him a lot of ribbing from the rest of the force, but he took it in stride. "Melted cheese and pizza sauce don't go with this suit."

Tom chuckled, then sobered. "So the PP 847 research didn't reveal anything?"

Puchalski shrugged. "We checked out addresses and license numbers, and those didn't pan out. There was something a little kinky, though."

"Kinky?" Tom raised an eyebrow as he wiped his fingers on a napkin. "How so?"

"Well, it's the part number of an oscilloscope."

"That doesn't sound too kinky."

"And it's also the code name of a swinging couples group called Party Possibilities 847." He winked at Tom. "PP 847."

"It always amazes me what you find online. Everything is there," Tom said.

"That's for sure."

"Did I tell you Johnson got a call from a guy that claimed to have seen a Ford Taurus at the entrance to the forest preserve the night of the fourteenth?" Tom got up for another piece of veggie pizza.

"What took him so long to call in? That's almost two weeks ago."

"Apparently he's been out of town. He works for Motorola and was in China."

"What made him remember the Taurus?" Puchalski reached over for another slice.

"He says he was on his way to the airport and pulled over to check that he had his passport. At the entrance to the forest preserve he noticed a car with Maryland plates turning into the service track. It struck him as odd since he remembered there's normally a heavy chain barring the entrance into the woods." Tom ate another bite of pizza. "We've got police officers from towns up and down the North Shore looking for a Ford Taurus with Maryland plates, but I'll tell you what."

"What?"

"I bet they're long gone."

231

By the time Francesca and the girl—Isabelle—got back to the *Banner Bee* office, Isabelle had begun to open up. She had kept her relationship with Brett Atkins bottled up inside for way too long. Before leading the way upstairs, Francesca stopped to order two hot chocolates from Yari Gonzales, who was manning the coffee bar. The woman greeted them cheerfully and Francesca introduced Isabelle. Then, they carried the frothy liquid upstairs.

"Let's sit over here." Francesca pointed to the round oak table. The sun was low in the sky, bathing the room in a rosy glow.

Francesca turned on the overhead light with the wide red shade and went behind the Chinese screen to get her cookie jar. There were some peanut butter crunch cookies inside. She offered the jar to Isabelle, who took one and placed it on a napkin.

"I'm starving," she said as she bit into the cookie, sprinkling crumbs on the table. "Ooo, these are really good."

"Have another one. That's what they're for." Francesca sipped her hot chocolate, gazing at Isabelle over the rim of her cup. "Do you know how I found you, Isabelle?"

The girl look surprised. "No."

"The teddy bears on your backpack. Brett's sister saw your backpack by the front door when she came home early from work one night."

Isabelle blushed. "I never saw her. I didn't think she knew who I was."

"She didn't. But she figured you were a freshman. That's why I was waiting outside the freshman exit today."

Isabelle told Francesca how she and Brett had met. She described their meetings on Mondays and Wednesdays, and explained why they kept it all a secret. Her face glowed when she recounted their times together. Then she talked about the night of the overdose—how Brett looked and sounded; how bewildered and frightened she was; how she'd called 911 and fled into the night.

"Brett was the best friend I ever had. But I didn't know what he was doing. I didn't know about the heroin. It's like I was blind." Tears ran down her cheeks. "I really miss him and I can't talk about it to anyone." Her naiveté was poignant.

"Well, you can talk to me when you need to."

"Can I?" Isabelle looked around the office. "Maybe I could come over here sometimes?"

"Sure you can." Francesca smiled at her new young friend. "But I think you're going to have to call your mom now, Isabelle. You understand that, don't you?"

"Yeah, I guess so."

"She's probably wondering why you're not home from school. Then we need to contact the police."

"The police? Are they going to want to arrest me, you know, because I ran away?"

"No, they're going to need your help. They want to find the person who sold the heroin to Brett."

Chapter 40
Wednesday Evening, November 29th

Martin had finally settled the kids in bed. After a supper of fish sticks, tater tots and applesauce, he had given them a bath. They'd had a great time splashing each other... Even though Stevie was only ten months old, he and Rosie loved being together. She would submerge her face in the water and then pop up, and Stevie would screech with delight. Once they were in their pjs and in bed, they fell right to sleep.

Kate was at another one of her meetings, which seemed to be occurring more frequently. She'd said she would be back by nine. Martin sat down at his computer in his study and tried to get to work. His syllabus was coming together slowly. For a while he lost himself in his work, checking references and clarifying certain points. This lecture would deal with the lucrative slave trade propagated by the Vikings. Few people knew that the word "slave" came from the word "Slav." During the Middle Ages the Vikings went up and down the rivers in Eastern Europe, destroying villages and capturing the Slavic people, whom they subsequently sold as slaves in Constantinople.

Jack came into the study and put his head on Martin's knee. He'd been restless earlier, pacing around like a caged lion. Maybe he needed to go outside. Martin got up and followed Jack through the kitchen to the back door. Jack began to growl. Martin unlocked the door and let the dog out into the fenced yard. Jack took off into the darkness, growling and barking. Was something out there?

Martin shut the door and reached for the back porch light. He flipped the switch but nothing happened. How could that be? He was sure he had put in a new bulb last week.

234

He went into the kitchen and took the flashlight from the utility drawer. Then he opened the back door and pointed the flashlight up at the wall sconce. No bulb. No wonder the light hadn't come on. This was crazy. Maybe he hadn't changed the bulb after all. A sick feeling crawled through his gut. He must be losing it.

He called Jack, who came bounding back into the house. Whatever creature had been out there must be gone. Martin looked in the hall cupboard where they kept the light bulbs. They'd run out. Kate would be ticked when she got home and she couldn't see her way in.

He felt vaguely restless, like Jack. He reached up over the fridge, took down the bottle of scotch, and poured a generous inch and a half into a heavy tumbler. He had been doing this more and more lately. He felt perpetually on edge. He'd told Kate that he thought someone was following him. She told him he was being paranoid.

At the tree lighting ceremony, he thought he'd seen the men from that awful night. Two strange men had been at the ceremony, staring at him. He couldn't be sure of their faces, of course, but there was something about the way they'd held their bodies and the angle of their heads. When Kate and Rosie came back carrying hot cider and cookies, he had looked away. By the time he turned back around, the men were gone. Were they stalking him?

He'd had multiple sightings over the past few weeks, apart from those in his nightmares. He thought he'd seen them lurking behind the magazine stand at the train station. Once he'd glimpsed them by the cars outside Rosie's school. Another time he had spotted them in the back row of St. Luke's church on Sunday morning. He knew these sightings were bogus, a trick of his imagination. But the glimpse of those two men in the dark by the glimmering tree seemed different.

235

Oh God, was he losing his mind? Chief Barnett had told him they thought the criminals were from Maryland. Someone had reported seeing a Maryland license plate on a car near the scene of the crime that night. The police department seemed to think the killers were long gone.

Maybe the police were right, but his uneasiness remained. Sometimes he felt that in losing the ability to recognize people, he had gained a psychic awareness of those around him; as though he had eyes in the back of his head. Of course he could just be paranoid, as Kate said.

Martin went to check again that the back door was locked. Next, he checked the front door. Then it hit him. The front light was out, too. He knew he had turned the porch light on when he'd gone upstairs with the kids. He opened the front door, only to find the light bulb had disappeared from there, too. Was this some prank?

He thought he heard a sound. He yelled, "Hello! Is anyone out here?" Jack growled again, and he quickly shut the door and bolted it.

Martin went back into the kitchen. He had to get ahold of himself. He carried his scotch and a book on Icelandic poetry into the living room. He was planning on assigning several poems to his students. He bent down and switched on the lamps at each side of the sofa. Behind the sofa was a picture window. Kate had never wanted to hang curtains in this room. She loved having the morning light pour in. At night Martin felt as though he was living in a fishbowl. He looked out at the darkness and shivered. Maybe he should call the police, but they would think he was being irrational.

Then like a bolt of lightning, Jack came hurtling into the room. He knocked into Martin, who fell over a Tonka truck left on the floor. Martin went down, hearing glass shatter amid Jack's wild barking as his tumbler of scotch struck the fireplace. Then shots burst out. Martin heard a crash as the picture window was blown to smithereens and Jack's last bark as the dog fell backwards from the sofa onto the floor. Jack whimpered and then fell silent. Cold air seeped into the room.

Martin thought he heard running feet and a car engine. Fearfully, he raised his head and looked around. The floor was covered with shards of glass. He looked over at Jack's inert body. Blood was pumping out of a wound in the dog's chest.

Chapter 41
Wednesday Evening, November 30th

Tom and Francesca sat across from each other in Tom's office. Mrs. Simmons and Isabelle had left a few minutes earlier. Now, an uneasy silence reigned.

"Good job with the teddy bear brigade," Tom said. "You found our girl."

"Yeah, she seems like a nice kid, a lonely kid." Francesca didn't meet Tom's eyes.

"It's kind of amazing her parents didn't have a clue where she was all those nights. Her mother seemed totally out of the loop." Tom looked at Francesca's bowed head. She was studying her nails intently.

He continued, "Luckily, she kept her cool, otherwise Isabelle might have clammed up."

She nodded.

"We've got to find Brett's drug dealer. I think he's the clue to this business."

"And maybe the clue to Carrie Landwehr, and Lewis as well. I really think these three crimes are connected," Francesca said.

Tom said nothing, merely watched her.

Francesca looked up at the clock on the wall. "I should get going." She made a move to leave.

Tom sighed. "Do you want to tell me what's wrong? I've never seen you like this. It's like there's a big wall between us." He got up and shut the office door. "You haven't answered my phone calls since you got home."

Francesca didn't turn around. She didn't know what to say. She didn't want to come across as the jealous female, but she hated

238

playing games. Tom deserved an explanation. She stood up and turned so they faced each other.

"I missed you while you were in California," he said.

"Did you? It's just, I—" Francesca began.

The phone rang. Tom reached over and picked up the receiver. As he listened, his eyes widened and then narrowed. "I know the address. I'm heading over there now. Thanks." He put down the phone and glanced at Francesca. His mood had changed, and he looked worried as he went to grab his jacket from the hanger behind the door. "There's been a shooting at the Marshalls'."

"What happened?" Francesca asked. "Was anyone killed?"

"So far, I only know about a dog. Someone shot through the front window and killed the dog." Tom ushered her out of the office. They walked quickly down the hallway.

"I'm going to follow you over there. Okay?" Francesca reached over and held his arm briefly. "Maybe I can be of help with Kate and the kids?"

"Sure, maybe you could take them to your house." He looked at Francesca as he headed out the back to his car. "Be careful. I'll see you over there."

Francesca went out the front door and walked to her car. She shivered, not from the encroaching cold, but from the menace once again threatening Banner Bluff.

Kate was driving home. They had met way west of town at a seedy motel in the sticks. Her body was sore and her mind was charged. Guilt and self-loathing permeated her brain. Why did she do this to herself? Why did she agree to meet Glen? She wasn't even sure if she liked him. Their lovemaking was passionate and violent. They pawed at each other like two wild animals. She gave him what he wanted. It wasn't good but she felt vindicated. He knew her. He saw her. She was real. At home, she felt like a ghost. Martin's eyes would follow her as she moved around the kitchen or upstairs in the bedroom, but he didn't really see her.

It was very dark out. The drive took almost forty-five minutes. She felt drowsy and had to concentrate on driving. They'd opened a bottle of champagne when they arrived at the motel and she had drunk more than two glasses. The lights from the oncoming cars momentarily blinded her.

Finally she arrived in Banner Bluff. The village green was aglow with the Christmas lights on the enormous fir tree. Garlands of pine and holly entwined the lamp posts. The shops were all decorated with twinkling lights and red bows. She sighed and felt relieved to be home. This was her safe harbor.

As she turned on to her own street, she saw police cars lining the road, lights flashing. What was going on? An ambulance was parked in front of a house. Her house? Dear God, what had happened?

She drove past the cars toward her driveway, where a patrol car was blocking the entrance. "Sorry, ma'am," the policeman said when she rolled down her window. "This is a crime scene. You'll have to park down the street."

"But I live here. This is my house. What happened?" Her voice rose. "I need to get in there. That's my family." She was screaming now.

"You can't park here; just park down there at the end of the block." He pointed with his gloved hand.

Anger swept through Kate. Who was this guy telling her she couldn't park in her own driveway? Fuming, she pulled away and drove fast down the street, parking in front of a fire hydrant. Who cared if she got a ticket? Then she was out of the car and running back to the house. When she got there, yellow caution tape blocked her path. They had cordoned off the entire property.

She bent down to slip under the yellow tape. An officer grabbed her arm.

"Hey, you! This area is off-limits."

Kate shouted at him. "I'm going in there!" She shook off his arm and raced towards the sidewalk leading up to the front porch. The picture window had been blown out. Several men dressed in white coveralls were combing the entire area, which was bathed in bright light. At the top of the steps, Detective Puchalski blocked her way. He reached out and held her arms.

"Kate, Kate, calm down. It's all right. Everyone is safe."

"Where are the children? I have to get to my children."

"They went to Francesca Antonelli's house with Emma Boucher. We didn't think they needed to see what happened here."

"And Martin, where is Martin?"

"He's in the kitchen. He's pretty shook up." Together they went into the house.

Kate looked into the living room as they went by. She could feel the cold air seeping in from the blown-out window. The sofa was covered in blood and glass.

"There's blood everywhere. Whose is it? I don't understand. You said Martin and the kids are all right?" Her voice cracked as she spoke. She looked up at Puchalski, desperate to read an answer in his eyes.

"Come into the kitchen. Let Martin tell you what happened."

They continued down the short hall. Martin was sitting at the kitchen table across from Tom Barnett.

"Martin," she said, her voice trembling.

He stood up and came to her. He enfolded her in his arms, pulling her close and kissing her hair.

"Thank goodness you weren't here. Thank goodness you didn't see what happened." He was trembling.

241

"What happened?" She stepped away, looking up at him. She didn't want to be in his embrace, not when she didn't deserve his love. Guilt washed over her. All Martin could think about was *her* safety. And yet *she* had been gone…committing adultery… thinking only of herself.

"It was Jack. He saved my life. He jumped onto the sofa just when the bullet came through the window." Martin looked at her, anguish evident on his face. "Oh, Kate." He moaned and pulled her again into his arms. They clung to each other, crying for Jack and for their marriage.

Chapter 42
Thursday Morning, November 30th

Tom Barnett and Ron Puchalski sat at a small table in the back corner of Churchill's restaurant. They had been up much of the night and had walked over from the police station to take a breather. The coffee here was a lot better than the thin brew in the break room at the station. They each had a mug, strong and black, along with a couple of doughnuts.

At the other tables were construction workers, mothers with preschool children and Christmas shoppers taking a break. The restaurant was alive with chatter and laughter. Greenery and sparkling lights festooned the front windows and the air was charged with holiday excitement, although Christmas was still three weeks away. It seemed like another world from the one they'd lived through the night before.

Tom blew on hot coffee and looked up as Frank Penfield approached their table. "May I join you, or are you talking shop?"

"We're always talking shop but you can certainly sit down." Tom smiled. "How are you feeling, Frank? It looks like you've put on a little weight. That's good."

"Thanks for asking. As a matter of fact I'm feeling great. I've got a blessed new start on life and I'm grateful." Frank set a cup of tea and a warm blueberry scone on the table, then sat. He smiled at the officers as he cut open the scone and smeared butter on one half. After taking a bite, he said, "Tell me about what happened last night. Francesca emailed me that there was an attack on Martin Marshall."

"Here's the problem," Tom said quietly. "Martin Marshall saw Carrie Landwehr's killers and they saw him. We kept this out of the press. But they've apparently figured out who Martin is and

243

where he lives. Last night there was an attempt on his life. They want to eliminate him so he can't identify them. They don't know he's face-blind and could never recognize them in a lineup."

Frank nodded. "What happened, exactly?"

"They were aiming for Martin, but Jack, the Marshalls' dog, jumped up on the sofa and knocked Martin down. Jack took the bullet in the chest," Tom said.

Puchalski toyed with his half-eaten doughnut. "The dog saved his life. There was a terrific amount of blood."

"Martin must be in a terrible state. The poor guy! He's a walking target for these murderers," Frank said.

"Last night he was talking about never leaving the house again. He's really freaked out, not only for himself but for his wife and kids. He thinks if those guys shot his dog, it could be a family member next." Puchalski swept crumbs from the table and placed them on his plate.

"What are you going to do?" Frank asked.

"First we're going to publicize that Martin is face-blind. Then he'll have protection twenty-four hours a day. He's not going back to the university until January. The problem is he's in charge of the kids and running the household while Kate is at school. He has to go out to take Rosie to ballet or to do the shopping, stuff like that."

"Maybe I could help out. I'll give him a buzz," Frank said.

"So are you back at work at the *Bee*?" Tom said.

"Yep, Francesca asked me to do some research into the construction project over at Hollyhock Farm."

"I've seen the trucks. We checked the permits displayed on the road. It all seems on the up and up," Puchalski said.

"What are they doing?" Tom asked, sipping his coffee. "We've been too busy with our murder investigations to talk to the Meriwethers. Is it improvements on their land?"

"It's all very hush-hush. It's about—" Frank began.

Tom put up his hand in a signal for quiet as he listened to a call on his headset. "Listen, Frank, we've got to go. Something came up." He stood abruptly and gestured to Puchalski. Both policemen placed their mugs and plates on the counter and headed for the door.

Chapter 43
Thursday Evening, November 30th

Francesca sat in her car outside Zimmerman's Mercedes. She was on a stakeout. If Tom found out what she was up to, he would not be happy. She smiled to herself. She had a small thermos of coffee and a California turkey sandwich. By 9 o'clock the dealership would close down and she could see if anything suspicious was going on.

She'd parked her vehicle a while ago among the used cars, where she figured no one would notice it. This area of the parking lot was unlit, plus she'd worn dark clothing—black jeans and a dark blue hoodie over a long-sleeved tee shirt and a sweater—and she felt well hidden. She had a pair of binoculars around her neck and a flashlight if she needed to get out and look around.

From here, she had a good view of the service department, the offices and even down the hallway to Dottie Muffie's cashier's office. Everything was lit up. She could see people coming to pick up their cars and the car-hikers bringing the vehicles around. The Captain moved in and out of the office while the service assistants talked to the clients.

She kept an eye on the action while her thoughts drifted back to the phone conversation she'd had with Dottie Muffie the previous morning. "I'm feeling on edge. I think something's up," Dottie had said, then lowered her voice. "I just don't think things are right around here, Francesca. I've got an itchy finger and that always happens when something's going wrong."

"What do you mean, exactly?" Francesca said.

"The Captain is a bear to work with these days. He's snapping at everyone. We're all walking on pins and needles."

"Did they hire an evening cashier?"

"Yeah, he's a retired accountant, very quiet guy. He listens to WFMT, you know, classical music, and reads books on presidential history. Definitely not my type."

Francesca laughed. "Well, that sounds good. Now you don't have to stay late."

Dottie paused, then whispered, "I think there are some shenanigans going on here at night. One night last week, I forgot my knitting and came back to get it. I wanted to finish this sweater for my niece's cute new baby. Did I tell you my niece had a baby?"

"No, you didn't," Francesca said patiently. "So you went back for your knitting and...?"

"Yes. See, there was a good movie on HBO and I thought I could knit while I watched." She paused. "So where was I? Oh yes, so the light was still on and I saw the Captain and one of the mechanics coming out of the service bays. They were carrying something. I knocked on the service door and he started yelling that I should wait till tomorrow and not bother him. He didn't even give me a chance to explain. He was just so rude." She stopped abruptly, then said, "I've got to go," and hung up.

In her mind Francesca was reminded of the conversation she had overheard at Jordanville Prison about Petroff, the Hook and something going down in Banner Bluff. Petroff, aka, the Captain had to be part of some nefarious scheme.

It was dark now. Francesca's stomach started growling, so she unwrapped her sandwich and took a big bite of creamy avocado and roasted turkey. It was just perfect. Her cell phone began to vibrate. She pulled it out of her pocket and checked the screen. It was Tom. She decided not to answer. He might ask where she was or what she was doing. She wasn't good at lying and he would know if she was being evasive. She put the phone back in her pocket and took another bite of sandwich.

247

Earlier, an enormous car-hauling truck carrying nine or ten cars had arrived and gone around to the side. How did they manage to balance all those cars on the truck bed? She took another bite and chewed slowly. Through her binoculars, she saw they were bringing some of those new cars into the service bays. The cars were still partially wrapped in some sort of plastic.

Pretty soon her sandwich was gone and she had drunk half the thermos of coffee. She was still hungry. Why hadn't she thought to pack a couple of peanut crunch cookies from the cookie jar? The other night, the Marshall kids had loved them.

It was fun having Rosie and Stevie spend the night, despite the circumstances that brought them there. Luckily, they were clueless about the shootings at their house. Rosie only recalled being woken by "a big noise," and Martin had kept her upstairs away from everything until Francesca and Emma arrived. They'd whisked both kids away out the back door, wrapped in blankets. They were half asleep. The children felt comfortable with Emma and knew Francesca pretty well. After some hot chocolate and a romp with the dogs, they had fallen back asleep in the guest bedroom. Emma had slept in Francesca's bed after a lot of coaxing and Francesca had taken the sofa.

A freight train rumbled by behind the dealership, its whistle blaring as it approached the crossing at Lakeview Avenue. A couple of engines were pulling it and she could feel the vibrations as the heavy train thundered by.

She gazed out the window at the dealership and thought about the last few weeks. First Carrie Landwehr's murder and Brett Atkins' overdose—or suicide. Whichever it was, drugs were involved. Then Officer Lewis's murder and the drive-by shooting at the Marshalls'. What had happened to Banner Bluff? It was the perfect small village full of caring people with a strong sense of community. Neighbors looked after each other. Citizens worked together to create a vibrant but safe town. Now their haven was being undermined by the drug trade that was insinuating itself into the very fabric of everyday life.

Outside, the temperature had dropped. Francesca's feet and nose were cold. No one seemed to be around, so she decided to turn on the engine for a few minutes and heat up the car. Inside the dealership she could see the elderly accountant getting ready to leave. Hopefully, he or anyone else venturing outside in the next few minutes would assume the low purr of her engine was coming from a nearby street. He walked down the hall and opened the glass door to the service entrance. He waved goodbye to the Captain, who barely looked up. Then he went out through the service door.

Francesca leaned back against the headrest, snuggling down. She almost dozed off and had to shake herself awake. It was nine o'clock and the car salesmen were leaving. She turned off the engine and hunkered down as two men came towards her car. She felt uncomfortable from sitting so long and she could really use a bathroom. How did the police handle that on a stakeout?

A few minutes later the dealership was looking closed down, but the Captain was still there. She had seen him go into the service bays earlier, and he hadn't come back to the office. The lights in the bay were on. She gave it ten more minutes, then decided to get out of the car and see what was going on inside. After that she could go home to the bathroom and to bed.

Flashlight and car keys in hand, Francesca opened the door and quickly clicked it shut. She dropped her keys in her pocket and pulled up her hood. Stadium lights lit up the parking lot closer to the building. She scurried across the driveway towards the wall along the service garage, where the building's shadow offered cover. She giggled nervously as she flattened herself against the hard surface. She felt like a spy. She stood tall and peered into the garage through the nearest window. A parked SUV blocked her view. She crept along the wall, crouching down as she passed three large windows. At the last one she slowly raised herself and looked into the garage. From here she could see down into the service bays. A couple of men were still working in there, though she couldn't see who they were from this distance. She extracted the binoculars from inside her sweatshirt and raised them to her eyes.

Now she could see down the long hangar. Several service bays contained the newly arrived cars. In one, the Captain and some other guy appeared to be working on the inside of the front door. The Captain stepped back, gesturing sharply with the tool in his hand. He looked like he was yelling at the other guy. Maybe they were getting the car ready for sale tomorrow. The other guy said something, and they turned back to their work.

Francesca set her flashlight on the ground and reached into her pocket for her phone. It wouldn't hurt to take a couple of pictures. Maybe she could study them later. The two men were crouched near the floor now, reaching underneath the car. Francesca snapped a picture. The mechanic handed something to the Captain. Francesca snapped another picture. The two men studied the object, whatever it was. She snapped another picture.

The mechanic dropped something. He retrieved it, then stood up and walked down the center aisle towards her. Could they see her, with the lights on in the bay and her in the dark outside? Before she could duck down just in case, he glanced up right at her. Surprise crossed his face. Then he shouted something to the Captain, who turned around and looked. Francesca's mouth went dry. Maybe the beam from the stadium lights illuminated her silhouette. Both men started running towards her.

Francesca shoved her phone into her pocket, picked up the flashlight and ran toward the nearest row of parked cars. Behind her, she heard the wheeze of the garage door opening. She stayed low to the ground as she ran across the aisle to the second row of cars. Now she heard shouting, and heavy footsteps running down the aisles as the men hunted for her. They were running away from her towards the front of the dealership. She doubled back along the last row of cars and headed for the rear of the building, away from the glowing lights toward the sheltering darkness beyond. Still keeping low, she took a chance running towards the woods on the other side of the service road and the railroad tracks.

A freight train approached from the south. The crossing gates were going down on Lakeview Avenue. Behind her, she heard shouts. She glanced over her shoulder and saw the two men running towards her. She picked up her pace. Could she make it across the tracks before the train got there? The heavy engines made the ground tremble under her feet. She climbed up onto the embankment and looked to her right. Bright lights nearly blinded her as the train bore down. It was now or never. Francesca leaped forward, skipping over the first set of tracks and then the second. Her foot slipped on the wooden tie. She fell sideways and rolled down the embankment. Then the train was upon her. The power and force of the engines pounded in her ears. It rumbled by, wheels clicking, and the ground shook. Francesca lay on her back, trying to catch her breath. She had to run for the woods, into the dark and safety.

Isabelle was in her room. She had a pile of books on the floor and her geometry book was open on her desk. She tried to study but her mind kept wandering. Her mother knocked gently on the door and then poked her head into the room.

"Do you need anything, honey? I could get you a drink, some milk and cookies." Her mom looked anxious and uncertain.

Isabelle looked up and smiled. "No thanks, Mom. I'm trying to get through my geometry problems."

"Well, don't stay up too late. You need your sleep." Her mom stood there as though trying to think of what to say next.

251

Isabelle tapped her pencil on the open page. "I don't have too much more to go."

Her mother came further in and puffed up the pillow on her bed. Then she turned down the comforter and smoothed the edges. "Is everything all right at school?"

"Uh-huh. Fine." Isabelle felt as though they were dancing around each other. Lately, her mother had been asking a bunch of questions. What was she worried about? Did she think Isabelle would sneak out? No way. That was over. She had nowhere to go. Besides, except for Rachel she barely had any friends these days. She didn't want any. She didn't need any.

"Well, I'm going to get ready for bed." Her mom paused at the door. "You know, Isabelle, you have a wonderful life ahead of you. You're going to get over all this."

Isabelle was losing patience. Every day it was the same mantra. That was a new word she'd learned in World Geography when they'd studied eastern religions. Mantra…her mother repeated the same song every day. But Mom didn't have a clue. Isabelle felt anger rising. "Could you please leave me alone now, Mom? I need to finish these problems." She tried to keep the irritation out of her voice, but wasn't successful.

Her mom shut the door. Isabelle heard her footsteps as she went down the hall.

Twenty minutes later Isabelle had finished her math problems. She put her book and her notebook into her backpack along with her English folder containing the paper she had written earlier on Romeo and Juliet. Isabelle had cried when she read the last act. It seemed so real to her. She knew how Juliet felt. Love and loss were so painful. Since Brett died, the light had gone out of her life. Maybe she should have taken some heroin, too. Then she could have died with Brett. In spite of what her mother said, she would never get over Brett.

Isabelle reached under her bed and pulled out last year's high school yearbook, The Banner Bluff Broadcaster. *She'd stolen it from the school library. She was going through every page, carefully looking for the name Mickey, or anything it might be a nickname for. Brett had mentioned Mickey several times. She was going to track him down.*

There were lots of Michaels. She'd gone through all the pictures at the front, reading the subtitles for each. Then she'd gone through the class pictures. No Mickeys. Now, she was looking at the activity pages in the back. There were pictures of all the cheerleaders, the sports teams, the language clubs, the chess club. She hadn't realized how many clubs there were. Looking at all the smiling faces made her feel like a loser. Maybe she should join one of these clubs? But they probably wouldn't want her.

There were only a few more pages to go. On the second to the last page were pictures from the Battle of the Bands. Sometime in January, everyone who was in a band performed on the stage at school and then the students voted for the best band. Probably just a big popularity contest. This year Brett might have been there, though. Him and his guitar.

Carefully, she read the names under each picture. There were the guys from Upstairs, all doing high fives. They thought they were so cool. In the next picture was another rock band called Tiger Eyes. They all wore black jeans, a black tee-shirt and a black baseball cap turned backwards. On the tee-shirts were printed two large yellow eyes. They looked menacing.

She read the names printed underneath. One was Mickey Sandhurst.

Isabelle looked long and hard at the photo. The picture was too small to really see him. She went to the index at the back of the book. There he was: Francis Michael Sandhurst, page 85. She turned to that page. He was there, smiling broadly. He'd been a junior last year so he was a senior this year. He had black curly hair, blue eyes and an arrogant smile. Like he thought he was super cool.

Isabelle went to the computer and typed in his name. She was going to find out who he was and where he lived. Then she'd pay him a visit.

Chapter 44
Thursday Evening, November 30th

Francesca ran limping into the woods. Her right leg was throbbing. The train was still clicking and clacking behind her. Thoughts raced through her brain. Where should she run? Would the two men follow her? To her left she saw cars stopped on Lakeview. Eventually she would have to go back to Zimmerman's and get her car.

Her first thought was to make her way through the woods and then into town to Tom's house. It would be a relief to share all this with him, to be safe. Then she could ask him to drive her back to the dealership. But did she want him to know what she'd been up to? Probably not. He would read her the riot act and she didn't have any hard evidence about whatever the Captain and his mechanic were up to. She needed to check out her pictures first.

Francesca made a quick decision. She turned left and stumbled through the bushes and tall grass towards the lights on Lakeview. What seemed like hours only took a few minutes; she was on the other side of Lakeview by the time the last freight car rolled by. She looked down the tracks but saw no one. When the guard rails went up, she crossed quickly and headed west towards the Granary restaurant. There was a strip mall and a bar along the road. She stepped into the shadows and went around behind the buildings.

The Granary, a popular spot for pizza and hamburgers, was built like a barn with an attached silo. The place was enormous and Francesca thought she could hang out there for a while, then go back to Zimmerman's and retrieve her car. She was shivering by the time she reached the restaurant. The temperature had dropped considerably and the wind had kicked up.

Inside, Francesca went immediately to the restroom to use the facilities and wash her face and hands. Looking in the mirror, she undid her ponytail and loosened her hair to form a shield. She didn't want to be recognized if those men came into the restaurant. Her jeans and sweatshirt were muddy. She wiped off her jeans with a paper towel and took off the sweatshirt. She wore a white fisherman's sweater underneath. Hopefully, she didn't look anything like the girl who'd been running through the parking lot at Zimmerman's.

The restaurant was still busy although it was a quarter to ten. At the front desk, she smiled at the hostess and asked for a booth at the back.

"Sure, honey." The woman smiled warmly. "Just follow me."

She led Francesca to a rear booth on the right side. Francesca sat down, facing the back wall so she wasn't visible from the entrance. Was she being paranoid? Fear was a crazy motivator.

"Here you go." The hostess handed Francesca a menu. "Everything is pretty much on here. There's minestrone tonight and the pulled pork special if you're so inclined."

A few minutes later, a waiter appeared. He was tall and thin with dark skin. Francesca thought he might be Indian or Pakistani. He introduced himself as Anil and began to launch into his spiel, but Francesca cut him off.

"Thanks, but could I please have a glass of the house cabernet?" Abruptly, Francesca realized she was starving. As long as she was going to sit here, she might as well eat something. "And an individual pizza; make it spinach and mushroom. Okay?" She smiled up at Anil and gave him back the menu.

"Certainly, lady. Spinach and mushroom! Good choice!" He headed back toward the kitchen to put in her order.

Francesca pulled out her phone and opened up the photo album. Slowly she studied each picture, using her fingers to enlarge the image. It looked as though the Captain and the other guy were either extracting something from the cars or putting something in. She couldn't really see what was in their hands.

Anil came by with her wine and a basket of warm breadsticks sprinkled with parmesan. "I thought you might enjoy these while you are waiting," he said.

"Great. Thanks so much." Francesca was too distracted to look up at him. She took a long sip of the red wine. It tasted wonderful, smooth and fruity. Finally, she felt her body relax. The adrenaline pumping through her system slowed down and she felt suddenly very tired. The thought of going back over to the dealership was both frightening and exhausting.

Francesca picked up her phone again and looked back at the pictures, nibbling on a breadstick. Unfortunately, her hand had moved when she took the shot of the mechanic heading towards her. It was too blurry to make out his face. Now she recalled, though, his demeanor had seemed vaguely familiar.

Francesca's pizza arrived. It was a delicious, gooey pie that could wreak havoc on a white sweater, so she began to eat it with a knife and a fork. As she ate, her mind trawled through recent experiences, trying to connect the mechanic with anyone she'd met. Maybe she'd seen him at the dealership when she was over there interviewing people.

When she'd finished her pizza, she picked up her phone again and checked her email. She sipped wine and waited another twenty minutes. It was 10:45 and the restaurant would be closing in fifteen minutes. When Anil, came back she told him she'd be paying with the Tabbed Out app on her phone. He handed her the check and told her to pay up at the counter.

"So are you a cop?" Anil asked as she stepped out of the booth.

Francesca raised her eyebrows in surprise. "A cop? No. What made you think that?"

"Well, I couldn't help seeing the picture on your phone." He gave her an apologetic look. "And it looked like a drug bust to me."

Francesca frowned. "A drug bust?"

"Yes. A favorite place to hide drugs is in a car door." He drew himself up with pride, his dark eyes intense. "I'm studying criminal justice and that's something I learned."

"Those are just pictures of men working at a dealership." As Francesca made a move to leave, she glanced across the room. Her gaze swept across a raised platform that held more tables. The men were there, the Captain and his associate, deep in conversation.

Francesca swung her hair over her face and started across the room. As she wove around some tables, she heard a voice calling her name. She looked up to see Ron Puchalski and his wife Bonnie seated near the entrance. With her back to the Captain and his crony, Francesca stopped to say hello.

Ron looked at her, concern in his voice. "You look like you've seen a ghost."

"I'm just exhausted. You know, big day…long day."

"Why don't you sit down and have a glass of wine with us. We've got a babysitter tonight and we're having a late date." Ron smiled at Bonnie.

"I'd love to, but I need to run. Maybe another time." Francesca smiled briefly and headed for the door.

Ron and Bonnie watched her go. "She looks stressed out of her mind," Bonnie said. "How are things going with her and Tom these days?"

"I don't know. He never talks about personal stuff." Ron reached over and held Bonnie's hand.

She squeezed his fingers. "You guys need to communicate more."

"Yeah right," he said, rolling his eyes.

Chapter 45
Friday Morning, December 1st

The Homicide Task Force met in the conference room at 8 AM. Everyone was drinking coffee and a box of mini cinnamon buns from Bonnie's Bakery sat in the middle of the table.

Tom Barnett brought the meeting to order. "Time to get started. We don't have all day." He felt irritated this morning. Maybe it was the weather, clear and cold. The pure icy light made him edgy. And then there was Francesca. Things hadn't been right between them since Thanksgiving. He couldn't put his finger on it, but she hadn't been the same. It hadn't helped when Ron mentioned seeing her last night at the Granary. Why was she out for a late dinner? Was she really there alone? He turned his mind back to the meeting. "Let's get through our agenda and then get to work."

He noticed Cindy Murray in a whispered conversation with Mark Sanders, and banged his fist on the table. "Hey, let's go." A hush fell over the room. He guessed they were all thinking they better step lightly around the boss. Good. They'd be on their best behavior.

Tentatively, Ramirez raised his hand. "Here's what I've got, Chief. I'm going to cover the three murders chronologically."

"Three murders?" Cindy frowned as she reached for a cinnamon bun.

"Yes, well, two humans plus one canine." He looked up, his expression bland. "Let's start with Carrie Landwehr. We've been back out to the murder site again and again. Monday morning a technician found a piece of torn material on a low branch. The lab says it could have come from an insulated coat or pants."

"How's that?" Cindy said, chewing.

Tom wished she would be quiet and listen. He watched her body language. She was perched on her seat, seemingly ready to pounce. He looked over at Sanders, who was checking out his cell phone. "Sanders, are you with us?"

"Yeah, Chief...sorry. My wife just texted me...her car broke down over on the highway."

"You need to go help her out?"

"No, she called Triple A."

"Okay." Tom nodded at Ramirez, who looked annoyed at the interruption, but continued.

"The fabric was a polyester-cotton blend, dark blue, with a bit of red nylon facing and a snatch of polyester fiberfill lining. The lab tech thinks this bit of material could have come from common work pants or a coat; something a construction worker might wear outside in the cold."

"You mean like workmen's winter coveralls?" Cindy was licking her fingers.

O'Connor rolled his eyes and flopped back in his chair, while Puchalski looked down and brushed crumbs from his freshly ironed pants.

Ramirez continued, "The branch in question is about three feet from the ground, along the route Martin Marshall said he took through the undergrowth while being pursued by the killers. There are other broken branches along the way, but we found this material right beyond a heavy log that barred the path. We're thinking one of the killers fell over the log and scraped against the branch with enough force to scratch his clothes. The lab's still analyzing to see where this material could have come from...brand, supplier, that kind of thing."

"So we've got someone who works outdoors, or in an unheated factory, maybe..." Cindy tapped her pencil.

"As for Jesse Lewis," Ramirez paused and looked down at his notes. "The lab lifted some DNA from the ear buds found on the platform above the train tracks. They're analyzing it and we'll look for a match. We also lifted fingerprints from Lewis's cellphone. We found his prints but also someone else's. From the angle, whoever left those prints might have tried to grab the phone out of Lewis's hand. Maybe when they were pushing him onto the track. But here's what's really interesting." He paused for effect. "We got a couple of prints from the wall sconce on the Marshalls' front porch. And—"

"And they're a match to the ones on the cell phone," Cindy cut in. Her foot was jiggling and she sounded excited.

Again, Ramirez squelched his irritation. "Yes. We're waiting for a match from the FBI database. We have no control over how long that will take."

"Good work, Ramirez," Tom said. "This should give us something to go on. Maybe we're seeing a tiny light at the end of the tunnel."

Cindy fiddled with her pencil some more. "So we're looking at someone who wears heavy work clothes, listens to music and is handy with a gun."

"And some gun," Puchalski said, "The dog was shot with a Makarov pistol."

"Makarov?"

He nodded. "A semi-automatic pistol adopted by the Russian military in 1951. It's become a favorite concealed handgun in this country."

"Here we go again. We've got the Russian connection," Sanders said. "We need to infiltrate the Russian criminal community. Who can we talk to? Who might give us an in?"

Chapter 46
Friday Morning, December 1st

Francesca woke up late. She had tossed and turned most of the night. This morning when she rolled over to look at the alarm clock, her whole body complained. It was almost eight. She rarely slept that late. Her right knee and right arm were sore, probably from the fall down the embankment beside the tracks.

What a night! After leaving the Granary, she had gone back over to Zimmerman's, staying in the shadows and avoiding the glare of the stadium lights until she reached her car. No one was around and the dealership was dark. Without turning on the headlights, she had driven out of the parking lot and down Lakeview. She'd glanced over her shoulder several times at the road behind her, but spotted no cars following.

In the morning light, last night seemed like a nightmare. What had she been thinking, going over there alone? Now, considering things in the light of day, she knew those men were up to no good. They wouldn't have chased her all the way to the train tracks if she hadn't witnessed something that compromised them. She dreaded telling Tom about her harrowing experience but she knew she must.

Francesca put on a sweatshirt and padded downstairs in her stocking feet. The dogs greeted her, running circles around the kitchen. She opened the back door and let them out. After only a minute they wanted back in again. It was freezing. The thermometer on the windowsill read twenty degrees, pretty cold for this time of year.

Francesca made herself a café latte and fed the dogs. She took the coffee into the sunny living room and curled up on the sofa, where she went through the pictures on the phone again.

Maybe that waiter, Anil, was right and the men were dealing in drugs. But where were the drugs coming from and where were they going?

Francesca switched to email and clicked on one from Frank: *I've got some news on the eminent domain case on the Meriwethers' property. I want to check on some details today. Would you like to take a stroll Saturday afternoon around the Village Green? I need to get out and move. See you soon.*

Francesca responded that she would be available at 2 o'clock tomorrow.

She flicked through her phone icons and scanned the *New York Times* site. A lead article about Haskell County, Kansas reported that intensive farming and continued drought were draining the High Plains aquifer that stretches from South Dakota clear down to the Texas Panhandle. Continuous pumping was draining the water. Refilling the aquifer would take hundreds if not thousands of years of rains. Francesca wondered if Emma had seen the article, which was proof of the U.S. water wars they'd discussed a few weeks ago. She emailed the article to Emma.

Next she checked out her calendar. Today was the League of Women Voters Breakfast at 9 AM. She would have to fly if she wanted to make the breakfast on time. Twenty minutes later she was out the door.

Colman Canfield had a bad feeling about his car. He knew he needed new tires now that winter was setting in. Roads were getting slick and icy. He felt safe driving around Banner Bluff and out to the college but not much further. At his advanced age of twenty, he had become a relatively cautious driver. That happened when you'd flirted with the law and had zero money. He didn't want to take his car out on the highway and drive down to Jordanville Prison but he'd promised his dad he would be there this weekend. What to do? Maybe he could hitch a ride with Anya Kozerski. It wouldn't hurt to ask.

He decided to take a half hour off from work and drive over to the hospital. He knew Anya worked in the oncology unit. At the hospital, the parking lot was full, so he had to park two blocks away on the street. Inside the hospital, he followed the signs to the Cancer Center and asked for Mrs. Kozerski at the reception desk. The woman behind the desk didn't know who he was talking about at first. She asked the other receptionist, who told her it was Anya's last name. "Why don't you sit down in the waiting room? I'll call Anya," the receptionist said to Colman.

Colman went into the waiting area and took a seat in the corner. To his right was an old guy with a walker who sat with his wife. His skin was pasty white. One of his gnarled hands held on to the walker. It was shaking uncontrollably. His wife, a plump woman with a soft, kind expression, held his other hand in both of hers. Colman saw her thumb gently caressing the back of his bony knuckles.

Across the room was a pretty young woman with a bald head. She wasn't wearing a wig or a scarf. He figured she was in for chemotherapy. She was texting someone on her phone. She looked up and eyed him defiantly. He quickly looked away.

The walls were painted a warm salmon color with framed flowered prints. The atmosphere was supposed to be soothing, but Colman was overcome with emotion. These people were fighting an intangible, elusive enemy that lurked within them…right inside their own cells. He wasn't sure if he had it in him to work in this environment day in and day out.

Anya Kozerski came into the room and smiled warmly at the old man. "Good morning, Mr. Johnson. It's your turn."

The man's face broke into a craggy smile. "Hey there, Anya. What's a pretty girl like you want with me?"

265

She walked over and helped him up. "We've been waiting for you. I want to hear another one of your jokes today."

Mr. Johnson held onto the walker and began to shuffle towards the treatment rooms. He turned briefly and waved to this wife. "See you later, Mary. Are you going to leave?"

"No, I'll be right here. I've got my knitting."

After her husband left, Mary's face fell. She stared out the window, her eyes filled with tears. Colman glanced at the young woman who was staring blindly ahead. Then he looked away and was about to reach for a magazine when Anya reappeared. She didn't look happy to see him. She came over and whispered, "What do you want?"

"I need to ask you a favor," he blurted out.

Anya glanced at the bald girl and Mrs. Johnson. "Please step out in the hall, so we can talk privately."

He followed her out. The hospital hallway was a busy place. Anya led him over to a corner behind a large potted ficus tree. "Why did you come here?" she asked, glancing over her shoulder.

"I wanted to see if I could drive down to the prison with you this Sunday."

"Shhh. Don't say 'prison'," she whispered. "No one knows I go there." She looked around again. "I don't tell anyone."

"I've got a problem with my car. I could really use a ride."

Anya put her hand to her throat. "Well, I guess you could," she said.

"I'll pay for gas," Colman said quickly before she could change her mind. "What time do you leave? I'll meet you wherever you want."

"Where do you live?"

"Up over Churchill's."

"I'll be there downstairs at six AM. Do not be late, please." She turned away and walked quickly back to the oncology unit.

Chapter 47
Late Friday Morning, December 1st

Francesca arrived at her office at 10:30. The speaker at the League of Women Voters' breakfast had been Susan Bagley, an Illinois State Representative. The gist of her talk concerned more transparency in the election process and in campaign donations, along with the need to establish funding limits. Feisty and smart, she often went head to head with Governor Crenshaw. Some credited her with coining the nickname "the Pharaoh." After the meeting Francesca, asked Ms. Bagley if they could get together sometime and discuss the difficulties and successes of women in politics. They agreed to meet after the holidays. All in all, a satisfying start to the day.

When Francesca arrived at Hero's, Colman and Hero were doing inventory. They'd stacked packages of Jell-O, jars of peanut butter and boxes of cereal on a cart while they wiped down the shelves and took a tally of the packaged goods.

"Francesca, you are late today." Hero pointed to his watch. "Colman is late also. I'm wondering if you've got the sleeping bug."

"I've been busy," Francesca said, smiling. "Looks like you guys are busy too."

"This is not a favorite part of my business, but it must be done." He handed Colman a small jar of mayonnaise and made a mark on a tablet.

"You know, I keep telling Hero he can do all this on a computer. He needs to set up his cash register and then we wouldn't have to go through this process," Colman said.

"Colman, this is how I have always done it. It has always worked fine."

"Yes, sir." Colman said, winking at Francesca as she headed for the stairs.

Upstairs in her office, she hung her coat on a peg and walked over to the desk, where she looked out the window at the street below. With the unseasonably cold weather, not many people were out. Two men walking across the green deep in conversation caught her attention. They wore work pants and jackets with heavy Timberland boots. The Captain and his mechanic? She shivered and wrapped her arms around her torso. As they approached, she saw it was Luis Gonzales and another village worker. She let out a slow breath and made her tense shoulders relax. Her mind was playing tricks on her.

Across the green she could see the Village Hall and the police station where Tom must be at work. Why didn't she just call him and tell him about her hair-raising evening? After she got a little work done, she would give him a buzz.

Francesca moved away from the window and sat down at her desk to write the article about the League of Women Voters breakfast. It wouldn't take long. Then she wanted to do some research about Mercedes-Benz. Where did the cars come from that arrived in Banner Bluff? If Anil was right, and the Captain and his partner were removing drugs from those vehicles, where and when were the drugs hidden in them? These were brand new cars. Could something be concealed at the plant where they were manufactured?

Her article was quickly dispensed with, and then she spent an hour googling Mercedes-Benz and studying the varieties of models. On Wikipedia she perused the history of the company. She learned that the cars were made all over the world. A plant near Tuscaloosa, Alabama produced primarily sport vehicles. So where did Zimmerman's Mercedes get their cars? Francesca leaned back in her chair and twisted a loose strand of hair around her finger. She looked out at the unadorned skeletons of the leafless trees.

Of course, she could just drop the whole thing. She looked down at her computer monitor. The daily quote she received each morning flashed on the screen. Today's was a quote from Will Rogers; somebody her grandmother used to talk about. It said: *Even if you are on the right track, you'll get run over if you just sit there.* Francesca smiled to herself. Talk about *a propos*!

She decided to call Paul Jenkins, the manager of the dealership. No way was she going to go over there. She shivered at the thought. But a call to Mr. Jenkins would be easy enough. She would have to dream up a reason.

"Good morning, Zimmerman's Mercedes," said a friendly, slightly nasal voice.

"Hello, this is Francesca Antonelli from the *Banner Bee.* Could I please speak to Mr. Jenkins?"

"Certainly, let me put you through." A few minutes went by. Francesca listened to a Beethoven sonata. It was nice; different from the usual Muzak.

A new voice, rushed and impatient, came over the line. "Good morning, Ms. Antonelli. Paul Jenkins here."

"Good morning, Mr. Jenkins."

"What can I do for you?" His aggressive tone belied his words. "I hope this isn't more questions about Carrie Landwehr. I think we've covered that."

"No, no. I'm calling with a couple of questions about your dealership, well, about Mercedes-Benz."

"In what regard?" He sounded cool now, a little wary.

"I thought I might do a series about local businesses. You know, encourage people to buy locally." Now she was embroidering. "I thought some background information…the history of the dealership…maybe some personal interest stories about the employees…"

"A series? Well, maybe." She could practically hear him thinking. Paul Jenkins was looking at this as free publicity. He had never advertised in the *Bee*.

"Maybe we could get together someday soon." Where was she going with this? She needed to figure that out, fast.

"You'll have to make an appointment with Sheba. I'm a busy man." Jenkins must be feeling more relaxed. He fairly puffed with pride.

"Oh, I'm sure you are…running such a large enterprise." Did she really just say that? "Oh, just one quick question…"

"Ask away."

"Where do the vehicles come from that I see rolling in on those giant car-haulers?"

"They come from Germany by way of Baltimore."

"Baltimore?" Francesca was surprised.

"Yes. Every day a thousand cars arrive from Germany on ships and are checked over before they're sent on to us." Jenkins was warming to his subject. "As a matter of fact, I recently went to Baltimore to view the shipyards and the processing procedure. I'm part of an elite group of dealership managers chosen to attend the event."

"Wow, what an honor." Francesca rolled her eyes as she tapped a pencil on the desk.

"It is impressive. Thousands of cars are individually processed in this giant plant. They're washed, checked over to make sure everything works, and then they get their Monroney sticker." He was on a roll and could probably go on all day.

"Do you order your cars from there?"

"No, I order the style, color and so on from Germany."

"When do you get the new arrivals?"

"Every Monday and Wednesday our shipments come in."

"So these cars aren't built in America."

"Well, no. They represent Germany's finest engineering."

"Hmm. I wonder if that would bother people here, you know, who want something made in America?"

That question was a mistake. Jenkins' tone changed. "Listen, Ms. Antonelli, I've got to get to work. Please make an appointment with Sheba and we'll talk further." He hung up.

Francesca leaned back in her chair and considered what she had learned. If drugs were being sent to Illinois in the door of a brand new car, then somebody in Baltimore must have hidden them there. Was it a Russian drug ring with Petroff acting as middleman here? And who was his contact at the other end? The hook?

Paul Jenkins dropped the phone into its cradle and looked up at the Captain, who sat across from him in his glass-enclosed office. "Those journalists try my patience."

"So she wants to know where our cars come from?" The Captain's eyes narrowed and he squeezed his knees with his stubby fingers. "Why would she want to know that?"

"She's going to write an article about the dealership."

"Is she?" The Captain's voice trailed off. He got up, shoved back the chair he had been sitting on, and left the office, lumbering down the hallway.

Paul Jenkins shook his head. The Captain could be rough around the edges. He turned to his computer, immediately forgetting Francesca Antonelli and her questions.

Chapter 48
Friday Afternoon, December 1st

Ramses Crenshaw walked down the stairs from the second floor of the governor's mansion. He had a busy afternoon ahead of him. There was a meeting with the members of the TRS, the Teachers' Retirement System. The cost of retirement benefits weighed heavily on the state budget. Crenshaw had handily reduced benefits for teachers, firemen, law enforcement and other government workers through some heavy politicking. He had called in his chits from various sources. But the battle continued. He would need to be his most solicitous self this afternoon.

Educators were a tricky group. People had a love-hate relationship with teachers. On the one hand they trusted and admired a teacher's selflessness. On the other hand they were jealous that they had the summer off. His dealings with the TRS demanded finesse. Today, he would be at his best.

Before Crenshaw entered the conference room, Harrison Rand came through the front door bringing in rain and wind. The door slammed shut behind him.

"Governor, sir. May I have a word?" He was out of breath.

Crenshaw paused, his hand on the door handle. He could hear the rumble of voices awaiting him. "I've got a meeting, Harrison. Can't this wait?"

"No sir, it can't. We've got problems." He approached and lowered his voice.

The governor was irritated. "That's your job...to take care of problems." His voice was brittle. "What is it...and be brief."

"Sir, someone's making inquiries into the agua corriente project. They could jeopardize your plans."

"Find out who it is. Then put Bielski and Stroik on it."
Crenshaw's eyes glowed with anger. "I'll want answers
tomorrow." As he turned back towards the door he said, "We will
destroy anyone who blocks our plans."

"Hey, Tom." Francesca's voice over the phone was
unnaturally low.

"Hey yourself." He waited. After all, she'd called him.

"Have you a got a window of time? You know, to talk?"

"Why?" He paused. "Did you want to meet over at the
Granary?" There was silence at the other end of the line. Why had
he said that?

"No, I wanted to come over to your place."

"What were you thinking?" He asked.

"I could stop at Marigold Heaven and get Thai."

"That would be great. Could I call you in a bit? I don't
know when I'll be finished. It *would* be good to go home for a
couple of hours."

"Okay. Call me when you're ready."

At 7 PM, Francesca sat across from Tom at his kitchen
table. She'd picked up *tom yum* soup, coconut shrimp, chicken *pad
Thai* and vegetarian fried rice. It was way more than they would
ever eat, but Tom would have leftovers.

Tom pushed back his plate. He leaned his forearms on the
table and looked at Francesca. Francesca sipped her glass of
chardonnay. Tom had stuck with green tea. He looked tired and
on edge, and didn't mince words when he spoke. "So tell me
what's going on. You've been different, withdrawn lately."

She took another sip as if to fortify herself. She still wasn't
ready to discuss their uncertain relationship, or whatever might be
going on between him and the redhead. "I wanted to tell you what

274

I was doing last night." She looked up briefly and then back down at her glass.

"And?"

Francesca took a deep breath. "And…I went on a stake-out."

Tom frowned and reached for her free hand. She let him take it, even though he would see she'd chewed her fingernails to the quick. She saw him notice the damage, his frown deepening. But all he said was, "Stake-out?"

"Yes, I went over to Zimmerman's late yesterday afternoon." His eyes narrowed in disbelief. In a sudden flood of words she told him about Dottie Muffie's fears, the long wait in the car and then what she'd seen in the garage. Tom let go of her hand, stood up and began pacing the room.

"Let me get this straight," he said when she paused for breath. "You went to Zimmerman's…alone…without telling me. God, Francesca. You should have told me what you'd learned that afternoon and we could have discussed Mrs. Muffie's concerns."

"I haven't finished." She wrapped her arms around her torso and stared at the ceiling. Tom stopped pacing and leaned against the kitchen sink, searching her face. She told him about getting out of her car, taking the pictures and the run across the parking lot. "A freight train was coming. I crossed the tracks just in time. I rolled down the other side and they didn't catch me." As she remembered the chase, her eyes widened and she started shaking.

Tom came over and pulled her into his arms. "My God, Francesca, you could have been killed."

She clung to him, her arms wrapped around his neck. She should have done this last night, she thought, feeling safe and secure for the first time since the stake-out. To hell with the redhead. Who knew what she'd really seen in the police station conference room, anyway? "I still haven't finished, Tom." Her

275

voice was muffled against his chest. She pulled away and sat down again. He sat across from her, a questioning look in his eyes.

"I made it to the Granary to kill time until I could go back and get my car. Anyway, I was going over the pictures I took and my waiter saw them over my shoulder. He asked me if I was a cop. He thought I'd been involved in a drug bust." Now Francesca looked up at Tom. "I think he's right. I think the drugs are coming into Banner Bluff in new Mercedes cars transported from Baltimore."

Tom got up and started pacing again. When he asked, Francesca went through her story a second time. She told him about her conversation with Paul Jenkins earlier in the day, describing what she'd learned about the Port of Baltimore Auto Terminal. Finally, she pulled out her phone to show him the pictures.

Tom frowned at them. "We can't really see what they've got in their hands. We'll need to send these in to the lab and have them blown up."

Francesca stood up and started to clear the table. Tom's back was to her as he stared out the kitchen window, his hands resting on the edge of the counter. His low voice vibrated with emotion. "Francesca, you were nearly killed." He paused. "And how do we know these guys won't come after you?"

"I had my hoodie on. It was dark and I wore dark clothing. They couldn't have recognized me from a distance. Even their security cameras won't show them much. " She was trying to reassure herself as well as Tom.

He was still looking out the window. Then he turned abruptly toward her and gestured at the take-out cartons. "Leave all this," he said. "Let's go into the den. Bring your wine. Maybe I'll have a sip of Glenlivet. We'll have a fire and cuddle." He smiled at her.

276

She smiled back. "Cuddling sounds like a great idea to me."

In the living room, he lit the gas fire and they settled on the sofa. "Isn't there some way you could check out some of those cars?" Francesca said, snuggling under Tom's arm.

"Not without a court order. We can't just barge in there and ask to inspect the vehicles. We don't really know what those men were doing, anyway. Maybe Mercedes puts information, I don't know, registration materials or pamphlets in the doors in Baltimore?"

"Come on, Tom. This was at night. They were sneaking around and when they saw me, they went nuts. That alone tells you something is going on."

He looked thoughtful as he sipped his scotch. "I could assign a detective to do what you did, do a little reconnaissance mission. When do the vehicles arrive from Baltimore?"

"Monday and Wednesday, according to Paul Jenkins."

"Let's see what we find on Monday night. You might be disappointed, though. You may have your suspicions, but some people in town really like that guy Petroff. They call him the Captain."

"I know. I think he's slime." She stared into the flames.

"So…" Tom sounded tentative. "Why have you been standoffish these last few weeks? What's going on?"

She took a breath. Here it was. "You want to know?"

"That's why I'm asking."

She felt a blush rising. "Because, well, because I was jealous."

"You? Gimme a break."

She felt defensive and knew she sounded it, but couldn't help herself. "On Thanksgiving I came home all happy to see you and there you were with someone else…down in the war room of the police department."

"Someone else? I don't know what the hell you're talking about." He was actually laughing.

"You were in close proximity to a red-haired lady. Very close."

Tom cocked his head. Then his brow furrowed. "A cute little redhead? You mean Cindy Murray? " He chuckled, shaking his head. "We were looking at cop humor on Facebook." He reached over and tousled her hair. "You're nuts, but I'm glad you were a little jealous. It does a guy good."

"Cute little redhead?"

"Yeah, and she has the personality to match. She's a spitfire."

Francesca didn't want to hear him extol Cindy Murray's virtues. "So, since you were busy with your little friend, I decided to accept a dinner invitation with a well-known gentleman."

His frown now was far from thoughtful. "Well-known gentleman...and who might that be?"

She grinned. "The Pharaoh!"

"As in RC the Third?"

"Yes. He called me out of the blue, said he wanted to talk about local issues with someone in the media." She pulled her knees up and wrapped her arms around them. "I think he had another agenda, though. Politicians always do, but something felt ominous about the entire evening. I can't explain it."

"You already knew he was a scumbag. I can't believe you went out with him."

"I thought I might learn something. You should have seen him work the restaurant. People adore him."

"So what did you learn?"

"I learned he's willing to do anything to win the next election. He said he would crush his opponent. He meant Bob Newhouse, even asked me how well I knew Bob; like he was hoping I'd dish up dirt or let something slip that he could use. And he has some…interesting views on local issues—like who owns Lake Michigan's water. He—"

Tom's phone rang. He answered it, hung up after a brief conversation. "Gotta go, sorry" he said.

She wanted to ask if it had anything to do with the murders or the shooting at the Marshalls', but decided against it. After last night, she could use a little break from the mayhem.

They kissed briefly. Then he got up and took his gun from the hallway safe, put it in its holster and pulled on his jacket.

After he left, Francesca put the leftover Thai food into the fridge, rinsed the dishes and put them in the nearly full dishwasher. As she worked, she thought about their brief get-together. They hadn't done much cuddling but she felt like they were back on track. She still felt annoyed that he'd referred to Cindy Murray as a "cute little redhead." Francesca certainly wasn't little or a redhead. She filled the cup with liquid dish detergent, shut the dishwasher door with a bang and started the machine. On the other hand, she definitely could be a spitfire.

Chapter 49
Saturday Afternoon, December 2nd

Martin was grateful for the bright sunny day. He didn't care how cold it was. The sunshine chased away the demons that swirled in his psyche at night. He couldn't imagine that anything bad could happen this afternoon. Kate had suggested they take the kids down to the ice-skating rink. Normally, the rinks were flooded toward the end of December, but the exceptionally cold weather had led Banner Bluff Buildings and Grounds to do it early. Kate had been a figure skater as a girl and had even won some competitions. As soon as the rink was frozen in Banner Bluff, she was ready to go.

While Kate skated around holding Rosie's hand, Martin took the stroller and walked the perimeter of the green. People were out walking, and several acquaintances stopped to say hello and to admire Stevie, who slept wrapped in several blankets. He looked angelic in his sleep, not his devilish self. A young police officer followed them, trying to look unobtrusive.

Martin thought about the last few days. The morning after the shooting he hadn't wanted to go downstairs. He'd felt safer upstairs in the darkened bedroom with the drapes drawn. He'd finally gone downstairs in the late afternoon, but the sight of the empty living room was a frightening reminder of the horrors of the night before. The sofa and Persian carpet, both heavily spattered with blood, had been removed. They'd decided to get a new sofa and Kate had ordered one online.

Emma Boucher and a couple of her friends had come over to scrub down the room. Harry Bliss from the hardware store had sent a fellow who'd installed a new picture window, and Emma and her crew had hung some curtains to block out the world.

Casseroles and salads, as well as a large chocolate cake, filled their refrigerator. All of this was done quietly and efficiently. These were their friends and neighbors in Banner Bluff, and these were the reasons it was an ideal place to live.

Chief Barnett had asked him to go over the evening several times. They found the front and back porch light bulbs had been removed. Unfortunately no one in the neighborhood had noticed anything unusual in the early evening. At the time of the shooting, no one had seen the getaway car, although several people had heard the shots.

Now, their house was under surveillance 24/7. It made Kate feel safer, though Martin still got nervous every time he heard a car drive by or an unfamiliar sound in the backyard. He realized he would have to get over his fear, which was compounded by his inability to recognize faces.

During the police interview after the shooting, Martin had told Chief Barnett his hunch that he'd seen the two murderers at the Christmas tree lighting ceremony. It was something about the way they stood, their posture and the way they looked at him, even the similarity in the lighting between the ceremony and the night of Carrie Landwehr's murder. He wondered if it could also be their aura. He knew it might sound nuts to some, but he could almost *feel* goodness and evil emanating from certain people. And the two men standing in front of the gazebo that Friday had vibrated with evil.

Francesca and Frank ambled along the path that meandered around the village green. The path bordered the ice-skating rink that was teeming with children of all ages. Music echoed from the little house that served as a warming shack on the edge of the rink. Smoke curled from the chimney. Today, the rink's opening day, there was hot chocolate for one and all.

Frank smiled at Francesca. "You know, with this brilliant sunshine and those happy voices, it's good to be alive, so very good to be alive."

Francesca knew those weren't just empty words. The past few months had been touch and go for Frank. The fact that he could walk around the perimeter of the green, albeit slowly, was a joyous thing. "You are so right, Frank. We have to be grateful for a sunny day like this even though it's absolutely freezing." She tightened the scarf around her neck. Both she and Frank were wrapped up like sausages with multiple layers of clothing. "So tell me what you found out about the Meriwethers' property."

"What I found was nothing."

"Nothing? What do you mean?"

"I found no record of any judgment to obtain that land. I checked at each level of government. Banner Bluff has no record of any request for that land, nor does Lake County, nor does the State of Illinois. Someone has to apply for the right to acquire the land." Frank took off his gloves and handed them to Francesca, then reached into his pocket and pulled out a folded piece of paper along with his reading glasses. "Let me read this to you: The law states that if the exercise of eminent domain is to acquire property for public ownership and control, then the condemning authority must prove the acquisition of the property is necessary for a public purpose and the acquired property will be owned and controlled by the condemning authority or another governmental entity." He turned towards her. "That means they have to prove, in court, the necessity of acquiring that land. And there is no record anywhere."

"But Carina told me she had to sign a whole raft of papers with the governor's signature on them. It was some state lawyer she was dealing with."

"Right, but I also called the Department of Natural Resources for the State of Illinois. They don't know anything about any pipeline bringing water from Lake Michigan to the western suburbs. They had no idea what I was talking about. There is absolutely no paper trail. And there should be."

Francesca stopped walking and turned to Frank. "You're telling me this whole thing is bogus?"

"Yes. There has to be a recorded document somewhere, there has to be a legal acquisition of the Meriwethers' land. But there's nothing."

She let out a breath and shook her head. "Here's what I don't understand. Carina got a check for five million dollars. Where does that money come from?"

"I think you need to go to the Meriwethers' farm and check out the documentation. Find out as much as you can."

Francesca stood still gazing at the twelve year-old boys that were smashing a puck around the ice. One kid wove his way across the rink; outmaneuvering the other boys, shifting to the left and the right, tightly controlling the puck. With a few deft moves he had scored a goal. The other kids didn't even know what had happened. Just like the Pharaoh, she thought, who knew exactly how to move his agenda through the labyrinth of state laws and regulations with no one else the wiser until the deal was done.

Colman had taken on another job. He loved skating and adored hockey. When Mr. Greenwood from the Park District called to ask him if he wanted to work at the skating rink, he had jumped at the chance.

Today, Colman was cruising around the rink. Earlier he'd helped a little girl learn to skate backwards and he'd refereed a hockey match for a group of eight year-olds. He saw Mrs. Martin skating hand in hand with Rosie and skated over.

"Look at me, Colman," Rosie shouted. She let go of her mother's hand and skated unsteadily on her own towards the middle of the rink. Then she lost control and fell backwards on her rump. Colman quickly skated over and pulled her back up.

"Good for you. You're getting better and better," he said.

"I'm not crying either," she said, her bottom lip trembling.

"Come on, Rosie-Posie," Mrs. Martin said. "Try it again."

This time Rosie took longer, smoother strides and skated evenly over the ice. "Wheee, this is fun," she chirped.

"Where's Mr. Martin today?" Colman asked. "Is he all right?"

"Yes, he's doing better today. He's right over there taking Stevie for a ride in the stroller." She pointed with her gloved hand.

Colman looked over and saw Martin Marshall pushing a stroller. A police officer walked along behind him.

"Martin is being watched twenty-four seven," Kate said. "Officer Czerny is following him around this afternoon." They watched as Czerny walked purposefully, his eyes scanning the street and the park.

"Why are they trying to kill Mr. Marshall, anyway? Don't these crazies know he can't recognize them?"

"Apparently not," she said. "Uh-oh, there goes Rosie, down again." She skated off to help her daughter get back on her feet.

Colman skated over to the warming shack and went in. He helped a little kid lace up his skates and then put another log in the potbellied stove.

When he came back outside he saw Mr. Marshall walking towards him on the west side of the rink. A woman had stopped Officer Czerny to talk to him. She had her hand on his arm. Behind them, a nondescript black car drove slowly along the road. The back window slid down, and Colman saw the long barrel of a shotgun.

Colman leaped onto the ice and skated faster than he ever had before, shouting and waving his arms. "Mr. Marshall! Down! Get down!"

The car was speeding up. Martin looked at Colman, a frown on his face. Then he glanced back at Officer Czerny, who was several steps behind now.

Colman watched it all as if in slow motion. He reached the edge of the rink and threw himself onto Mr. Marshall, knocking him to the ground and tipping over the stroller. He heard Mr. Marshall's head hitting the pavement and the crisp, sharp sound of a gunshot. Stevie started to scream. Martin Marshall was groaning. Pandemonium exploded on the rink as everyone skated for cover, charging towards the trees or into the shack.

"Are you all right?" Colman yelled.

"Yeah." Mr. Marshall sounded shaky, but okay. "What happened?"

"Somebody in that car tried to shoot you." Colman pushed himself up and looked back at Officer Czerny, who was lying on the ground. The black car had raced by, headed for the underpass under the train tracks, and was out of sight.

Colman helped Mr. Marshall up. The man staggered to his feet, breathing unevenly. Stevie was still screaming from being suddenly awakened and thrown on his side. They bent over to set the stroller upright.

Kate Marshall rushed over, dragging Rosie behind her. She was frantic. "Martin, are you all right?" She reached up and touched his cheek. Then her gaze darted to the stroller. She bent down and pulled Stevie into her arms. The little boy whimpered and stuck his thumb in his mouth.

"Mommy, what happened?" Rosie shouted. No one was paying any attention to her.

Chapter 50
Saturday Late Afternoon, December 2nd

Tom Barnett conferred with Detective Puchalski in the lobby of the recreation center, which stood at the edge of the village green a short distance from the skating rink. Colman had come in to give an account of what he'd seen and done. After saving Martin's life, he'd shepherded the unaccompanied children into the warming shack and called 911. He shivered a bit as he spoke even though he was warmly dressed—probably from shock.

"Are you sure you don't want to take a trip to the ER and make sure you're alright? Tom asked.

"No,sir. I'm fine. I'll probably have a couple of bruises. Colman said.

"If you hadn't acted so fast, Martin Marshall would have been a goner." Puchalski said.

Although only a short time had passed since the drive-by, the Banner Bluff Police Department had alerted surrounding communities to be on the alert for the suspect's car. Several people had witnessed the shooting, though most only remembered a dark-colored sedan. Tommy Schroeder, one of the kids on the hockey team, said it looked like his Uncle Harry's car, which they learned was a black Ford Taurus. Then Jeremy Gresham, an electrician out skating with his daughter, swore it was a dark blue Chevy Malibu. Now Greta Nielson had asked to speak to them. She bustled through the door looking like a cheerful, aging teletubby in a bright purple ski outfit and a purple-and-pink knit cap with a large pink pompom that bobbled as she walked.

"I've got the answer to your prayers," she said as she reached them. She pulled a camera out of her multi-striped bag and plopped it on the table. "This is a Canon VIXIA camcorder. It's high-definition with a zoom. I filmed your shooter along with my granddaughter Lucie."

She turned the camera on, clicked play and held it up for Ron and Tom to view. In the foreground seven year-old Lucie glided smoothly across the ice. Behind her on the walkway, they saw Martin Marshall pushing a stroller and a car moving slowly down the street. Then Colman Canfield appeared, flying through the air and crashing into Marshall. The car sped up and left the camera frame.

"Could you show that again and zoom in on the car?" Ron asked.

She reset the film roll and enlarged the picture. "That's a dark blue Impala," Ron said. "Needs a wash, but I'd bet my life on it." He looked closer nodding.

Tom turned to him. "Notify the surrounding villages." He turned to Greta. "We'll need to take that camera and get a copy made of the video. We'll get it back to you pronto."

"Sure thing," she said, already turning towards the door. "I've got to get Lucie home now."

Chapter 51
Saturday Night, December 2nd

It was 9:30 when Isabelle left the house. Her parents had gone down to Chicago to the symphony. They had left early so they could have dinner in the city. Since they'd taken the train they wouldn't be back until after 11.

Her mother hadn't been able to decide whether to go to the concert or not. All week long she'd gone back and forth trying to make up her mind. Could she leave Isabelle home alone?

"Honey, how about if I ask Margie Mansfield over to have dinner with you. You girls could rent a movie and have popcorn."

"Mom, I don't need a babysitter and I can't stand Margie."

"Don't say that, Isabelle. She's my best friend's daughter. She's a nice girl." Her mom was folding laundry on the kitchen table. She turned and frowned at Isabelle. "She is only four years older than you."

"Mom, she's a dork. Even though she's in college, she's still living at home." Isabelle opened the pantry and helped herself to three Oreo cookies. She opened one to lick off the white frosting. Without looking at her mother she said, "Don't you trust me? I am fourteen years old."

Her mom looked flustered and didn't answer right away. Isabelle left the room nibbling on the dark chocolate cookie.

Eventually, her parents decided to leave her home alone. There was a plate in the fridge with baked chicken, gravy and mashed potatoes, her favorite meal. Of course her mom also included broccoli and carrots. She was nervous and could barely eat. She ended up scraping the remains into a plastic bag and putting it outside in the garbage. Waiting until nine-thirty was a drag. She felt too nervous to do anything to pass the time.

She knew where Mickey Sandhurst lived. His house was on a cul-de-sac looking over a ravine one block from Lake Michigan. It was a ten minute walk from her house. If he was there, she'd talk to him. She wasn't afraid. He owed her an explanation about what happened to Brett. She put on her jacket and a knitted hat, then stepped outside.

It was a cold, dry night. The black sky was brittle with sharp stars and a cleanly etched slice of moon. Isabelle walked down Elm over to Apple Tree and then three blocks to the entrance to the cul-de-sac, Lake Point Drive. The short street contained three houses, each hidden in a forest of trees. She found the number she wanted and walked up the winding path to the front door. Lights illuminated the trees and the walkway. The front door was lit up and there was a large wreath decorated with bright red cardinals as though the birds had just alighted on the branches. It was really pretty.

Isabelle rang the bell and waited. Inside, the house was dark. If the parents came to the door she would just ask for Mickey. She had already made up her speech. She rang the bell again, but no one came. She stood there trying to think what to do. In the still night she could hear waves breaking down on the beach. What else? Nearby she heard muffled voices, laughter and music.

Isabelle went back down the walk to the driveway and around to the right side of the house. Back here, the voices and music were louder. A path along the side of the house led down into the ravine. It was lit up just like the front with small pathway lights, and the trees were illuminated with spotlights.

Isabelle started down the path, listening as the music grew louder. Somewhere down here was a party. The path led to a deck over the ravine. She stepped onto the deck. It was dark here but to her left was a row of tall windows covered with curtains. She could see chinks of light from between them. The music was blasting and there was a lot of laughing. This must be Mickey's hangout. This must be where Brett came on the weekends before he died.

She wondered how all the kids got here. She hadn't seen any cars up on Lake Point Drive or on Apple Tree. She walked over to the edge of the deck and looked over the wooden railing. Down below she spotted a path coming up from the ravine. Maybe the kids parked over on the other side. She turned back to the windows and tried to peek between the curtains. It was hard to see who was in there, just bodies in jeans and t-shirts. Further down the row of windows was a set of French doors. That must be the way in.

Someone grabbed her from behind and pinned her arms to her body. It was a big guy, she could tell. He picked her up off the deck and carried her towards the French doors. She smelled beer on his breath and his body reeked of sweat.

He kicked the doors a couple of times and someone opened up. She recognized Smoothie Connolly, the quarterback of the football team. The guy holding her spun her around against his hip and carried her in with one arm.

"Hey, look what the cat dragged in." The voice, high and rasping. He started to laugh, a mean, snarly laugh. "This girl must weigh ninety pounds or less." He flipped her around against his other hip. She drooped like a rag doll in his grasp, her head hanging down. She turned her head to look up at her abductor. It was Razor Wilder, one of the biggest football players on the Banner Bluff team.

"Come on, Razor. Put her down. You're going to scare her to death," Smoothie said.

Razor obeyed, placing her on her own two feet. The music had stopped and everyone was looking at her."

"Hey, we could have some fun with her. Maybe she came here to get some. Hey, baby, is that what you want? " Razor put his arm around her waist and spun her around. Then he bent down and kissed her, putting his tongue deep inside her mouth, his arms holding her prisoner while he moved his hips back and forth.

Isabelle gagged. She smacked his arm and tried to kick him. He tasted and smelled disgusting. Everyone was laughing. She must look ridiculous. Then she heard a commanding voice from the back of the room.

"Razor, let her go."

Razor put her down and pushed her further into the room. At the back she saw Mickey Sandhurst. He was leaning against the back wall. Beside him was a door into a bedroom. The room they were in was enormous, all paneled in wood with a vaulted ceiling. A mini-kitchen ran along one wall with a bar and stools. Empty bottles of beer were lined up on the counter like soldiers. Kids lounged around on leather sofas; sweet smoke from their reefers filled the air.

In a corner, several guys from different bands were standing, clutching their instruments. She spotted some other football players and a couple of girls. She didn't know any of them well. They must be seniors.

"What are you doing here?" Mickey asked from across the room.

"I came to see you." Her voice wobbled.

"Me?"

"Yes, I need to talk to you." She sounded stronger now. He pushed himself off from the wall. "Okay, talk!"

"No, in private." Isabelle pulled off her knitted cap and undid her coat, like she meant to stick around. She pointed to the bedroom. "Can we go in there?"

Everyone cracked up. "Look at this little freshman." "She wants you, Mickey. She wants your bod." Isabelle didn't care what they said or what they thought.

291

Mickey had a wry smile on his face. "Sure babe, come on into my man-cave."

Isabelle walked across the room and into the bedroom. Mickey waved at everyone, smirking, and followed her in. He wasn't too steady on his feet. They were all laughing when he shut the door.

The bedroom was a mess, clothes all over the floor. Mickey walked over and flopped down on the unmade bed. He lay there spread-eagled and reached down to unzip his pants. "If you want to hook up, you're going to have to take off that coat."

Isabelle walked over and looked down at him. "I want to know if you killed Brett."

Mickey looked perplexed. "What?" He zipped his pants back up and slowly sat up, frowning. "What are you talking about?"

"I know you sold him the drugs that killed him. I want to know if you sold him some bad stuff."

"I don't know what you're talking about," he repeated.

"Yes, you do. Half the kids out there are drugged up and you sold the stuff to them. Brett told me you were a dealer."

He sniggered. "Come on. I just have parties here. A little beer, maybe a little pot, that's all. Your friend Brett got his shit from somewhere else."

"You're lying. I know it was you." All of a sudden, anger welled up inside of her. She bent over and punched him. Then she was screaming; hitting him; kicking him. "You killed him. You killed him."

Mickey grabbed her wrists and forced her down on her knees. She kept wriggling, moving sideways, trying to escape his grip. He pushed her harder and forced her flat on her back. Then he was lying on top of her, flattening her with his body. Isabelle couldn't breathe. She tried to push him off with her fists, but he didn't budge.

292

"Listen, you little cunt. I did not kill Brett.*" He*
enunciated each word, spitting them out. "Think about it. He was
a miserable kid." *Mickey took a breath.* "He killed himself."

*Isabelle felt her anger slipping away like blood draining
from her body. She stopped fighting and went dead inside, lying
there inert except for her jagged breaths.*

*Mickey rolled off and lay beside her, panting. He was
breathing hard too.* "Man, you're nuts."

*Isabelle lay there, unmoving. Tears streamed down her
face. She took another ragged breath.* "But he had me. I loved
him."

After a moment Mickey said quietly, "Well, maybe that
wasn't enough." *Then he pulled himself up and left the room,
shutting the door behind him.*

Chapter 52
Late Saturday Night, December 2nd

Tom was still at the station; would probably be there into the wee hours. They were on the hunt for the car in the drive-by shooting. Francesca knew he was interviewing everyone at the rink and probably meeting with the Task Force. What were they going to do to keep Martin safe? These people were fearless. They had attacked Martin at home and in a public place. It was crazy. She had written a story that covered the shooting but reiterated the fact that Martin was face-blind and could not recognize his assailants. Didn't they read the news?

Francesca was cuddled up in her UCLA pajamas and fuzzy slippers, and had made herself a hot toddy. None of it helped, not even the blazing fire. She was still freezing from the afternoon at the skating rink. She pulled a crimson fleece throw around her legs and opened a worn copy of *Pride and Prejudice*. Jane Austen was something she turned to when she was tired. After a chapter or two she would be ready for bed and her dreams would be sweet. She hoped.

After only a page or two, she could barely keep awake. She leaned back against the sofa pillows and closed her eyes. Visions of Elizabeth sparring with Mr. Darcy at the Bingleys' estate filled her mind. She was just dozing off when a timid knock sounded at her door and jarred her awake. The dogs started barking and jumping around. *Who could that be?* She stood up, tripping over the throw. She kicked it off and stumbled to the door.

She looked through the peephole and at first saw nothing. Then she glanced down and saw the frantic, tear-stained face of Isabelle Simmons. Francesca unlocked the bolt, drew Isabelle into the house and shut the front door. The dogs nuzzled Isabelle in welcome. "What's happened?"

The girl pulled off a boot and nearly lost her balance. She limped over to the stairs and sat down to take off the other boot. Her hands shook as she tugged at it. "I—I went to Mickey's….It was terrible…I just want to die."

Francesca helped her up and took her coat, then led Isabelle into the living room and sat her on the sofa. The girl looked small and limp. Francesca covered her with the crimson throw and sat in the armchair across from her. "Why don't you start at the beginning?"

In fits and starts, Isabelle told her. "I decided to go over and confront Mickey 'cause he killed Brett…I wanted him to feel bad…But it was terrible…He doesn't even care." When she looked up at Francesca, her eyes enormous and sad; she looked like a little child.

"Start even more at the beginning. Who's Mickey?"

"He's a kid at school. He's a dealer and he has parties and they all do drugs."

"How did you find out about him?"

"Brett talked about him and he was on Brett's phone."

Slowly, with Francesca's prompts, she told the whole story. Razor carrying her around like a rag doll; the kids laughing; Mickey inviting her into the bedroom and their confrontation. Then she began to sob, her face in her hands. "You know what Mickey said? He said I couldn't save Brett. That Brett committed suicide." She turned to Francesca. "But I loved Brett. Didn't he want to be with me?"

Francesca had no answer. The words hung in the air.

Then Isabelle said, "He left me all alone." Her face crumpled in hopelessness.

Francesca moved over and sat beside her on the sofa, hugging her and crooning that it would be all right. She felt at a loss, unable to assuage the girl's deep pain.

After a while Isabelle took a long, last sob. "I didn't know where else to go."

"I'm glad you came here. Let me make you some cocoa and then I'll drive you home."

As Isabelle sipped the cocoa they talked together about Brett and about school. After she calmed down Francesca decided to ask the question that was hanging in the air.

"Isabelle. You have Brett's phone, don't you?"

"Yeah."

"You've got to give that to the police. They've been looking for it."

"I know." She said turning pale. But I needed it to feel close to Brett."

Then Isabelle looked around. "Do you know what time it is?"

Francesca glanced at her phone. "It's almost midnight."

"Oh my God, I've got to get home. My parents will kill me."

"Okay, calm down. I'll drive you."

When they arrived at the Simmons residence, Isabelle's parents had just pulled up. She told them Isabelle had come over for a chat and she was sorry to bring her home so late. They seemed to accept that, and she left Isabelle with a quiet good-bye.

Back on the road, she pulled over and called Tom. He picked up immediately. "Hey, Francesca. We've just found the car. It was stolen from a guy in Lindenville. They dumped it in the Cherrywood Mall parking lot. With all the Christmas shoppers, it wasn't spotted right away."

"Tom, Isabelle Simmons came to my house this evening. She told me about an underage party going on with drugs and alcohol in a house on Lake Point Drive. The Sandhurst residence. The parents aren't there and the party is down in back on the ravine."

"Okay, we'll check it out."

"You need to bring in Mickey Sandhurst. Isabelle tells me he's the one who supplied Brett with drugs."

"Why didn't she tell us this before?"

"I don't know. I didn't ask her. She went there tonight and got roughed up by some upper-classmen, but she's safe at home now."

"And Tom, she's got Brett's phone."

"We'll go over there and get it. Why was she hiding it?"

"She said she needed to feel close to him. She's been sleeping with it."

"Great. Thanks. We'll get on it right away. And Francesca?"

"Yes?"

"Make sure your doors are locked. Okay?" He hung up.

Chapter 53
Early Sunday, December 3rd

It was 2 AM. Chief Barnett and Detective Puchalski were in the interview room with Mickey Sandhurst. The police had raided the Sandhurst home and arrested about ten kids. Apparently before they arrived, there was a fight and a bunch of kids had already left.

After booking the teenagers, the police called their parents, who arrived at the station to take their youngsters home. Some were angry with their children, others were angry with the police. Tom soon tired of their belligerent attitude. A couple of kids were sloppy drunk and mouthed off to their parents. One girl got a slap across her face. Another mother couldn't stop crying, "What will my friends at the garden club say?" Tom could write a book about the freaky family dynamics.

Now it was quiet. Just them and Mickey Sandhurst, seated across the round table in his cargo shorts and soccer jersey. They had read him his rights. He'd said he didn't want a lawyer because his parents would go nuts if they found out. He seemed to think he could just walk away from this whole thing. Puchalski switched on the video camera and they began the interview.

"Please state your name for the record," Puchalski said.

"Frances Michael Sandhurst." The kid smiled easily, sure of himself.

"What do your friends call you?"

"Mickey. Everyone calls me Mickey." He flashed another self-assured smile.

He was a handsome young man, Tom admitted to himself, although he reeked of cigarette smoke, pot, beer and sweat. He looked cocky as Puchalski ran him through the softball questions. "Please state your age."

"I'm eighteen. My birthday was two weeks ago." Mickey leaned back in his chair.

"What was the date?"

"November twenty-first."

"Where are your parents, Mickey?"

"Hawaii."

"Are you home alone?"

"Well, tonight I was. Usually, Sarah is there. She's our housekeeper. But she's cool. When I have a party, she always comes down and cleans up before my parents come home."

Puchalski kept it low-key as he shifted subjects. "Do your parents know about the parties?"

"Yeah, I think they do. But, you know, they're cool. They know kids just want to have fun."

"What happened tonight?" Puchalski's tone was conversational. He smiled as he took notes.

"Well, all these kids came over. I mean, I didn't invite them. They just kinda found out about it."

"Where did the beer come from, Mickey? You're all underage."

Mickey shrugged. "My dad always gets a couple of cases along with the hard stuff he drinks. It's delivered every couple of weeks. I don't think he even notices if a little beer is gone." He started drumming his fingers on the table and looked around. "Hey, I gotta take a leak."

Puchalski got up and turned off the camera. "It's down the hall." He went with the kid and waited for him, leaning against the wall, his arms folded. When the two of them came back to the interview room, Tom restarted the tape.

Mickey propped his right foot on his left knee and started playing with his shoelaces. "How much longer will I be here?"

Puchalski's answer was crisp. "Until we've got all the answers we want."

Mickey looked at Tom and smirked. "Aren't you going to ask me questions?"

"All in good time, Mr. Sandhurst." Tom crossed his arms and leaned back in his chair. *Throw the kid off balance a little.*

Puchalski reached down and pulled out a small bag of white powder. It bore a label depicting the three of diamonds. "We found this in your room. How about you tell us where it came from."

"I don't know. Hell, some kid must have brought it over."

"What kid?"

"I don't know. Jesus, you've got to know kids can buy heroin anywhere. I had a bunch of kids at my house."

"How did you know it was heroin?"

For the first time, he looked uneasy. "I just figured. I've seen it around."

"Like in the back of your closet?" Puchalski pulled out three similar bags. "What about these? They just suddenly appeared too?"

Mickey scowled. "Did you have a search warrant to go through my stuff?"

Tom leaned forward, elbows on the table. "Cut the crap. Where are you getting the drugs?"

"I don't know what you're talking about." He was tense now, his cocky smirk gone.

"Who's your supplier?"

"*I don't know!*" Sandhurst stood up suddenly, so fast his chair crashed to the floor behind him.

Both officers jumped to their feet and grabbed Mickey's arms. He tried to fight them off at first, but then went slack. Tom reached down and picked up the chair, and Puchalski pushed him back down in it.

"I've had enough of this," Mickey said. "I want to go home."

Tom leaned in and spoke, enunciating every word. "We're going to book you on possession. In addition, some of these so-called friends of yours are going to spill the beans, Mickey. We'll get to the bottom of it."

The kid leaned over the table, covered his face with his hands and mumbled something.

"What did you say?" Tom said.

Mickey raised his eyes. The smirk was gone. "I just pick it up at the post office. I don't know where it comes from. Okay?"

"The post office? It arrives through the mail?" Tom asked.

"No, someone texts me and puts it in a post office box." He mumbled looking down and rubbing his hands together between his knees. "Number 847."

Tom looked at Puchalski.

"Did you say post office box 847?" He was excited.

"Yeah." Mickey looked up, his eyes questioning.

"PP 847. He must have slipped up on the letters." Tom said.

Puchalski nodded. "Right. Lewis must have seen the pick-up!"

Mickey looked from one cop to the other and yawned. "Can I go home now?"

Chapter 54
Sunday Afternoon, December 3rd

Colman and Anya were on their way back from Jordanville prison. On the trip down, Colman had tried to start a conversation several times but Anya seemed too agitated to respond. Only when he asked her about her patients at the hospital did she begin to open up. Her voice grew animated as she told stories about the people she helped. He asked questions and she spoke of the difficulties cancer patients faced. How brave and hopeful they were. She also spoke of the doctors and nurses who gave exceptional care.

"I know you're a favorite there, Anya. Like, Mr. Penfield is one of your biggest fans."

"Oh yes, he is a wonderful, kind person. I like him so much. Now, we do not see him…and that is good."

By the time they reached Jordanville, they had become tentative friends. The visit passed quickly. Colman played chess with Royce for much of the time. They reminisced about Colman's childhood in Banner Bluff and about all the years he'd played baseball and hockey as a kid. This discussion segued into Colman's hair-raising experience the day before at the skating rink.

"After I knew Mr. Martin was all right, I looked back and saw Officer Czerny was down. He took a bullet. Luckily he was wearing a Kevlar vest. I didn't know that then. I thought he was a goner. I ran into the skating shack and called the direct line. Before I knew it the place was crawling with police and paramedics. Luckily, no one was hurt."

Royce looked at his son with pride and awe. "I'm so proud of you, Colman. That's the second time you've saved someone's life." Tentatively, he patted Colman on the back, a rare moment of physical contact. Then he threw his arm around his son and hugged him briefly. They looked at each other in wary surprise. Then Colman looked up and saw Anya and Alexei watching them. He quickly pulled away.

Now, on the way back, he and Anya lapsed into silence. The prison visit was always exhausting. Lulled by the radio turned low to a classical music station and the warmth of the car, Colman quickly fell asleep. Not until Anya brought the car to a stop outside a busy truck stop did Colman wake up. He had slept for an hour.

He rubbed his eyes and sat up, "Hey, I'm sorry. I couldn't stay awake. I'm not very good company, I guess."

"Do not worry, Colman. You work hard, I know. You need to sleep. I understand."

She looked pretty tired herself, he thought. "Are we stopping for gas? Remember, I want to pay."

"You may pump the gas. Then let's go inside for dinner."

Colman quickly got out of the car and walked in to pay cash. As he stood there pumping gas he looked at the other people bundled in heavy coats. Where were they all coming from on a cold Sunday night? Not from prison, he'd bet.

Inside, the truck stop was busy. They headed for the restaurant and were seated in a booth. After they sat down, Colman looked across the table at Anya, who was unwinding a grey-blue scarf from around her neck. She smiled at him and he smiled back. She was so beautiful in a simple unadorned way. He felt himself blushing and quickly looked down at his menu. He had never felt this way around her before.

"I always have the Reuben sandwich and sweet potato fries. When I leave that horrible place, I am starving. Every time, I stop here to eat," Anya said.

Colman kept staring at the menu. He didn't have enough money left for dinner after buying the gas. Maybe he could just get a bowl of soup. That seemed to be the cheapest thing on the menu. He looked up again. Anya was watching him. He could feel himself reacting to her. Jesus, she was a married woman. He had better get control of himself. "I'm not so hungry. I'll just have the chicken noodle soup," he said, shrugging out of his coat.

Anya looked surprised and then frowned. When the waitress came to their table, Anya ordered before he could say anything. "We will both have the Reuben sandwich with sweet potato fries and we would like two strawberry milkshakes with that." She handed the waitress her menu, grabbed Colman's and handed it over, patting his hand. "You are hungry too. I am going to buy you dinner. How do you say? It is my treat." She beamed with pleasure.

"Thank you, Anya." He grinned. "I'm starving!"

Outside the window by their booth, they could see several semis parked in the lot. Even through the glass, Colman heard the muffled throb of the motors in the cold air.

"I think being a truck driver would be a terrible profession. I hate driving on the highway each week. I would not like to do it every day," Anya said.

"You could listen to music or talk radio. No one would bother you."

"Yes, but I like people. I need to talk to somebody and feel needed. It would be so lonely."

Colman reached for his water glass and took a sip. "You probably are alone a lot though, aren't you? I mean, when you leave work?" He knew this was none of his business but he plunged ahead. "Do you have friends you hang out with, or family?"

She gazed across the restaurant. Colman admired her perfect profile with its small neat nose and full lips. Her straight blond hair was tucked behind a delicate shell-shaped ear. Her voice was low when she responded, "Yes, I am often lonely." She put her hand to her neck, a familiar gesture.

"I don't tell people about Alexei. I keep my life a secret. No one at the hospital really knows about me." She turned to face him. "You are my friend, now, right? You know about me."

"Well, I don't know much," Colman said.

Anya began to tell him about her childhood in Russia and her immigration to the States. She told him how she met Alexei and about the crime he committed. She told him about her move to Banner Bluff and the hardships she had experienced at first. During her narrative, the waitress brought their platters piled with food. Colman gobbled down his sandwich, listening to every word and prompting Anya with questions. She spoke between bites, eating neatly and patting her mouth with the napkin. When she had finished, she looked at Colman's empty plate and pushed hers over. "Do you want to finish my fries?"

"Sure," he said. "Food shouldn't go to waste." He poured some ketchup on the plate and proceeded to finish every last French fry on Anya's plate while she continued to pour out her life's story. He figured it must have been bottled up inside her for years.

When the waitress brought the check, Anya grabbed it and smiled. "My treat, remember?"

They continued to talk and laugh, sipping on their milkshakes until Anya looked down at her phone. "We better get going. It is late."

Back in the car, they continued to share their stories. Colman told Anya about his high school years and his dependence on drugs and alcohol. Even now, he didn't know how he had slipped into that pit of addiction. He told her how he stole money from Hero's Market and how Hero Papadopoulos had saved him and given him a purpose in life. "Even though I stole from him, he trusted me to come and work for him. At first I was angry with him and with the world. But now he's a friend and an advisor. And his granddaughter, Vicki, we're kind of like going together."

"Where are your mother and sister?" Anya asked.

"We're not in touch."

"Why?" Anya glanced over at him. The headlights from the oncoming cars lit up her face.

"My mom divorced my dad. She won't visit him or let my sister visit him. She can't forgive him for what he did, you know, stealing from so many people."

"And it isn't a problem for you?"

"Well, I know there are people in Banner Bluff who are probably still furious with my dad. They turn their backs on me when I meet them on the street. But I had to forgive my dad. He's not perfect and he made a giant mistake." He cleared his throat. "And I'm not perfect either, and I'm not that different from him." He went quiet then and looked out the window.

For a while they just listened to music. The interior of the small car felt to Colman like it was filled with their thoughts and shared secrets. As they approached Banner Bluff, Anya interrupted the silence. "I think I know who is trying to shoot, Mr. Martin."

"Oh my God, you do?" Colman sat up fast, pulling on the seatbelt so it locked tight.

"Yes, I'm sure I do."

"You have to tell the police. Martin Marshall is in great danger."

"I can't," she said, her voice shaking. "They will kill me. Or worse, they will go after Alexei. I cannot tell anyone."

Chapter 55
Sunday Evening, December 3rd

Francesca was invited for dinner at Hollyhock Farm. She'd called Carina on Saturday, thinking they would meet for coffee in the village somewhere, but Carina suggested dinner instead. Francesca hoped to have a private discussion with her concerning what she had learned from Frank. She would just have to pick her moment during the evening.

"Why don't you bring your man in blue?" Carina had said, teasing. When Francesca called Tom, he said he would have to meet her there. Right now, too much was going on to promise a leisurely evening, but he would show up for part of the dinner. Francesca relayed the message, and Carina said that would be fine.

When Francesca arrived at Hollyhock, there were a couple of cars in the parking area in front of the house. The home was aglow with Christmas lights, the porch roof and columns outlined with strings of blue, red and green. As she mounted the front steps, Francesca could see through the windows into the front room where a bright fire was burning and a tall Christmas tree stood, bright with fairy lights and sparkling balls. The scene reminded her of a Currier and Ives Christmas print.

She rang the bell and Carina swung open the door. Her perfectly cut red dress must have cost a fortune. It looked fabulous on Carina's tall, slim frame. Carina smiled and pulled Francesca into a warm hug. She smelled of some exotic scent and of alcohol, maybe gin? "How wonderful to see you, Francesca! Please come in," she said, a bit too loudly.

"Carina, you look fabulous. I love the dress."

"Here, let me take your coat." Carina hung it in the front hall closet and drew Francesca into the living room. A tall, unfamiliar man stood near the fireplace. Standing by the drinks cart was a couple she recognized from town. They were part of the horsey set. Francesca had seen the woman dressed in a velvet-collared riding jacket and jodhpurs shopping in town or striding across the village green. She was large and strongly built with a horse-like, homely face that was redeemed by a genuine smile that lit up her eyes. Tonight she wore a brown, tailored suit and low-heeled brown pumps.

Next to her was her husband, a perfect match: tall, large and homely. Like his wife, he radiated kindness and bonhomie.

"Francesca, let me introduce Harold and Hazel Landers," Carina said.

They've even got matching names, Francesca thought. "Harold Landers, wait a minute...are you Lorinda's nephew?"

"That I am. Why? What have you heard? Nothing bad, I hope." He laughed uproariously.

"Well, I recently admired a pretty sweater you gave her."

"I bet she said I only visited her so I could inherit her money." Still grinning, he raised his eyebrows in inquiry.

"Well..." Francesca felt herself blushing.

"Ah-ha!" Harold said, and turned to Hazel. "Aunt Lorinda is true to form." She responded with a low-pitched, barking laugh identical to her husband's.

"Aunt Lorinda is a card. Let me tell you, we don't need her money. But we do worry about her in that big house. Thank goodness for Sadie," Hazel said.

"Yes, isn't she a gem? I think the two of them are really great friends," Francesca said.

She turned to the man standing by the fireplace. He was holding a martini but put it down to come forward and introduce himself. "I'm Harrison Rand," he said, one hand outstretched. "I'm an acquaintance of the Meriwethers'."

308

"Francesca Antonelli." She shook hands. He held on when she tried to pull away.

"Are you the famous editor of the *Banner Bee*?"

"Famous, no, editor of the *Bee*, yes!" She gently slid her hand from his and turned to Carina.

"Francesca, what would you like to drink? The Landers are having sherry and Harrison made a pitcher of fabulous martinis. Would you like one?"

"I'll bet they're fabulous but I'll stick with the sherry."

Carina poured her a small glass of Manzanilla sherry and picked up her own martini. "Please, sit down."

"How's your mother? Will she be down for dinner?" Francesca asked.

"She's in the kitchen, checking on things. We have a new cook. Somebody you know," Carina said. "Yahaira Gonzales agreed to work here full-time."

"How wonderful! I know she's a good cook. Has she left Hero's Market and Appleby's?"

"Yes," Carina said. "Weekdays she's here from eight to four, so she can get home to her boys after school. She makes dinner before she leaves and we just heat it up. Tonight is an exception since we're having a party."

The Landers were seated in matching chevron-patterned armchairs, striped in red, pink and green. Carina and Harrison sat on the rose-colored sofa, only inches apart. Francesca took a seat on a matching striped loveseat. "What a pretty room," she said. "I don't remember being in here before."

"We've had this part of the house closed off for the last two years. It was too expensive to heat in the winter, but..." Carina glanced up and stopped talking in mid-sentence. Daphne Meriwether stood in the doorway, looking around the room.

"Mother, there you are." Carina rose, as did Harrison. "Come sit down."

309

Daphne ignored them. She turned towards Francesca, who stood up as well and went forward to greet her. They hugged each other warmly. "How wonderful to see you, my dear," Daphne said. She turned to the group. "Here's my adopted daughter." She took Francesca's arm and they went to sit together on the loveseat.

"Mother, would you like a martini? Harrison made them."

"Heavens, no. I'll have a glass of sherry," Daphne said with barely veiled distaste.

A moment of silence ensued as Carina poured the sherry. She turned and asked Francesca about her plans for Christmas. Would she be going home to California?

"No I was there for Thanksgiving. I'm going to stay here. There's always a lot going on at this time of year that I need to report on. It's hard to cover stories from San Diego."

"That almost makes you a prisoner in Banner Bluff," Mr. Rand said.

"Not at all. I love it here. Home is where the heart is and all that." Francesca smiled at him. "How about you? Where is home?"

"I'm from downstate Illinois, from a dumpy, little town…and I am oh so happy to have escaped it. The people there are hicks. I've pulled myself up by the bootstraps and now I'm a lawyer. A successful one, too."

Silence fell again. Francesca wasn't certain how to respond to this, and apparently neither did anyone else.

"Well, good for you," Carina said finally. "I'm sure you've had to work really hard."

"With very little scruples, I bet," Daphne said, so low that only Francesca could hear.

"Do you have any plans to go away, Hazel?" Carina asked.

"Not for Christmas. We love all the goings-on in Banner Bluff. We'll be here until mid-January. Then Harold and I are off to Florida. We've got some horses down there and Harold likes to play polo with his buddies."

"Where do you go in Florida?" Mr. Rand asked.

Francesca turned to look at him. He was lounging against the back of the sofa, his arm stretched behind Carina like he was châtelain of the castle. A handsome guy with a powerful sense of self-worth. A little too powerful. No wonder Daphne didn't like him.

"Vero Beach," Harold said. "We've got a pied-à-terre that's just perfect for the winter months. Hazel can get down to Palm Beach and visit her friends while I ride."

"Mother and I are planning a trip to Morocco in February," Carina said. "I booked it yesterday. We're going to visit Marrakech, Casablanca and Fez, and even take a camel trip into the Sahara."

"How exciting! Considering I don't even know how to ride a horse, I don't know how I would fare on top of a camel," Francesca said.

"I've heard some people get motion sickness from the movement of the camel. It's like riding the waves in a boat," Carina said.

Yahaira came into the room. "Dinner is served," she said.

"Thank you, Yari." Carina stood and the others followed suit. They went down the hall to the dining room. The table was set with festive Mexican placemats and colorful pottery. On the sideboard was a selection of Mexican-inspired dishes: chicken enchiladas, chiles rellenos, *tampiquena* steak, black beans and rice, and freshly made tortillas.

"Please take a plate and help yourself," Carina said.

"My oh my, this looks wonderful." Hazel turned to Yari, who lingered nervously by the sideboard. "You have created a masterpiece."

Yari beamed as the guests helped themselves. There were bottles of beer in a bucket and bottles of wine on the table. Carina had carried in the dregs of her martini, which she downed before sitting. Francesca didn't remember Carina drinking much of anything in the past.

As they served up and got settled, the doorbell rang. "That must be Tom," Francesca said.

Yari went to answer the door, and returned after a moment with Tom in her wake. He looked worn out, Francesca noticed. She felt a pang of guilt for having roped him into coming, but his smile when he saw her held its usual warmth. He served himself and sat down in an empty seat next to her. Conversation flowed around the table, a discussion of dressage rules—something the Landers and the Meriwethers knew well and better known in general since Mitt Romney ran for president.

Francesca listened as she ate, not paying full attention until Hazel Landers turned to Tom and asked how his investigation was coming. He'd barely answered the standard *I'm not at liberty to discuss it*, when Harold joined in and it became a tag-team interrogation. Tom handled it well, though Francesca could tell he was getting irritated. The Banner Bluff police had been working flat out for a month without getting anywhere. By now, the Village Council must be breathing down Tom's neck.

Poor Tom. Before she could bail him out, he turned the conversation to Harrison Rand and what he did for a living. Rand looked less than happy to be questioned. "I'm involved in the legal ramifications of bills before the legislature," he said after a moment. Then he recovered himself and winked at Francesca. "I won't bore you with all the minutiae I deal with day in and day out."

"But you work with the governor, don't you?" Carina said.

"Not always." He looked irritated again. "Just like the Chief here doesn't want to talk about his unsuccessful investigation, I don't want to talk about the ins and outs of my job." He stood abruptly and headed back to the buffet. The subject was officially dropped.

Chapter 56
Sunday Evening, December 3rd

After a delicious tangerine flan, crispy biscochitos and coffee, they returned to the living room. The fire was warm and everyone was comfortably satiated. Tom and Francesca shared the love seat, their hands joined loosely.

"I've been so involved with the murder investigations that I haven't been following the construction on your property," Tom said to Carina. "The sign on the street says it's a State of Illinois project and 'keep out'. What's going on that it's so hush-hush?"

Carina looked like a deer caught in the headlights. She eyed Harrison and then her mother. After a moment, she cleared her throat. "It's—"

Tom's beeper went off. He excused himself and left the room. Carina looked relieved. Francesca wondered what she'd been about to say, considering what Frank Penfield had learned in his research concerning Hollyhock farm and the lack of a ruling on eminent domain.

Tom stepped briefly back into the room and said he had to go. Just routine police business, Francesca judged from his face. He thanked the Meriwethers for dinner, made his apologies and left.

Twenty minutes later, the Landers left, followed by Harrison Rand. Francesca heard the door shut on the Landers' booming voices. Out in the hall, Carina and Harrison lingered in quiet conversation. Francesca tried not to listen, and turned to Daphne to discuss the upcoming St. Nicholas night in Banner Bluff. "I love that evening," she said. "That's when I get most of my Christmas shopping done. I love all the special gifts I find in town. And the music…it's magical."

The front door shut with a bang. A sudden silence fell in the house. Then Francesca heard the click-click of Carina's high heels as she came across the hall.

Carina smiled brightly at her mother and Francesca. Her lipstick was smeared and she was wobbling slightly. She put her hand on the door frame for balance and kicked off her shoes, then crossed to the sofa and collapsed. "Ouf! I'm exhausted." She curled up in the corner and lolled her head against the cushions. "I've been fussing with this party all day."

"You did an excellent job," Francesca said. "Everyone had a wonderful time and Yari's dinner was fabulous."

"Yes, dear," Daphne said. "Your dinner party was a great success." She smiled at her daughter and stood up. The tension Francesca had sensed between them earlier was gone. They seemed to have reached a truce now that Harrison Rand was out of the house. "I'm going up to bed. Tomorrow, I want to work with the Johansson's' filly."

"Are you sure you're up to it, Mom?"

"Yes. I'm ready to get back in the saddle, as they say." Daphne's smile deepened as she glanced Francesca's way. "It's always lovely to see you, Francesca. Come again soon."

Francesca got up and gave Daphne a hug. When her mother was gone, Carina went over to the drinks cart. She took a bottle of champagne from an insulated wine bucket and removed the silver paper around the cork. "Join me in a glass, Francesca. I forgot about this earlier."

"I don't really need anything else to drink." Francesca said. "Let's just sit and talk for a while."

"Come on, I want to celebrate my new life. I want *you* to celebrate with *me*." She started crooning, her voice slurred and boozy: "'Pack up all my cares and woe, here I go/Singing low, Bye-bye blackbird.'" She turned the cork with one hand and then let it pop. The cork sailed across the room and into the fireplace.

"Wah hoo!" Carina giggled. "Bull's eye." She took two flutes and filled each to the rim, spilling some on her hand. She handed Francesca a flute and then licked the back of her hand. "Can't waste a drop." She stood with her legs apart, tears in her eyes. "Let's drink to no more cares and woes." She drank down half of her glass of champagne.

Was this a celebration or a breakdown? What was bothering Carina? Was it her relationship with Rand? Francesca patted the seat next to her. "Sit down, Carina. Tell me what's going on."

"What's going on is we are out of the hole. We're into the money; Hollyhock is saved." She did a little dance and spilled champagne on the carpet.

"We need to talk about this." Francesca took a small sip of her own champagne while she figured out how to start. "Frank Penfield's been doing a little research."

"Research? What in the world for?"

"Because I asked him to. Actually, you asked me to look into it, remember?" Francesca put down her glass. "Carina, there is no court order for taking that stretch of land on Hollyhock Farm, no record anywhere. When eminent domain is invoked, there has to be a court judgment to prove the land is necessary for the public good. There's nothing."

"I saw the papers. I signed the papers and the governor's name was there. I don't know what you're talking about." Carina sat down on a footstool, hugging her knees.

"Not only that, but Frank contacted the Illinois Department of Natural Resources and—"

"*And*, Miss Busybody…" Carina said, her voice dripping with sarcasm.

"And no one knows anything about a water pipeline going to the western suburbs. This whole thing is very fishy."

"Francesca, it's a government project. The governor signed the papers. There must be some reason it's hush-hush."

Francesca shook her head. "There's a Canadian-American agreement in place. Water can't be siphoned out of Lake Michigan, or any other of the Great Lakes. So where is this water really going, if it's not going to the western suburbs?"

"I don't know." Carina got up and walked over to the fireplace. She stood facing the fire, rubbing her arms. "Why don't you mind your own business?"

Francesca closed her eyes and leaned back against the sofa cushions. "Because I think the Pharaoh is up to something. I think you're a pawn in some devious scheme."

There was a long moment of silence. Finally, Carina said, "But what about the money? We *need* the money."

She spoke so quietly, Francesca could barely hear her. Then Carina turned around and faced Francesca. Her face was flushed from the heat. "I will not give up the money that is saving the farm. Maybe I've made a deal with the devil and I'm going to hell, but I'll live with it."

Chapter 57
Monday, December 4th

Francesca pulled on her winter running gear. She'd decided to leave the dogs at home and do a long loop through town and down to the beach. There was so much going on in her world. She needed to think creatively. Running would help. When she was moving, she could organize her thoughts.

She placed her water bottle in her fanny pack along with a couple of tissues. Just as she was putting her phone in, it began to ring. It was Colman.

"Hey, are you going running?" He sounded out of breath.

"Hey, Colman. Yeah, I'm just taking off. How are you?"

"Could I run with you?"

"Sure." She didn't really want company, but he always pulled at her heart-strings.

"Where are you headed?" he asked.

"I'm doing a big loop: Eastern, Lakeview, down to the lake and back up, then over to Ridgeway."

"Okay, I'll be coming down on Elm. I'll meet you at the beach and we can run back up together." He hung up without waiting for an answer.

Outside the wind careened through the trees and the air sparkled crystalline. Initially, the cold penetrated Francesca's clothes and skin, and zeroed in on her bones. But after twenty minutes she felt warm and strong and powerful. The adrenaline was kicking in and she felt as though she could run forever.

What to do about the Pharaoh and Carina? Where had that money come from, and where was the precious Lake Michigan water going? She remembered her conversation with Governor Crenshaw when they'd had dinner in Chicago. He said Lake

Michigan water did not belong to Illinois or to the other states surrounding the Great Lakes, but to the entire United States. Was he willing to break a federal law? Why would he tempt fate? His career would be over if all this came out in the press.

Hmm, she *was* the press and this would be a scoop. But she was hesitant to make the story public. She felt...what? Afraid? Yes, afraid. She wasn't yet ready to confront him. She needed to know more. She needed to talk to Connie and get her opinion.

At the lake she looked over at the vacant mansion that clung precariously to the bluff. *No Trespassing* signs were displayed on each side of the driveway. The ownership of the property was in litigation, so the massive stone house stood empty.

Colman was there, jogging in place at the top of the service road that led down to the beach. His cheeks were bright red from the cold. He wore only shorts and a sleeveless sweatshirt. There were dark circles under his eyes and he looked worried. He nodded at her and they started down the road to the beach.

"Thanks for meeting up with me. I don't have much time 'cause I should be at work soon."

"What's up, Colman...something with your dad?" She knew he'd been planning to visit his dad on Sunday.

"No, it's Anya. You know, Anya Kozerski?"

"Right. From the hospital. I know her." The mention of Anya's name brought to mind the uncomfortable conversation they'd had at Jordanville prison.

"Well, she drove me down to Jordanville yesterday. My car isn't so reliable right now."

"That was nice of her." Where this was going, Francesca wondered.

At the bottom of the incline the road widened into a broad parking area. A wall of piled rough-hewn stones formed a breakwater against the lake. Angry waves dashed themselves against the stones and spray climbed five feet into the air. They stepped back from the violence of the crashing waves. Francesca turned to look at Colman. The wind blew his hair around his face, which had gone pale.

"Francesca. Anya knows who's trying to kill Mr. Marshall. She knows, but she won't tell. You've got to help."

Monday Morning   December 4th 20__
The Cimarron Missive
A Blog Serving Cimarron, Texas and Beaver Counties, Oklahoma

A local informer reports that construction is moving along on the fortified castle being built twenty miles outside of town. "It's unbelievable! It will be like one of those castles in Europe with stone walls, turrets, and a moat," we're told. At this point, they've started massive excavations. "It will be a fortified city like Carcassonne in France." The construction workers are being housed out near the site. They haven't been into town and have had no interaction with the locals. Who bought and owns this land continues to be a mystery. Our informant tells us, "They're spending a fortune bringing in all the materials, workers and living supplies. They've even got tank trucks delivering water to the crew." Which brings up an important point: where's the water going to come from to fill the moat? Cimarron County is a desert. Looks like they'll need to do a Chickasaw water dance.

Chapter 58
Monday Morning, December 4th

Martin lay in bed. The blinds were drawn and he was curled up in a fetal position deep under the covers. He kept his eyes closed. He felt safer that way.

"Martin, are you coming down? I've got to leave for school!"

He didn't respond to Kate's call. He didn't want to leave this cocoon and face the day. He knew he should get up, but his alternate-self held him prisoner in bed. He was finding it harder to think rationally. He hated himself for letting fear rule his psyche.

He heard Kate's light tread as she came up the stairs. When she entered the room, she switched on the bedside light. He felt the bed dip as she sat down beside him. Her voice was warm...not like it had been these last few months. "Darling, I know how you're feeling. Or maybe I don't really understand." She faltered. "But you need to fight this depression or fear or whatever blackness has descended upon you. It's like a vortex and it will swirl you down into oblivion." She caressed his shoulder. "The kids need you, Martin. I need you."

He made no response. He wanted to, but he couldn't. His body stayed inert and his brain managed to tune her out.

"Okay, Martin. Okay." She sighed. "Just for today stay up here." He heard resignation in her voice. She left and shut the door.

When she had gone back downstairs, he got up. He felt dizzy and sat back down. Then he slowly stood up again. At the foot of the bed was an antique hope chest. He got down on all fours and began to slide the heavy chest towards the door. Leaning back against the bedstead and using his feet, he pushed the chest flush against the door jamb. Now no one could get in. Sweat covered his brow. He went back to bed, turned off the light and took refuge under the covers.

Downstairs in the kitchen, Stevie was in his highchair. Cheerios and pieces of banana were smooshed on his face and on the plastic tray. He was giggling at Rosie, who was hiding around the corner in the pantry. She popped out, holding a thick wooden spoon pointed at Stevie.

"Bang, bang!" she shouted, and went back inside the pantry. Stevie squealed with delight. Then she peered around the corner and pointed her spoon at him again. "Bang, bang!"

Kate flew across the room and grabbed the spoon out of Rosie's hands. "What in the world are you doing?" Her voice throbbed with anger. "Rose Marie Marshall, don't you ever shoot at your brother again."

Rosie gaped at her in shock. "Mommy, it's not a real gun. It's pretend."

She took a deep, calming breath. "I know, Rosie. I know. But shooting is dangerous."

"We were just playing," Rosie was scowling, her chubby hands in tight fists.

"I know, dear heart, I know." Kate put the spoon on top of the refrigerator.

"Anyway they shot at Daddy and he didn't get hurt," Rosie grumbled.

Kate slumped into a kitchen chair and rested her head in her hands. "Oh, my God. What's happening to us?"

Chapter 59
Early Monday Afternoon, December 4th

Francesca was writing an article on the virulent flu epidemic that was on the horizon. According to Dr. Reynolds, this year's strain was likely to be one of the worst. The gist of her article was to encourage senior citizens, expectant mothers and tiny tots to get their flu shots pronto. It seemed to her that every year the flu season got longer and more people succumbed to the disease. As she was wrapping up her piece, the desk phone rang. She picked up.

"Hi, Francesca. It's Julie...Julie Robinson."

Delighted and surprised, Francesca leaned back in her chair. "Julie! How are you?"

Julie was in Elmhurst, she said, living with her aunt and working at a local branch of the Modern Method. Then she said, "So, I'm calling because I woke up in the middle of the night and thought of something about Carrie."

Francesca sat up straight. "You did? What?"

"Remember how you said the police didn't find any incriminating pictures on her phone?"

"Yes, that's right."

"I just remembered about the spy pen."

"Spy pen?" Francesca grabbed a pencil.

"Carrie found it online. See, people at work didn't want her taking pictures without warning. But she said she wanted more natural poses... she wanted to catch them unawares. So she found this pen that was really a camera."

"What did it look like?"

"It was black, like a regular pen, but fatter."

"Where did she keep it?"

"Sometimes in her purse, or when she worked the desk, she would carry it around like a regular pen."

"This could be a big deal. I'll call Chief Barnett and they can check out her purse and the apartment again."

As soon as they'd said good-bye, Francesca called Tom. Her news intrigued him, but he was too tied up at the moment to go to Carrie's place. "We had another drug overdose Saturday night, and I'm still dealing with that. Could you go over to the apartment and check it out? We're swamped here. I can only spare one officer to go with you. They'll meet you at the apartment."

"Okay. I'll head over there right now."

Harrison Rand and Ramses Crenshaw were closeted in the governor's office at the Thompson Center in Chicago. Crenshaw had told his secretary to hold all phone calls. Harrison was perched on the edge of his chair, jiggling his foot. Crenshaw paced the floor, his voice raised in anger. Harrison felt like a recalcitrant school boy brought before the principal.

"You *don't know* who's been making inquiries? *This* is what I'm paying you for?"

"It's someone in Banner Bluff. A man, I'm told."

The governor turned to look at him. "How did your informant know that much?"

"The guy showed ID. The clerk remembered his license said Banner Bluff because they started talking about what a nice town it is…blah, blah, blah. But she didn't remember the name."

"Banner Bluff. I'm wondering if it isn't Newhouse or his campaign manager. That old hag is a real busybody. She's been around the block too many times to count."

"Connie Munster?"

"Yeah. She might have sent someone to check on us. Maybe Bielski and Stroik could get into Newhouse's campaign office and check around on the computer."

"I was in Banner Bluff last night, sir." As soon as he said it, he wondered if he should have. He'd prefer the governor didn't know about his relationship with Carina Meriwether.

"You were?" Crenshaw stopped pacing and spun around to face him.

Harrison nodded. He'd have to be careful. "The Meriwethers invited me for dinner to thank me for my help. I couldn't refuse."

The governor chuckled. "As though you had anything to do with it." His voice hardened. "You didn't say anything, right?"

"Of course not." Harrison shrugged. "There was a lot of horse talk. Oh, and that Antonelli woman was there. She's eye candy and sharp." He didn't mention the police chief. That would have made the governor anxious.

"Francesca Antonelli." Crenshaw pursed his lips. "She's a looker, all right…and maybe too smart for her own good." The governor went to the window and looked out at the bustling city. "You need to delve into this some more. Go back and talk to the Meriwether woman, the daughter. Use your charm. See if she's talked to anybody." He rubbed his chin. "And get into Newhouse's office. I want a report by Wednesday."

When Francesca arrived at the Landwehr mansion, a police car was parked at the head of the driveway in front of the garage. She drove up and parked next to it. As she got out, the occupant of the police car flung open the driver's side door. Francesca spotted a mop of red curls and a smiling face as a petite woman in police uniform climbed out of the vehicle.

"Hi, you must be Francesca. I'm so glad to meet you." The woman came around Francesca's car and stuck out her hand, blue eyes sparkling. Francesca guessed who she was and wanted to dislike her, but those feelings quickly ebbed under the onslaught of friendliness.

"Yes, and you must be Cindy Murray. I've heard about you."

Cindy laughed. "Probably that I'm a pain in the butt! I think half the guys on the task force wish I'd crawl back under a rock."

Francesca couldn't help grinning. "It must be hard working with all those macho he-men."

"Macho he-men…we're talking cavemen." She winked. "The Chief's all right though. He's a gentleman, through and through."

Francesca smiled. "Let's go up and see what we can find. This is really your job but I'll keep my eyes sharp."

"I've got the key." Cindy started up the rickety staircase along the side of the garage. Francesca followed her up. At the top Cindy removed the yellow tape and unlocked the door. When they stepped inside, they halted in shock. The front room looked as though a cyclone had blown through.

"This place is a disaster," Cindy said. "Did the evidence techs do this?"

"No. I was in here with Tom after the tech team got done. It didn't look anything like this."

Cindy surveyed the mess. "Well, somebody was in here looking for something."

"Where shall we start?" Francesca asked.

"How about the bedroom?"

Sweaters and pants were strewn on the bedroom floor. They went carefully through every piece of clothing, searching pockets. They upended the bed so they could look between the mattresses and underneath. Francesca went through the chest of drawers while Cindy checked out the closet, tapping on the walls in search of a secret hiding place for a small object. They found nothing.

Then they went into the bathroom. The white lacquered table Francesca recalled from her first visit there, with make-up and jewelry on it, had been smashed and the jewelry scattered around. Poking out from behind one of the bathtub's claw feet was a large black pen.

"Voilà," Francesca said as she picked it up. She remembered the pen now, hanging incongruously among the earrings and necklaces on the little jewelry tree. "Carrie hid this in full view."

The visitor sat facing Petroff in the Captain's office. He was posing as a parts salesman, but the Captain could see the bulge of the man's pistol under his black leather jacket.

"The Hook says you must clean up your business. You caught this woman on tape. She's calling and asking questions. We don't know what she knows. It's time to act. He is not worried about another body. You pick her up tonight and get her off the street."

"What about the delivery?" Petroff said.

"The cars have arrived. You will extract the packages as usual and make the deliveries tomorrow. Collect the money. I'll be here tomorrow afternoon.

The visitor spoke with authority. Petroff knew not to question the emissary.

Chapter 60
Monday Night, December 4th

At 6:30 PM, Francesca was sitting alone in the back room of Churchill's Café. Colman had gone to pick up Anya at the hospital. During the drive back from Jordanville on Sunday he had offered to make Anya his fabulous meatball sandwich and she had agreed to come over tonight on the condition that Colman come get her in his car. Apparently, she feared her own car might be followed.

Anya must really be afraid, Francesca thought. She was seated on a chintz loveseat decorated with pink and red cabbage roses. The back room also held a matching armchair, and the desk chair sported a lace trimmed pillow. The shades on the porcelain lamps were trimmed with fringes of glass beads. In contrast to this cozy Victorian-style furniture was the stainless steel desk, computers, copy machine and file cabinets…all very business-like.

This room was Marion Churchill's domain. Her husband ran the restaurant and she did the books. Colman had assured Francesca that the Churchills never came back in the evening. Francesca felt uncomfortable being there, but she had agreed to talk to Anya at Colman's request.

She unwrapped the raspberry pink scarf from around her neck and laid it next to her coat. Colman and Anya should be here any minute. She looked down at her brand-new leather boots, black Rose Petals Portland boots with a 3 ½-inch heel. She didn't need the extra height but she'd fallen in love with the boots on sight.

Headlights swung into view behind the restaurant. Doors slammed and Francesca heard voices, then the ding of the key pad at the back door. She got up as Colman came around the corner into the office. Anya was in his shadow, still in her light blue work scrubs. When she stepped forward, she saw Francesca. "Why are you here?" Then it dawned on her. She turned with flashing eyes to Colman.

"You are playing a trick on me, Colman. That is not nice."

Colman looked at Francesca, mutely beseeching her help.

Francesca stepped toward her. "We did trick you, Anya. And it *isn't* very nice. But we need your help."

Anya looked around the room as though looking for an escape.

"This is a life-and-death situation. You know what I'm talking about, don't you?" Francesca continued.

Anya's face crumpled and her eyes filled with tears. She clutched Francesca's arm with both hands as though grabbing a lifeline. "You do not understand. I cannot do anything that would hurt Alexei. He is not safe in prison and I am not safe in Banner Bluff."

Francesca drew her over to the loveseat and they sat down. Anya perched on the edge, her elbows on her knees and her hands covering her face. Francesca reached out tentatively and patted her shoulder. Anya didn't pull away. It struck Francesca that Anya probably received very few hugs. She had no family around, no husband to share her life. She must be very lonely. Francesca reached over and put her arm around Anya's trembling shoulders.

Colman stood there, looking uncertain. "Hey, I'll make us all a sandwich. Okay?" He went down the hall toward the restaurant.

Timidly, Anya glanced up, wiping her eyes with her palms. She was still leaning into Francesca.

"I'm sure you're scared to death," Francesca said. "You've been carrying this information around for a long time with no one to talk to. You've got to trust me and Colman." She continued as Anya turned to look at her. "We won't do anything that would harm you or Alexei. But we need to find a way to stop these men who are terrorizing Martin Marshall."

"You cannot stop them…it is the whole family…they are very powerful." Anya's voice rose. "You are innocents, you and Colman. With them, it is playing to the death. They are wild…wild like wolves…cunning and sly."

"Then we must be even more cunning; beat them at their own game; hunt them down."

Anya shook her head and pulled away from Francesca.

Colman called from the front room. "Come on, dinner's ready."

They went into the restaurant and found him standing at the counter with three plates before him. He'd drawn the blinds across the front windows so no one could look in. When asked what they wanted to drink, Anya requested water while Francesca opted for a Diet Coke. She needed the caffeine. She had a feeling this was going to be a long night.

Colman carried all three plates to a table, balancing one on his outstretched arm. He had made three meatball sandwiches on French bread, covered with marinara sauce and melted mozzarella. They had coleslaw and chips as well. It was a veritable feast.

For a while, they tried talking about Anya's work at the hospital, Colman's exams coming up and the St. Nicholas festival on December sixth.

But none of this conversation prevented them from thinking about Anya's predicament. When they'd eaten every last bite of their supper, Francesca leaned forward in her chair, her elbows on the table. "Anya, what are you going to do?"

Anya swallowed hard, not looking up.

Francesca prodded her. "Do we know these people?"

Anya shook her head. "Probably not."

Then Francesca took a chance. "Is one of them Petroff, the man they call the Captain?"

330

Color drained from Anya's face.

"And what about the Hook?" Francesca asked.

She still made no answer, but terror filled her eyes.

Detective Ron Puchalski sat in the used-car portion of Zimmerman's lot and kept an eye on the service entrance. The Chief had apprised him of Francesca's misadventure at Zimmerman's Mercedes on Thursday, and though neither man was convinced that Francesca had seen a drug transfer, the Captain and his henchman were definitely up to something.

Earlier in the day, new cars had arrived on a car carrier. At the end of the work day, several vehicles were brought into the service bays. The service department closed at eight o'clock and everyone went home. Puchalski saw Petroff taking off with a tall mechanic, in a car with dealer's plates. He figured the mechanic must be the same guy Francesca had seen the previous Thursday. At nine PM the dealership closed down and the building went dark.

Puchalski decided to stick around and see what transpired. Ten o'clock went by and then eleven. He was dozing at midnight when a sound woke him. Two men walked past his car carrying flashlights. One was tall, the other short and stocky. He was pretty sure it was Petroff and the mechanic. Petroff was yelling at the other guy, but Puchalski couldn't understand a word. It must have been Russian. They were heading towards the service door.

Once they went inside the building, Puchalski left his vehicle and moved quietly over to the windows along the service garage. He couldn't see much in the dark interior. The bobbing flashlight beams showed him glimpses of Petroff carrying a large duffle bag. The other guy had a purse and a pink scarf over his shoulder. The scarf stood out against his dark blue padded jumpsuit. Puchalski remembered the scrap of material Officer Ramirez had found in the woods, dark blue, from a workman's coverall. Everything was coming together.

331

Just as Francesca had described, the two men went to work on the new cars. They were definitely removing something. From what little he could see in the occasional glow of the flashlights, it looked as though they were searching under the seats and inside the doors. Whatever they removed, they placed in the duffel bag. *Why not the purse too*, Puchalski wondered. The mechanic had tossed it and the scarf on the floor before getting down to business.

After they'd gone over all the new cars, Petroff zipped up the duffel bag. He motioned to the mechanic, who picked up the purse and scarf and gave them to him. Puchalski watched Petroff stuff the scarf in the purse and walk briskly to his office, followed by the mechanic. He opened the door and went over to a file cabinet, shoved the duffel bag in the bottom drawer, and threw the purse into the top drawer. He locked the cabinet, then double-locked his office door. As Petroff and the mechanic headed back toward the service entrance, the Captain continued to gesture and yell at his flunky. Puchalski slipped around the corner and waited out of sight until the men drove away.

Chapter 61
Tuesday Morning, December 5th

Dark, cold, pain...where was she? Francesca opened her eyes a crack and then closed them. Her surroundings were grey and dim. Her head ached and she felt woozy. Her mouth was bound. A piece of tape. Duct tape. She could smell it.

Panic struck her. What if she choked? What if her nose clogged up? How would she breathe? She had to calm down. She made herself breathe through her nose, slowly and regularly.

How long had she been here? The last thing she remembered was stepping out of Churchill's restaurant and heading down the darkened street to her car. She whimpered, but the duct tape muffled the sound.

She tried to move her arms and discovered they were pinned behind her. Her wrists were held fast with more duct tape. She wiggled her fingers and felt the smooth, hard surface she was lying on. Maybe tile? Again, she opened her eyes. Above her a neat square formed where the ceiling and walls met. The room wasn't large, maybe eight by eight feet. For several moments she contemplated the neat square above her.

She tried to move, but it was hard without her hands for leverage. Her feet weren't bound, and she was still wearing her stiletto boots. She tapped her foot. The sound reverberated off the hard walls and floor.

She swiveled on her back, towards the corner of the room. Struggling to gain purchase, she snaked her back up the wall, leaning in at the corner and pushing with her fingers until she achieved a sitting position. She closed her eyes again and let a wave of nausea pass. Then she looked up at the room's source of light. Bright sunshine filtered through the dirty glass of a high transom window. It could be late morning or early afternoon.

She looked around her prison. The walls were unfinished, the floor tiled just as she'd guessed. Except for a water pipe running vertically up the wall opposite her, the room was empty.

She must have been here all night. Someone had grabbed her, conked her out and thrown her into this room. Probably drugged her, which would explain her woozy head and nausea. They had taken her coat and purse. She wore only her heavy beige sweater and jeans, plus her boots. Who had abducted her, and why? Another bout of nausea pushed up her throat. She swallowed hard to keep it down, feeling close to panic.

A faint, rhythmic sound caught her ear. She slowed her breathing to listen. She knew that sound—waves crashing against a breakwater. She'd heard it only yesterday when she met Colman down at the beach. Lake Michigan must be right nearby.

Her mouth felt lined with sandpaper. Fear rose again, threatening to choke her. She had to get out of here before they came back, but how? There was nothing in here she could use to free herself. Nothing but cold floor tile and that pipe across the room.

She eyed the pipe and noticed it was attached to the wall with clamps. Screws and nuts held them fast. A screw protruded through each clamp. Would it be sharp enough to cut through the tape on her wrists?

Francesca slipped to her knees and inched across the floor, holding her body rigid so she wouldn't fall forward. It would be difficult to get back up if that happened. When she reached the opposite side of the small room, she turned and used the wall to snake her way to her feet. The middle pipe fitting was just about at wrist level. She stepped in front of the clamp and began to move her arms up and down against the protruding screw. She felt the tape catch. The screw scratched its surface, and also the tender pads below her thumbs. After a while she felt blood seeping into the cuffs of her sweater. She kept going, ignoring the pain and the tedium. She wouldn't stop until her hands were free.

Chapter 62
Tuesday Morning, December 5th

"So you didn't see what they put in the duffel bags?" Tom asked.

Puchalski shook his head. "No, it was way too dark."

"Talk to Francesca and compare notes." Tom frowned. "I've tried to call her several times, but she hasn't picked up. This isn't like her." He felt uneasy, though he couldn't put his finger on why. Francesca was fine; she was probably just busy.

"Chief, if we're right, last night a new shipment of heroin arrived. Mickey Sandhurst told us he picked up his supply at the post office box on Tuesday and Thursday nights and left a cash payment. Those are the days following the arrival of new vehicles at Zimmerman's."

"Right. I've had the post office under surveillance since Sunday morning but there's been no action. If we're right, they'll deliver the goods sometime today. I'll put another man inside the post office this morning."

Someone knocked on the office door. "Come in," Tom called.

Ramirez stepped into the office with a file folder in his hands. "I posted these in the Landwehr file online but I thought you'd like to see a hard copy." He laid the folder on the conference table in front of Tom. Tom opened the file and studied the series of pictures that Carrie Landwehr had taken with her spy pen. They were close- ups of an evening drug transfer in the auto dealership's service bays: small plastic bags filled with white powder being extracted from new cars, snapshots of the Captain's file cabinet. More pictures showed a man carrying a smallish white box into the post office.

"This confirms what Puchalski saw last night," Tom said, looking up at Ramirez.

Puchalski tapped the photo of the courier. "Once we nab this guy, we can blow this case apart."

"Right," Tom said. He stared at the pictures, thinking of Francesca and what she'd seen at the dealership Thursday night. Where could she be?

Chapter 63
Tuesday Afternoon, December 5th

Time crept by. Francesca wobbled in her high-heeled boots. Her feet were cramping. Periodically she stopped and slid down the wall, crouching on the floor to rest. Then she wriggled back up. Her thighs were throbbing and shivers racked her body.

At last one hand came free. She stepped away from the wall and pulled at the tape, removing it from one wrist and then the other. Her wrists were raw and bloody where she'd scraped them. Steadying herself, she reached up and yanked at the tape across her mouth. It hurt like blazes but the tape came free, along with strands of hair. She took big mouthfuls of air and rubbed at the sore skin around her lips. Tears of relief filled her eyes.

How much time had gone by? Outside, the light was fading. Dark would fall soon. She had to get out of here.

Francesca went to the door and twisted the knob. The door wouldn't budge. It was locked from the outside. She looked around the barren room. They had taken her purse, so she couldn't use a credit card or a nail file to get out. What could she do? She studied the door again. The hinges were on this side. Could she remove the pins? She needed a screwdriver and a hammer for that, though.

Think, Francesca, think. What about a pipe clamp? She went over and began unscrewing the one she'd rubbed against, which was looser than the rest. After it fell into her hand, she maneuvered the clamp from around the pipe. Then she went over to the door and wedged the clamp between the knuckle and the pin of the hinge. Now she needed a hammer. Ah-hah! She reached down and pulled off her boots. Using the sharp stiletto heel, she banged at the pin until she could wedge it out of the hinge. She

338

worked at each hinge, stopping to listen periodically. The heel of her right boot broke off. She threw it down and switched to her left boot. At long last all the pins were removed.

Francesca pried open the door. In her stocking feet, she squeezed through the opening. So far she had heard no voices or sounds other than the constant movement of the waves crashing on the rocks. She was in an unlit corridor with doors on each side. After a few moments her eyes adjusted to the dimness. She made her way toward cement stairs, barely visible at the end of the hall.

Just as she reached the stairs, she heard a door slam up above. Then voices and footsteps. Were they coming back to finish her off? Panicked, she opened the nearest door and looked inside. Muted late-afternoon light filtered in through a single window. Lake Michigan was visible below.

Cindy Murray sat by the window of Sorrel's Bar across the street from the post office, nursing a tonic water and lime. She'd relieved Officer Smith, who'd spent the morning surveying the post office from the coffee shop in Hero's Market. Cindy wore civilian clothes: wool pants a black turtleneck and a loose jacket that concealed her weapon. Inside the post office at the back, two more officers were at the ready. Once they nabbed the "delivery boy", they would raid the service department at Zimmerman's Mercedes.

She sipped her water and kept an eye on the street. Nothing had happened yet. She hoped something would before too long.

Tom had tried to work, but felt too distracted. He'd called Francesca off and on all morning. At 2 o'clock after they'd finalized the plan for the drug raid on Zimmerman's, he went over to her office but Hero told him she hadn't come in that day.

He drove over to her condo. He rang the bell several times, but got no response except for the dogs barking frantically and scratching at the door. He took out his key and let himself in. Both dogs pushed past him, running outside to do their business. There were puddles on the floor by the door.

Calling out for Francesca, he went through the house and into the kitchen to get some paper towels to clean up.

When the dogs came back, he took them into the kitchen. Their water bowl was empty. He filled it and they drank greedily. He filled it again and then he fed them. They ate like they were starving. Clearly Francesca had not come home last night.

Tom went through the rest of the condo. The bedrooms were empty and Francesca's car wasn't in the garage. He locked the door and left. Back at the station, he sent out an APB alerting police to be on the lookout for Francesca's car. Then he sat and stewed. He wanted to tear Banner Bluff apart looking for her, but had no idea where to start.

Francesca shut and locked the door quietly. This room was similar to her prison, with white tiled floors and unadorned walls. The window had a Pella sticker in the right-hand corner. She walked over and unhitched the latch. As she pulled up the lower sash, she was buffeted by a gust of icy wind. Far below, a massive pile of boulders fortified the house against the wrath of Lake Michigan. Waves battered the rocks and sent spray into the air. The boulders glistened with a thin coat of ice. Just above them, Francesca made out a foot-wide ledge that wrapped around the house. Could she reach it without falling onto the slippery rocks? Did she have a choice?

Behind her in the hallway, she heard heavy footsteps stomping down the stairs. In a minute or two they would see she was gone and start looking for her. It was now or never. She bent down and pulled off her socks, thinking she would have better traction. Then she turned around and went out the window, sliding backwards on her stomach, her arms bracing her movement. Outside, she slid down gripping the windowsill with her fingers while she felt with her toes along the rough surface of the house's stone walls. She glanced down and spotted the ledge about a foot below her.

*One, two, three…*She let go of the windowsill and dropped to the ledge below, scraping her hands and feet. Above, she heard banging on the door. She stood still for a moment, gasping for breath and clinging to the wall like Spider-woman. Then she crept along the ledge, clutching the wall. It was slow going. As she came around the corner, she saw the Banner Bluff beach further down the bluff. She'd been held captive in the vacant mansion at the north end of the beach.

She crept around the ledge until she reached the front portico. Her first thought was to run to Lorinda Landers' house, just a few short blocks away. She stepped off the ledge onto the driveway, and stopped dead. Visible through the open door of the unfinished garage was a black Mercedes with dealer plates.

Chapter 64
Tuesday Afternoon and Evening, December 5th

Arlyne, the daytime dispatcher, appeared at the door. "Chief, there's a lady out front who came to see you, but she doesn't want to come in until Francesca gets here."

"Francesca?"

"Yeah, she says she agreed to meet Ms. Antonelli here at five o'clock."

Tom got up from his desk and strode down the hall. He opened the security door and went into the foyer. Sitting on a bench along the wall was an attractive blond woman of slim build. He knew her from somewhere, but couldn't place her at the moment. She looked frightened as he approached.

He held out his hand. "Hello, I'm Chief Barnett. Can I help you?"

The woman stood up, looking ready to take flight. "I don't know. I was going to meet Francesca here, but she has not showed up."

She spoke with an accent, he noted. "Can I ask what this is about?"

"I had better leave." She started towards the door.

He moved to bar her way. "Please don't go. I'm worried about Ms. Antonelli. Maybe you know something. Come in to my office and we'll get you a cup of coffee." He nodded to Arlyne, who was observing them. Arlyne stepped forward. The woman looked at them, at the door, and then back at Tom. She seemed to be making a tremendous decision. "Well, just until she gets here. Okay?"

"Of course," Tom said. He shepherded her into the hallway and down to his office, while Arlyne went for the coffee.

Once the woman was seated, he plunged in. "Have you talked to Francesca today?"

"No, last night. We had dinner with Colman."

"With Colman?" Tom felt totally in the dark.

"Yes, he made dinner for Francesca and me in his restaurant."

"Churchill's?"

"Yes."

"Where did Francesca go after dinner?"

"I don't know. Maybe home? Colman drove me back to the hospital. I work there."

He knew who she was now. Anya Kozerski, an oncology nurse. "So Francesca left Churchill's when you did?"

"Yes."

"What time was that?"

"Maybe nine o'clock." She looked frightened again.

"Was she going somewhere?"

"I don't know. I know nothing."

He tamped down his desire to drag the story out of her. "What was this dinner about?" Arlyne appeared in the doorway with a mug of coffee, but he waved her off.

Anya looked down at her hands, which lay knotted together in her lap. "It was about what I know."

"What do you know?"

The woman was trembling. She looked up. Fear filled her eyes.

"Tell me. Don't be afraid." Tom was on the edge of his chair.

"I know who is trying to kill Mr. Marshall, the face-blind man."

When she saw the Mercedes, Francesca started running. She sprinted down the long pebble driveway and made for the street. From behind her came voices and the sound of the front door slamming. She veered left and ran along the road beside the bluff. There were two homes in the first block—an old Victorian with a weather vane on the roof that was spinning and creaking in the wind, and a grand Georgian bright with welcoming Christmas lights. She ran past them to Elm.

Behind her, an engine roared into life. Had they seen her? She raced diagonally across Elm Street and headed for the backyard of the corner house, a Shaker cottage with an extensive garden. If she cut through this yard, she'd end up behind Lorinda Landers' house. Her feet felt like they'd been put through a shredder. Her breath came in ragged gasps.

Head lights flashed in her direction, and she heard the screech of brakes. She pushed through high shrubs. Stealthily she crossed the broad yard, moving towards the cover of bushes on the other side of the lawn. The slam of car doors echoed in the cold air.

The bushes scratched her face and hands. On the other side was Lorinda's house. She shoved the rest of the way through and found herself in front of a walled vegetable garden adjacent to Lorinda's kitchen. It had miniature turrets at four corners, each crowned with a conical slate roof. Francesca thought of secret gardens in fairy tales. There was even an old wooden door with a lattice top.

Francesca pulled at the door. At first it wouldn't budge. Then the hinges squeaked and it began to move.

The garden was stubble now and Francesca tripped over dried stalks, painful on her raw feet. Through the window she saw Sadie, sitting at the kitchen table reading. Warm light from an overhead lamp fell on her bowed head. Her lips were moving as she turned a page. Francesca went to the window and tapped gently. Sadie looked up, her eyes searching in the darkness.

Francesca moved closer to the glass. Then Sadie's face broke out in a big smile. She came around and opened the kitchen door.

"Land sakes, Francesca, what are you doing here?"

"No time to explain." She hurried inside. "Go back to your reading. I'm going to lie on the floor. Pretend I'm not here."

Sadie gave her a questioning look, but nodded without a word. Francesca threw herself on the kitchen floor, pressing the length of her body along the cabinets under the sink so she couldn't be seen from the windows. In a wavering voice, Sadie began to recite.

"'The Lord is my shepherd; I shall not want. He maketh me to lie down in green pastures; He leadeth me beside still waters. He restoreth my soul: He leadeth me in the paths of righteousness for His name's sake.'"

The garden gate squeaked. Sadie stopped reading. "Someone's out there. I can't see who it is," she whispered.

"Keep reading. Pretend you didn't hear," Francesca whispered back.

"'Yea, though I walk through the valley of the shadow of death, I will fear no evil; for Thou art with me; Thy rod and Thy staff, they comfort me...'" Sadie broke off.

The gate squeaked again. Francesca listened, but heard only silence from outside. Then a car engine, muted, fading into the distance. After a moment Sadie said, "My Lord, we've been saved. Hallelujah!"

"Yes, hallelujah." Francesca rolled over and lay on her back. Tears ran down into her hair.

Sadie looked at Francesca's bloody bare feet and torn clothing. "What happened?"

"It's a long story," Francesca said. She was shivering now, more from relief than from her trek in the cold. "Would you please call the police station and ask for Chief Barnett? Don't call nine-one-one. Just tell Tom to come over here and get me."

345

Chapter 65
Tuesday Evening, December 5th

Banner Bluff was quiet tonight, Cindy Murray thought. The streets were empty and the shops were closed. There were only a few customers in Sorrel's dining room. Cindy sat on a high bar stool nursing her drink. Facing near-starvation after several hours on stake-out duty, she'd ordered a small plate of fried calamari to quiet her growling stomach. A man walked by, being pulled down the street by a gigantic wolfhound. Briefly, she followed their progress. *Who's walking whom?*

Her gaze returned to the post office. A tall man with longish hair was approaching the door. He wore padded dark blue coveralls and work boots. He entered the building, carrying two small white mailers with red and blue trim. The post office was closed at this hour; only the P. O. boxes were accessible.

Hunger and boredom forgotten, Cindy radioed O'Connor and Rodriguez, who were waiting in a back room at the post office. Her message went to the police department and the S.W.A.T. teams at the ready near Zimmerman's Mercedes. "Suspect entering post office carrying package." She hopped off her stool and headed for the door.

"Miss," the waiter called after her. "Miss, your calamari…"

"You eat 'em," she said without looking back.

The suspect had disappeared inside the post office. She whipped across the street, pulling out her service revolver. Cindy heard shots as she pushed through the door. She took cover beside a wall of P. O. boxes, hunkering down behind a stamp machine. Then she peered around the corner.

Rodriguez was down, moaning softly. A ragged patch of red showed through his shirt, high up on the shoulder. The suspect,

346

his back to her, held O'Connor at bay. She motioned to O'Connor and touched her finger to her lips. He kept his face blank and didn't acknowledge her presence.

"Come on," he said to the suspect. "We know who you are. You won't get away with this. Put down your gun and you'll have a better chance." In the distance, they heard sirens approaching.

Silently, crouching down, Cindy moved forward. A few feet from the suspect, she exploded into motion, ramming into him shoulder-first and wrapping her arms around his legs. He went down like a ton of bricks. O'Connor sprang forward and together they managed to handcuff the guy.

"Nice tackle!" O'Connor said. "Where did you learn to do that?"

Cindy shrugged. "I had four older brothers."

They heard police cars pulling up out front. Cindy knelt by Rodriguez and felt his pulse. His shoulder was bleeding and his breathing was ragged, but he was alert. She smiled at him. "You're going to be all right."

The minute Puchalski walked into the post office, he recognized the suspect. It was the mechanic he'd seen last night; the man in Carrie Landwehr's pictures, and undoubtedly, the man who'd taken shots at Martin Marshall. He called Barnett. "We've got our man, Chief. We can go ahead with the raid."

At the station, Tom sent the go-ahead to the S.W.A.T. team standing ready near Zimmerman's, then he grabbed his jacket and headed for the door. He wanted to be there when the raid went down. As he headed down the hall to the parking lot in back, Arlyne yelled out to him. "Call on line three, Chief. For you."

"I'm on my way out. Can't someone else handle it?"

"It's Sadie from over at the Landers house. She says she must talk to you."

347

"You'll have to take a message. I'm gone." He continued down the hall.

"But sir…"

Tom yanked open the back door with unnecessary force. "God damn it, Arlyne, nothing takes precedence over this drug bust."

He stormed out to his car, angry with himself. He'd never used language like that with Arlyne. He should be thrilled; he was about to crack the drug trade and put the bad guys behind bars. But deep down he was thinking about Francesca, and whether she was alive or dead.

Chapter 66
Tuesday Evening, December 5th

Sadie put down the phone. "He's not available. It sounds like something is going on over there. He'll call back."

Francesca nodded. Maybe they were looking for her.

Sadie helped Francesca up the stairs to the big, old-fashioned bathroom. She ran a tub of hot water and laid out a silk nightgown and a flannel robe in a style from a bygone era. "Ring this bell when you're finished and I'll come and take care of your feet. Miss Lorinda is already asleep and she won't hear a thing."

Francesca soaked in the hot tub until her skin was wrinkled and she was warm to the bone. After drying off, she put on the nightgown and robe. Sadie came up and sat on a stool with Francesca's feet propped on her lap. She massaged them with a creamy, antiseptic unguent and wrapped them loosely with gauze. Then she helped Francesca downstairs to the parlor where a fire was burning in the fireplace.

Francesca sat on a flowery satin chaise lounge, her legs covered with a soft wool blanket. Sadie brought her a bowl of thick minestrone and two fat slices of homemade bread slathered with butter. Francesca hadn't realized how hungry she was. She devoured the entire meal, wiping up the last drops of soup with a piece of bread. Sadie watched her with pleasure.

"You sure were hungry, girl." She picked up the tray and placed it on a table near the door. Then she sat down on the settee across from Francesca. "Now tell me what all this is about."

Francesca told Sadie the whole story of her kidnapping and escape. Sadie's eyes widened and shock crossed her face more than once, but in the end all she said was, "Thank the Lord you're safe and sound."

349

Francesca felt so exhausted she couldn't keep her eyes open. "I think I'll just curl up here and wait for Tom to find me. Why don't you go to bed, Sadie?"

"No, honey, I'll sit right here and watch over you."

Chapter 67
Early Wednesday Morning, December 6th

When the phone rang, Martin and Kate were asleep. Martin had taken a sleeping pill and was dead to the world. The ringing woke Kate, who reached for the phone on the bedside table. Fumbling for it, she knocked over a stack of books, which banged into the lamp and sent it crashing to the floor. Martin never budged.

"Hello," Kate said, groggy.

"Mrs. Martin, it's Chief Barnett."

Kate instantly came wide awake. "Yes?"

"It's over." He spoke gently. "It's over, Kate. We've got the bad guys. They'll never threaten Martin again."

Kate began to cry. "You've caught them all?" she said shakily.

"Yes. I wanted you to know right away so you can sleep safe. Is Martin awake? I'd talk to him."

"No, he took a pill and he's deep asleep."

"Good. Well, you can relay the message. I can come over tomorrow and go through everything."

"Yes, please do that." Her voice caught. "And thanks, Tom, thanks for everything."

She lay there in the dark, feeling the tears running down her cheeks while a lightness and warmth streamed through her body. Was it happiness? Then she turned to Martin and wrapped her arms around him, pushing her head under his chin, pressing herself as close to him as she could.

Martin smiled in his sleep and said, "Kate, darling Kate."

In the early morning hours when Tom finally came to get Francesca, he apologized over and over. "I should have taken Sadie's call. Then I would have known that you were all right. I should have come here first thing."

"No, you had to do your job. By the time Sadie called you, the worst was over and I was safe."

"You called specifically for me and I wouldn't listen to Arlyne. I even swore at her."

"Tom, stop it! You just closed down a drug ring. You saved Martin Marshall's life and probably the lives of countless other citizens."

He sat on the edge of the sofa. "I guess this *is* one of the biggest cases of my career." Then his gaze met hers, his face so open and unmasked that she could see into his soul. "But you are terrifically important to me. Maybe the most important thing in my life." His voice had an urgency to it she'd never heard before.

She looked at him in wonderment, "And you are…" *Could she say it?* "…the most important person in my life."

Tom enfolded her in his arms. Then he picked her up and carried her out to his car.

When they arrived at his house, Tom carried her in and set her gently on the sofa. Then he went to get them each a glass of Calvados. They sat side by side for a long time, sipping the liquor and swapping stories about what had transpired in the last twenty-four hours.

Francesca told him how she'd escaped the locked room. They both laughed at the demise of her stiletto heels that weren't fit to walk in; but that made excellent hammers. When she described her fall to the ledge surrounding the vacant house, high up over the boulders and the lake, she shook her head. "I would never dare to do that in my right mind."

"Can you describe your captors?" he asked.

"No. I never saw them."

He told her about Anya's arrival at the station. "She's going to be a lot of help in identifying these guys."

"What about her husband, Alexei? She's frightened about the repercussions…"

"He'll be moved to a secure location. Maybe some deal can be worked out if he agrees to turn state's evidence."

At one point, in his recounting of the raid on the Mercedes dealership, Tom got up and went out to the hall. He came back and tossed Francesca her purse and pink scarf.

"We found these in Petroff's file cabinet. That's when I wanted to kill him. Puchalski had to pull me off of the guy."

Francesca fingered the scarf. "So he was there when the raid went down?"

"Yeah. He was in his office, preparing more packets for drop-offs in the area. We nailed him in the act."

"So what did you think when you found my purse?"

He shook his head and stared up at the wall. "God, Francesca, I thought they'd killed you." He turned to face her and she reached out as he came closer.

"I wonder why they didn't kill me," Francesca whispered against his shoulder. "Maybe they had other plans for me?" She shuddered.

Later when they were upstairs in bed, holding hands under the sheets, Francesca turned to face Tom in the dark. She could see the outline of his profile.

"Tom?"

"Hmm?"

"I was thinking about face blindness."

"Yeah?" He drew her closer.

"I was thinking that we are all face blind at times. We don't always see the face in front of us. We see what we want to

353

see. We superimpose our own feelings and desires on that face, on that person."

He was quiet for a time. "You're right. And sometimes we put on masks so no one can see what we're thinking or feeling."

For a moment Francesca thought about this. "Let's not hide behind a mask. Let's be open and transparent. Always." She reached up and caressed his cheek. He brought her hand to his mouth and kissed her palm.

Chapter 68
Wednesday Night, December 6th

Banner Bluff was bustling. The small downtown had been closed off to traffic and holiday shoppers filled the streets. Earlier, the Mothers' League had organized a treasure hunt. Groups of children went from store to store looking for the holiday items on their lists. At the Gazebo, Santa Claus held court and children lined up to tell him their special wishes and receive a candy cane.

Now the children were home with babysitters and their parents were out shopping. The Toy Chest was doing a brisk business selling dolls, dinosaurs, action figures and the latest electronic games. The Baby Boat had toys and clothes for toddlers that grandparents couldn't resist. Then there was Henrietta's Boutique, with the latest fashions for teenagers and moms alike.

Churchill's was open for a light supper, as well as Sorrel's for something more substantial. The Banner Bluff Brewery was jammed with menfolk who could take just so much shopping and much preferred watching a hockey game. Even Hero's Market stayed open late. They served tea, coffee and hot chocolate served with warm sugar-buns. Colman was helping out as barista, happy at the chance to spend more time with Vicki.

Upstairs, Francesca was huddled over her computer trying to catch up on work. The door to her office was locked. She knew her fear was probably irrational, but she didn't feel safe even with all kinds of people downstairs. Laughter and chatter drifted up to her office. She looked out the window at the throngs below. News had got around, she figured, that the drug ring had been brought down and their village was again a peaceful place.

That morning when she woke up, Tom was gone. It was nine o'clock and the sun was shining. She looked around his bedroom, so neat and impersonal. No pictures on the dresser or the bedside tables…no tchotchkes, either. The clean surfaces made her think of a hotel room.

She sat up and opened the drawer in the nearest bedside table. A framed picture lay in it, face-down. She turned it over. It was the photo of a lovely, blue-eyed blonde woman. This must be Candace, Tom's deceased wife. Carefully, she put the photo back. Did this mean he was healing and ready to move on?

He'd left a note on the other bedside table, saying he'd taken care of the dogs so she could sleep in and that he had a long day ahead of reports, interviews and meetings. He would call her when he could. He'd signed it: *I love you, Tom.*

She brushed her fingers over those words. This was a first. In one night they had catapulted from a close relationship to something much more. They had revealed a need for each other that they hadn't wanted to admit before. Francesca smiled. She liked this new beginning.

Remembering that morning, Francesca felt warm and happy. She saved the article she'd been writing on the drug raid and shut down her computer. She would post it tomorrow. Right now she needed to get downstairs, rub shoulders with her fellow Banner Bluffers and share some holiday cheer. Frank had offered to write a story about the St. Nicholas Festival and David, her photographer, was out there taking candid pictures of families enjoying the evening. She decided to walk down the street a bit and mix with the crowd.

She put on her brown sheepskin boots. With a pair of cotton socks and the boots' soft lining, she could manage to walk on her tender feet. She pulled on her coat, unlocked the door and tromped down the stairs.

356

Downstairs, the atmosphere was buoyant. The aroma of coffee and hot chocolate filled the air. Francesca smiled at Colman. He didn't know about her nightmare adventure. She would tell him when she was ready. He beckoned her over.

"So did Anya come in?" he asked.

"Yes. They have her in protective custody right now...just until things calm down."

He nodded. "Good, I worry about her." He turned as a customer came up to the counter.

Francesca waved. "Okay, I'm off to join the bustling crowd."

Colman turned back to the coffee machine.

Outside the weather was cold and brisk. Snowflakes danced in the air. At the corner, the Rotary Club was selling roasted chestnuts. Francesca walked towards the Toy Chest, stopping to talk to people she knew. She wandered into the store and looked at the latest toys with her niece and nephew in mind. There was an Ultra Stomp Rocket and a Perplexus puzzle she was sure Timmy would love. For Betsy, she found a Singer sewing machine for kids. The girl who waited on her was wearing a red stocking cap and looked like one of Santa's elves.

"Everything is fifteen percent off tonight", she said as she scanned the items.

"Could I have these shipped to California?"

"Sure. No problemo. Just give me the address and we'll wrap 'em up and send 'em."

Francesca wrote a note to each child on a gift card for enclosure. As she left the store, she ran into the Marshalls. Kate had her hand tucked under Martin's arm. She looked radiant, and Martin looked tired but jovial.

"Hi, Francesca. Beautiful night!" he said.

"Yes, it is. Where are the kids?"

"Home with Emma. She offered to babysit so we could get some early shopping done," Kate said.

"We just had dinner at the Noodle Hut. It was great to be out without the kids and talk." Martin smiled at Kate and patted her hand.

Francesca decided not to bring up the raid on Zimmerman's. Martin probably needed to digest the news slowly and recalibrate his life. She said goodbye and continued back towards her office, then past it and on towards the Brewery. The crowd there had spilled out onto the street. She saw Susan and Marcus standing on the sidewalk, each with a glass of wine in hand. Susan reached out and the two friends hugged. Francesca smiled at Marcus.

"How are the wedding plans coming along?"

"It's all going to be very low-key, but I do want you to be my maid-of-honor," Susan said. She studied her friend. "What happened to your face? Did you try some new make-up? It looks raw."

She pulled her scarf up. "Oh, it's nothing…a little wind-burn."

Marcus held up his glass. "Can I get you a glass of wine?"

She smiled at him, her gaze taking in the windows above the Brewery and Bonnie's Bakery. She saw a light moving around in Bob Newhouse's darkened campaign headquarters. She frowned. Bob, Alicia, and Connie Munster were in Peoria. She'd written a piece about Bob's plans to run for governor and she knew he was giving a speech to an agro-business consortium tonight.

"Francesca? Would you like a glass of wine?" Marcus repeated, turning to follow her gaze. "What are you looking at?"

"Oh, nothing. Listen, thanks but no thanks. I better get going. We'll talk soon, Susan." Francesca walked away. She pushed through the crowd toward a passageway between Banner Bluff Bank and Grand and Lambert's real estate office. When she reached it, she pulled out her phone and dialed Tom. He didn't answer, so she tried the station number. "Could you please get the Chief on the phone?" she said when the night dispatcher answered. It's urgent."

"They're in a meeting with the FBI. This case has blown sky-high."

"Please, Gerry. I need to talk to him briefly."

"Okay, I'll try."

A few minutes later, Tom came on the line. "Hi. This has to be quick."

"Somebody's up in Bob Newhouse's campaign headquarters. They've got a flashlight. I know the whole crew is out of town. Something fishy is going on."

"We're swamped here, Francesca. I'll get someone to contact Lister and Romano. They should be in the vicinity. One of them can check it out."

"Okay, tell him to come around back and meet me in the passageway between the bank and Green and Lambert's—and to be careful. Whoever's up there could very well have a lookout down here somewhere."

Francesca hung up and stepped out into the street, eyeing the passers-by. The crowd had thinned. She wandered back and forth, keeping her eye on the walkway and glancing up at the window. The light continued to bounce around. Across the street, under the trees on the green, she thought she spied the glow of a cigarette.

She glanced back at the passageway and saw a figure moving forward. It must be Officer Lister or Romano. She hurried back over and stepped into the passage. Someone grabbed her arm, pulling her into the darkness and covering her mouth with his hand. A gun poked into her back. Her captor dragged her towards a car parked behind the buildings.

Anger coursed through her. *No. It would not happen again.* She let her body go limp. When her attacker's grip loosened, she whipped around and jammed her knee into his crotch. He screamed and doubled over. She turned to run. Someone blocked her way. Fear froze her for an instant until she saw the uniform. It was Lister.

"That guy just attacked me." Francesca gestured behind her. "And there's someone across the street on the green."

He nodded. "I've called for backup. Go inside the Brewery. Get off the street."

Francesca hobbled out of the passageway. She went down to the door of the Brewery and stepped inside, then glued herself to the window. Outside, a police car drove slowly down the street clearing pedestrians out of the way. She heard sirens coming from the back alley. Another car appeared, and she saw two police officers climb out of it and head for the stairs up to the Newhouse campaign headquarters.

Francesca turned away from the window and saw Susan and Marcus across the room, looking fearful and perplexed. She walked over to them. "Sorry about earlier. I'll take a glass of wine now, Marcus."

"You look like you've seen a ghost," he said.

"Maybe I have…my own." She murmured.

Susan stared at her, visibly concerned.

They stood together making small talk while Francesca kept one eye on the street outside the window. She didn't explain her remark or tell them about her close call. She didn't want to discuss it right now. After yesterday, she'd thought her life would settle down, but since the attack in the passageway she felt off-kilter. It made her think of those horror movies where everyone thinks the monster blob is dead and then it rises up again. These last two days had been her own private horror movie.

Ten minutes later, Francesca saw Officer Lister dragging a burly guy across the street. Something about his walk was familiar, and she belatedly recognized him as one of the Pharaoh's bodyguards. A few minutes later, Officer Romano escorted another man across the street: Roscoe, the governor's chauffeur. The real surprise came after that—two more police officers hauling Harrison Rand away in cuffs. She guessed he'd been the one nosing around upstairs.

Her brain was going a mile a minute. What was Rand looking for? Some dirt to stain Bob Newhouse's campaign? Or maybe they were planting listening devices so they could learn Connie Munster's campaign secrets. Why had they taken such a chance? Maybe they thought no one would notice with all the hullabaloo of St. Nick's night.

Marcus nudged her. "I think you know more than you're telling us. What's going on?"

Francesca thought for a moment. "We just witnessed Banner Bluff's Watergate scandal."

The Cimarron Missive

A Blog Serving Cimarron, Texas and Beaver Counties, Oklahoma
Monday January 1st 20__

Today's Stories

It's a mystery. Construction on the Cimarron Castle has ceased. The crew cleared out last week, but left behind the bricks and mortar. Stone walls, parapets and crenellations; it's all there. When you approach the site across the windswept prairie, the castle glimmers like a Disney chimera.

There's lots of talk in town. Some say an Arab sheik was building the castle to host camel races across the prairie. Others claim a Chinese consortium wants to drill for oil to feed China's gargantuan economy. I even heard a Russian financier was planning on housing a casino.

Whoever they are, it seems they changed their mind or ran out of money. Now we have our very own medieval ruins in the middle of the Oklahoma panhandle. Les Lindquist plans on taking his history class out there next week.

Chapter 69
Sunday Afternoon, May 20th

Francesca gazed out at the backyard through the kitchen window. It was late afternoon. Bright sun filtered through a thick canopy of leaves. The flowerbeds surrounding the lawn were vivid with spring blooms. She was looking at their friends and thinking about all that had happened in the last six months.

Yari and Luis Gonzales were helping themselves to sangria and chatting with Carina and Daphne Meriwether; all four of them laughing about something. Carina and her mother wore flowery frocks and wide-brimmed, beribboned hats. They made Francesca think of a Monet tableau. Carina had been instrumental in securing a loan for Yari, who would be opening up a small Mexican restaurant on the village green between Hero's Market and the Banner Bluff Brewery. The Gonzales family was currently busy fixing up the space with the help of friends. It would probably go live in August.

At Carina's elbow was Jacques Rostand, a Paris-born Frenchman who had recently moved to Banner Bluff. He worked at Aftat Labs, a pharmaceutical company located nearby on the North-South highway. As well as being a biotech engineer, he was an experienced horseman and participated in equestrian competitions. He boarded several horses with the Meriwethers and seemed to have become Carina's very special friend.

Hollyhock Farm was back to normal. Work had stopped on the pumping station at the beach. It had never become clear what the Pharaoh intended to do with the water to be siphoned out of Lake Michigan. Those close to him remained silent on the project. After Harrison Rand and his cronies were arrested for breaking and entering, the governor must have gotten a heads-up. By the next morning, all signs of the construction crew had disappeared, including the signboards on the road. That same afternoon, while Carina and Daphne were down at the barn, someone broke into their house and took the copy of the bogus eminent domain judgment from the file cabinets in the library. When the state troopers came to collect the fake documents, they found nothing bearing the governor's signature.

In court Ramses Crenshaw claimed to know nothing about the writ of eminent domain and maintained that Harrison Rand had acted on his own. Rand never disputed the fact, but he refused to admit any knowledge of the purpose of the pumping station. It remained a mystery that incited much debate and fanciful imaginings.

Then there was the five million dollars. Where had it come from? Again Crenshaw claimed to have no knowledge of the check. Rand claimed an anonymous donor had contributed the money. The state didn't seem anxious to investigate the issue as all proof of the transaction had vanished into thin air. The Meriwethers didn't press the matter and eventually interest in the mystery money died down.

Bob Newhouse's campaign was going gang-busters. He was the media's darling, along with his wife and two adorable children. He projected honesty and decency. The latest polls showed him as a sure winner in the fall election. Although no one had managed to pin anything on the Pharaoh, he had lost his allure.

Over on the grass the Gonzales boys and Rosie Marshall were blowing giant bubbles and watching them disappear into the air. Little Stevie watched too, wide-eyed, seated on the grass with a frosted sugar cookie in each hand. Next to him was Isabelle Simmons. She had agreed to watch the little boy so his parents could relax and enjoy the party.

They had planned the event to celebrate Colman's graduation from junior college. He was on his way to Stanford next year in a premed program. Francesca would miss him. He was sitting at the wrought iron garden table with Hero and his granddaughter Vicki. They each had a piece of the chocolate ganache cake before them. Vicki would graduate from Banner Bluff High School in June and was on her way to the University of Illinois in the fall. Who knew if their high school romance would make it through the vicissitudes of college life? But Francesca would bet on it. They had already been through a lot in their young lives and had gained a certain degree of maturity.

Marcus and Susan Reynolds sat in the shade talking to Kate and Martin Marshall. Susan and Kate had their heads together, undoubtedly discussing maternity matters and baby paraphernalia. Both of them were due in late September, and glowed with happiness.

Martin had pulled out his phone to show Marcus the facial scanning app he'd recently acquired. With great excitement, he'd told Francesca he was participating in a test trial of a system originally developed by the Department of Homeland Security to scan crowds for possible terrorists. Martin used it to scan students and Banner Bluff acquaintances into his phone. The app would give him the ability to recognize people and respond to them appropriately.

The only one missing was Anya Kozerski. Shortly after the raid on Zimmerman's Mercedes, she and her husband Alexei had disappeared, courtesy of the witness protection program. The Captain and his crew were in prison awaiting trial, and Alexei had agreed to turn state's evidence against them. Francesca had recently read about an explosion in Baltimore near the waterfront Mercedes vehicle-processing plant. Authorities said a bomb had been set off inside a car. The three bodies inside were incinerated and a hook prosthesis was found near the explosion. That information had given her pause. *The Hook* had been the name of the notorious leader of the Russian mob. His grisly demise seemed justified.

Emma, Frank, Lorinda and Sadie were sitting on the back porch, close enough for Francesca to hear bits of their conversation. They were reminiscing about the good old days. Emma's well-modulated voice rose above the rest, saying, "But friends, life is good in Banner Bluff today." They all laughed in agreement.

Francesca felt Tom's arms encircle her from behind and his cheek pressed against hers. Together they gazed out at the backyard.

"Hey beautiful, are you having a good time at your party?" he whispered in her ear.

She turned her face toward his, and they kissed lightly.

"Yes," she murmured. "Everything is perfect."

His name is Rob. He's really, really cute and really, really nice. Isabelle met him at the Math Team competition. He basically won the tournament for the Banner Bluff team. Lately, he's been coming over to do homework after school.

They like to sit at the kitchen table and study and talk. Her mom doesn't mind at all. Sometimes she even invites Rob to stay for dinner.

Last night Rob invited Isabelle to go to the Spring Dance. This is her first real date and tonight she can't sleep. She can see herself dancing, her dress swirling around her and Rob looking down at her, his eyes full of amazement.

Made in United States
Orlando, FL
16 June 2024